HEREAFTER

C.K. CRIGGER

WOLFPACK
PUBLISHING
— EST 2013 —

WOLFPACK PUBLISHING
— EST 2013 —

Hereafter

Paperback Edition
Copyright © 2020 (As Revised) C.K. Crigger

Wolfpack Publishing
6032 Wheat Penny Avenue
Las Vegas, NV 89122

wolfpackpublishing.com

Paperback ISBN 978-1-64734-090-2
eBook ISBN 978-1-64734-087-2

HEREAFTER

Chapter 1
October 31, 2020

Stakeouts. God, how she hated stakeouts. What a crappy way to spend Halloween night.

Twitchy as a small dog lost in an alligator swamp, Border Patrol Agent Lily Turnbow huddled under the drooping branches of a scraggly nine-bark bush freezing her ass off. Rain drizzled down the back of her neck.

One item in the credit column—her packer boots, warm and waterproof, left some feeling in her toes. It seemed unnaturally cold for October until she remembered shivering in those lightweight costumes on trick or treat night as a kid.

A small sigh sent a puff of air jetting out in front of her, steaming in the chill. One thing stayed the same. Halloween remained a time of ghoulies and ghosties and it was, at this point, not so far off from the witching hour. A pregnant vibe of tense waiting trembled in the air.

The luminous dial of Lily's watch showed the time as eleven-thirty, with the minute hand crawling toward midnight. As though to add even more atmosphere to the situation, a nocturnal bird cooed from the old cemetery on the hill above her, sounding almost human in its misery.

She shivered, a goose walking over her grave. When the hell was anyone going to show up? Had their informant been wrong? He'd seemed sure of his facts two days ago, when the call came in. A loaded plane, he said, flying low and without a flight plan over the most desolate part of the Canadian/U.S. border where it crossed into Washington.

After standing almost immobile for the better part of two hours, the coffee she drank before coming on duty cried for release. Trying to take her mind off the increasingly pressing need, she made plans for her next days off. First on the docket, take Heathen, her mustang, home for Grandpa to trim the mare's feet and put on new shoes. Something to look forward to.

Unfortunately, the slosh of waves lapping at the lakeshore not thirty feet away refused to let her ignore physical needs. How did some of the guys handle it? Pitt, her counterpart from the western side of the county, had been known to go six hours, sipping from the bottomless cup of coffee in his hand the whole time.

Shifting from foot to foot, she reached for her zipper determined to squat when a crashing sound in the brush on the hill to her right stilled the motion. None of *her* team would make that much noise. They all knew better—or were supposed to. Something must be happening at long last.

Bladder forgotten, she faded deeper into the shrubby nine-bark which, even this late in the season, was thick with leaves and desiccated flower-heads. Crud shattered into her hair. Excitement quickened her heart; her blood ran faster.

The crashing turned into the sound of running footsteps. The person headed toward her seemed in a tearing hurry, skidding on rain-slicked pine needles and falling onto one knee not five feet from her hiding place. The size of the dimly seen body and a whispered curse told her the runner was a man. Picking himself up, he galloped on without spotting her.

Releasing an indrawn breath, Lily took her hand from the Glock she carried tonight in a hip holster and cocked her head, listening with all senses alert. Lopez had stationed her nearest the landing, and within seconds she heard the runner's footsteps thumping a hollowed cadence over the dock. A bump sounded, then the buzz of a little electric motor as the fourteen-foot fishing boat tied up there pulled away. In the distance, the hum of a small plane coming in low above the lake became audible.

Her mom always used to say Lily had preternaturally acute hearing—and then a look of dread would fill her eyes. Mom never mentioned that other thing, though. Not after the first time. It took Lily years to figure out why. Probably lots of people could hear the things she did, but nobody could do the other.

Even as the odd memory drifted in and right back out of her mind, Lily heard the plane, still unseen, begin circling. She bet a person with night-vision glasses was up there in it, searching the ground for anybody who shouldn't be out on a night like this. Anybody like the DEA or Border Patrol. In other words, Lopez, Lily, and the rest of the team.

Lopez's voice murmured through the speaker in her ear. "Turnbow, you awake? Get ready. Pitt says the plane's coming in to land. When I say go, go. No dragging along hiding behind the guys."

Anger flared along her nerves. Asshat! Lopez disliked having women in the department. In particular he resented having them along on an action like this one, and he truly hated having a female second-in-command. That wasn't omniscience on her part. God knows his complaints had been loud enough for everyone to hear.

Or maybe, not that she cared, he just hated Lily Turnbow. If so, the feelings were mutual and dated from their first meeting when he looked down at her and said, "Jesus, if we've got to fill our minority quota, couldn't we at least have somebody full-sized?"

So she wasn't exactly a full-figured woman. So what? And minority quota? What was up with that?

Lily eked out her reply, waiting almost long enough to make him speak again before she whispered into the mic, "The plane's coming around to the north. Give it time to sit down. A small boat has gone out to meet it."

"Out of the north?" His raspy baritone shouted into her ear. "Are you sure?"

"Yes."

"How do you know these things, Turnbow?"

What did he want to do, carry on a whole conversation? Maybe give away her position? Or was he accusing her of something. Hah! He wished.

"The boat has one man in it," she said, ignoring a question she suspected was rhetorical anyway. "There are more bodies stirring around on the hill above us. Looks like they're going to come down through the cemetery. Let'em all get on the dock before you make your move. Stay quiet and wait until I give the word."

She could only imagine how much he hated the plane coming in on her side of the little bay. Now it became her job to call in the troops, since she had a better view than Pitt on the other side.

Nevertheless, Lopez took the hint as the plane's drone grew loud enough even he must have heard it. The plane itself remained invisible against the cloud-covered night sky, flying without lights while out on the lake the man in the boat uncapped a lantern and flashed a signal.

"See that?" she asked.

"Saw something."

She heard another voice talking to him before he said, "Okay. I've got it pegged."

Lily tracked the plane by sound as it flew in low over the point and landed a couple hundred yards away with a soft splash of its pontoons. The pilot must be an expert—or he'd done this several times before and knew the layout.

"The plane's down," she murmured into the shoulder mic. "Wait."

Voices carry well over water. Distinct differences in tone and tempo identified three men who didn't seem too worried over the noise they were making. Grunts and curses spoke of heavy lifting as they emptied the plane of its cargo and packed it into the small boat. The area was private property, most of it belonging to some big developer out of Coeur d'Alene. The summer houses were empty at this time of year.

The team's DEA contingent assumed the cargo was B.C. bud or cocaine or, more likely, heroin smuggled into the U.S. from Canada. Homeland Security thought a new group of terrorists or illegal aliens sneaking into the country more likely. Border Patrol just wanted to protect U.S. citizens. If they didn't find one or the other, they were in the sewer or, at best, wasting their time.

Lily had no doubt they were on to something. Intuition shouted so.

Soon, out on the lake the trolling motor started again, whining with strain as it pushed the fishing boat, riding low in the water, toward the dock. Even through the rain Lily could see the boat was overloaded, and instead of one man, it now carried three people and several bulky cartons. Her stomach clenched as the lantern flickered another signal before it went dark.

"Get ready, guys," she breathed, excitement building a knot in her own stomach. "They'll dock in two minutes."

Hard on the heels of her warning, a couple more figures ghosted past her, hurrying onto the dock to join the people coming in. They stood silent, dark silhouettes against the water. Lily waited, her breathing shallow and even.

A man in the boat said, "Catch the line," and she saw one of the new arrivals reach for the rope. The engine cut off, the boat bumped against the wooden dock, and two of the figures in it clambered out to join the others. The final man started manhandling boxes.

This looked like an opportune moment to round up the whole bunch.

"Begin moving in now," Lily said into her mic, and almost before the words were out of her mouth people began running toward the dock both from below her position and from the other side of the bay.

Too fast. Too fast and too noisy. What did Lopez think he was doing?

Only because she knew his stakeout position, she saw him appear from inside an old rock gazebo fifty feet farther down the beach; Pitt moved from under the trees thirty yards to her right up the hill. The DEA guy scooted out of an old car he'd broken into and used for cover—quite illegally, considering his situation. Another of his contingent, the guy guarding the agency's black van a quarter mile up the road, could be heard pounding along on the pavement. He needed to put on his skates if he wanted to be in time for the capture.

Lily started forward as Lopez hollered, "Everybody freeze. This is the United States Border Patrol speaking."

But her sharp ears heard something more. Someone else still out there in the dark. Someone Lily couldn't account for and whom she hadn't heard until now. A curse and a clatter of metal signaled their trap had been sprung a few seconds early. Too late now to call the team back. Heart pounding, Lily turned to face the new threat in time to catch the flare of a powerful flashlight.

She whispered into the speaker on her mic. "There's another of them on the hill," she told Lopez. "He's signaling the plane. I'm going after him."

She could tell by the way Lopez gasped for air he was running and breathing hard. Out of shape loser.

"Right. Don't let him get away," he choked.

Lily shrugged out from under the clinging nine-bark branches. Unlike Lopez, she wasn't out of shape. Excitement quickened her steps as she sped up the slope, the traction soles of her packer boots carrying her along the hill without much slippage. Up ahead, the signaler flashed code-like bursts of light. The plane had already come around, motor revving to get it back in the air.

She thought the spotter's attention all on the plane, but though she was quiet as anyone could be while sloshing through mud, something—a small noise, a sense of movement—drew his attention. He directed a strong beam of light at her, catching her in it even as gunshots cracked from the dock area. A rattle of weaponry from the beach returned fire.

"Hellfire!" Fumbling for the Glock, she ran. It seemed as though the person with the flashlight was deliberately showing his position. *Deliberately!* Realization of the danger made her dart out of the beam a fraction of a second before a bullet whipped past her head. Another followed her into the dark.

In the stress of the moment, Lily forgot to unsnap the tab on her holster. And even when she remembered, the pistol managed to hang up. She tugged at it, at the same time bending her knees like a slalom skier and jigging the other way. The shooter missed twice more, muzzle flashes showing as he changed his position.

Finally tearing the Glock from the holster, she aimed where her assailant had been. Although she had yet to fire a shot, as though the threat were enough she saw him retreating up through the graveyard, using the taller of the old stones as cover. But not complete cover. He seemed to be egging her on, trying to separate her from the rest of the force so to finish her off.

Lily stumbled at that thought, then ran on. It took two to play cat and mouse. Though on her own, so was he.

Dodging behind the towering wing of an adult-sized angel monument, she stopped, taking time to ready her weapon and catch her breath. Down on the beach, Lopez hollered something in a language neither English nor Spanish. She couldn't understand the words, but he sure in hell said it loud enough to carry all the way up the hill. The gunfire dwindled, then died. Lopez must've turned off his mic, too, because she couldn't hear him through it anymore.

Looked like she was the only one with an opponent still in action. Risking a peek around the marble angel, she glimpsed the man darting into a mausoleum near the cemetery gates. His light went out, leaving the night darker than before. Clearly, he planned on bushwhacking her, catching her from behind when she went past him. That didn't fit with her plan.

Backing away from the angel, she sought the dark like a hunting cat, grateful now for the rain. The patter as it hit the ground covered most of the small sounds she made creeping through the tangled grass matting the unkempt old graveyard. She approached the last few yards to his hideout on her hands and knees.

Only one way led in or out of the mausoleum, the same low doorway the suspect had gone through. From an earlier, daylight scouting expedition over the ground, she knew no windows broke the walls of the plain stone box. She crept to the corner of the structure and stopped. Things might get a bit touchy now. Wait him out, or force his hand?

Lopez decided her. "Turnbow. Can you hear me? Turnbow?" His voice came through her shoulder speaker loud enough to bounce off her eardrums.

Idiot! She winced. Was he *trying* to get her killed? Anybody within twenty feet could hear him, let alone a mere six feet—all that separated her from the man inside the mausoleum. She knew when the man stirred, his feet shuffling the debris littering the floor inside. Dirt, gravel, rat scat and rotting leaves. She knew that from earlier, too.

Lily not only ignored Lopez, she unclipped the mic and tossed it a few yards to her left where it landed feather-light in some sodden weeds. To hell with him. Let him yell. Maybe the racket would distract the man inside the structure long enough for her to get the drop on him. "Concentrate Turnbow," she told herself.

Flattening onto her stomach, she grimaced at the touch of cold mud. Instructors at training school said people nearly always shot high when someone came at them. They advised agents to go in on their bellies. This was her first opportunity to try the lesson out under genuine battle conditions. Fear prickled in her veins. She hoped those instructors knew what they were talking about.

Clenching the Glock in her right hand, she inched forward to the mausoleum's doorway. Trusting the person inside couldn't smell her fear or hear her heart pounding away like a hammer on steel, she slithered into the building through the ridge of sodden leaves glued to the step by dirt and the rain.

She knew the instructors were right the moment the stale stench of a dank dirt floor rose up to meet her because the bullets from his gun passed well over her head. One took a chunk out of the stone door jamb at about where her belly would've been had she come in on her feet.

But they were wrong, too, because they hadn't mentioned the enemy probably read from the same instruction book. Not only that, *she* had forgotten the flashlight, which he snapped on and shone down at the floor, the glare momentarily blinding her. The beam followed as she rolled for cover. With another shot chasing her, she dived behind a rough stone altar in the center of the tiny room.

She crashed hard against the corner of the altar. Pain zinged with agonizing ferocity, paralyzing her whole arm as her right elbow took the brunt of the blow. The pistol dropped from her nerveless fingers and skittered away into the dark. Despite herself, she cried out, earning another shot in her direction that kicked sharp little stone shards into the side of her face.

Her chest felt filled to exploding as panic set in. He had her now. He must be wondering why she didn't return fire, the uncertainty probably all that kept him from standing up and pumping shot after shot into her. It wouldn't take long before he figured it out.

Lily cowered behind the altar hoping for a little more time, hoping the guy would die of a heart attack, hoping he hadn't seen what happened—and maybe he hadn't, because the flashlight beam still shined a little high as he snapped off a couple more shots. They sparked off the stone, mercifully without lethal ricochet. The noise thundered in the confined space, wounding her sensitive ear drums.

How many shots had that been? She snorted internally. Did it matter? The answer came as she heard the dry click of his semi-automatic hitting on empty.

Yes. It mattered.

Shaking in her muddy boots, she stood up, folded her hands together like there was a gun between them, and said, "Drop your weapon. You're under arrest." It was the biggest bluff sr ever heard of anyone running. If only it worked.

There wasn't time for her to see much of him. A medium-tall, skinny man wearing dark clothes and something on his head. One of those Arab kind of things, a scarf tied on with strings. *Kaffiyeh*. The word shot through her mind. And then the light flickered and went out.

Though she knew he understood her, he still hadn't said a word.

She sensed him moving, coming at her in a rush. She stood her ground, fending him off as he grappled with her. His hands sought her neck in an assassin's choking grip. First falling backward, she tucked her head to protect her throat before rearing forward, butting him hard in the chest and chin. The sharp smack pushed him back, a little. Enough to make him stumble.

She whirled, tripping him with a leg sweep before he regained his balance. The sweep did little good for, wily as a cat, he recovered and came at her again, clawed fingers catching in her hair.

This time she tried the old knee-him-in-the-groin trick, which seemed to earn her a little respect and teach him caution. Made him angry, too. He grunted and yelled something obscene in a furious, rapid-fire spate of words.

Not that Lily comprehended a thing he said but, in some strange fashion, she did understand he wasn't yelling at her. About her, maybe, but not at her.

That's when she realized he wore a speaker on his shoulder just like the one she'd chucked moments earlier. And really bizarre thing was that the voice coming out of the mic sounded identical to the one bellowing in hers before she threw it away.

Lopez?

"Kill her," Lopez yelled in English. "Kill her now!"

The shock—call it stunned realization—almost paralyzed her. A traitor. Lopez was a traitor. All that gunfire, earlier—was any of the team left alive, or had there been a slaughter? And now he wanted this guy to kill her. She didn't need to speak the language to figure that much out.

Desperation lent Lily strength. Adrenaline poured through her. While the Arab bent over his abused gonads, she darted behind the altar and, miracle of miracles stepped right on top of her gun. She snatched it up in that stretched moment, all the breather she got, because when he straightened, he held a knife in his right hand. She saw him and his hurken big knife silhouetted in the strangely wavering light, and then he charged, swarming over the top of the crumbling altar.

"Shoot him!" Her mind screamed the order at her, and this time, her arm moved to obey. Too late. She tried to dodge, but his knife plunged downward, sliding along her left arm and slicing through the tough fabric of her jacket to her flesh.

Fire seethed through her, ran down her forearm. Hot blood flooded over her hand. Retaliating, Lily slugged him on the side of his head with the Glock, and if the blow lacked power, at least she managed to keep hold of the gun. He jerked aside, but she hit him again, this time connecting with a solid thud.

The blow didn't stop him. Slowed him a little maybe. The pale hand she saw him brush across his eyes came away wet and dark. Good. She hoped his own blood blinded him.

Lunging to the side, she kicked up some of the rubble littering the floor under his feet. He slipped on a sodden spot, but nothing would hold him now. His teeth flashed in a contemptuous grin. Why could she see this? Hadn't it been dark in here a second ago? Was that son-of-a-bitch Lopez here already, bringing more light to help finish her off?

Lily smelled the Arab as he grabbed her gun arm. Sharp, acrid sweat; an odd, cheesy odor; clothes worn several days too long.

The blade of his knife looked like watered silk as it plunged downward, toward her neck. Apparently he knew she wore a ballistic vest. Instructors had taught what to do in these situations. Better to take a wound in the arm or shoulder than the neck, they said. Better to take *two* wounds in the arm or shoulder.

Lily dropped. Had a second in which to see the rage grow on his face, and hate glitter in his eyes before a blaze of pain lashed her senses. She kept willing her finger to pull the Glock's trigger.

As from far away she heard Lopez screaming on a single long note.

Funny. Beyond the mausoleum walls, the sun had already risen. The marble angel stood outlined behind her attacker's head, its wings spread against a red and orange sky. How could that be? As if that weren't weird enough, her ears felt stuffed to bursting with foam.

Then they weren't. Nothing could stop a gargantuan crack of sound louder than any thunder she'd ever heard— so loud it couldn't possibly be real. And though her eyes closed, nothing could shut out the burst of white light across her retinas.

What the hell?

The Arab bore her to earth behind the altar, but suddenly she couldn't smell him anymore. She must have pushed him off because he seemed to have disappeared, even though she felt no lightening of the pressure on her body.

And then—nothing. Not even pain. Her last halfway coherent thought said she was disintegrating.

Chapter 2
November 2, 2120

Cattle lowed mournful protest, their heads swinging on outstretched necks as if sheer yearning would bring them to water sooner. Dust rose over the herd, but scenting water nearby, the parched animals drove forward through the choking cloud.

Selkirk O'Quinn, leader of the O'Quinn clan, sat his horse on a small rise. At his motion, herders and their dogs drew in closer, holding the herd back to keep it from over-running the dozen home wagons lumbering just ahead of the cattle. Under his watchful eye, the water-wagon, high-sided and filled with large round kegs stacked two layers high, broke a path around the families. Three ten-year-old boys rode on top of the load, already unwinding the hoses of hand pumps in preparation of refilling the kegs. Should the cattle beat them to it, the water would be muddy and befouled for the next hour or so, and useless to the humans.

O'Quinn whistled, the shrill sound carrying above the squeal of dry wagon wheels, barking dogs, and complaining cattle. Its lilt summoned his cousin Bannion, also O'Quinn, who reined toward him, riding a horse too tired to break out of a trot.

Bannion didn't force the animal, most likely because he was as weary as the horse. There'd been a skirmish yesterday morning, and constant scouting since.

"Surprised you have the spit to pucker up for that whistle," Bannion said, drawing in beside the clan leader.

"I've been wallowing a rock around in my mouth. Helps a little." Selkirk grimaced. "Has Nate reported in?"

"About five minutes ago."

"He see any sign of Harrison?"

"Said not." Bannion removed his floppy hat, an old one made of beaver pelt, and wiped sweat off his forehead with a filthy shirt sleeve, oblivious to the muddy tracks left behind. There hadn't been water to wash with for the last two days as they traveled through the wastelands. Everyone in the clan was suffering.

His dark eyes, never still, squinted against the dust and glaring sunlight, scanning the hills rising over the broad valley as though to see to its end. Although he bragged of keen eyesight, nothing stirred in the distance. The clan's winter quarters were over there, on the banks of a small lake. Harrison Bell, yet another shirttail relative was the summer caretaker, holding the clan's title over the land by right of possession. That he hadn't showed up at the ford to welcome the nomads home was cause for worry. That they'd been attacked twice on the way, in the wastelands, no less, cause for more.

Bloodstains made dark patches on the front of Bannion's shirt. This particular blood had once belonged to someone else, although the splatters on his leg were all his. A raw gash on his calf showed through a rent in his homespun britches.

Bannion's gaze shifted back to his cousin who was trying to keep his concern from becoming too clear. "Don't worry, Selkirk. He'll be here. He's never failed us yet."

Selkirk cocked him a look out of red-rimmed eyes. "He's getting old, Bannion. Too old to fight. The broken leg he had in the spring didn't do him any good. Slowed him down too much, if you ask me. I should've had somebody stay with him."

"He didn't want anybody. Just his dog." Bannion hesitated. "Speaking of his dog—"

Selkirk flinched, but to his relief, Bannion shook his head without finishing his thought.

"More at stake here than Harrison's feelings," Selkirk said, and repeated almost fretfully, "Somebody should've stayed."

"Soon as we cross I'll have Nate scout ahead," Bannion offered. "Circle around the foothills and make a sweep down to the ranch from there. Just in case. This is not the time to get careless."

"I agree. Especially after what happened yesterday. Although how we were to know the Mags were going to start a war is beyond me. The Farmers should've sent word after first blood." Selkirk spat out the little stone he held under his tongue in hopes it would alleviate thirst. "Wait until dawn, Bannion. Eat and have the men rest first." His sharp eyes examined his cousin. "Wash. Maybe Harrison will show up this evening. You're worn out. The horses are worn out, and the troops are frazzled. If there's more fighting to be done, it'll go better after a night's sleep."

"And a decent hot meal. For all of us. Won't hurt for the whole company to have a day of rest before the last push to headquarters."

Selkirk had no trouble deciphering Bannion's hint. "Don't worry. I won't let them head out until we have a report. No sense in walking into trouble blind."

Their minds were traveling the same path. Nudging his horse in the ribs with his heel, Bannion nodded and rode after the water wagon, leaving his cousin to manage the cows.

*****

Neila Bell, nee O'Quinn, drove the water wagon with a strength and expertise belied by her thin, almost bony frame. Selkirk's sister, she enjoyed a status in the clan above older, more settled women. Aside from birthright, she earned the standing by her own efforts, being an excellent doctor and when necessary, a canny fighter.

Harrison Bell was her father-in-law—or he had been. A widow these last three years, her husband had been killed in a clash with Mags. Since then she'd grown harder, leaner, more militant.

Her son, along with two boys, rode atop the kegs in the wagon.

"Harmon, no fooling around up there, showing how brave you are," she yelled to him. "Those cattle need water and the drovers can't hold them forever. It's your job to fill water barrels, not play. Get in and get out. Take too long and those cattle will run right up your ass—and mine. Hustle! You, too, Pak. No slacking, Benji."

"No, ma'am. No slacking," Benji answered for all three.

Neila delivered these reminders and instructions rapid fire, while at the same time guiding the dray horses pulling the wagon—light now, but soon to be very heavy indeed—down the incline and splashing into the ford. Neither her driving, nor her demands upon the children stopped her inner worries. Where was Harrison? Why wasn't he here? Was he dead?

The last question moved through her mind before she could stop it, no matter how she tried to convince herself he was a tough old varmint. Tough—but not invincible.

About mid-way across the river, she pulled the horses to a halt and eased the reins, allowing the animals to lower their heads and drink. Leaning around to see behind her, she waved the following wagons around the dray.

"Chop, chop!" she told the boys, who sprang into action, climbing monkey-like over the kegs. They dropped the pump tubes into the river and cranked like their young lives depended on it, wiry muscles straining. Within moments the pumps began drawing fresh, clean water into the kegs.

"That's it," Neila said. "Keep it up." Reins loose in her hands, she stretched out her back and shoulders. Give her a couple copper pennies, she thought, and watch her jump into the water right now and bathe the dirt and sweat from her body. Soak moisture in through her skin until she felt something different than a desiccated grape. But that wouldn't be fair to the others, especially the men and boys bringing up the rear with the cattle, so she made herself a promise for later, after the kegs were filled, and everyone safely crossed into O'Quinn territory.

Between the kids' grunts and competitive taunts to one another, the clack of pump cranks, and the liquid gurgle of the stream, she failed to hear the splash of Bannion's horse until he showed up at her side.

His horse lowered its head, snuffling through its nose as though to clear the dust before sucking in great gulps of water.

Her cousin Bannion, head of defense and sheriff of the clan, grinned at her, his teeth very white in his filthy face. "If I looked as bad as you do, Cuz, the Techs would never recognize us as full human."

"They prefer not to recognize us anyway, the sciffy bastards." She reined in the horses who'd made a sudden move. Didn't want to throw the boys off the top of the kegs, after all. It was a long way down. "And don't remind me how I look—or smell. I've got a pretty good idea." The moment of what passed for levity with her nowadays faded. "Has anyone seen Harrison? Is he here?"

Bannion shook his head. "Not a sign. I'm sending Nate on ahead as soon as we have something to eat. He'll see what's holding him up."

"Nate won't go alone." It wasn't a question.

"Now, Cuz. Don't you go trying to be his mom. He's traveled all over this country by himself. He wouldn't appreciate your fretting."

"I know." She fiddled with the reins. "But I worry. I worry about you all. O'Quinns sometimes aren't all that good about taking care of their own skins."

"But they ain't stupid. Not Nate and not me."

Neila's smile stretched thin. "I know you aren't. You and Nate and Selkirk—all O'Quinn and a mile wide, graced by the spirits and made better than other men. Even if Nate's last name is different."

At this he laughed. "Finally—she admits it."

"Yes," she said, not smiling now, "and my son, though only half an O'Quinn, has inherited the same traits as his uncles and his cousins. It's enough to make a woman wish she'd married into the Techs. Or the Farmers. Anything but the damn Warrior clan."

"Bullshit," Bannion said above the noise of thirsty cattle growing louder and more imperative. "You wouldn't have it any other way. I don't need to remind you that we wouldn't need warriors if those Techs or Cits would leave us alone, do I?"

"Humph," she said. "And Mags and who know what else." Agreement of a sort.

He pulled his horse's nose from the river, looking toward the bank where the herd milled in increasing impatience. "That's it, boys," he hollered to the three atop the kegs. "Cattle are coming. Get this wagon out of the way, Neila. Camp over there by the cottonwood grove. It's safe enough."

She knew he hadn't scouted across. "How do you know?"

He winked. "A little birdy told me."

Damn him. One probably really had. "Crazy O'Quinn shaman!" she said. "If it can tell you that much, why can't it tell you everything?"

Her question was a reference to Harrison, which she knew Bannion caught. He merely shrugged, kneeing his horse and pushing through the river to the other side.

Aware of a strong dose of self-pity, Neila recalled her complaint had been oft-repeated during her years of widowhood. Too often, perhaps, her rant brought on by outrage against fate as she railed against her husband Caleb's death. The O'Quinn men didn't hold her attitude against her, or even mention it. They just tightened up and ignored it.

Besides, there was nothing any of them could do to alter what had happened. Everyone alive was what they were, and had been since the old world died a hundred years ago.

With a slight sense of shock, she realized the clan had missed the Big Bang commemoration. A centennial, she believed the old ones had called it, although the word was lost in time. They were a few days late reaching their winter homeland, slowed down by unprecedented Mag attacks as they made their way from the mountains where the cattle had grazed through the summer in the upland meadows. The event would be "remembered" a few days late, after they had settled into the safety of their winter homes. If they made it that far.

Why wasn't Harrison here waiting for them?

Neila watched her cousin as he swam his horse into deep water, then urged it onto the river bank nearest the cottonwoods. Sure enough, a flock of small black birds swarmed out of the tree tops, calling in raucous confusion. Bannion waved at them, as though saluting. Safety there, she thought, reading the signs. Just as he promised. Her unconscious tension eased.

She turned around. "You kids got your pumps stowed and secured?" she demanded.

"Yep," Harmon yelled, grinning down at her from the top-most keg. "I was done first."

The other boys, Benji and Pal groaned, but without denying his claim.

A proud mama feeling welled inside her. Harm was a good boy. Too serious and subdued since his father's death, his grin just now a rarity. Too driven and doing his best to take on a man's role. Regret for his shortened youth nagged her beyond reason. Damn those Mags. Someday they'd rid the world of the last of them, then maybe they could live in peace, get back a little of what they'd lost. If the Techs and the Cits let them.

She shook the crazy thought aside.

"Hang on, guys." She snapped the reins over the team, their thirst quenched now, and they settled into their collars, grunting with the effort of moving the heavy load, wheels lumbering through the sandy river bottom. With her sure hand guiding them, they pulled their dripping burden up the gentle incline from the river, following the other O'Quinn clan wagons onto home territory.

Behind her, as soon as everyone had crossed, the barking of dogs and shouts of men marked the progress of the herd as it scattered out along the river bank. Though only three in the afternoon, it would be full dark before the animals settled down and folks could get to their bathing. Time enough to fix a real meal instead of a hodge podge of whatever was quick and easy.

Neila smacked her lips, planning ahead. And then, with the other women, a bath in the usual secluded cove formed before the river took a turn. They were almost home. What joy!

*****

Selkirk lifted his arm and made a circling motion, signaling the drovers to push the cattle into the river. They'd take it slow and allow the animals time to slake their thirst during the crossing. From there, the herd would be hazed out of the water into the meadows a little farther on.

A quick survey showed dried pasture grasses standing tall, a good crop this year. There'd been two decent rainy periods during the growing season and the bottom land was rich with naturally cured hay, full of nutrients that would keep the animals fat all winter. Tomorrow, he'd start some of the men cutting loads of it to be brought in and stacked at headquarters in case winter grew severe. A precaution. He didn't expect it would be needed. For now the supply looked ample.

One worry off his back.

He was thankful to be home. Now, if only Harrison would appear, hale and hearty and as though planning to live forever, he could dismiss the visualized, though not realized, dreams that had haunted him these last two days.

Why should he dream of the old times as if he were present for them? He hadn't been alive then. All he knew came from stories handed down from his great-grandparent's time. That, and the sometimes odd artifacts Nate brought back from his scouting excursions into far-off territories.

He made up his mind to ask Neila for help. Driver of the first wagon in, she and Harmon had the horses out of harness and hobbled on the nearby pasture before the wagon even quit dripping water from immersion in the river. As leader of the women, her responsibility included the selection of a prime location to park the family wagons. She ordered camp set up beneath the sheltering branches of cottonwood trees, barren now with the coming of autumn, but with a thick golden carpet of fallen leaves to cushion their bedrolls. The air was redolent with a sharp, nutty smell.

Neila was waiting for him as he rode up, even though her fire-building techniques never missed a beat.

"Get down. Ease yourself. I'll have tea ready soon," she

greeted him, blowing on sparks thrown from her flint and steel. After all these years, it was still the quickest and most reliable way to make fire. Once, so the lore went, there'd been other, easier ways.

"Plain water is fine," he said. "Though it'll take a gallon before I'm filled." He dismounted, leaning against the sturdy brown gelding with a smothered groan. Stiff enough he could hardly walk, and sore along with it, his muscles protested the long hours in the saddle. When feeling returned to his legs, he limped over to the cask at the side of the wagon and filled a dipper. Taking only small sips for fear his stomach would rebel if he drank too fast, he watched his sister.

"I can't rest long," he said. "There's a lot to do."

She waved a negligent hand. "*Phfft.* Every last one of us is aware of proper procedure, eldest down to the youngest. Don't take yourself so seriously, Selk. You're entitled to a moment and everyone knows it."

He smiled. His people ought to. She told them at least once every day.

A wisp of smoke rose from the small pile of kindling and dry cedar shavings Neila used as tinder. She grunted as she sat back on her heels, piling larger sticks over the fire, teepee fashion.

When flames began snapping at the sticks, she looked over at him and said, "I'll bring a chair. You can take a load off on something softer than that saddle."

"Thanks."

The chair she brought was made of alder, smooth with a patina of age and fine workmanship, one of six in a matched set she carried around in her and Harmon's personal wagon. The wood felt warm under hand. The chairs folded down to almost nothing and when set up, were cushioned with quilted pillows filled with sheep wool. Selkirk sat his abused behind down on one and sighed.

"Feels good. The Bell clan always has been the best

woodworkers and furniture makers I know. These chairs are clever. Who made them, Harrison or Caleb?"

"Harrison," she said. "They're old, maybe forty years, from a pattern designed long before the Big Bang. He gave them to Caleb and me when we married."

"As good as ever," he replied.

She set a metal rod, anchored at either end in Y-shaped posts, over the already-blazing fire and hung a water-filled kettle on it to heat. "You're not here to talk of chairs, Selkirk. What's on your mind?"

"Dreams."

The word captured her full attention, her dirty face in sharp contrast to her thoroughly washed hands.

Wary, she repeated, "Dreams? Yours or somebody else's?"

"Well, they're in my head. I guess that makes them mine."

"What do they say, these dreams?"

He stared into the fire, avoiding her eyes. "It isn't so much what they say, Neila. It's what they show. Maybe you can figure out what they mean."

"Show?" She frowned.

Selkirk nodded. He often had visions inside his head that were portents of things to come. It was no secret. The clanfolk all knew of this odd talent, and since what he saw was never downright wrong—although he failed sometimes to interpret the meaning correctly—they were part of the reason he, and his family, remained clan leaders after all these years. He and his dreams, Bannion with his animals, their cousin Nate with his uncanny weather-sense. Neila had her healing and her wisdom, seeing things in his dreams even he missed. Other extraordinary talents showed within their bloodline. A rarity in their world, one that so far as he knew had not existed anywhere before the event. Moreover, the O'Quinn gifts seemed to be growing stronger, which in his case, made his head ache.

As though called, a portion of the earlier vision appeared

behind his eyes. The woman. The blood. The dog.

It was Harrison's dog.

He looked up to find Neila handing him a steaming cup of spiced tea. Around them, quiet laughter sounded as fires were built, tea made, food prepared. Relieved laughter. They were almost home.

"You went off for a moment," she said. "What is it? Have you seen Harrison in a dream?"

He drew breath to tell her, but the three boys running toward him interrupted his flow of thought.

"Mom, Mom," Harmon called, his young voice soft for all the excitement and alarm the boys were unable to hide. "Come quick. Uncle Selkirk, we've found something you need to see."

He was a smart boy, wise enough not to disturb the whole camp, just now settling into a comfortable nightly routine.

Selkirk got his legs under him and rose, envious of the grace Neila used in rising from her knees on the ground. She was on her feet well before him.

"What is it?" she asked. Plainly her son was safe, so there was no alarm in her voice either.

The boys reached them, Benji and Pak hanging back letting Harmon do the telling.

"We found a body," Harmon whispered. "Of a man." The other boys nodded, solemn as young soldiers.

Harrison? Selkirk's heart sank. "A body? Is it . . ."

Harmon's voice dropper lower. "I think it's a Mag."

The other boys' heads bobbed agreement.

Behind him, Selkirk heard Neila's breath catch. "Show me," he said.

Chapter 3

Pain, running bone deep and raw throughout her body, awakened Lily Turnbow. It didn't help that her bed was the hardest, lumpiest piece of crap imaginable. She wondered, in fact, if someone had played a joke on her by placing a bunch of jagged rocks beneath her mattress. Some joke.

More logically, given the amount of pain, the torture was on purpose. Something like an electric shock jolted through her, eliciting a moan.

Where the hell am I? Not at home in my own bed, that's for sure.

She tried to think, her memory searching for information like a computer with one of those antique dial-up Internet connections. The facts were there, accessing them slow if not impossible. Nothing made sense.

There'd been a fight, shots fired. That much came back to her. *Okay. Good.*

Or not so good, maybe, because the fight had been with someone who was almost certainly a terrorist. He shot at her, and when that failed, stabbed her, cutting her arm.

Lily groaned. From the feel of things, he almost succeeded in killing her during their last struggle, but then—

Then? For the life of her, she couldn't remember what happened next. She was alive. Did that mean she'd won?

Her body twisted under the strength of another surge of…what? Life force? Something that left her gasping, hard put to stifle screaming aloud. She felt as if her blood was burning a new course through long dried arteries and veins, and it hurt. Lord, how it hurt.

She lay still, panting, until after a time the worst pain backed off. Her heartbeat pulsed in her ears, perfectly audible to her sharpened hearing. An errant thought came to her, one that said at least the rain had stopped.

Rain?

Last she remembered it had been dark, the rain pouring out of a leaden sky. Lopez, her superior officer, had revealed himself as a traitor. She remembered hearing him talk to the Arab, urging him to kill her.

Rat bastard.

Her sense of urgency grew. She had to get word to Border Patrol; to Homeland Security; the FBI. Hell, the local cops. She had to tell them not to trust Lopez. He'd put something serious in motion. Something bad for the country.

And something bad for him? The last she heard of him had been a scream.

Hot sunlight beat down on Lily's eyelids. To her surprise, when she forced her eyes open she found blue sky—a summer sky—forming a bright canopy overhead. A few lacy clouds drifted in the high atmosphere.

Had someone moved her from the mausoleum? If so, why had they put her outside by herself and left her in the middle of a hip-high rock pile? Why hadn't they loaded her in the ambulance that must be waiting up on the road?

But she heard nothing. No voices. No motors running.

Where is everybody?

Lily, her muscles and joints creaking like they'd been frozen in place for the last umpty-dozen years, raised herself on one shaking elbow. The movement brought her forearm, the one the Arab had cut with his knife into her line of sight. Stiff with dried blood, the cut sleeve of her jacket flopped open.

Her heartbeat increased, thudding in her ears as she stared, unbelieving. She expected to find an open, bleeding wound, by preference infection free, which she would consider real lucky considering the mausoleum's rat scat infested dirt floor.

What she saw was a double scar about six inches long, one of which bore the raised surface of pale, ridged keloid tissue. Quite ugly, really, nothing any self-respecting physician would show to advertise his surgical prowess. The other scar lay flat, wide, and white. But their appearance didn't bother her as much as the fact she had them at all. To her untrained eye, they looked old. Years old, not weeks, or days—*or hours.*

Which was impossible.

Wasn't it?

How much time had passed since the fight anyway? A glance at her watch showed the battery had died at ten seconds before midnight. Another puzzle since the battery had been replaced only a couple months ago. How weird was that? No weirder, on second thought, than the scars.

But wait. The Arab must have stabbed her as she went down beneath him, scoring her side with that big knife he took such pleasure in flourishing in her face. She remembered the pain, more fear than agony, just as the—what? Thunder? Lightning? Earthquake?—hit. Her mind shied away from thinking of anything else.

Fumbling, she reached around, finding no trace of other wounds. Just the arm. Then why did she feel so weak? What in the hammered hell was going on? Had she come down with some sickness? Dementia, per chance?

Her elbow collapsed beneath her. She flopped down hard enough to take her breath away, forcing a moan from her dry throat.

"Help." Her voice scratched and wavered as though it had forgotten how to speak. She coughed, the pressure causing her insides to blaze with new fire, and tried again. "Help. Anybody? Where are you?"

The raucous caw of a crow sitting on a tree branch arching over her head answered, its cry sounding as if the bird were laughing at her. Damn, she hated crows. Too Edgar Allen Poeish, by far. Or were those ravens? Not that it mattered.

"Hello?" A few seconds later she tried again, a little stronger, a little louder, still shaky. "Hello!"

But although she listened with all her being, only the bird answered. It seemed she was the lone human in this little universe.

After a while, she sat up, feeling as if every little gray cell inside her brain was doing a sit-spin on ice skates. But after a few moments, her vision settled down and she could see again. And think—after a fashion. And oh yes, she could feel. Every pain, every stone and shard of old concrete on which she sat bruising her butt, every toe inside her mud-caked packer boots. She even felt pangs of hunger. Moreover, thoughts of a simple drink of water almost made her weep with longing. Which meant all of this must be real.

But where in this world was she, if not still on the scene of last night's mission?

And what about the lake? She ought to be able to catch a glimpse from here. Or a smell, at least. Hear the gentle lap of waves on shore. But she didn't.

Maybe she'd gone rat's ass crazy. Been gassed with some mind altering crap that screwed up her perceptions. Not a lethal poison gas, because she wasn't, after all, dead. Something peculiar, though, that's for sure. Unless she wasn't alive. Maybe she was walking around in some kind of hell.

Lily grabbed the crumpled edge of what once had been a concrete wall. A piece broke off in her hand, but the rest supported her weight as she pulled herself to her feet. She stood there dizzy, ears buzzing, waiting while her equilibrium reasserted itself.

No. Definitely not dead. Too much pain for that.

So if you're not dead, you're not in hell, right? Right?

"Help!" she called. A moment later, the crow mocked her cry, if not the actual word. "Help." Her arm throbbed.

She knew her problem. Some asswipe had stuck the blade of his ninja knife in her, and the loss of blood had weakened and disoriented her. Made her plumb goofy. As for the scars—

Don't think about the scars. Think about the asswipe.

A terrorist, trying to sneak into the country over the border from Canada, that's who he was, and she the patriot making certain he didn't succeed. Looks like she won—although that might be up for grabs. Still, he must be dead if she wasn't.

Keeping a grip on the wall, she stared wildly around. In that case, what had happened to his body? She shuffled her feet, which is when she realized what she'd taken for a yellowish, rounded rock nudged up against her foot was actually an old human skull, its eye sockets and nose reduced to open holes in the bone. The jawbone, separated from the skull's top, grinned up at her from a foot away, it's teeth out of line and rattling loosely. A few of the other bones scattered about might have belonged to a ribcage. The longest one probably a femur. Closer examination of the skull showed an extra hole in the middle of what had been a forehead.

No. Not possible.

She kicked the skull away, aware of sweat running into her eyes.

Better to study her surroundings. She made out the familiar backdrop of mountains covered in timber. Closer, deciduous trees, some with leaves miraculously reattached since last night, shimmered in greens and golds. Jack pines loomed overhead, the crow still perched on a high branch where it yammered at her. At some time, long ago by the look, several of the pines had fallen criss-crossed like matchsticks, their roots torn out of the ground by a fearsome kind of cataclysm. The one lying across the broken end of the mausoleum showed charred bark as from a forest fire. A very old forest fire.

Not how she remembered the terrain. And yet—

She went to sleep, so to speak, in a mausoleum, and awakened sheltered by worn down stone. The tall angel monument she took cover behind last night—*last night?*—had disappeared. She didn't see a single tombstone. Nothing added up. *Where was everyone?*

Lily checked her pockets, nearly crying when she found her cell phone still in one piece. What a relief to find hints of herself remained with her.

Fingers clumsy in their eagerness, she snapped the tiny case open, touching the key pad to turn it on. And although she tried and tried, pounding the tiny switch two, three, four times, the device did not respond, its battery as dead as the one in her watch.

Everything was wrong. Just wrong.

Her sense of the uncanny increased. Somehow, the phone's demise did not even surprise her. She put the useless instrument back in her pocket and called, "Hello? Can anyone hear me?"

No answer.

The discovery of her Border Patrol badge, a supply of plastic tie handcuffs, and the Glock 9mm that had been half-hidden under her left thigh came as a relief. Nothing electronic about them, thank God. No batteries to die. She looked down and saw something else, too. Something as hard and unyielding as her semi-automatic—the assassin's knife. One of those huge survival gadgets with a hidey-hole in the haft that concealed, among other things, a garrote capable of everything from sawing wood to cutting someone's throat. But this knife must've been custom made, because the blade's sheen, except stains here and there of what she suspected was her blood, glowed bright as new in the sun's glare.

After a while she realized no one was coming no matter how long or how loudly she called.

Holding onto the low wall, she bent and gathered her things, including the knife, and distributed them around her person. Then she started walking, lurching along like someone suffering the most gawd-awful hangover of all time. Each step brought a new wave of pain inside her. Eventually, she reached a break in the trees and caught sight of the lake, a mile or so distant.

A fluttering sensation shook in her belly. Who, she wondered, had cleaned up all traces of the shooting and then, then moved the whole damn lake?

*****

An hour later Lily finally reached the shore. Ignoring the rocks grinding into her kneecaps, she knelt on the gravely beach, sucking water out of her cupped hands with all the greed of a hummingbird at a feeder.

Did *giardiasis* grow in lakes, she wondered, or was the parasite active only in streams? She had some pills in one of her pockets that were supposed to kill a full spectrum of boogers, but she couldn't—absodamnlutely could not—wait twenty minutes for it to work before she drank. Besides, she had no container to put water in. Where were the cast off Dasani bottles or Pepsi cans when she needed one?

She cupped her hands again, alternating scoops to her mouth and splashing her face, which seemed to glow with heat.

The lack of a container—it was odd, now she thought about it. Normally she would be complaining about the junk everyone left scattered about, not the lack thereof, but in this case, without finding something to carry water her range of exploration was limited. It meant she dare not wander far from her water source.

All thought stopped when a wave of nausea swept through her. Stomach twisting, Lily bent over, and barfed up the water. That soon turned into dry heaves, great surges that felt like they were wringing her inside out. The siege, which lasted several minutes, left her sweating, shaken, and hurting more than ever. Weaker, too.

After almost diving headfirst in the lake when she tried washing her face again, Lily sat back, looked to the horizon and took a single sip of water, holding it in her mouth to warm before letting it hit bottom. It tasted fine—like good water should taste. Eyes closed, she swallowed and let her head sink onto her knees, hoping the liquid would stay down. Although the idea increased her queasiness, she knew she needed food to anchor the moisture. Food and a sign of civilization. Hunger—more—a desperate craving for nourishment almost overwhelmed her.

"Concentrate on something else," she told herself. "Something good." The trouble being nothing good came to mind. Only more questions. Impossible questions.

Lily knew most people would've said they heard nothing in the deserted countryside. Complete silence. With her formidable hearing, Lily heard more. The rhythmic sound of waves reaching the shore, the regular movement soothing. To her relief, the clamorous crows had been left back in what had once—last night?—been a cemetery. Birds called here, too, but the species were different; soft cooing doves, a few noisy gulls, a sprightly bunch of sparrows and finch. A faint breeze stirred the colored leaves of bushes.

How can that be, when yesterday—

Inside her head, Lily shied away from remembering last night. *Or the last night she remembered.*

What she didn't hear were people sounds; dogs barking, children playing, car engines revving, sounds of construction. Wasn't someone always hammering on bright days like this?

A sudden disturbance behind her caused Lily's head to whip around. Momentary dizziness blurred her eyesight, but then the iridescent feathers of a cock pheasant became clear. A big male, as unafraid as though he'd never seen a person before, fluttered down not twenty feet away from where she sat and flapped its wings.

Food.

Though not the best choice for hunting birds, Lily drew her Glock. Easing it out of the shoulder holster, she brought the back sight to bear. Take off the bird's head and leave good meat. Her mouth salivated at the thought; her belly burned with need.

Sucking in a breath, she held it, then squeezed the trigger. The hammer snapped down…and nothing happened. Except the pheasant turned toward her, beady-eyed and angry look-ing. It squawked, a rasping call, as if giving her the bird.

A misfire, strange with the reliable Glock.

Undisturbed, the pheasant ignored her, too busy pecking at something on the ground. Lily took deliberate aim, held her breath, squeezed the trigger. And again, nothing happened, except a dry click. She stared down at the gun. The Glock had always been dependable before, and it didn't seem jammed now. Its failure was just another sign of the wrongness she felt everywhere. Working the slide manually took effort but finally, she ejected a round, pressing it between her fingers. The metal cartridge dented, powder spilled. Worthless.

Curious, the bird ambled over to investigate one of the bright brass shell casing the Glock ejected while Lily cursed inaudibly. The ammo may have gone kaput, but she still had the assassin's knife. Maybe she could catch and whack off the pheasant's head before it knew what happened.

Reaching down, she withdrew the big knife from the one of the loops on her duty belt.

"Nice birdy," she whispered, taking a careful step forward.

The bird eyed her, continuing to peck at the cartridge, until she was within a half-dozen feet. With a sudden whirr of wings that made her jump, it took flight. Lily hurled the knife, as much in frustration as in hope of a hit, but her aim held true. The blade hit the pheasant in the head, knocking it out of midair. Unfortunately, the blow wasn't lethal. Squawking and fluttering, going in circles, the pheasant crashed into a bush a few dozen feet up from the shore and disappeared from sight in a cluster of trees where she heard it rattling around.

"Crap!" As fast as she could, Lily followed, bending to pick up both the unfired cartridges and the knife as she came to them. Another wave of dizziness shook her, the weakness more disconcerting than ever after her brief moments of clarity during the hunt.

Reaching the grove gave some relief. The tree trunks provided her with something to hang onto; the shade cooled her sweating face.

"Here birdy, birdy," she called. This time she wanted to frighten the animal into motion; something to show her where it had gone. "Come on. Where are you? Give me a little hint."

The woods smelled alive, lush with a combination of pine resin and the nutty odor of autumn leaves. There were ferns underfoot, adding a green freshness as she crushed them, and she caught the fragrance of mint. No clue where that had come from, but even the smell eased her empty, aching stomach.

A flurry of movement in the underbrush a little to her left snapped her head around.

"Aha," she said. "Gotcha, you little sucker. You're toast." A smile cracked. "Or roast."

A gap in the bushes invited her to burrow through, then a few feet of crawling brought her to an opening. Raising the knife, she pulled a last clump of foliage aside and prepared to separate the pheasant from its head.

Instead, her eyes widening, she froze.

Chapter 4

Smoke from Neila's cooking fire rose straight into the graying sky, passing through the branches of the cottonwood tree before dissipating. Water bubbled in a kettle set over the flames; enough for a hot drink. Scattered around the campsite, other fires flickered as the members of Bannion's patrol rolled out of warm sleeping bags and caught their horses.

Bannion sat beside his cousin's fire, warming his hands and breathing in the fragrant steam of her special morning tea, something, he thought, containing rose hips. His horse, a dun gelding with a dark strip down its back, was already saddled and ground-hitched behind him, nibbling at his shoulder in a friendly way.

Neila waved away the smoke that followed her every move, pulled the tea kettle to the side and set a frying pan in its place. She found a mug and filled it from the kettle, shaking her head as she handed it to him. "You look like forty miles of burned over road. I take it you didn't sleep."

He eyed her right back. "Did you?"

"You know I didn't." She grimaced. "They're getting worse. More of them, and they're bolder. Did you notice . . ."

She had no need to finish her sentence. Bannion knew. In particular, he noticed the way she cut her sentence short, as though she couldn't bear to voice her horror. He answered the unasked question with a short nod.

Last night, every person, man, woman, and child, had filed past the body Harm and the other boys had found outside camp. They'd been a sober bunch, their shock and disgust holding them silent. As a lesson in self-preservation, the viewing worked a treat judging by the clan's horrified reaction.

"This is one of them," he heard one mother tell her children. "If you see something looks like this and you can't kill it, run."

But the Mags were getting harder to kill. Stronger, tougher, and although he didn't want to believe it, wilier. And a whole lot uglier. This one, for instance, the shape of his head all skewed like something half-melted. Three eyes, for Christ's sake. Nate mentioned seeing one with three before, but this was his first. A new twist, and not one he liked. The third eye was only hinted at, like a stutter. Nothing functional, or not yet, anyway. The Mag's bones were growing strangely elongated, too. Had been for a while, the last fifteen years. What new and gruesome trick was fate about to play on them now?

"Been a jump in their evolution," he said, grateful for the warmth of the tea. "Doesn't look like it's for the better."

"Why don't they just die?" Neila burst out. "They're freaks. If a cow drops a bad calf, it dies. We find dead birds, other animals. *Our* babies die!"

"The human species is stubborn," Selkirk said, coming up behind her and putting his hands on her shoulders as though his touch could soothe her. "Even its mutants. And whatever the Mags are now, once they were human." Then, in a shift of subject, "Bannion, your eyes are so red they're almost bleeding. Are you up to leading the patrol? Nate can go in your stead, you know."

Bannion blinked, glad of the clan leader's intervention. He'd heard Neila's lament before, many times. Not that he didn't sympathize, he did, but there wasn't a single thing he could do to ease her mind.

"He's already gone," he said. "If I'd caught him earlier, I'd've put him in charge. Anyway, my eyes are dust burned, is all. And sunburned. The section of cattle trail we were on day before yesterday is still tainted. It'll pass. I'll be all right."

"Is your wound bothering you?"

"Have you had a healer look at your leg?" Neila asked.

"It's fine." The wound was clean, just sore. Anyway, if he wanted to bother a healer, Neila would've been his first choice.

The scent of fried ham and berry muffins fresh out of the Dutch oven had his mouth watering before Neila could fill his plate. He stuffed himself, hurrying to get his patrol underway before the sun full rose. Be out of range before he had to contend with Harm begging to go with him.

"I want to help find Grandpa," he announced last night. "I'm a good finder. I found that Mag, didn't I? Something led me right to it."

Probably the stench of a decaying body, Bannion thought. But yeah. It was beginning to look like Harmon did have real talent as a locator. Bannion would still as soon the boy stuck close to camp for now. It'd save Neila some fretting, he knew, since the signs didn't portend well for finding Harrison alive. What else they would discover at the valley's head was anybody's guess and he didn't want to be thinking about his nephew if it came to a fight.

As though reading his thoughts, Neila said, "The arrow that killed the Mag. It was Harrison's, wasn't it? Even with the fletching broken off and the painted pattern almost obliterated, I'm sure I recognize the colors and those chevrons."

Selkirk cocked his head questioningly at Bannion, who reached around and fed the last of his muffin to his horse.

Bannion nodded. As the clan's sheriff and captain of his people's defense, he knew everyone's patterns. "Yeah. It was Harrison's arrow. One more Mag's hash he's settled.

"The question is, did the Mag also settle Harrison's?" Selkirk asked.

Bannion shrugged. "That's what we're going to find out."

Deeper worry lines crinkled Neila's brow. "Where did the mutant come from, do you suppose? Was he shot here? In that case, alive or dead, where is Harrison? Or did a bunch of them attack the stronghold? In which case, how on earth did one so badly wounded manage to travel this far?"

Brushing muffin crumbs from his shirt, Bannion stood up. "Don't bust a pustlegut trying to guess, Neila. We'll know soon." He turned to Selkirk. "You'll keep everyone close until we come back, won't you? Don't let the kids wander."

Selkirk's face turned somber. "Already got it planned. Kids, as always, are first priority. I'll spot some guards a half-mile from of camp. They'll give us warning if we need to barricade for a fight."

"Good enough." Bannion swung astride his horse and settled his butt on cold saddle leather. "If we're not back by nightfall, double the guards and pull them back to a quarter-mile."

"Will do."

"And if Nate gets back, send him on ahead."

Selkirk nodded.

With the members of his patrol forming up at the edge of camp, Bannion reined his horse toward them, but Neila stepped forward, catching the nose piece on the dun's hackamore.

"Be careful," she begged.

He grinned. Leave it to Neila. Always trying to be his big sister—when she wasn't busy trying to mother him. "I'm always careful," he said.

She gave him one of *those* looks. "No, you're not, cuz, and I try to live with that. But this time…" She swallowed what she started to say. "Be careful and stay alert. I've got a feeling."

"A feeling?"

"Go," she said without elaborating, and swatted his horse on the hindquarters to start him off. She was noted for her feelings, and wisdom dictated a man pay attention.

He soon put Neila's concern from his mind. Dwelling on what could happen did no good. In a fight, it muddled a warrior's thinking, making him cautious when he should be bold, making him bold when he should be cautious. He preferred to rely on his troops training than to be thinking of his cousin's "feeling."

Day broke as the patrollers got underway, horses snorting, equipment rattling. Chief Deputy Zelnor, riding the length of the column, soon had quivers and swords battened down. Wispy clouds tinged pinky orange at the horizon predicted a wind storm in the afternoon. Bannion eyed the weather phenomenon with displeasure. If there were Mags about, they'd be sure to use a storm for cover. Weather didn't bother them much, unlike his patrollers.

Except for Deputy Rongo Zelnor, the members of his patrol were young and inexperienced. One boy from the Bell side of the family riding with them was only sixteen. But a man in his strength, Bannion conceded. This was the patrol's first exercise as a group. They'd seen combat on the way down from the summer pastures, but then they'd been fighting next to hardened warriors. In some cases, they'd been bloodied. All had fought well.

Today they deserved a chance to prove themselves. They'd be riding hard all the way to the head of the valley. These were the strongest of his young patrollers, and those with the fastest horses. Not the steadiest, perhaps, he thought, watching as they spread out along the well-beaten trail leading toward their winter quarters, but give them points for being the most eager. Laughing and calling to one another, they bragged what they'd do when they caught up with more Mags.

"You, Cameron House." He hailed one of the more rambunctious young men.

Cameron broke off his flirtation with a female patroller and spurred his mount over to Bannion's side. The kid was fairer of skin than most of the clan, and he blushed at the slightest provocation. He was blushing now. God only knows what line the girl had been feeding him.

"Yessir?" Cameron made an offhand salute, the casual brush of his first two fingers across his forehead. It annoyed Bannion.

"Damn it, House, no saluting. Hasn't Deputy Zelnor taught you better than that?"

The flush bathed Cameron's face anew, coloring him nearly as bright as the sunrise. "Yessir. He has. Forgot, sir. Won't do it again."

"I'd be grateful," Bannion said. "Do you remember the part about why patrollers don't salute?"

"Yessir. Because if the enemy sees one of us saluting, he'll know who the officer is and do his best to pick him off."

"All right. Seeing as how I have no desire to be shot by a sniper, keep it in mind. And you can cease with the yessir thing, too. Our enemies can hear, as well as see."

"Yessir," House said. "Yes, Mr. O'Quinn, boss. Okay."

Bannion's eyes narrowed as he searched the hillside to his left. The forested ground seemed quiet, but the Mags were good at that. One could be lying doggo until a warrior's horse nearly stepped on him. Then he'd jump up and disembowel the horse, or break its legs if he could, and drag the rider off to kill later.

"Take two people, House," he said, "and scout the hillside through that band of trees. The flight of birds indicates the area's clear, but I don't want to ride into a trap. You know what to watch for?"

"You bet, sir." Excitement at riding point flooded Cameron House's face. "Kris and Bevee, come with me," he called.

Bevee was the girl who'd been flirting with him.

"Stay quiet and keep your proscribed distance from each other," Bannion reminded him. "Rejoin us over by Mallard Landing." At Mallard Landing, the river they were following ran into Frying Pan Lake, the lake so named because if its round shape, the handle being the river that fed it.

"Yessir," House said again. "Yes, Mr. O'Quinn." He stopped another salute before completion and galloped off to relay his orders to the other two.

Bannion grinned, wondering if House'd read about all that sir and salute stuff in one of the books Nate brought home. Looked like the kid had been practicing the salute in front of a mirror, he was so enamored of it. Probably thought it would impress the girls.

As though Bannion's recent thought of him had been a summons, Deputy Zelnor, the grizzled senior scout trotted his horse up beside him. Rongo's mount, a mountain-bred mare, had short legs, which sat its rider well below Bannion's eye level.

As usual, Rongo was grumbling his dissatisfaction with the new crop of patrollers. "This is as rowdy a bunch of hellions as I've seen in a while. Undisciplined young whelps. Listen to them brag now, but mark my words, they'll forget everything they've learned if it comes to a fight."

"They do and it'll be their last time."

"Yeah." Rongo grunted. "Young fools'll all be dead as electric lights."

"Not all of them, I hope. But they'll sure as hell be drummed off patrol." He motioned one laggard girl to close up the spacing between her and the lad to her left. "Are you doubting your own training program, Rongo?"

"I doubt everything until these kids have seen enough of battle to be afraid. Why didn't you order out some of the experienced warriors and leave these kids to guard camp?"

"Are you forgetting we've been fighting a running battle almost since we left the summer lands?" Bannion rubbed the sore spot on his calf, a reminder of the Mag's constant threat. "The older troops are tired; the kids fresh. They've been training, guarding camp, and pushing cattle. Easy stuff. Safe stuff. Not a one of them hurt. Now they get their chance to prove themselves."

Bannion hid the roil of displeasure Rongo's question raised in him. Rongo was good with the young recruits, but he wished to hell the man would stop second-guessing his every move. He got tired of explaining.

As a rule, the patrollers connected with the deputy, a tough man, but fair in his training, able to instill confidence in the kids. When it came to combat, they would've learned tricks from him that had kept more than one of those now experienced people alive long enough to get that way. He was also damn good at following orders. However, he lived only in the moment and wasn't worth a hoot when it came to planning longer term strategy. Fortunately, he left that to Bannion or Nate.

Rongo nodded as though Bannion's explanation had been cribbed from inside his head. "Makes sense, I suppose. Still, it's good knowing help is only a few miles away if we run into trouble."

"Crying for help is not my intention, Rongo," Bannion said. "My intention is for these patrollers to fight their own battles." He sighed. "They've got to be blooded sometime. Might as well be defending their home ground."

This drew a sharp glance from the deputy. "You think there's going to be trouble?"

"Don't you? Didn't that dead Mag tell you anything?"

"Told me Harrison Bell killed him," Rongo said, but now

his gaze had gone to searching the surrounding hills. "Didn't say whether there were more of the bastards around."

Bannion snorted. "When did you ever see just one Mag? Besides, one Mag is dangerous enough. And it means there's probably two more either sneaking up on your backside, or is ready to drop on top of you from above."

Glancing up, Rongo pondered a moment. "Good point. Sonsabitches hunt in packs like wolves."

"They'll come at you from all sides," Bannion agreed. "Means you need a good rear guard. Take one warrior with you and show him how it's done. It'll be a good lesson."

Rongo wore an unwilling grin. "Cagey, ain't you, boss?" He pulled his horse to the side to let the next rider go past and, with a side glance at Bannion, pointed a finger at a brown-haired girl. "You, come with me."

Squinting, Bannion saw that House's group had reached the hills without incident. Birds flew up, calling a raucous warning of the invaders as the three entered the woods and disappeared. He winced. Damn kids were clumsy as a herd of yearling colts.

Bannion nosed his horse into line somewhere in the middle of the patrol. They trotted single file along the grassy path following the riverbank. Insects droned in the dried weeds, water tumbled around boulders shaping the river's flow. An hour passed. Two. A few of the younger riders slumped in their saddles. Bannion gritted his teeth, stifling a reprimand. They'd learn how dangerous slacking off could be soon enough.

Wind, as promised by the crimson-streaked sunrise, kicked up, raising dust devils in the dry meadows stretching away from the river. A red-tail hawk flew overhead, dipping and gliding as it followed the thermals.

They were approaching a copse of trees that shaded the confluence of river and lake when a flock of small, black-winged birds exploded into the sky, making their own thunder. Prickles inched along Bannion's spine. The smaller birds were ignoring the hawk, and the only thing likely to scare them enough to ignore the predator was the presence of humans. Who those humans might be, Bannion couldn't say, but it sure wasn't his group who'd set off the alarm. Not House's, either, just now riding out of the foothills, the three patrollers separated by the standard thirty feet.

It was unlikely anybody hiding amongst the shrubbery would be a friend. For one thing, they were on O'Quinn land. Anyone seeking peace would meet them in the open, arms sheathed, and more often than not, bearing gifts. That left either Mags or Techs, which one didn't much matter. What mattered was how large a war party his posse had to face. Logic told him it couldn't be many. The grove wasn't big enough to hide more than a few.

House's squad had seen the larger patrol, and one of them waved as though to say all is well. They hadn't paid attention to the birds' panic. Bannion's impatience grew. Hadn't Rongo taught them to always watch the birds?

The squad came on, oblivious.

Bannion's sharp whistle drew his patrol to a halt. The girl at the head of the column spun her horse and trotted back down the line. She stopped beside each rider, never letting on that one might be more important than another.

Smart girl, he thought, making a mental note alongside her name. Unlike House, she hadn't forgotten the rules for protecting the commander's ID. Pretty girl, too, he decided as she stopped beside him. And old enough to consider becoming a partner if her bloodline checked out, which it should. Her name was Kira Shandy, another of the Bell family cousins.

"The birds?" she asked, her mouth barely moving.

"Did you see where they rose?"

Although her head never moved, her eyes swiveled toward the trees. "Twenty yards to the left of that lightning-struck cedar."

"Good work. Take two men. You'll find whatever disturbed the birds will have moved. If it's Mags, they'll slip deeper into the woods, hoping to trap our mounts. Get around them and flush'em out."

Her face turned pink. "Me?"

He smiled. "And two men. Go now, before House blunders into them. As soon as you're in position, the rest of us will ride in from the front. We'll catch'em between us. House'll flank them." If the young bugger could be trusted to read the situation as it developed.

Kira nudged her horse in the ribs, turning and lifting it into a lope. She selected the youngster in front of Bannion as one of her crew, picking up another as she rode back to the head of the column. The three of them charged the woods, drawing their swords and dropping the reins as they rode, guiding their horses by knee. But where an ambusher might have expected a frontal attack, the girl directed her riders into a wider circle. Bannion thought he saw a flash of brown body turning to meet them before it became invisible against the underbrush.

He gave them a couple minutes, then his whistle pierced the air on a three-note, and the rest of the patrol lifted their horses into a headlong gallop—except for Rongo and the brown-haired girl, still watching the patrol's rear. Even as he drew his sword from the saddle scabbard, Bannion saw House pull up. The three squad members seemed to confer, and then they, too, broke into a run, riding on a tangent into the fray.

Good boy. Whoever was there would be trapped between his patrol and the river.

"Kill them," Bannion yelled. It was always open season on Mags, but anyone found in clan territory without prior permission came under a death sentence. The clan's safety lay in destroying all enemies, and no quarter was the only way to assure that.

He led his patrol into the trees, heading for the area from which the birds had taken flight. Knee pressure alone gave Nog direction, but the horse, an agile beast, choose the way. The gelding slipped between trees with inches to spare, ears pricked at the prospect of battle.

Bannion held his short sword in his left hand, his fighting knife ready in his right. When the first Mag rose almost beneath Nog's hooves, an iron-tipped wooden spear aimed at the horse's belly, a quick thrust of Bannion's sword drove the mutant backward before he could strike. Blood spurted from a deep slash across his chest. The creature stumbled, screaming his pain and suddenly Kira was there, an arrow nocked in her bow. She released it, catching the Mag in the throat, shutting off the noise.

Except for that, the Mags fought with silent ferocity for the most part, as did the patrollers. Only the clash of steel, snorts and grunts of horses, and a few cries of, "ware" when a Mag got too close sundered the hush.

House's patrollers arrived and ran into immediate trouble. The young squad leader was unhorsed, his mount kicking out its life with another Mag spear in its gut. Two Mags, as though conjured from dirt, appeared one on each side of the boy. Before Bannion could spur Nog toward him, the girl, Bevee, flung herself off her horse onto one of the Mags, attacking him from behind before he could plunge his knife into House's left kidney. She rammed her knee into the Mag's buttocks, grabbed the pigtail hanging down his back and, before he could twist away, slashed his throat in one smooth motion. Blood splashed, but not on her. It was one of Rongo's best moves, classically performed.

House, Bannion noted, also had his opponent well in hand. Other than that, only a single mutant remained alive, running away fast as its thin legs could move. Nog, with little urging, followed.

The Mag, a female, darted from tree to tree, leaping over a windfall with a grace more animal than human. She headed toward the river, seeking the steep banks and cover to be found there. If she made it, her escape was assured.

"Go, Nog." Bannion spurred the horse, forcing him to jump the windfall while trusting a safe landing lay on the other side.

It did. They gained several strides on the Mag, but she was fast enough to have already reached the riverbank and one of the huge boulders scattered there. She ran out on the boulder, but instead of jumping, she turned and flashed a triumphant grin at Bannion, her filed teeth showing razor sharp.

Without pause, he hurled his fighting knife, burying the foot long length of steel in her stomach, just below the ribs. Her eyes widened before she collapsed, still soundless, in a heap atop the rock.

It had been, he thought, a pretty good throw from the back of a running horse.

Chapter 5

Caught off guard by the . . . the *thing* in front of her, Lily Turnbow recoiled in horror as she gazed through a cluster of green-scented ferns at her intended prey. Instead of a pheasant, she'd found a . . . what?

Her vision wavered. Blinking, she reared backward out of reach of the sharply pointed object thrust at her face. On automatic, she fended the jab off with a quick backstroke, and followed up with a downward thrust of the big survival knife already in her hand. The blade must've been razor sharp, slicing through the creature's hand...paw... appendage...and digging deep into a bony chest. The thing threshed its feet a couple times. Then it went still with a bubbling, choked breath. The eyes—were there truly three of them?—remained open.

The stench of putrefying flesh rose, overwhelming the smell of forest and earth.

Lily yanked her knife from the body as though afraid it would catch fire. That, or fizz away into nothing in a kind of chemical reaction. She lurched out of the brush and retching, fell to her knees.

"What the hell?" The red blood dripping from the knife blade appeared ordinary enough, but in a frenzy of revulsion, she plunged the steel time and time again into the soft ground until wrenching tremors called a halt.

What if were more of those awful—creatures? Staring into the nearby woods, her eardrums pulsated in the effort to sharpen her hearing in case anyone—a monster—might be creeping up on her.

Holy crap! That thing hadn't been real, had it? In an already unreal day, maybe her mind was playing tricks. Hunger and dehydration were liable to do that to a person.

What had she actually killed? She needed a second look.

Taking a firm grip on the hilt of the knife, Lily drew in a deep breath and wiggled through the bushes, dry leaves raining down on her head. Ice seemed to incase her innards. Why? She wasn't afraid the damn thing would come back to life, was she?

Logic told her nothing came back from a knife stuck through the heart, but that didn't prevent replays of every horror movie she'd ever seen from running through her head. She closed her eyes, half-hoping the body would be gone when she opened them.

No such luck. The corpse sprawled in a bed of greenery, smelling worse by the moment, as if the rot had already spread. She pinched her nose and drew a minimum of air in through her teeth.

The creature wore clumsy looking sandals, tied on with bands of leather. Narrow at the heel and wide at the toes, sort of like a duck's, the calloused foot seemed out of proportion. Walking, it would make very strange looking tracks indeed. Her inspection continued, moving up the body.

Upright, it must've stood well over six and a half feet upon thin elongated bones. Strangely mottled brown skin covered legs sticking out of short pants. And the skin appeared tough, less like a human's and more like the hide of an animal.

The middle part of its body looked normal, both in size and proportion, although again, with inordinately long arm and finger bones. The spear with which it had tried to skewer her, lay fallen beside an out-flung hand. Though pointed and sharp, the broken haft had no added tip, she saw. Old blood showed in the dry crevices of the wood. Releasing a bit of air from her lungs, the examination toiled on.

The thing's head gave her the collywobbles. Stretched and misshapen as though fused when squeezed through a narrow birth canal, it had apparently never assumed a proper shape. But the third eye is what really startled her. Set in a shallow socket, it was a milky blue color, although the other two eyes were brown.

Her stomach lurched again and the rest of her air gushed out. A freak. Living out here in the woods, evidently alone. Why? How could such a thing happen and nobody know?

Lily sucked in a tiny breath through gritted teeth.

He wore no shirt. No boobs, she thought, so it must be male. On the other hand, with anything this screwed up, there was probably only one way to be sure. Using the knife, Lily popped loose the single button holding the britches closed, and flipped back one side.

Yes, definitely male, but the source of the gawd-awful smell also lay revealed. Sometime in the recent past, he'd been wounded in the groin. A frightful wound. From what she could tell, some kind of stab, or shot, or arrow had become infected, then turned gangrenous. Not that she had ever actually seen gangrene, but the pus, the smell, and the angry, discolored flesh was just as reported.

Something like relief flooded through her. Already dying, killing him had probably been an act of mercy. Unintentional perhaps, but a mercy all the same. Hard on the heels of this thought came another. Who, then, had dealt him the first wound?

The smell made the sickness rise again, and with her empty stomach she couldn't afford any more dry heaves. Gagging, Lily retreated. Her back was still turned when a deep, long-drawn rumble sounded behind her. Whirling to face this new threat, she drew the knife into fighting position.

A medium-sized black-and-white dog sat on its haunches looking at her. He had the pheasant—her pheasant—in his mouth.

Lily extended her free hand. "Good dog," she said. "That's my bird. Give it to me."

The dog's head tilted. The rumble came again from deep in his throat.

"Drop it," she commanded, her voice stern.

The dog got up, to all appearances sneering at her around the limp carcass, and trotted away.

"Hey, you. Drop it."

His curled, white-tipped tail waving, the dog went from a trot to a lope.

Well, dang! She needed that pheasant, and had every intention of eating it all by herself. Putting the strange, dead creature from her mind, she ran after the dog, calling every command she could think of. "Stay; sit; down." She gave them all a try. Once, after perhaps half a mile, he looked back at her when she hollered "whoa" and even slowed for a moment, but seeing her laboring after him, turned and kept going.

Finally, after climbing a semi-steep hill, which felt like a true mountain to Lily's trembling legs, she discovered the terrain leveled out at the top and turned into a meadow. Dry grass waved in a breeze that, to her surprise, had picked up and turned a little cold. Across the meadow lay a band of trees, deciduous for the most part, like white-barked birch and golden-leaved aspen. She stopped to catch her breath.

Strange. As she recalled, the leaves, except for some of the bushes like the nine-bark she sheltered under last night as she waited for the plane, had already dropped, but here they were in leaf. Some kind of micro-climate, she supposed, but extreme for this part of the country. That had to be the reason. Any other explanation made no sense.

The dog, far enough ahead of her by now that distance diminished him, stopped and turned his head toward her.

"Yeah," she muttered, as though replying to a question. "I'm coming."

He found a road and padded along it at a good clip. Not a real road, but something resembling an ATV trail without paving or even gravel,. Except there was no ATV. No tire tracks, either. The dog's footprints were the only distinguishable marks she saw in a layer of powdery dust.

How could there be dust when it had poured bucketsful last night? Unable to think of a good answer, holding her aching side, Lily straggled on. The meadow must've been at least a mile across, but thankfully, the dog stayed on the trail. After a few minutes, he disappeared around a bend. She hurried to catch up, and when she, too, had passed the high outcropping of basalt rock broken by small, twisted evergreen trees and sage-like shrubs, found herself at the head of a separate hidden valley.

The dog had disappeared.

"Hey, dog," she called. "Good boy. Where are you?" She wasn't quite sure what she expected. For him to speak to her? And yet, why not, considering the freakishness of everything else encountered today?

Lily snorted, disgusted with herself. What was she doing, anyway, following a black-and-white dog that by now had probably holed up somewhere and eaten her pheasant? Wasting her time, that what, when she ought to find someone in authority to tell about the gruesome being she'd killed. Finished killing, at any rate.

Nevertheless, she pressed on, following the dog's paw prints. His trail showed where he crossed a wide ditch. Or a canal, she thought, that in springtime would drain excess water from the meadow into the lake. An ordinary cattle guard barred the far side, although she had not, as yet, seen any cattle.

Squinting ahead, what she did see lifted her heart. Clustered at the near end of the valley, a group of ranch buildings stood sheltered by hills rising above the meadow and lake. There were a couple of good-sized barns with rock foundations and log sides; three large barracks-like buildings similar to the barns; and several smaller structures of uncertain use, one of which appeared to be a house.

"Thank God!" Lily's exclamation burst out as relief flooded through her. First thing on the docket, demand use of the rancher's phone and call the local sheriff. The longer she waited, the worse her report of the dead creature would appear. Second thing, and here dread filled her, call her boss and report Lopez's treachery. Everybody knew she and Lopez detested each other. Would Smith even believe her?

Clutching her back, which had acquired a deep-centered ache around her kidneys, she shuffled on, sweat pouring down her face, until she came to the first of the smaller buildings. Upon close examination, it seemed oddly built. More like an 1800's fortified outpost than anything else. In fact—craning her neck, she squinted upward—were those portholes in what must be a second or third story? Nah. Ventilation system of some sort. Had to be.

"Hello," she called out. "Anybody here?" She was pretty sure there wasn't or she would've heard them.

Abandoning her pursuit of the dog, she continued on, her destination being the older of the two barns. It bore a decided resemblance in shape, size and location to the one where she stabled Heathen, her formerly wild mustang, before joining the team last night. Thinking about the little mare brought a smile to Lily's face, lightening her mood for a moment. The Border Patrol had incorporated several mustangs into their arsenal of defense, and the animals had proved an excellent investment. Sturdy, and canny, the trail horses performed well in the woods and on rough, off-road terrain. Heathen—regardless of her name—was the best of the lot.

Pushing aside her uneasy feeling about the ranch's familiarity, Lily came to the first of the barracks. She ended up standing in front of a chained and padlocked door made of heavy, rough planks.

This part of the place was nothing like the O'Quinn homestead, the well-kept and prosperous ranch where she stabled Heathen. Heavy silence wrapped the area, which seemed totally deserted. Only the rustle of leaves on some of the trees, and the rush of water in what must be a small stream just beyond her sight broke the stillness.

No telephone, no food, no help.

Lily hadn't cried in years, but she damn well felt like crying now. Sitting down and bawling her eyes out.

Exhausted, she lowered herself to the rock steps in front of the barracks and sat. She was shaking again, harder than ever, and hunger gnawed with a deep, gut-wrenching need. Putting her head on her knees, she rested, trying to will the tremors to stop. There was no need to explore further. Her keen ears and a sharp sense of smell told her she wouldn't find anyone here; the barns were empty of livestock and had been for a while. The barracks doors behind her bore the same heavy chains as the rest of the buildings.

Desolate. Forsaken. Empty of life except for a stray dog.

And no frigging phone.

Gradually, her shaking eased. The sweat dried on her face, leaving her skin feeling sticky and tight. She really did feel rocky, which made her wonder if she was coming down with something—something more than a recent stab with the knife. The ill feeling could hardly be caused by water drunk straight from the lake. Not this fast.

Horror suddenly shook her. Crap! What if the knife had been contaminated with some kind of bacteria or virus. Anthraces, Ebola, bird or swine flu. It had, after all, been in the possession of a man she figured was a terrorist.

A heartfelt groan escaped her, a noise almost in tandem with an echoing kind of groan coming from no more than ten feet away. Her head shot up.

"You. What do you want now?" She eyed the black-and-white dog with some disfavor. He dropped her pheasant between his front legs, all the while staring at her out of beady brown eyes.

The dog huffed, standing above the bird as if in protection. Then, delicately, he picked up the flop-necked pheasant and walked a few steps before turning to look back at her.

"Not again. Who do you think you are?" Lily asked, her eyes narrowing. "Lassie or somebody? Hah! Knowing my luck you're Cujo."

Emitting that funny huffing sound, he took another three or four strides, and paused again.

Lily took a breath, wincing at the pain in her back, and got up. "What? For two cents I'd say you're asking me to follow you." And fooling herself, she suspected, because while the dog wasn't threatening, he didn't appear all that friendly either.

As though reading her mind, the dog wagged its curly tail—once. "Okay," she said, moving toward him. "I'll bite. You lead and I'll follow. But this had better not be a game. I'm not up to playing tag."

The dog darted away, leading her along an almost invisible footpath winding through the woods behind one of the barns. Dry grass and late-blooming weeds grew up in the path, showing no one had been this way for some days. An acrid scent rose up as her footsteps broke stems and leaves and she sneezed, an outburst that caused the dog to stop.

She waved. "Go on," she said, mightily surprised when he did.

Soon she heard the gurgle of running water, which she surmised came from one of the small streams feeding the lake. The sound grew louder as she went until, momentarily losing sight of the dog, she slipped around one of the many large rock outcroppings and found its source. Although no more than four feet wide from bank to grassy bank, the creek swirled over a stony bed, clear and clean.

Lily licked dry lips, but before she could kneel and taste the water, the dog gave a commanding bark, clearly a demand for attention. Looking around, she couldn't see him until, Genie-like, he popped into sight as though spurted from solid rock. She squinted into the shade and, as the dog moved, he exposed what appeared to be the narrow entrance to a cave or a deep crevice in the stone. He huffed again.

"What? You want me to look in there?"

The dog's stare compelled her into taking a few steps toward him.

"There aren't any rattlesnakes in that den, are there?" She shuddered. "Or another thing like that creature down by the lake?"

The dog cocked its head and barked once before darting inside.

Reaching down, she drew the survival knife from her belt. "Better not be," she whispered. Whispered, because, although muffled, she heard sounds from inside the cave, sounds she identified as a man talking. A few words were actually decipherable. Three in particular. "Sliver, no. Hush."

Sliver, huh? An odd name for a dog, even if spoken in a hoarse, fading kind of voice. Still, Lily thought, once was enough for her to have learned a lesson when it came to blundering into blind spots.

As she had done last night when fighting the terrorist—

was it really only last night?—she lowered herself to the ground and crept forward on elbows and knees. And just like last night, it was a good thing she did, for as she peeked into the cave, her shadow bobbing in front of her, she heard the unmistakable twang of a crossbow string as a bolt flew just above her head.

"Hey!" An involuntary yell escaped her as she ducked to the side of the cave opening where the stone offered protection. "Stupid dog, trying to get me killed."

As though protesting this estimation, inside the cave, the dog whined.

She sat up, gasping as fresh pain gripped her back and traveled around her side. Lily listened, her superlative hearing centered on deciphering any sounds. She couldn't help wondering if some weird monster was going to jump out at her with another bolt in his crossbow. If he did, she was as good as dead. She would never be able to bring the knife into play. *Play*. Right.

The dog whined again, louder, imperious. This time there was no admonition to remain quiet. No response at all.

Lily didn't move, trying to breathe through her mouth without making a noise. She could hear the dog panting just a few feet beyond the cave entrance, but no other indication of life or movement. It began to look as though the man who'd shot at her was holding his breath as diligently as she.

The dog's—Sliver's—sudden howl caused her to jump. Pathos seemed to steer his cry, raising goosebumps on her arms. She couldn't bear it.

"Mister," she said, "your dog stole my pheasant. I'm hungry and I'd like it back." Had she gone crazy, saying such a silly thing? "I'm not out to hurt anybody," she continued. "Please. I just want the bird."

Silly or not, nobody laughed. She drew no response at all beyond Sliver's short "huff." Strange. After going so far as to shoot at her, you'd think the guy in the cave would respond somehow, if only to loose another bolt.

"Mister?" Her earlier thought of how the dog was acting like Lassie came back. Movie dogs always brought help to their master when he was in trouble, using actions similar to Sliver's to fetch someone. And of course, the rescuers never arrived until it was almost too late. Could this possibly be the situation?

"Mister? Do you need help?"

She waited, taking in her surroundings while she had the chance. The cave was well-hidden. If it hadn't been for the dog she would never have found it. Never even suspected it existed. She saw no sign of people going in and out for water or other bodily needs, and the dog wasn't big enough to leave much trace of his presence.

So what did that mean? Did it mean whoever was in there was hurt? The creature she killed—he of the gangrenous wound. He lived for a while, there by the lake. Was it possible whoever was in the cave had done the damage and then, also wounded, denned up here?

"Mister," she called into the cave, "I'm coming in. Please don't shoot me."

She wasn't stupid. She dove in low and fast, rolling as she hit the ground, coming to a stop against the dog where he sat guarding a man.

And her bird.

Chapter 6

Lily finished her wild dive into the cave, landing on her sore side and pulling already cramping muscles. She lay still, half paralyzed with pain.

"Ouch. Oh, Lord. Just shoot me."

She stared into the black-and-white dog eyes. In return, it peered down its nose at her before slinking around to lie beside the man who half-sat, half-lay against the far wall of the cave.

The man hadn't moved, a lucky thing for her since she couldn't have stopped him from plugging her. The crossbow had dropped from his hands and fallen on the ground out of his reach.

"Crap," she said, squinting at the body. After the sunshine outdoors she could barely see in the cave's dark interior. "Tell me this isn't another of those freaky things like I found down by the lake."

Sliver rested his chin on the man's leg and uttered a pitiful whine.

"Well, hell." Lily, having seen enough dead bodies for one day, didn't want to get anywhere near this one. Wouldn't have, except those for old Lassie stories as seen on cable reruns returning to her mind.

"Is this why you stole my pheasant?" she asked the dog. "You wanted me to come here? Because you almost got me killed, which I can't say I appreciate. Looks like you ought to make prior arrangements with the host before you lead people on."

Sliver blinked at her.

As Lily's eyes grew accustomed to the gloom, she finally made out the man's features, which thankfully, at least at first glance, looked as normal as her own. Two eyes, a nose, a mouth, a jaw bristling with a week or two's growth of white whiskers. A heavy set of wrinkles indicated he was quite old—maybe seventy or so—and he had the point of one those truly ugly spears stuck in him right where the shoulder and chest go together. She couldn't imagine how he ever managed to cock the crossbow to shoot at her.

Lily crawled to his side, leaning to allow the maximum of outdoor light to shine past her. Putting her middle finger on his carotid, she checked for a pulse. Shallow, thready—but there. She didn't need a thermometer to tell he was running a fever. Heat radiated from his skin.

"You blew it, pooch," she told the dog. "You picked the wrong person to help him. I'm a Border Patrol agent with just enough medical training to know my limitations. Sorry, buddy, this is way out of my league."

Her explanation had no discernible effect on the dog. He leaned over and swiped her hand with his tongue, before doing the same to his master's face. Maybe, she thought, the poor animal had run into a difficulty similar to hers—that of not being able to find anyone else. Maybe she was a last resort to him, too.

Groaning, the man made a slight movement. In her help-lessness, she almost groaned along with him. What on earth should she do now? Any fool could see what he needed was a medi-vac helicopter and a trauma unit. What he got was a tired and sick Border Patrol agent lacking fundamental resources.

Shivering a little, she dug out her cell phone and tried for a signal. Nothing had changed. It was still dead as the proverbial doornail, with nary a single blink or flicker of light. She set the useless piece of junk aside.

"What do you think, Sliver? Should I boil some water? Maybe I should clean and cook that pheasant. Maybe he's as hungry as we are." On second thought, she doubted it. Nobody could be hungrier than she.

The dog tilted its head sidewise, watching as she leaned over to peer at the man's wound. Buried deep in his body, the point of the spear had gone almost far enough to pierce his back on the other side. Someone had broken off the long end. Pus leaked out around the edges, leaving a thin, greenish-gold trail running down his ribs. She sniffed. Maybe it was just the dirt and generally skanky smell of the cave, but she believed the wound might be starting to turn bad. Not as far gone as the creature down by the lake, but bad enough.

"Phew, that's gross." Swallowing heavily, she sat back on her heels. Judging by the bright red flesh, she figured infection had set in. "I'm afraid your master has blood poisoning," she informed the dog. Bits from historical novels came back to her. "I'll bet part of his shirt is trapped in the wound. That spear head needs to come out."

"You do it," he said.

Lily sprawled on her butt in the dirt, crying out in surprise.

"I can't do it myself," His deep voice was weak and halting. "I tried. Can't wait for the clan. You do it."

"Me?" she squeaked. "No. no. Beyond my capabilities, I'm afraid.

His eyes, shut until now, drifted open. They were a very dark blue, she saw, and his hair was snowy white. His unfocused gaze sought her face. "What family?" he asked, his bewilderment plain. Then louder, as if alarmed, "Are you Techno?"

Techno? What the hell was he talking about? "I'm Lily Turn-bow," she said. "I'm with the Border Patrol out of Metaline."

He shook his head, as though she spoke a foreign language and he couldn't understand her words. "Take it out," he demanded. "It's killing me." He slumped, trailing into unconsciousness again.

Sliver huffed a soft whine, sticking his nose under his master's hand and lifting it, as though he were beseeching her on the man's behalf.

Struck dumb by the mere thought of doing what he asked, Lily jumped to her feet, cracking her head a solid whack on the cave's low roof. It served as a reality check. Digging that chunk of lumber out of him would be nothing less than full-fledged surgery. He must be nuts to even suggest such a thing.

Or desperate, an inner voice amended. And it was true she'd seen no one else anywhere, except the three-eyed dead man, if he had been, in fact, a man at all. And the dog. Even the nearby buildings were closed up tight and inaccessible. Damn! If only her cell phone worked and she could call for help. She tried to ignore what her overworked inner voice was asking now. For instance: What help? Where is everybody? Why does everything, from the landscape to the quality of the air, seem skewed? What was that weird creature I killed? *Where the hell am I?*

Sliver's impatient pawing at her leg brought her out of her funk. Could be the dog was smarter than she. She thought he was agreeing with his master, urging her to do something.

Lily brushed dirt and grit from her hands. "Water," she said. "Preferably boiled. Isn't that always the first thing?" She provided an answer for herself. "No. First thing is a fire."

In examining the cave, she found evidence that it had seen use before as a shelter. A circle of blackened stones formed a fire pit over which hung the only amenity, a small kettle. There wasn't much else. No food, and only a small supply of bolts for the man's crossbow. That was it. Certainly no medical equipment that she could find. When she went through his pockets, she discovered he wasn't even carrying a knife.

At least finding dry wood for a fire was no problem; the area was full of it. She gathered an armload and found some cedar punk for tinder. Sanitizing came first, she decided, feeling a little cheered as she dropped the load inside the cave. Then would come the bad part. But after laying the fire, she ran into a major obstacle. Although she searched every pocket in her jacket and cargo pants, she found no matches and, worse luck, the wounded man had none either. With a trace of panic spreading through her, Lily calmed herself by dragging out the terrorist's big survival knife. These things had a waterproof storage cavity in the hilt for matches, didn't they?

They did.

But this one, although she found the cavity, was empty except for a faded note written in Arabic characters that she couldn't even begin to read.

She hunkered beside the fire pit, frustrated and growing madder by the minute.

"You're no help." She glared at the black-and-white dog still guarding the rather bedraggled pheasant. "Seeing as how you can eat it raw, you might as well take that damn bird out of here. I'm sure it's not fit for human consumption by now anyway."

The sound of her voice must have roused the man, because his arms began threshing, and he moaned pitifully. When she went over and felt of him, his face felt hotter than it'd been even a few minutes ago, his skin faded to the color of ashes. The seconds of his life were ticking past with every moment she delayed.

Lily hunkered beside her well-laid fire and stared hopelessly into its center. Now what? One tiny match, that's all she needed. One little spark to bring flame.

She snorted. If the anger searing through her veins was any indication, she ought to have a conflagration going by now. Disgusted, she flipped her hand, meaning to tear down the sticks. Her heart almost stopped as a ball of white light no larger than a pea slid from her fingers to the pile of wood. A tendril of smoke rose from the cedar punk, followed in short order by flickering yellow flames.

"Oh. My. God!" She stared at tiny blaze, her mouth hanging open although transformed into the village idiot. Her heart thumped and she pressed her hand against her chest as though to still the heavy pressure.

That other thing. The thing her mom denied happened on that long ago day, and then told her never to tell anyone about. She'd done it again. But how?

The man spoke from across the fire. "Not a Techno. Not the clan. A Cross-up woman."

She whirled, surprised he still had strength enough to speak. "A Cross-up woman? What do you mean?"

"You know." His eyes closed.

"No, I'm afraid I don't." Lily shook her head. But she saw the discussion was moot as he drifted back into La-La land.

As the fire rose higher, she took the kettle and went to the stream, filling it with water. Within fifteen minutes, water steaming, she dropped the knife in to boil and sterilize. When the time came, she stripped off her t-shirt and tore several inches off the bottom into strips, some for bandages, some for washing cloths. She hadn't realized she planned on going through with it until then. That she actually planned on operating on her new-found friend.

She bet they wouldn't remain friends long.

*****

An hour later, Lily emerged from the cave drooping with exhaustion, yet euphoric, too. So far, the man had survived her rudimentary surgery. Some kind of miracle, she was sure. Taking a deep breath to clear her lungs of campfire smoke, she saw, to her surprise, the twilight shadows already reaching into the trees. A definite chill was in the air. Hunger gnawed at her stomach, fiercer now, painful and urgent.

Sliver, the dog, accompanied her, leaving his master immobile in the cave. The dog's first action was to lift his leg against a weed. Smiling, Lily followed suit—not lifting her leg exactly, but performing a like function.

"Where's that bird?" she asked the dog. "I've changed my mind. I'm not going to worry about food-borne illness. I don't care if it's teeming with salmonella. I'll just cook it well done."

After a short argument with the animal over property rights, she spent the next few minutes moving in and out of the cave preparing the small meal. Wild onions, a little dried at this time of year, still grew along the banks of the creek. So did a fiddlehead fern, and a second crop of asparagus, both remarkably free of frost. Lily harvested them while there was still enough light to see, washed the curling fern sprouts free of brown crusties, then dumped everything together into the washed pot.

Later, as she gathered more wood for the fire, Sliver's behavior arrested her attention. She saw the dog, standing immobile at the edge of the woods where it was darkest. He was staring off to where the locked buildings lay just out of sight. A ridge of hair stood straight up along his spine and he looked, if she wanted to try and describe him, as though he were about to do battle.

To tell the truth, her short hairs rose up and saluted, too, when an unearthly scream reached her sensitive eardrums.

What the hell?

"Sliver! Come here," she whispered harshly. He looked toward her, then, ignoring the summons and with his attention riveted on something beyond her sight, he dropped to his belly, creeping forward with an awkward paddling motion. In seconds, the pattern of his black-and-white coat blended into the background and he disappeared. Shaken, she headed into the cave, seeking at least an illusion of safety.

The eerie, ululating cry sounded again, from a different direction this time, the strangeness of it raising goose bumps on Lily's arms. Instinct told her these sounds could only be coming from the throat of another of those "things." Hands trembling, she set out her small store of defensive paraphernalia. The knife; the garrote from its storage cavity; the wounded man's crossbow and three bolts—no leeway for missing there—and last, her Glock.

Her Glock with its worthless bullets.

Maybe if she willed hard enough, it would work. Yeah. Just like her equally worthless cell phone; like her watch, as dead as the cell. Panting with effort, she began stacking her collection of firewood in the cave's opening, adding a few loose stones from the cave's floor in a kind of barricade. Leave room for Sliver to get in, she reminded herself.

"Mags . . ."

The wounded man's whisper caught her by surprise. "What?" She turned to find his eyes open, with him struggling to sit up. "Lie down." Her command emerged sharper than intended. Voice softening, she said, "You'll start the bleeding again."

Her own jacket, tucked around him against the chill, slipped from his shoulders. "Won't matter if I'm already dead," he said. "Can you manage the crossbow?"

"I can manage." She saw him staring at her Glock, and then he blinked up at her.

"Is that a working unit?" he asked.

"What? My gun?"

He nodded.

"Unfortunately, no. I tried. It misfired twice, the ammunition's fault. It's disintegrated to powder."

"I thought so." His eyes fluttered shut. "That's always the case."

"It is? Why?" She froze as another scream, sounding as if it were just outside, echoed against the walls of the cave. Brush crashed. She heard grunts nearby. "They're here."

"Help me up," he commanded in a weak whisper. "Cock the bow and give it to me."

"You . . ." she started, but why not? Depending on how many of those creatures were ranging the woods, they stood no chance at all unless he fought, too. Besides, the bow belonged to him. Hurrying, she cocked the weapon and put it in his hands.

"Stay awake with that thing," she told him with a faint smile. She took the knife in her right hand, and grasped a fist-sized stone in the left. "I'd just as soon not get an arrow in the back."

One of his bushy white eyebrows lifted. "A sense of humor. I didn't know Cross-ups had any."

"Cro—" she started to say, but at that moment Sliver appeared in the mouth of the cave and with a rattle of loosely piled rocks, scrambled over the inadequate barricade. She caught sight of blood staining his muzzle before he whirled around to meet his pursuers.

There was no more time. The lithe body of a boy—young man—dived into the cave, and Lily leapt to grapple with him, the knife alive in her hand.

From behind her, the man cried out. "No!"

Chapter 7

Twisting in midair, Lily diverted the upward swoop of her knife from the newcomer's midsection. Her blade missed by the narrowest of margins. Besides the frantic entreaty in the wounded man's voice, two other things penetrated her concentration. First, shocking agony as her muscles strained to the breaking point and second, the kid's ordinary brown eyes as he crouched staring at her.

"Crap! Ouch!" She tripped over Sliver, spilled to the ground panting, and stared back at the boy.

"Who're you?" he asked.

"I'm Lily Turnbow. Who're you?"

"Jacob Felix."

His name meant as little to her as her own must to him. He peered into the recesses of the cave where Lily's patient lay and said, "Mr. Bell? Is that you?"

"Me," Bell replied.

"We been lookin' for you. You hurt bad?"

"'Fraid so. Better now. This woman helped me." Bell's voice shook. "The family?"

"Almost here. So are the Mags." The kid, Jacob, scrambled over to Lily's makeshift barricade, already crumbling from the way he flung himself over the top. He squinted into the darkening night. "I'm scout," he told Bell. "A patrol is doggin' my heels. They'll be here soon."

"Praise be." Bell's eyelids fluttered shut and with a soft sigh he lapsed into unconsciousness again.

Lily duck-walked over to him, laying her hand on his forehead. "He's burning up with fever," she said to the boy. "I hope your folks know a good doctor. They need to get this man to the nearest hospital."

Jacob, who was carrying what had to be a custom-made recurve bow strung and ready to shoot, reached behind him for an arrow and nocked it. His attention focused outside the cave, he didn't turn around. "Hospital? I think they got one in the city."

Lily frowned. "Well, sure, but there's a small one in Colville. I guess that's closest. They could stabilize him there before sending him to town."

He made a phtting sound. "Shoot, there's nothin' much in Colville except burned bones. Neila does our doctorin'. Keep him alive until she gets here and she'll pull him through. She's the clan healer."

Healer? Clan? And what else had he said? Something about him being a scout with the patrol right behind him. What did all that mean? What kind of war zone had she happened into, for God's sake? Her mind couldn't seem to focus on what was happening.

"You don't understand," she said. "He's in bad shape. Can you give the hospital a call on your cell? Tell 'em we need an air ambulance out here."

"What's a cell?" His bowstring twanged as he released an arrow into a stand of bushes.

She jerked around. "What are you shooting at? Who is out there?"

"I'm shooting Mags." Reaching into his quiver, he pulled out another arrow. It had a serrated hunting tip suitable for large game. "Wish I knew how many there are. I backtracked the one we found dead in the woods to the compound, then a bunch of them almost caught me. Sliver found me about then and I followed him here. I couldn't remember where the cave was, coming at it from a different angle."

Lily's head buzzed. Here were more allusions she didn't understand. She chose one. "Mags being those weird looking guys."

"Well, yeah." His intonation implied she was some kind of idiot.

An arrow zoomed between them, the wooden shaft splintering against the rock wall above Bell's head. Lily squeaked in surprise.

Before she could blink, Jacob snapped off another shot and from outside, an unearthly scream raised the hairs on Lily's arms.

"Sounds like you got one." She swallowed, her dry throat convulsing.

Angry, unintelligible muttering rose outside.

"Nicked him pretty good, anyway." He glanced at her. "Better put out the fire. Don't want it backlighting us."

Lily, already thinking along the same lines, had a moment of regret. She created that fire out of nothing. It went against the grain to smother it now.

"I made soup," she said. "For Mr. Bell and me. It's been a while since either of us had had anything to eat."

Jacob grimaced. "Yeah. I smelled cooking. Probably what drew the Mags."

Accompanied by the rise of snarling voices, another missile, a hard-thrown rock the size of Lily's fist, caromed into the cave where it ricocheted into her boot with surprising force.

"Ow! Goddammit!" Snatching up the soup pot, she set it against the wall where it would hopefully be out of reach.

Using a stick of wood, she scattered the fire and stamped out the flames. Afterward, it seemed very dark.

"That's better," Jacob said after a couple minutes. "Got my night vision workin'. They won't be takin' us by surprise now."

As if somebody out there was disputing his confidence, the creepy, ululating cry heard earlier grated across her eardrums.

"Ma'am," the boy shifted lower behind his pile of rubble, "do you know how to use a crossbow? Looks like they're plannin' on rushin' us. Don't know if I can keep'em out by myself."

For all Jacob's supposed calm and his air of seasoned combat veteran, Lily heard a quaver. He's just a kid, she reminded herself. A boy.

"I can shoot the bow," she assured him. "But I'm not sure I can reload without seeing what I'm doing. Crossbows aren't something I'm real familiar with. I've got my knife, though, if they get that close." She remembered her Glock and felt around in the dark until she found it. "And this.

He peered at the pistol, a rising moon lending enough ambient light to see. "That old thing," he said, his disinterest clear. "Won't do you any good."

Just like Bell, he somehow divined the pistol's condition at a glance.

"Huh. If they get close enough, I can bean them with it. At least it's made of good quality steel."

Jacob's teeth flashed white. "Guess that'll work. Stab with your knife and jab with your gun. Give'em something to think about. Sliver and I'll take care of the rest."

"Sliver will?"

As if they'd risen from the earth itself, a dozen or so mostly naked beings came dashing toward the mouth of the cave. A frontal attack, Lily thought. Stupid. Or it would've been stupid if her pistol had worked and she could've mowed them down like rabbits. Or if there'd been more defenders in the cave. As it was, the two of them were in danger of being overwhelmed.

She discovered the dog's role when Sliver rushed out to meet the enemy, his sharp white teeth slashing at Achilles tendons, at thin calf muscles, at extraordinarily long arms. Lily saw him in action, a racing whirlwind in attack mode. For a smallish-sized dog, he did an extraordinary amount of damage. One of the attackers tripped over him and fell heavily. Sliver was on him in an instant, grabbing for the Mag's throat. Wishing for a stout set of ear plugs about then, Lily heard a choked off scream and a gurgle.

Another of the creatures went down with one of Jacob's arrows high in her chest. That one lay on the ground writhing and sobbing. A second dropped out with a bolt from Bell's crossbow stuck in his arm. Lily hadn't even realized she'd pulled the trigger until she saw the damage done.

But the rest reached the mouth of the cave. Spears and knives and rocks flew through the air like lethal rain. From the corner of her eye, she saw Jacob drop his bow and ward off a fellow with one of the spears a Mag had thrown.

Another Mag, horribly scarred, shouted something un-intelligible as he jumped over the loose barricade, only to stumble as a piece of firewood rolled beneath his feet. He thumped to the ground in front of her, slashing about wildly with a sword. Lily slammed her Glock down on his head, once, twice. In a sickening thud, the steel connected with his temple, at which he went into a wild sort of prone dance. Dodging his kicking legs, she brandished the big survival knife in every direction with as much vigor her tiring arm allowed. About the time the Mag's legs went still, she became conscious of cutting nothing but air, her opponents gone, and the night quiet except for Jacob gasping for air.

Or was that herself she heard?

Both, she realized. But at least the awful gurgle echoing throughout the cave was coming from a Mag wearing his own spear as a belt buckle—Jacob's work—and not from either of them.

Abruptly, her legs gave out under her and she sat. Her butt met the earth with a spine jolting snap. "Holy crap," she muttered, fighting an almost overwhelming urge to pee her pants. "Are they gone?"

"For now." Jacob frowned. "Ma'am, your face is white as bleached bone. That little skirmish scare you?"

Lily pushed herself up on quivering knees. "Hell, yes, it scared me. What do you think? Weren't you scared?"

"Me, ma'am? No. Not much." A stray moonbeam striking his face just then showed her he was lying.

"You should've been." Her tirade went on. "Anytime I got someone trying kill me, I'm scared. I'm a Border Patrol agent, not a marine, not a ninja, not a Wonder Woman." Plus it had been her first experience of real hand-to-hand combat.

Yet she realized that wasn't quite true. There'd been the Arab. Everything else had been practice. There wasn't, she was discovering, much similarity between training and the real thing. "As for you," her pointed finger demanded honesty, "you're a kid. Where'd you learn to fight?"

"Sergeant Deputy Zelnor. He's our training officer," he said, which only confused her further. He could've been talking about Genghis Khan for all she knew.

Giving up for the moment and leaving him to drag the two Mags they'd killed outside, she edged over to Bell. She was afraid of finding him dead, if not succumbed to his older wound, then re-injured during the fight. He hadn't, she found, although his fever still raged. It was as she pulled her jacket closer around his neck that the thin rustle of cellophane jogged a memory.

Reaching into one of the shoulder pockets, she dug out a sample package of an extra-strength analgesic, one a grocery store clerk had palmed off on her when she went in to buy a candy bar to bring along on the stakeout.

She positively salivated, longing for that Snickers right now; chocolate, peanuts, caramel. Energy. Her stomach grumbled. But the aspirin was a godsend, too.

Tapping the man on his stubbled cheek, she called his name. "Mr. Bell, wake up. Can you hear me? I need you to wake up."

"Are you supposed to do that?" Jacob asked. Finished with his body-removal task, he shuffled over until he was facing her across Bell. "Neila always says people should rest if they've been hurt."

Lily tapped harder. "He's not resting, he's unconscious. If I can get this aspirin down him, he can rest afterward. But he's got to wake up in order to swallow the pills."

"What did you say they're for?"

"They'll help bring his temperature down."

"Neila's got stuff for that," he informed her. "Some stuff she makes from tree bark."

"And do you see Neila, whoever she may be, in this cave right now?" She caught herself as her voice shrilled. "Make yourself useful. Help me sit him up. And then keep watch in case more of those damn Maggots come back."

His snigger reminded her of his youth. Just a kid, really. "Maggots? Nah. They ain't coming back anymore tonight. There's only one or two of 'em left."

"We killed that many?" Lily asked, shocked.

"Well, hell," Jacob said, as if it were nothing. "There weren't more than half a dozen."

So much for Lily's head count.

Harrison Bell groaned, lids fluttering as between them Lily and Jacob picked him up and propped him against the cave wall. "Did we run them off?" He clutched Lily's coat around him like a lifeline as he opened hazy eyes.

"We're good." Jacob answered the unfinished question.

"Here, Mr. Bell," Lily said, "I have a couple aspirin and I want you to swallow them. They'll be bitter, but they'll soon make you feel better. Water?" She looked at Jacob. "Pills are better washed down with liquid."

He jumped up. "I'll get some."

"Neila here?" Bell looked up at her as if hoping.

There was that name again. Lily was working up a regular database on the woman. "No," she said. "But trust me. These will help. They can be hard on an empty stomach, so we'll follow up with a bite of soup." Or they would as long as it hadn't spilled.

Bell's eyelids fluttered. "Not hungry," he muttered.

Lily felt sure that was a bad sign. "The soup'll warm you from the inside out," she said. "Make you feel better." It was something her grandma used to say on the rare occasion Lily came down with an illness.

A tin cup of water dripped on her shoulder, courtesy of Jacob. "Thanks." She dropped the pills into Bell's mouth, open like a baby bird's beak, and pressed the cup to his lips until he sipped a little water. Stream water, she realized, and untreated. It must be safe, after all.

"Bitter," he complained, but afterward he managed a few bites of soup from the still upright pot before firming his lips and refusing more. Settling back with Lily's coat snuggled around him, his eyes closed.

Lily's stomach lurched as, at last, it was her turn at the soup. Remembering her bout of sickness with the water earlier, she borrowed Jacob's cup and drank broth, leaving the pot with the bulk of meat and greens to the boy and Sliver.

Closing her eyes at the first mouthful, she savored the taste. Salty, although she hadn't added any. Had none to add, actually. At the second sip, a long trembling started in her belly and traveled all the way through her. By the time she finished, the tremble had abated. Some of the pain eased. Setting down the cup, she watched Jacob and the dog polish off the fruits of her labor while she checked Bell once more.

Good, he was still breathing. Let the old man sleep. She had the boy to question, and if she couldn't get more information out of him than she could from a wounded man, she was better off in different line of business.

From the moment she awakened this morning, she felt as if she were living a dream. Or had stepped into another world. The feeling continued even now, seeing Jacob lying at the cave's entrance where he had a clear view of the surrounding area. Her ally, for God's sake, was a boy with a bow and arrows, going up against freaks with swords and rocks and sharp teeth. Maybe she was in shock, because how could all this be true?

Wishing for a toothbrush and some minty fresh toothpaste, she cleared her throat. "You're apt to think I'm a little crazy, but these Mags…they…" she stopped. Oh, yeah. He was bound to question her sanity. Hell, she was questioning it herself right now.

He didn't look around. "What about them?"

What could she do? Ask if they were real. She knew they were. Even in the dark of the cave she could see blood splatters on her ballistic vest, and it hadn't come from either her or the pheasant. She shuddered and changed her mind.

"I don't want to talk about Mags, after all," she said. "Tell me about Neila. Who is she?"

Jacob burped. "Good soup," he said, adding, "Neila is our healer."

"Yeah. So you said. But what does that mean? Is she a doctor? A witchy woman? Old woman in an herb patch?"

Jacob scowled. "Watch it. We all respect Neila, and you'd better too."

Hmm. Sensitive young soul, wasn't he? "Sorry. I don't mean to be disrespectful. I just want to know about her, aside from the fact she's a healer. That's all. Is she young? Old? Pretty?"

He ducked his neck in a universal sign indicating he hadn't given the matter any thought. "Pretty old."

What a card.

"She's got a kid. His name is Harmon. She's an O'Quinn, so she's sister to the clan chief. Cousin to my boss, too," he volunteered, pride apparent. "Bannion O'Quinn," he explained at Lily's quick stare. "He's the sheriff and war captain."

War captain? She didn't want to even go there, not yet.

"O'Quinn?" O'Quinn. She knew the name. Knew it well. Lily's mind stuttered over this, but Jacob didn't wait for her to assimilate the information.

"She cleans up nice, I guess," he continued. "She's so much older than me I never thought about it. She's older than you, too. Neila is just Neila." He went quiet a moment. "Neila knows things other folks don't. All the O'Quinns do. It's like—"

"Like what?" She tensed.

Lily heard Sliver panting as he lay by his sleeping master, the dog's breathing loud.

"Magic," Jacob finally said, but he hurried to add, "They're not magicians, though. I'm not saying they are. They'd never go along with that bunch of Cross-ups. Honest."

That bunch of Cross-ups? Lily was not reassured. Harrison Bell believed *she* was a Cross-up.

*****

Bannion rose in his stirrups, easing his tired butt and stretching stiff legs. His eyes rested on the vista of dark green water spreading all the way to the mountains. The wind promised at sunrise had arrived, frosting choppy waves with whitecaps.

From the site of this morning's skirmish, to the turn-off leading to clan headquarters had taken most of the afternoon. Moving slowly, the posse found traces of Mags all along the way; some of which the mutants hadn't bothered to hide.

Bones, shit, cooking fires, broken weapons. And blood, of course. Anywhere you found a Mag, you also found blood.

They'd flushed two more only a couple miles from here, a male and female still bearing vestiges of humanness. Zelnor had quietly dispatched them. He couldn't say it eased his mind, finding so many this close to headquarters, and with no trace of Harrison Bell. The Mags hadn't come this close in years. What had emboldened them now?

Bannion figured he knew. He figured the Mags had gotten Harrison.

"Mr. O'Quinn, sir, we've found something you need to see." Kira Shandy loped up to Bannion, spinning her horse to fall in beside Nog. Although she sounded calm enough, her cheeks were flushed and her brown eyes flashed.

She was a pretty girl whose excitement added to her charm, and Bannion admitted he got a little stirred just looking at her. A patrol wasn't the time to pursue, or even to think of that twitchy fellow in his britches however, and he accepted her report with appropriate gravity.

"What is it, Miss Shandy? Have you found Harrison Bell?"

"No, sir. We've found another dead Mag. It looks like he was killed this morning, but there's something kind of strange."

"Strange? Show me," Bannion said.

Kira kneed her horse, leading the way to a narrow strip of beach where bushes grew within a few yards of the water. When they got to the undergrowth, she slid to the ground, saying, "In here, sir. Watch your head. We have to crawl."

Bannion followed her, aware of her firm bottom moving just ahead. So admirable was the sight, he nearly ran into her when she stopped after only a few feet. Not nearly long enough, considering the view. But then, he already knew what lay ahead. The buzz of a thousand flies along with the prevailing stink of death warned him. The only question was who—or what.

He wriggled up until they were even. The brown-haired girl who'd been riding drag with Rondo Zelnor earlier was already there, ducked under low-hanging foliage and squatting by the body of a male Mag, one of the three-eyed variety, intent on examining the wound in its ribs. Fresh blood, still sticky, bathed the Mag's thin chest.

"Report," Bannion said.

Kira took the lead. "As ordered, sir, me and Dulce and Luke were scouting ahead. Dulce saw a bunch of magpies diving into these bushes and chattering away, which made her curious. Then we smelled something rotten, so I sent her and Luke to investigate while I kept watch. They found this dead Mag."

Flies, in a loudly buzzing swarm of iridescent green, rose up in a cloud from the body as Dulce waved them away. She pointed at the wound, her voice rising in excitement. "Look here, Mr. O'Quinn. This one right here is a fresh wound. He's only been dead a little while. But he was hurt bad before that, and holed up here, probably waiting for more of his kind to come find him."

"Is that so?" Bannion moved up beside her for a closer look. The smell rising from the body was horrific. Gangrene, enticing to flies, sickening to humans.

"Yes," Dulce replied, gagging a little. "See here. Here's the first wound, the sick one."

"Do you think he killed himself when the pain got too bad?"

"No, sir," Dulce said confidently. "See here? What killed him was this stab wound. See the marks of a blade? But the only weapon here is a broken end of a spear, and it has a round head."

Bannion, whose first glance had told him as much, smiled at the girl. "An excellent observation, Dulce. I believe you're right. Is there anything to show who finished him off?" The kids had been in here, moving around, muddling the scene. He expected there'd be little to find by now, even by as seasoned a tracker as Nate or himself.

"No weapon left behind," Kira said. "Whoever it was took the weapon with him. But look…" Like a prideful magician, she motioned him over to the side, and pointed at some marks showing on the soft ground. "Have you ever seen anything like this, sir?"

Bannion peered down at a sharply delineated track imprinted in dew-dampened soil.

"Never have," he said. A footprint, sure, but one shod in gear new to him. Not a moccasin, like everyone—including Mags—here in the hinterlands wore at one time or another. Nor had it been made by a riding boot, with a heel mark distinct from the ball and toe. It wasn't like the smooth-soled shoes worn by the Techs and Cits, either.

Looking up, he found the girls focused on his reaction. There was something else, he noticed, besides the odd cuts made in the sole. "What's your take on size?"

Kira set her foot down beside the track. "Smaller than mine. Do you think it might be a woman, sir?"

He shrugged. "Or a boy."

"Or a small man," Dulce added and, as the other two stared at her, "Well, it could be. Maybe."

"Maybe." Bannion winked at her, leaving her flustered, before shifting his attention to the other girl. "Kira, detail someone from your squad who's good at tracking to see where this person went. The rest of us will stay here until he reports."

Kira's face lit up. "Already done, sir. Jacob Felix is the best in our squad, and he's on it."

Bannion started backing out of the shrubbery. "Well done, patrollers, I'm proud of you. I'll speak of you all at the next clan meeting—a graduation ceremony seems in order."

He pretended not to notice the look the girls exchanged, or the delight they tried to hide. Graduation meant coveted warrior status, better than just regular patrollers or posse members. It meant you were someone in the clan. That he should promote them on their first exercise was special, but they deserved it. He had experienced men in his troop who were not as observant, nor as able to draw accurate conclusions from those observations. Rondo had done a good job with this batch of kids, even Cameron House once the boy got over his first battle wobblies.

Out in the open again, Bannion called Sergeant Zelnor, who had allowed the patrollers to dismount, to him. "Check out the body Miss Shandy's squad found, Rondo. Then have somebody bury it. Can't stand the stink."

Rondo gawked at him. "Another Mag, boss?"

"Yep. This one is more interesting than the other. You'll see." He motioned the sergeant over to what was becoming a well-worn path into the bushes.

In seconds, Rondo reappeared, his rear skinny in baggy homespun britches. The older man grunted as he stood up. "Shall we camp upwind, boss? Or do you want to wait a while to see if Felix shows up. We've got another hour of daylight. Time enough to make headquarters."

"We'll wait on Felix's report. We know we've been driving a few Mags in front of us. I don't want to run into a bunch of them in the dark. Don't want to stampede them into Felix, or Harrison, either, if he's still alive."

Rondo nodded. "Gotcha." He lifted his voice, calling in a couple of weary kids who, their legs stiff, mounted up and rode out a hundred yards—perimeter guards for the camp. He set a couple others to setting up a picket line for the horses, one to digging a latrine, and three to fixing a cold meal. No fire to warn the Mags of their range, and it wouldn't hurt the kids any. They were all healthy and young, and had been eating regularly.

Bannion hitched Nog in the middle of the picket line. Experience had shown if a mount was stolen, it was almost always one on the end, and he never took chances with his best war horse. After that he found a relatively smooth spot near the beach on which to sit and eat his bread and jerky. Trail rations. Good, though not inspiring. He had no doubt that tomorrow the rest of the clan would be cleared to come forward, they'd settle into winter quarters, and food would be plentiful during the winter months.

What he didn't expect was the wait for Jacob Felix to go on through the night until the next morning when, at daylight, writing the youngest of the patrol off as dead, the troop saddled up and rode on. Bannion, grim-faced, sent a line of scouts fanning out into the meadow, moving slow and careful, until at last the headquarters buildings came into sight.

Chapter 8

Rongo Zelnor's hand on his shoulder woke Bannion an hour before dawn. The sergeant's eyes were glassy from hours spent staring into the dark during his watch. His chin bristled with graying whiskers, but his report bid fair. "Mags have vanished, boss, with nary a smell of one all night. Looks like we got'em on the run."

Bannion grunted a reply. Pushing his blanket aside, he sat up and yawned. He felt as weary this morning as when he went to bed. Too many nights short on sleep. Last night before retiring, he spoke with each member of the posse. Imbuing his young recruits with confidence, he figured, was more important than an hour in the sack. By the time he gave several commendations for work well done, then made a few suggestions on ways to formulate a better performance, the hour had grown late. Hell, he even stuck his nose into a couple's personal zone regarding the impropriety of romance on the trail. Affairs of the heart were not his forte, he admitted, remembering the girl's tears.

"Get Jacob Felix up and send him to me," he said, stretching arms above his head and twisting, trying to dekink his spine. "I want his report first thing. Meanwhile, rouse the troops and have them saddle their horses. I want to arrive at headquarters by daybreak."

Zelnor nodded, but didn't move. "The kid didn't make it back, boss."

Teeth gritting, Bannion reached beneath the saddle he used as a pillow, found his knife and rammed it into the sheath at his side. "That's not good," he said finally, soul flinching from his next duty. He dreaded giving bad news to the boy's mother.

"Nope, not good," Rongo agreed. "Best situation is he found Bell and Bell made him stay the night. Would've been the smart thing to do, considering the number of Mags we ran into yesterday."

"Those weren't Felix's orders." Shaking his head, Bannion rose to his feet. "He was to scout and return ASAP. Do you think he would've disobeyed?"

"Not on purpose."

"I don't think so either. House or one of the others might, but not the Felix kid. Being the youngest, he's always trying harder to prove himself."

"Have some experience with that yourself, don't you, boss?"

Bannion snorted. "Once upon a time." He bent, picked up his blanket and shook the dirt off before rolling it to fit behind his saddle. "Time is wasting, Sergeant Zelnor. Let's get moving."

Five minutes later they were trotting along a trail lined with thirty-year-old timber, the patrol in a double column, a configuration Rongo complained about until Bannion assured him it was safe.

The deputy scowled. "How do you know? Granted, we ain't seen a Mag all night, but that don't necessarily mean they aren't around."

Bannion knew they were around. Just not on this trail.

So he sighed and gave Zelnor a straight answer. "The birds, Rongo. They told me."

Rongo glared. "Wish to hell you wouldn't say stuff like that. It's creepy. Makes me think you're one of those Cross-up people."

"But the birds did tell me. They'd tell you, too, if you'd listen."

"Then they'd better talk in words. I don't understand anything but plain speaking."

"That's the point. They're talking, singing, chattering… whatever you want to call it." Bannion pretended he hadn't heard Rongo's crack about the Cross-ups.

To his credit, Rongo cocked his head and did a minute of the recommended listening. "Gotcha," he said at last. "I hear the horses, and the jingle of tack. Should do something about that, I suspect. We're getting careless. I hear a breeze rattling in the trees and bushes. I also hear some kid—probably House—talking when he ought to have his mouth shut. And you're right. I hear birds. Never hear any birds around Mags. I don't know why."

He didn't mention the smell of dust, of dew, of trees, and people and horses. Perhaps it didn't occur to him that if bodies had been lying in ambush, there'd also have been the scent of crushed ferns, the acrid odor of bruised wormwood, and the sweet smell of dog fennel. Bannion felt bad about the sergeant's lack. It meant Rongo was getting old and losing his edge.

He knew Zelnor's admission was an apology of sorts, contrition for overstepping the line. A little punishment wouldn't hurt the old fart, seeing Rongo would keep harping on the subject of Bannion's differences from the rest of the clan until he ran it in the ground.

He switched to commander mode. "Take one trooper and watch our back-trail, if you please, sergeant."

"Me?" Rongo protested. "What for? I should be out front leading. Send that girl, Kira Shandy. She can guard our rear. Probably be thrilled."

"Back trail, mister. Consider it a position of honor."

As if saying her name brought her, Kira Shandy appeared at Bannion's side just as Rongo huffed a reply and swung his horse around. The young woman's eyes bore dark rings beneath them, worry lay plain upon her pretty face.

"Mr. O'Quinn," she said, "permission to ride ahead and look for Jacob Felix?"

"Denied. We're staying together the rest of the way to headquarters. I don't want anymore stragglers." Without his being conscious of it, anger had crept into Bannion's voice.

"I should've sent someone else." Kira was staring straight ahead. "Someone with more experience. It's just that Jacob—"

"You made the right decision. If he's the best tracker in the unit, he's the logical choice. Don't beat yourself up, Miss Shandy."

"But, his mother—" she faltered to a stop.

They all, Bannion realized, were writing the boy off. Maybe Zelnor was correct. Maybe Harrison Bell had— A sudden frisson caused him to sit forward in the saddle. He flung up a hand to stop Kira from speaking and, listening intently, scanned the silent woods around them, and the sky above, with a sharp eye.

"Ride to the head of the column," he told Kira after a moment. "Now. At a canter. Weapons at the ready."

"Sir?" Her tired eyes widened. "Mags?"

"Yes. Now."

The girl loped off, crashing through the weeds at the side of the trail as she went around the column, raising not only dust, but the smells previously missing. Nog's yellow teeth scratched the horse ahead of him as Bannion gigged him in the flanks. A silent arm gesture drew those behind him forward, warning them to keep up. Soon there would be screams, blood and death. He knew. The birds had told him.

*****

"We should rig up a litter," Lily said to Jacob. "He can't walk."

"If we're carrying him, we can't fight." Jacob, his face too tired and drawn for a sixteen-year-old, stared out into the clearing in front of the cave. Light in the sky above the distant mountains raised a ragged silhouette, but here it was still dark and quiet. Too quiet? The birds, a comfortable nocturnal accompaniment, had fallen silent.

"Maybe we should just stay here." Lily's eyes scratched as though full of sand, the lack of sleep getting to her. On top of that, her innards still hurt, and so did her heart. But it was her mind that agonized, ran amok with bewilderment. Where was she? How had she gotten here? What the hell was going on? Had she gone out of her mind? The fire . . . *what was she*?

Drawing herself back from that particular edge, she made her argument. "We fought those things off before. Your people will be out looking for you, won't they? Why not let them catch up to us?"

"They'll be along," Jacob said. "Which is why we need to go now. We got to warn them. Don't want them riding into a trap."

Riding into a trap. He sounded like a character out of one of the western novels her Grandpa used to spend his evenings reading. She liked the sound of cavalry to the rescue better than his take on the subject, but facts were facts.

"What makes you think we can avoid a trap? Aren't they out there waiting for us?"

"Sure. But they think they have us bottled up. If we can just get out of here now, and into the woods, Sliver can smell them out and guide us through them. But not if we're carrying a litter. We'll be too noisy, too slow. Can't tell where to put our feet."

"Mr. Bell can't possibly—" she began, only to have her opinion overridden.

"Jacob's right. We can't stay here." Harrison Bell had awakened after all. "I can walk on my own. I'll have to."

Lily turned to look at him, seeing no more than an indistinct white face as he struggled to sit. From beside him, the dog stared at Lily as if distrustful of her. Probably still miffed over losing the pheasant.

"Well?" Bell extended his good arm. "Help me up. By the way, thank you for the loan of your coat, young lady. I expect you could've used it yourself, last night."

She hurried forward to help him, noticing that Jacob never once took his eyes from the outside.

"My vest kept me warm," she lied, drawing Bell to his feet. Warming her was the only thing it was good for, seeing it appeared to have lost the qualities that made it bulletproof. Gone flaccid, she wasn't any too sure it could stop a butter knife, let alone one of those sharp-chiseled spears or an arrow. Looked like she might find out.

Standing on his own, Bell panted in short gasps. He propped himself against the cave wall, his eyes unfocused. Then he asked, "See anything, Jacob?"

"Nah. All quiet. I think they're sleeping."

"We'll soon see." Although Bell said nothing Lily could hear, in some way he called Sliver to him. "I'm sending the dog out. Let him get into the woods, then we'll follow him. Bring my bow. I don't want to leave it for a Mag to find. You ready?"

Lily zipped her coat, hooked Bell's crossbow, now without bolts, to her belt, and took up the Arab's knife. "I'm good."

She didn't see how the old man directed the dog. Osmosis, perhaps, but Sliver dashed out and across the clearing, his belly near the ground, his white and black colors blurring. At the edge he stopped, waiting for the people. Lily and Bell, his good arm across her left shoulder, staggered out next. Jacob, light as a ballet dancer and just as nimble, brought up the rear, his head constantly swiveling, trying to see all ways at once.

They couldn't run. Lily hadn't been prepared for Bell's weight, and she thought he had underestimated his weakness. After a time that seemed everlasting, sheer determination got them into the trees beyond the cave.

Behind them, Jacob whispered, "We're movin' too slow. We gotta hurry."

Bell managed to stay upright while Lily waited for her heartbeat to ease. "Straight through the woods," he mouthed, at which Jacob nodded. A motion of Bell's hand sent Sliver on ahead again. They followed.

This route was different from the one Lily had taken to the cave yesterday. There'd been a path from the other direction. Here, they cut through the woods, stumbling over downed logs hidden in tall grasses and dying weeds, catching their toes in animal burrows sprouting from the ground, avoiding snags and clusters of thorny wild rose bushes. It was hard work, and they weren't up for it. Or only, perhaps, Jacob, who in his youth appeared bred for wilderness tactics.

Once the boy grabbed her arm, stopping her in mid-step. He squatted low, indicating she and Bell do the same. The maneuver almost brought them all down in a heap. But then she scarcely dared blink, for no more than twenty feet away four Mags snaked through the forest, headed in the same direction as they. The creatures made no attempt at silence, for which she was grateful.

In what appeared at first to be bad timing, Sliver chose that moment to show himself. One of the Mags pointed and said something. Another raised his spear, took a couple running steps, and cast it at the dog.

Lily gasped, choking back a scream. Only Bell's soft, "shh," prevented the outcry.

As it happened, no warning was necessary. As if he were afraid of the Mags, Sliver darted into the brush, the spear missing by a good four feet. Rushing ahead, the Mags gave chase, laughing now, and yelling, "Kill, kill. Debil dog."

So, she thought, more than a little shocked, they did speak. Moreover, they spoke English—of a sort. What in God's name were they? Where had they come from?

When the creatures were out of sight—if not out of hearing—Jacob scrambled to his feet, pulling Harrison Bell with him. The old man's face was chalk white, but he was game to go on, grabbing hold of Lily once more and gesturing Jacob to take point.

"Go," he murmured, "Go, go." As if any of them needed urging. Sliver, in running away, had cleared a trail for them. Crouching low and trying to stay below the taller bushes, they lurched along. Perspiration poured down Lily's face and between her breasts. Bell was sweating like a horse, his shirt wet where his underarm rested on her shoulder.

Ahead, a small clearing of about an acre beckoned. Jacob stopped at the edge and said, "I'll go first. If nothing happens, when I'm about twenty yards out, you follow. I'll cover you."

Bell nodded. "Go."

Lily's heart thundered. Having never been so weak in her life, here she was trying, in effect, to carry the old man. Grateful for even so slight a respite as the time it took Jacob to reach his objective, she wheezed, realizing she was holding her breath.

Hearing tuned to her surroundings, voices and the sound of pounding feet warned her the Mags were only seconds behind them. Without waiting for Jacob to gesture to them, she took firm hold of Bell and plunged onward. Another of those weird trilling cries announced they'd been spotted. The center of her back quivered, waiting for one of the Mag's primitive spears.

They reached Jacob without being hit, passing him without stopping. His bowstring twanged. Behind them, a shrill wail rose.

"Got her," he grunted, and ran past them, stopped again, turned and loosed another arrow. "Sonuvabitch. Move, move!"

Bell stumbled, taking Lily to the ground with him, but immediately he clambered to his feet. "Drag me if you have to," he panted. "But don't leave me unless you kill me first."

Shock ran along Lily's nerves. "They're closing in," Jacob yelled. "Look out ahead."

Lily took a firmer grip on the big knife, wishing with all her heart for a semi-auto AK-47 or even her Glock. This hand-to-hand crap was for the birds.

No sooner did that thought flash through her mind than, like a giant lizard, a being with sharpened teeth rose up in front of her. It had a three foot sword in its hand, and seemed intent on stabbing her. Sweat flicked from his forehead, his odor rank as any wild beast.

Letting Bell slide to the ground at her side, she stepped forward in front of him and crouched. The . . . the Mag . . . moved awkwardly, perhaps the fault of his oddly bowed legs. Lily feinted right, then dodged left. Darting closer, she slashing wildly with her foot-long blade. A deep gash opened across the being's ribcage, and he emitted a startling, agonized screech. As he stumbled, sheer terror made Lily reach out and cut into his neck. Blood spurted with a coppery stench.

Without waiting to see if the Mag was dead, she grabbed Bell and hoisted him up again. Fresh blood welled from his wound, soaking through his bandage.

The clearing, she saw now, ended at the edge of the same creek that had run in front of the cave. At the realization, she became aware of Bell saying, "Cross. Not deep. Meadow on other side."

"We'll make it," Jacob panted.

Using what must be a dwindling supply of adrenaline-powered energy, Bell managed to keep his legs moving. They slid down a soft, muddy bank, splashed through a foot or so of slow-moving water, and struggled up the steeper bank on the other side.

A Mag rose up almost at Lily's feet. To her horror, this one was armed with a spear tipped with gleaming steel. He was not so strangely formed as the other had been which, seeing him weave out of reach of her flicking knife, made him all the more dangerous.

Sliver, darting out of the deep meadow grass, leapt for the Mag's spear arm. Sharp teeth tore at the meat of its wrist. The Mag yelled, shook the dog away and in the same movement, switched the spear to his other hand. He prodded at Lily, his spear point locking with her knife blade.

His sharpened teeth showed in a grin as a twist of his wrist flicked the knife from her hand.

Holy crap! Where had Jacob disappeared to?

Lily's heartbeat pulsed in her ears. She was aware of Bell crawling through the grass beside her, his hand patting the ground as he tried to find her knife. A little farther away, Sliver whimpered. Somewhere in the distance a horse neighed and people yelled. That weird, gurgling call the Mags made shivered around the field.

Her eyes locked with the Mag's, his grin widening.

Disarmed. Defenseless. Powerless.

Bell yelled at her, something that made no sense. Run… ate? What?

She never knew what made her think she could do it, but

as the spear jabbed toward her heart, she flung a handful of fear at the Mag. A handful of fear mixed with fury mixed with—*fire*. A splattering ball of fire that flashed in his face, searing his eyes and setting his hair aflame.

Suddenly Jacob was beside her; his bowstring thrummed and the burning Mag lay still and silent on the ground.

"Sonuvabitch!" Jacob stared at her, his mouth open.

Bell was up, Lily's knife gripped in his fist. "C'mon," he said, his whisper roaring as loud as a shout.

Jacob's quiver was empty of arrows. He took over assisting Harrison Bell, leaving Lily to run elbow to elbow with him on one side of her.

"I hope you can you repeat that trick," he said. "Look."

Lily's gaze followed where he pointed. Pouring out of the forest beyond the meadow were people on horseback. Armed people on horseback, carrying short spears and gleaming sword blades. Spears and swords? Sweet Jesus!

"The riders are our people." Jacob sounded jubilant. "We've got to keep Mr. Bell safe until they reach us."

What did he mean? People didn't ride horses into battle. This wasn't the freaking Nineteenth Century. The cavalry rode in Humvees nowadays. Nevertheless, the squeal of horses and the pounding of their hooves took the place of racing engines.

Squinting into the light, she wondered when day had broken. As soon as they'd passed out of the tree belt, she supposed, because now the sun shone down on the broad meadow spread in front of them. The meadow was filled with tall, drying grasses, a field of overgrown hay. Dew frosted grass steamed lightly under the golden glow. It smelled of autumn.

But she hadn't time to think of that. Jacob had shown her a more pressing problem. The stirring of the tall grasses didn't come from a freshened morning breeze. No. It came from the gangling brown bodies of a dozen or more Mags wiggling through the grass separating them from the riders. The mutant's movement startled at least a hundred birds, starlings or the like, into the morning sky, all of them calling warning to the others. As though a signal had been passed, the Mags leapt to their feet, no longer silent.

Jacob looked at her. "I sure hope you have some more of those fireballs up your sleeve, Lily Turnbow."

Chapter 9

Bannion O'Quinn urged his troops forward, their horses galloping over the uneven terrain at greater speed than prudence decreed. Bannion put his trust in the shrieking flights of birds swooping across the sky over toward headquarters. They'd find trouble there, he knew, not along the road.

When they reached the edge of the meadow, he threw up his hand to halt the riders, holding them until the last patroller caught up. From atop Nog, he had a clear view of the far edge of the meadow where a fight raged between three of his people and a plentiful scattering of Mags. His three fought silently, the mutants yipped like coyotes.

Rongo reined in beside him. "That's Bell and Felix," he said, squinting into the distance, "but who's that with them?"

Drawing his cavalry style saber from its sheath, Bannion shook his head. "Damned if I know. Looks like whoever it is, is fighting like a tiger." He knotted the reins and let them fall loose on Nog's neck. A quick inspection showed the patrollers armed and ready.

"Watch the deep grass," he reminded the young troops. "Mags will be hiding there. Get our people away first thing.

They're top priority even before finishing off the enemy. Kira, take Felix up behind you. Rongo, grab Bell. House, you get the other one. If one of you falls, next person in line takes over. Got that?"

Heads nodded.

"Let's go. At a run." Pressure from his left knee spun Nog; a toe in the ribs urged the horse into a sprint, the time-honored breeding program of the O'Quinns proving the quarter horse/mustang cross a good one as they burst from the belt of trees into the meadow. A hidden flock of quail exploded almost under their feet, causing the horses to shy and the troop's planned order to straggle. Bannion heard one of the patrollers curse.

Fifty yards into the meadow, he saw Jacob Felix push Bell onto the stranger's shoulder while the boy tackled the mutant leading the attack.

"Kira," he shouted, pointing, and the girl followed him as Nog bore down on the struggling pair. Faster, faster, for God's sake. His patrollers broke into two groups, a few following him, the rest following Rongo and House.

He sensed when Kira's horse broke stride as they caught up with a female Mag. Kira's blade slashed out. The Mag screamed and went down, rolling into the bloodied weeds. Kira and her horse, unscathed by the encounter, rode on.

Nog charged ahead until Bannion dragged at the reins and the horse sat on its haunches, sliding to a stop in the dry grass beside the kid. Felix, in danger of loosing this combat, struggled beneath a wiry Mag trying to scalp him. Writhing like a rattlesnake, the boy stabbed at the mutant's eyes with his belt knife. Putting up a fierce fight, he kept the Mag at a distance despite the blood coursing down his face from a cut along his hairline.

A scar to be proud of, Bannion thought before the tip of his saber sliced through the Mag's spinal cord, preventing any worse damage to the boy. And then Kira was there, reaching for the kid's outstretched hand and yanking him to his feet. Although he must have been almost blinded by blood from his forehead, he managed to spring up behind his rescuer.

Already on the hunt for his next foe, Bannion spun Nog again. A quick glance showed Rongo and House riding side-by-side, the girl Bevee following close behind House as they raced toward Harrison Bell and the stranger.

A naked brown body rose up almost directly under House's horse, too close for the mutant to get any leverage on his spear, but enough to startle the horse into shying out from beneath its rider.

House, his concentration all on the Mag, slid from the right side of his saddle and bounded into the tall grass. Yelling like a crazy man, he stabbed wildly with his sword. Bevee, shooting past him, whirled her horse and came back.

Bad tactics. Bannion made note of a reprimand to be issued at a private meeting after the fight. If either of the kids lived, he meant.

Rongo, oblivious to the drama taking place behind him, sped on, his job now to retrieve Bell.

That's when Bannion, hurrying to provide backup, became aware of two items of crucial importance. One, the person protecting Bell was not only a woman but also a total stranger, and two, unless his eyes had gone bad on him, she was lobbing fireballs at the Mags. They weren't fireballs made of any natural material either, like lighted balls of pitch, because, as he got closer, he saw a tiny sphere of flame start at the ends of her fingers. The flames grew larger, until she hurled it at the nearest Mag. It splashed against the mutant's bare chest.

Wonder jolted through him. The stranger was a god-rotted magician and—here dismay joined the wonder chortling inside him—and, for good or bad, the O'Quinns had her.

On second thought, they didn't. Not yet. Rongo, oblivious to everything except his mission to rescue Harrison Bell, had a mutant impaled on the end of his sword and was shouting at the woman to "get a move on and boost the old man up."

Just for a moment it looked like she might protest, but Bell must've affirmed this truly was a rescue and not another assault. With Rongo pulling and her pushing, they soon got the wounded man up behind the scout.

That left the woman standing by herself and looking very small and forlorn. Four Mags, two male and two female, surrounded her. Rongo, following his orders to save Bell, spurred his horse viciously, pushing a way between them. Grinning and yapping, they let him go, sure now of easier prey.

"Go, Nog," Bannion said, leaning forward in the saddle. Looked like he was closest to the woman as the rest of the patrol had scattered. Individual groups were busy chasing down remnants of the mutant battle force.

Nog's shod hooves beat the dusty earth. Dry plants whispered against Bannion's pant legs. His breath whistled in his lungs as he shifted his saber to his left hand and gripped his long fighting knife with the other. A raven flew over him, arrowing toward the Mags and the woman.

Another fireball leapt from the woman's fingers and splashed into a female Mag's hair. A twitch of her fingers and another, smaller one followed. It hit a bare brown breast. Clung as if glued while the Mag screamed.

Then a third fireball, smaller yet, lit the cloth covering the Mag's crotch. Routed, she ran. Fire engulfed her whole body.

Bannion just had time to see the sick expression on the magician's face before one of the males darted forward, driving his short knife toward her chest. Bannion almost drew Nog to a halt then, figuring the woman was done for.

She never faltered.

Evading the stab as if it were nothing, she danced around the mutant. When close enough, she dropped to one haunch and pivoted in a circle, her free leg taking both the Mag's legs out from beneath him. The creature fell hard. Immediately the woman was up. She snatched the Mag's own knife from his loosened grasp, raised it high. Brought it down hard between ribs.

It was a move that showed training in the art of war.

So, she was a warrior magician. A rare creature indeed.

Another horse and rider shot between them before Bannion could get there, running a Mag into the ground as he did so. The horse squealed as other rider pulled him to a quick stop. *Nate.*

"Get up," he heard Nate snarl to the woman.

Bannion nodded approval to his cousin and threw his knife at the other male Mag, the thin haft almost going all the way through its body. "Take her," he shouted above the Mags' caterwauling. "I've got these."

The woman, her eyes, wide and shocked looking, flinched from the horse rearing above her head, but she reached out with her arm and let Nate grab onto it. Bannion figured his cousin'd have to pull her over the withers in front of him—those Outsider people never knew which end of a horse pooped—but she stepped on his foot and threw her leg over the back of the saddle, perching there like a bird about to take flight.

"Hang on," Nate said and the woman nodded.

Busy watching the magic woman with Nate, Bannion got a little careless, ignoring the last Mag. Fortunately for him, the woman had not. As he put Nog into a spin, another of those molten fireballs slid from her fingers, hitting the Mag in the face. That one screamed and ran blindly until Nog trampled her beneath his sharp-shod hooves.

The sound stopped.

Reaching for the whistle on the string around his neck, Bannion blew three sharp notes. "Fall back to the woods," he bellowed. "Regroup. Begin a sweep. Somebody bring me a prisoner, one that looks like it can talk. The rest die." A smudge of smoke reminded him. "And put out any fires."

The magician had succeeded in setting the meadow on fire.

*****

Lily Turnbow hardly knew what to think. Everything that had happened since she woke up yesterday seemed unreal. Downright preposterous, really. Especially this last battle. It was almost as if she was watching a poorly acted Sci/Fi movie on cable television. But the fearsome screams heard during the conflict had certainly sounded real enough. And the smell of blood and stench of unwashed bodies lingered after all the rest had gone.

Black flashes hovered at the edges of her vision, so that when she closed her eyes, the last thing seen was imprinted on her retina. Things like inkblot daubs of blood, a woman turning into a pillar of fire, a horse charging at her with its nostrils flaring red. A war-horse, for God's sake, like from medieval days only smaller and fleeter of foot. And a grim-faced man atop the horse, almost casual in his actions as he swooped her up.

Her head swam. Words sounded like gibberish. Nothing made sense. Who had started this war? Who and what were these strange enemies? And were the others truly her allies?

Lily's stomach, disturbed by the motion of the horse, churned dangerously. "Let me down," she demanded of her rescuer as they reached the woods. "Quick."

"You're safe for now, magician," the rider said, confusing her even further, but she had no time to bother with that. Before the horse fully stopped she slid from its back and bent over, once again losing the contents of her stomach, sparse as it was. The pain in her gut eased by an infinitesimal amount.

"Are you hurt?" the man on the horse asked.

"Just a little sick," she managed, staggering over to a fallen log and sitting on it. She trembled, deep tremors running through her, wet with sweat, yet feeling cold. Noises from the field grew fainter, until she heard only horses moving about, and then, finally, voices and once, laughter. The pain in her stomach eased, the shaking slowed, then stopped. Breath drew comfortably into her lungs.

Meanwhile, the man sat astride his horse and watched over everything, including her. Oh, yes. Her most of all. Although she avoided meeting his eyes, she felt the weight of his gaze, probing like a scientist examining a bug. Once in a while he shouted greeting to someone in the field. A relief to her in those moments, because for at least then his attention was elsewhere.

When Harrison Bell, helped along by Jacob Felix and a girl, came looking for her, she greeted the old man with distinct relief.

"Mr. Bell, you look better." Her lips curved in a faint smile. "Did you find the healer Jacob told me about? Did you find Neila?"

Bell sank down beside her on the log. "Not yet. But being safe among friends has proved a great restorative."

"I can imagine." Lily turned to Jacob. "And you, kid. I thought you were a goner when that…that…thing had hold of you. You're a good fighter."

"You ain't so bad yourself, Lily," Jacob said, grinning at her compliment. "How'd you do that, anyway?"

Lily shook her head. "Do what?"

"You know." He flicked his fingers. "The fireballs."

Lily swallowed with a dry clicking in her throat. She wished her little trick had passed without notice. Hard to do with spot fires and burned bodies all over the meadow, she supposed. But how in the world was she to attempt an explanation, especially when she couldn't explain the phenomenon to herself?

"Yes, Lily," Bell said, "I'd like to know, too. That's quite an addition to anyone's arsenal."

The man on the horse watched her, his odd, dark amber eyes unblinking as he waited for her answer.

Nope. Not a chance of passing what'd happened off as a figment of their imagination. Smoke still rising from the field prohibited that. And now she had to disappoint them all. Too bad.

"Nobody wants to know more than me." Spurious honesty oozed from her every pore. "But actually I have no idea. I just thought fire, and there it was." She looked at each of them in turn, even the strange girl—young woman, rather. Studying her fingers, she crooked a smile. "You know what's really weird? It didn't burn me."

Nothing would do but that Jacob see for himself. "Nope. No burns," he said, backing her up.

Still the man on the horse said nothing, his silence an ominous part of his strong presence. His steady regard made Lily uncomfortable.

"Does anyone have drinking water?" she asked, then was surprised when the man himself, evidently somebody important in this weird troop of antique-equipped soldiers, passed a horn vessel with a carved plug over to her.

"Thanks." This time she took care to take only small sips. After several such, she felt better, the black borders fading from her vision. Dehydrated, she thought. Strange it had happened so quickly, but she showed the symptoms.

Looking up, she found the young woman's stare, only a degree less intense than the horseman's, riveted on her like she was a specimen in a zoo. Until she narrowed her eyes at the girl, at which the girl looked away.

"Are there any questions I can answer for you?" she asked civilly. Might as well get this ball rolling. According to her experience, you learn as much from what people want to know about you as from what you ask about them. And then, once they finished, it would be her turn. At last she was on the verge of enlightenment. Where was she? How long had she been here? What had happened to Lopez and the terrorists? And most of all, what in the hell were these pitiable, though obviously dangerous mutant creatures?

The girl's first question, one that sparked approval in the horseman's eyes, took her by surprise.

"Are there many like you?" The girl stepped down from her horse and came nearer, keeping a wary eye on Lily's right hand. "Are you from the eastern lands? We've never seen any of your tribe before. Where are the rest of them?"

"My tribe?" Lily hoped she was mistaken, but there seemed something just a little threatening about the line of questioning. "I'm not tribal police. I'm Border Patrol. Federal law enforcement," she added, making sure there was no misunderstanding. Lurching to her feet, she reached in her pocket and fumbled for her I.D. and badge, only to have the girl nock an arrow faster than most people could cock a six-gun. "Easy. I'm only pulling my identification."

Impossible to miss the wary exchange of signal between the girl and the horseman, whose left shoulder hitched a mere fraction. Which left it up to Jacob and Bell to try to smooth things over.

"Kira," Bell said to the girl, "your arrow is not necessary. And you, Nate. Don't be hasty in your decisions. I think . . . I think not all is as it seems."

"No?" The rider, after a long moment motioned the girl to lower her bow.

"She saved my life," Bell said.

"I saw," the man, Nate, said.

"She saved me more than once. Last night, then again today."

"Saved me, too." Jacob reddened in embarrassment in admitting it.

"I think we're pretty even on that score, Jacob." Though she managed a smile, Lily was beginning to worry. Did she need these champions?

"And in addition," Harrison added, as though this were the final commendation, "Sliver brought her to me. That must count for something."

The girl, Kira, opened her eyes wide. "Sliver did?"

Ignoring the fact the dog's behavior had startled her, too, Lily nodded. "Why not? I get along with dogs pretty well and most of them are good at sensing when their master is in trouble. I suppose he thought I was the only help around."

They all looked at her, Bell with a faint smile. "As you were."

"Do you know what kind of dog Sliver is?" Jacob asked.

Lily shrugged. "He's a Karelian bear dog, isn't he? A breed noted for its loyalty to its master. I remember…" She frowned, not quite sure what she did actually remember. "And I understand they can be quite ferocious, if need be. Which Sliver—" She cut off. Yes. Ferocious, indeed.

"I would never have survived if you hadn't showed up with him," Bell said. "He drove off a wounded Mag. I don't know what happened then, but luckily for me, Sliver came back with you."

"Ahh." Lily nodded. "So that explains the creature I found down by the lake."

Jacob's words were not quite so delicate. "You're the one killed that sonovabitch? We saw your tracks and wondered."

Nodding, Lily took no pride in the death. "He was in bad shape already. Gangrene, spread beyond any chance of cure."

"Nobody would want to cure him," Kira put in, her lip curling.

Lily pressed her hand to her stomach and found her seat on the log again. "No. Excuse me. Of course not. They're wild things, aren't they? A mutated people of some sort, hidden away from the rest of the world. And very dangerous. I can't believe I've never heard of them, since they're in my territory. Apparently, they're a very well-kept secret." As were these people, in truth. She'd have something strong to say to her superiors about that, as soon as she reported in. "Are they what we've always called Bigfoot? Although they're not particularly hairy or big, and I wouldn't call these specimens exactly retiring."

When she looked up again, four, make that five—a man on a huge dun horse had joined the party—sets of eyes stared at her as if she were stark raving mad. More proof, if she needed it, that the whole world had skewed somehow. Her heart started an uncomfortable tripping again. "What? What did I say?"

Yeah. What was she saying, because of course, these people she sat among right now were every bit as mysterious as the mutants. A tribe, for lack of a better word, of horse-man warriors, nomads from the look of things, right here in northeastern Washington State. And even after covering most of this country in detail, she'd never seen hide nor hair or heard of them before.

Including right here on this spot. Lily's vision started up with the sparkles again.

Thankfully, the new man ignored her and motioned to Kira with a jerk of his head. "Select one trooper to ride with you," he said. "I want the pair of you to go back and bring up the rest of the clan quick as the wagon wheels will turn. Be on the lookout for Mag stragglers and warn Selkirk of the same."

Ah, the commander of this strange troop.

The girl's face glowed. "Yes, boss. I'll take Bevee." She was astride her horse almost before the words were out of her mouth, leaving the man grinning. "Now there's a patrol-ler who knows how to follow orders," he said, apparently to no one in particular. "Lets hope she can pry Bevee away from House long enough to get the job done."

Lily had no idea what he was talking about, and had no chance to ask, because he began issuing a new set of orders to the troopers who, at the completion of the their assigned tasks, gathered around him, and perforce her, for further instruction.

"Everyone accounted for?" he asked squad leaders.

"All here," the one called House said. "No deaths, only a couple slight wounds."

"Something they can brag about," an older man called Rongo, added. "It was a smooth mission. One of the kids has that captive you asked for, boss. A two-eyed specimen, and it seems he can talk a little."

Bannion nodded. "Watch him close so he doesn't kill himself. I'll deal with him later. Right now I want to the posse to push on to headquarters and have everything set up for the rest of the folks." He drew a leather thong from under his shirt, raising it over his head. A key hung suspended from it, which he handed to Rongo. "Open the kitchens first, please. Then start airing out the barracks. House, your squad goes along to guard him, and I don't want anybody—anybody, you hear?—taking off alone for any reason. You've drawn guard duty. That's it."

"Yes, boss," House snapped smartly, restraining, judging by the hand angling toward his forehead, a half-formed salute.

"One more thing." Bannion stopped the two men when they would've ridden off. "Clear out the medical department and put up a sterile field. Neila's going to want everything ready for Harrison and the wounded patrollers when she gets here."

"Will do," Rongo said, and ignoring the dead mutant bodies littering the field, led the way toward the buildings Lily had found deserted yesterday. Only yesterday? Already, it seemed a week had passed.

She slumped and closed her eyes, resting her head on her knees.

"Are you sure you're not hurt?" Nate's voice was less harsh than the commander's.

Lily started, staring toward where he seemed caught in a vortex that included his horse's head. "I don't know," she admitted. "I can't keep track of what is happening. In fact . . ."

After a wait, Nate said, "In fact what?"

Lily closed her eyes, which only increased her vertigo. "I wish I knew what was going on. I don't understand any of this."

Bannion snorted. "One way or another, I think understanding will come."

"Bannion." Just the one word from Harrison Bell sounded a warning, causing Bannion to shrug. "You wouldn't deny the necessity, would you, Harrison?"

"No," the older man said, "but there's no need to push right now."

For the first time, Bannion's anger became apparent, leaking around his tight control. "No. And for that we can thank the guardian spirits there are no fatalities to report to weeping mothers tonight."

Harrison's next words sounded weaker when he replied, "Guardian spirits, yes. But I believe there's some credit goes to Miss Lily Turnbow. If only we knew where she came from."

"We'll find out," Bannion promised grimly. "Neila will have a look at her after she's taken care of you. We need to be sure—" He broke off. "Nate, you look after her. I want her kept under observation at all times. Don't leave her alone for a minute."

Nate the laconic, as Lily had named him to herself, nodded. And nodded again when Bannion said he wanted a report on his scout as soon as possible.

Though she was having a hard time keeping up with what they were saying, Lily didn't quite like the tone of this particular promise. But it didn't stop her from fading into unconsciousness and falling off the log.

Chapter 10

Lily jerked awake as if zapped with an electric cattle prod. Muscles protested as she sat up, dizzy, her vision whirling.

In the few seconds it took her equilibrium to right itself, she stared around the room trying to make sense of these strange surroundings. Nothing struck her as familiar. Not the cot, layered in fresh linens, in which she lay. Not the wooden ceiling or log walls. Small and dimly lit by a single kerosene-type lamp, the chamber smelled medicinally of rubbing alcohol and sharp herbs, all overlaid by the scent of food. Her nose twitched. Her stomach growled with need.

Where am I? The old saw was true, she discovered. Bewildered people did ask themselves that question. More importantly, how had she gotten here?

She perceived the presence of someone else in the room. Quiet breathing drew her attention to a cot separated from her own by a curtaining sheet hung between them and a small nightstand. On her half of the stand sat a half-filled bowl of soup with a clean spoon at its side. A brown bottle closed by a glass stopper struck her as vaguely threatening. Gauze pads and bandages took up the little remaining table space.

Whole body aching, Lily leaned on her elbow and rolled until she could reach the curtain and pull it aside. The person in the other bed had his back to her, but she knew it was a man by the shape under the covers. Bandages swathed his upper body.

Okay. This must be a hospital of sorts. But where? What kind of facility put a man and a woman in the same room? She must've been airlifted to some rural facility short on space or personnel after the scrap last night, but she didn't remember the flight. What she did remember were disturbing, yet realistic nightmares of three-eyed mutants, a black-and-white dog, and a man—no, two men—on horseback. One of the men had amber colored eyes. The other dark.

Oh, yeah. And hunger. But that was no figment of her imagination. Her stomach growled again, more forcefully this time.

Overwhelmed by the empty gnawing, Lily reached across the nightstand and snatched up the soup bowl in a shaking hand. The contents, still lukewarm and floating chunks of carrot and minced beef, only reached midway up the sides. Just as well since otherwise she would've spilled it over the patchwork quilt covering her. Which would be a pity as the soup was too good to waste. Using both hands, she tilted the bowl to her mouth and swallowed greedily, the salty taste feeding a deep need. Why did she feel so starved?

The why didn't matter. Her stomach accepted the food with a grateful rumble and asked for more. She set the empty bowl back on the stand, the clink of pottery against wood joined by a whisper of movement hidden by the other bed. Ears pricked, a black-and-white dog peeped around the edge of the bed at her, the dog in her dreams. Lily almost strangled on her sharply indrawn breath.

"Sliver," she said, as if from far away, and the dog's ears moved forward and backward, acknowledging his name. Not a dream then, which meant the mutants and the men on horseback and everything else probably weren't either.

Despite herself, she groaned. Across from her, the man's even breathing sounded a different note. Good. Someone around here damn well better be able to answer the questions cluttering her brain before she went crazy—if she wasn't already.

"Mr. Bell?" she said to the occupant of the other bed, her voice loud in the quiet room. "Is that you?" Lily swept the curtain back on jangling rings, removing the barrier. If the rest of what she remembered was real, then the man in the other bed could be no other than Harrison, the gleam of his snowy hair the deciding tip-off.

Turns out she was correct, not that being right did anything but puzzle her further.

Bell shifted in the bed, grunting a little as he rolled over and scooted himself higher on the pillows. "It's me. About time you woke up, Lily Turnbow. The family's been wanting to talk to you. I'll call Neila." A pull cord dangled above his bed. Despite her staying motion, he reached up and yanked. "That'll bring her."

Lily heard a mellow pealing in the distance; a few seconds later footsteps headed their way. Make that two sets of footsteps, one set a whisper, one set the clomp of boot heels. Memory flooded back. She bet she knew who the boot heels belonged to.

She won the bet, glimpsing the patrol leader or sheriff or whatever he called himself. Not the man who'd brought her in, the other one. They'd called him Bannion, she remembered. He hovered in the shadows behind the woman, riding shotgun. But it was the healer who garnered Lily's attention. From everyone's respect and implied awe she expected someone larger-than-life, but instead of stately, the rather hard-faced woman who entered the room mostly looked tired and worried.

"Lily Turnbow," Harrison Bell said, "meet Neila Bell, our healer." He struggled to sit upright.

Neila, a woman no more than ten years older than Lily, nodded civilly before motioning Bannion forward to help Bell. It allowed Lily a moment of observation. Neila, she saw, was about her own size. Sporting no discernible make-up, and her dark brown hair bound into a low ponytail with a strip of leather, she wore an apron with filled pockets tied around her trim waist. She had a pair of leather, fur-lined slippers on her feet, and carried a pitcher of water in one hand, a glass tumbler in the other.

Lily licked her dry lips, happy to see the water. She wasn't so sure about the people.

Lifting the pitcher in a kind of salute, Neila said, "Thirsty, Lily? When we put you to bed, I noticed you're considerably dehydrated."

"I'm parched. Thank you."

Unsmiling, Neila nodded.

Lily's hands trembled as she took the glass of water Neila poured and guzzled it down in a few gulps. It had an artificial citrus tang, but in a moment she felt stronger.

Neila set down the pitcher and went to Harrison's side, bending to pull back the bandage and sniff the wound.

"Better," she pronounced. A brief smile flashed. "You'll do, father-in-law. We thought we'd lost you, you know."

Apparently Neila was related to the old man by marriage, her husband someone other than the patrol leader. Hopefully, Lily's care of Mr. Bell the night before would weigh in her favor.

Bell nodded. "Told you I'd be fine. Lily Turnbow did good, getting that piece of spear out."

It was credit Lily didn't believe she deserved. Bannion may not have thought so either, for he stepped closer to her bed and stared down at her.

"You ready to have that discussion we talked about?" he asked. "I have a question or two."

Her hold on the water glass tightened. If she disliked show-ing weakness in front of the healer, which she did, showing it to the sheriff tried her even more. He never took his eyes off her, as she'd disappear if not pinned by his gaze. She had a hunch he'd find some way to use any failings against her. Why?

"Sure," she said. "Ask away. But I could use more water."

"I'll get it." Neila lifted the pitcher. Water splashed.

"Thanks." Going slower this time, she drank down the whole glass, making Bannion wait.

A flash in his dark eyes indicated impatience. "If you're all comfy, how about telling us who you are and where you're from? And what you're doing here?"

"That's three. Three questions," Lily pointed out, her head growing lighter by the second.

A muscle in his jaw flexed.

"I've already answered the first," she added. "I told you my name is Lily Turnbow. I'm a United States Border Patrol officer based out of Metaline. My team saw action last night—No. Make that two nights ago—when we got a tip about a plane flying in from Canada. The tip was good, because along about midnight a plane landed on the lake. Since we'd been warned of something big but non-specific, we were a mixed bunch, FBI, DEA, Border Patrol, County Sheriff's office. We weren't sure who we'd be dealing with, you see. Drug dealers or terrorists or what. But then every-thing went to hell. Got in the middle of a firefight." She fell silent a moment, remembering, then continued. "We lost, I think. Had a collaborator in our bunch. I got in a hand-to-hand, then this guy wearing a *kafiyah* stabbed me with his knife a few seconds before that big noise and the flash."

Bannion and Neila exchanged a wary glance as Lily rattled on.

"What was that noise and flash, anyway? Do you know? No?" She frowned. "I thought I was a goner. Anyway, I guess I was unconscious until I woke up this morning sick as hell." She paused, thinking. "No. Make that I woke up yesterday morning."

"What's she saying?" Neila asked before Bannion held up a warning finger and silenced her.

Talk about running off at the mouth. Short of stuffing it full of blanket, Lily couldn't seem to stem the flow of words. It was as if she'd been injected with a truth serum. Even as the thought occurred that the admirable Neila had slipped a drug into the water, her mouth kept right on flapping.

"That's when I staggered out of the mausoleum and found everything was different from the night before." She peered up at Bannion. Weak, totally uncharacteristic tears flooded her eyes. She dashed them away. "I couldn't . . . can't figure out what happened! How can everything change like that overnight, huh? Answer me that."

No one stepped forward to speak, so she rambled on. "Then I had to kill that miserable creature in the bushes. Then the dog stole my pheasant so I followed him—do you know his name is Sliver? Isn't that a strange name for a dog? I followed him, trying to get my bird back. After the longest time I came to a cave where I met Mr. Bell and then Jacob Felix, and we all got into another fight with those awful creatures and here I am." She took a breath. "Where am I?"

Bannion flicked a glance toward Bell. "I thought you said she didn't talk much."

Bell chuckled and shook his head. "What did you put in the water, Neila?"

"Oh, a little herbal something. Nothing harmful, I assure you. I've never seen it affect anyone like this. It's a relaxant, is all."

"I'm probably super sensitive because my stomach is empty," Lily announced, her words slurring. "It's like I haven't eaten or drank in a lifetime. I'd better warn you folks that you could be in trouble. I didn't give permission to treat me with any quack drugs. I happen to have an idiosyncrasy to several things. They sometimes have weird side effects." She thought she sounded quite calm considering her brain was chattering like a fear-crazed monkey.

"Now what's she saying?" Neila asked again, whereupon Lily threw back the quilt, and stood up, swaying. She was clad in her bra and panties. Well, thank God for that. Better than bare skin, anyway. Even so, she heard a couple surprised gasps.

"I've got to pee," she announced. "Right now."

"Damn it, Neila." The sheriff, his lip curling as though the sight of her disgusted him, turned away after a brief look. "You gave her too much juice. Send somebody for me when it wears off."

On his way out, the man's boot heels pounded the wooden floor loud enough to make Lily's ears ring.

*****

Leaving the hospital, Bannion crossed the compound, silent and still at this hour, on his way to headquarters to confer with his cousin Selkirk. Yellow light shone through the windows of the big barn as he passed. A quick arpeggio of song spilled from the open door. Someone, probably his cousin Mallie's husband, tuning his fiddle in preparation of sawing out dance music at the party later on tonight.

On top of the victory this morning, clan folk had a homecoming to celebrate. He planned on joining them a little later, but first he needed a word with the clan leader. Selkirk had left the matter of the stranger to him and the interrogation hadn't gone all that smoothly.

"You're in charge of clan safety. Do whatever seems right," Selkirk had told him a few hours ago as the last of the camp wagons rolled into the ranch yard and drew to a stop. Being the head honcho, Selkirk's immediate concerns centered on settling his people. That meant every one of the home place buildings was open and aired, fires lit and the kitchens up and running. Next came turning the livestock out to pasture, and arbitrating any quarrels arising from who got what rooms for the winter.

Bannion grimaced as he walked, glad the responsibility didn't lie on his shoulders. But disposing of the bodies scattered in the woods and across the big meadow, that chore did land squarely on him.

"You," he instructed a few men taking their ease listening to the youngsters talk about their first battle, "lug those Mag's bodies out to the pit yonder and set them on fire while the wind is right. I don't want them raising a stink later."

They got the job done with only a little grumbling. Not too many argued with a warrior of Bannion's mettle, a matter of some pride to him. He snorted. Couldn't count his Cousin Nate Quick in that group of non-arguers. Nate feared no one and did what he wanted, when he wanted, consistently ignoring Bannion's orders unless they agreed with his agenda. Funny he turned up just in time to save the woman today.

Nate spent most of his time off somewhere scouting or exploring. And he was damn good—no, the best ever in O'Quinn legend—at both those things. Selkirk's forte was making sure his people worked together for the good of everyone. He left defense and espionage problems to Bannion and the patrollers, quipping that he was glad to do so.

Feeling the weight of his cousin's trust, Bannion ended up outside Selkirk's headquarters. He cut across the side yard to the rear of the house. Before knocking lightly and slipping through the back door, he took a moment to survey the yard. All quiet, praise be. Herd dogs patrolled the hills tonight, and at this moment everything was peaceful. He figured the victory over the Mags today should keep the mutants quiet until spring, except, perhaps, for the occasional stray.

Bannion found Selkirk in the act of sitting down at the kitchen table to a hot, though delayed dinner of elk steak and fresh bread rolls.

"Fetch a plate," his cousin said, waving him in. "There's plenty keeping hot on the stove."

Bannion sniffed the aromatic air. "Who cooked? Not Neila, for sure. She's been busy. Besides, nothing is burned." They had a standing joke that it always took Neila a full week to relearn the art of cooking on a wood-burning kitchen range instead of over a campfire with her trusty Dutch ovens.

Grinning, Selkirk stabbed a slice of roast and dragged it through the rich, brown gravy. "Auntie Doris cooked. These rolls are so light they practically float."

Bannion needed no more encouragement, finding himself a thick crockery plate and piling it with meat, assorted fresh vegetables and four of the rolls. "Been a long time," he said, sitting in a chair as if wary it might collapse. But the height eased his knees. Some different than finding a convenient stump to sit on, he thought.

"I haven't been in a house since spring," Selkirk said. "You?"

"Once. A farmer invited me in." Bannion savored a forkful of steak.

"You oughta go with Nate sometime. Farmers regularly ask him in to eat with them."

Bannion nodded. "He's a good ambassador. Good at taking care of any wandering Mags might be hanging around the farms, too."

"He is. And they show their appreciation." Replete, Selkirk sat back and sipped his tea. "Harrison's female have anything to say for herself?"

"Oh, yeah. Plenty to say."

"And?"

"I don't know what to make of her, Selk." Bannion crammed half a roll in his mouth. Chewing gave him a moment to compose his thoughts. He didn't want his cousin thinking he was weak, but the woman's dark haunted eyes and worried demeanor struck a chord in him. She seemed as bewildered about her place here as he. Where had she come from? Her wild words earlier came back to him. Eerie.

All she had going for her was Bell's and Felix's championship, and in the scope of the clan's survival, that didn't count for much.

"The kids in the fight, they're telling me things about her that don't hardly seem likely," Selkirk said. "Surprised you haven't mentioned anything."

Bannion smeared the rest of his roll with wild strawberry preserves. "You're talking about the fireballs."

"Of course I'm talking about the fireballs. What else? So what are they? How did she pull off that ruse?"

"I don't know. Neila took her clothes, all but some damn skimpy underwear, and we went through them together. We found some peculiar things, all right, but nothing that accounts for the fireballs. The woman says they were just there when she needed them. We didn't see anything that makes her a liar."

"You mean any trick fire lighters or the like." Selkirk took a careful sip of steaming tea. "Came when she needed them, eh? I guess we know what that means? She's magic, like Felix is saying. Another damn Cross-up after all this time. What's it been since the last one, fifty years?"

"Damned if I know." Bannion poked a bite of meat in his mouth and chewed with enthusiasm. "But I saw some of those fireballs with my own eyes. They were real, Selk."

"You aren't leaving it there, are you? What's next?"

"No, I'm not leaving it there. What do you think? Neila and I, we thought to use some fairy weed on her. Didn't work."

Selkirk scowled. "She immune to it?"

"God no. The opposite. She drank two glasses of the stuff and you couldn't shut her up. Trouble is, nothing she said makes sense. Except one thing." Bannion waited for his cousin to ask the inevitable.

"What?"

"Said she had to pee. Then a couple minutes later, I'm told, she had to go again." In spite of his chagrin, Bannion chuckled. "One of fairy weed's lesser known side effects, as I recall. I told Neila to call me when it wears off and we'll try questioning her again."

Selkirk laughed out loud. "What does Harrison have to say?"

"He says she saved his life a couple times and he owes her. Says she's a good person and wants us to lay off. He's getting old—and soft."

"Yeah." Selkirk got up and took his dishes over to the bucket standing in the old, chipped enamel sink and dropped them into the soapy water. Somebody, Auntie Doris or Neila or one of the girls would wash them in the morning. A clan leader didn't concern himself with actual kitchen chores, just, sometimes, the allotment of them. "Time was," he said, obviously still thinking of the Harrison Bell of his own youth, "he'd've showed no mercy to a stranger appearing out of nowhere the way she has."

Bannion mopped up a final spoonful of gravy with his last roll and pushed away from the table. "What do you want me to do?"

"Sic Nate onto her. Getting information out of someone like her should be easy for him. Listen close to what she has to say. Ask smart questions and hope her answers add up."

"Hope? Cousin, we don't survive by hope. We need the truth."

"Yes. We do. That's your job. Yours and Nate's." Selkirk yawned wide enough for Bannion to see his back molars. "I'm giving the party a miss and going to bed. I plan on sleeping a solid eight hours on a real mattress and not worrying about a thing. I'll leave that to you."

"Thanks." Bannion grinned openly for the first time since he met Lily Turnbow this morning.

"You're welcome." Even as he headed for the back stairway leading up from the kitchen to the second floor bedroom, Selkirk had the last word. "Just remember, cousin. Disarming somebody who conjures fireballs out of nothing might prove a real chore."

"No lie." Despite the feather lightness of Auntie Doris's rolls, the clan leader's last warning made Bannion's dinner lay heavy in his stomach. It reminded him again of the young woman's hunger and the way her skin pulled over sharp bones as though resurrected from a husk.

Though he might be forcing the conviviality, he'd join the patrollers celebration in the big barn, he decided, walking out into the cold, clear night. A sky filled with a million brilliant stars showed the way. There'd be 'shine and hard cider at the party, and probably even beer if Harrison had managed his annual end-of-harvest trade for barley from some of the farmers.

He planned to have a word with Harrison tomorrow. Time the old bugger passed his recipe for Artesian spring-brewed onto the younger generation. Harm was old enough to learn, if only Neila could be persuaded.

Warmth and music and laughter poured from the barn as he entered. Kira Shandy was there, wearing a swirly red skirt and light moccasins. She bore a pitcher of foaming beer, which answered one of his questions, and carried a handful of real glass glasses.

"Join us, boss" she said, laughing up at him, "we're tying one on."

He wasn't adverse to tying one on, especially with her.

"We're not on patrol now, Kira," he said, taking one of the glasses and holding it out for her to fill. "Call me Bannion."

Chapter 11

Early this morning, as Lily played possum, Neila Bell had awakened her father-in-law, helped him dress, and taken him away in a wheelchair whose tires creaked. She left the bedroom door open afterward, possibly to make it easier to keep Lily under observation.

Lily guessed the healer would've been surprised to learn that by so doing, nearly every word spoken in the tiny hospital was audible to one blessed with extra keen hearing. Even activity in another room couldn't drown out the discussion between Neila and Bannion when the patrol leader joined the healer in the hospital kitchen. Lily knew they were in the kitchen because she heard pots rattling and smelled food cooking. But nothing, including the rumble of her empty stomach, could keep her from listening to their conversation. Why should it when she was the object of debate?

First came the mutual "mornings," good or otherwise. Neila offered tea and Bannion accepted. Another man, one with an altogether softer voice than the patrol leader's, also murmured assent. Regular stuff. Conversation between the trio became more personal, some making Lily almost smile, like when Neila said, "Looks like you didn't get enough sleep, Bannion. Too much partying?"

Her use of the common phrase eased Lily with its normalcy. These people were strange, almost foreign seeming, but at least one thing was familiar.

"I tried," Bannion replied. "Turns out I wasn't in the partying mood."

"Kira Shandy, the girl in the pretty red skirt was," the other man said on a teasing note. "And you didn't seem to be objecting too strenuously."

"Shut up, Nate," Bannion replied. He didn't actually sound mad, though.

Ah, yes, Lily thought. Nate. The amber-eyed man who'd rescued her. That's why his voice was familiar.

Listening intently, she heard Neila's sigh. "You did get laid, didn't you? I saw you eyeing the Shandy girl yesterday. She didn't strike me as unwilling, and she'd make a good match for you."

A clatter of breaking glass was overlaid by Neila's titter, and Bannion exclaimed, " 'Sus, Neila! Get personal, why don't you?"

Nate chuckled.

"Well, did you?" Neila asked again.

"No, as a matter of fact, although I think Kira—" Silence, then, "I drank a few beers before going back to the barracks, is all. Too much on my mind to begin courting a woman."

Lily snorted to herself. Courting a woman? *Courting*?

"Too much on your mind, my ass," Neila scoffed. "First I ever heard men had anything *but* getting laid on their minds, especially after winning a battle."

This time Nate laughed out loud, and Neila said, "You better hush yourself, Mr. Quick. You need a woman to keep you warm, too."

"Don't start matchmaking for me, Neila," Nate said. "You know I'm immune."

"We'll see," she replied.

Bannion, having ignored that last byplay, turned serious. "I'm not so sure we did win that battle. Mags got beat, all right, but I'm thinking a certain stranger's unusual abilities had about as much to do with the victory as our armament. Speaking of the woman, is she awake? That damn fairy weed you gave her wear off yet?"

Lily didn't smile this time. *The woman.* He meant her.

"I think so," Neila said. "Bren, she's night nurse this week, said the woman hasn't been up for a few hours." Metal banged on metal. "Her clothes. They belong in the museum."

"What about them?" Nate asked.

"Let me show you." Light footsteps hurried across a floor. "Look, Nate. Her pants and coat have clasps—I seem to remember they were called zippers. And they actually work. Fabrics that never came off of any loom I ever heard of. A coat light as a cloud, but warm as an April day. And for closures, instead of buttons or hooks and eyes, there's this stuff that sticks to itself when you press two sides together."

Duck down and Velcro, you simple woman, Lily answered in her mind. *And don't kid me. People have been using down for hundreds, maybe even thousands of years to keep warm.*

"Where do you think she got them?" Neila went on. "Do you think she found a stash somewhere, hidden away these last hundred years?"

Nate answered first. "You've talked to Harrison, Neila. You know what his idea is and I think he's right. Or maybe somebody oughta just ask *her.*"

Now Bannion sounded hard. "Which is my intention, cousin. I'll add that to my list of questions."

Astonished, Lily froze, missing most of the cousin's next exchange. She was stuck somewhere around the stash comment. What did Neila mean, hidden away for a hundred years? And what were they doing, going through her things?

They were treating her like an enemy. Made her wonder what they had planned for her, that's for sure. Her heart pounded uncomfortably hard.

She wasn't prepared for a third degree. Her mind seemed incapable of thinking straight right now, with everything out of whack. Trying to convince these people she was not a threat seemed an insurmountable task. And maybe it wasn't true, anyway. Maybe she was a threat. It all depended on them. One thing for certain; she wasn't going to roll over just because they outnumbered her.

Beneath the quilt, Lily touched her breast. She still had on her bra and, yes, her panties, which left her wondering again if this was a real medical facility. Who ever heard of a hospital that didn't supply a gown that left the patient's bare bottom sticking out? The fact she wasn't wearing such a gown was, perhaps, a hopeful sign. Had these people intended total intimidation, they would've stripped her naked and taken away her blanket. Having her most intimate parts covered, if only by lacy underwear, provided a measure of reassurance. An errant memory of leaping from bed in front of them all returned to her. What the hell was in the stuff Bannion called "fairy weed," urging her to such uncharacteristic abandon?

She found herself wishing for a more of that false courage, so that instead of being forced to act the invalid in this narrow bed she could stand up straight and meet them face-to-face. Or maybe "in your face." What was she, anyway? A player? Or a victim?

The answer to that was one of many things she needed to get up and discover. But how? There was no closet here, only a couple pegs for hanging things. Empty pegs, in this case, because as she now knew, they'd taken her clothing to examine and not left even a robe behind for her to cover herself with. They'd even taken her packer boots.

From visits to a rudimentary bath facility during the night, Lily knew there were four doors opening off the hall. If she occupied one room, another patient the second, and the third was the bath, that left one other; the kitchen where these people sat around gabbing. Everything happened in kitchens in these old-timey places, didn't it? That's where her clothes would be.

Scowling, she got out of bed, shivering a little. Was there no heat in this place for God's sake? Stripping the blanket from the cot, she wrapped it around herself and padded barefoot to the door and peeped around the edge.

No one in sight.

Curling her toes against the cold floor, Lily stepped into the hall and tiptoed toward the kitchen. If she hoped to get her clothing back, there was only one way to do so.

Confrontation and demand—all very politely, of course.

"When can we expect Selkirk?" Neila was saying. "I'm surprised he hasn't been over to see this woman."

"You know how Selkirk is about the Cross-up people," Bannion said. "They make him powerful nervous. For that matter, so do the traders. And the Techs. And the Mags."

Lily understood nothing of that bit of yappity yap.

Neila laughed a little. "That's my brother. An organizer and wise leader for his people, but not a diplomat or a warrior. That's why he has you. He trusts you to be the public face of the clan."

"Yeah," Bannion muttered, "which puts the target directly on me."

"I never noticed it bothered you before. Are you afraid of her? One small woman?"

"You're damn right I am," he said, sounding grim. "You didn't see her in action, cousin. If you had—"

Lily figured that must be her cue.

"Good morning, folks. Is breakfast ready?" she asked brightly, striding into the kitchen as if she were an honored guest instead of a suspect, or a prisoner, or God only knew what else. Made her day when everyone jumped as though guilty of nefarious deeds. And so they were. Clothing theft, if nothing else.

Deliberately, she allowed the blanket to slip, exposing her shoulders. "I'd like my clothes and my shoes back before I eat, please."

She caught Neila's glance toward a tall armoire set against the far wall. Before either of the two men or the woman could stop her—not that they tried—Lily sidestepped and flung open the cupboard doors. Her clothes hung from wooden hooks. The packer boots sat side-by-side beneath.

"Thank you," she said, as if they'd handed them over with their complements. Dropping the blanket to the floor, Lily first snatched her britches, yanking them over blue bikini panties. Next came her T-shirt, hiding the matching blue Victoria's Secret bra. Her goose bumps flattened. Satisfied with that much, she leaned against the wall and jammed her feet into socks and shoes. After that, she took her time, tying the laces into precise double bows.

The O'Quinns, silent as porch posts, stood back and watched her dress. Eyes hard and intent, Bannion folded his arms across his chest and stared. Neila pursed her lips. The other man—he of the roan horse who'd snatched her out of the midst of mutants creatures—seemed only amused.

Had her near nudity offended them? Lily wondered. Nah, she decided in the next moment. She'd heard them talking about getting laid. Nothing prudish about that.

Finished with the shoe strings, she looked up. "You aren't burning those eggs, are you, Neila?" Smelled like she might be, but even so, her belly rumbled.

Neila leapt into action, jerking the cast iron frying pan from an old wood-burning stove that looked familiar to Lily. Flipping the bread toasting in the half-open oven, the woman cast a perturbed glance at her cousins. "Sit," she said, finding her voice. "All of you. I'll have this on the table in a moment." She added, "Burned or not."

Lily didn't care about the quality. At this point, she was ready to eat anything. Clomping over to the table, she sat in the chair Nate, in a surprising display of manners, pulled out for her. Bannion sat opposite, silent and wary.

Pleased with the reception she got with her assumed aggression, she folded her hands to hide a tremor and looked Bannion in the eye. "You have something to ask me? Fine. I'll answer if I can. I have questions for you, too."

Neila slid a plate of eggs and toast and a small piece of what smelled like venison steak in front of her, and pushed a pot of honey closer.

"Eat up," Neila said. Plates, heaped high, clattered onto the table for Bannion and Nate.

Lily picked up her fork and knife. "I'm starved. You go ahead and talk if you think you must." She cut into the steak. Yeah. Venison, for sure, with plenty of garlic and pepper for seasoning. The first bite almost melted between her molars. Umm, bliss.

"Generous of you," Bannion said dryly. He loaded his fork with egg, but didn't put it in his mouth. "Who are you? That's what we need to know. Where are you from? What sect? And why are you here? Is it about that trouble with the Techs?"

Lily crammed toast into her mouth, chewing as she tried to make sense of all that. Sect? Techs? What in the world was he talking about? The only question that made sense was the one asking who she was. *Again.* Had no one been listening yesterday?

"Who," she asked after swallowing the toast, "are the techs?" Although concentrating on her first real meal in at least three days, Lily didn't miss the cockeyed look Neila sent her cousins. She had the feeling they were adept at reading each other's nonverbal signals.

"Just tell the truth." Bannion said. "Let's go at this as cooperatively as we can." He ate, finally, as though he were almost as hungry as she.

Neila carried four cups of dark tea smelling of herbs and spices over to the table. She set them down and pulled out a chair for herself. Her hair was loose this morning, silver strands glinting at her temples.

"Do you have coffee?" Lily asked, longing for a jolt of caffeine. "I'm not much of a tea drinker. Not that this doesn't smell nice."

"Coffee?"

The woman's startled expression was hard to miss, and the way her glance shifted to Nate, who shrugged.

"Sorry," Lily said. "If drinking coffee is against your religion, I don't mean to offend by the mention of it."

Neila clicked her cup onto the bare wooden table. "We know we owe you for Harrison's life, Ms. Turnbow. But don't think that gives you any special privileges. You've been sick and I've cared for you. We're even, I think."

"Grudging hospitality," Lily corrected, as though talking to herself. "And since when does "care" include dosing one with psycho drugs?" Then louder, "I'm sorry. I didn't realize I was asking for the moon."

"Not the moon," Nate cut in almost apologetically. "But coffee is in short supply. The Traders haven't been around yet. Maybe later this week."

In Lily's opinion, his explanation, or apology, however he meant it, was pretty lame. Not to mention downright weird. What was with these people, anyway? Harrison Bell, and to a lesser degree the young fighter, Jacob Felix, were the most normal she'd met, and that wasn't saying much.

She ran Nate's words through her mind again. Traders? Did he mean they only bought coffee from some outfit like Craven's? Why did she find that unlikely?

"I'm not fussy," she said, pushing a little harder. "Grocery store brands are plenty good enough." Tensing, she waited to hear what he had to say, but there was only another meaningful exchange of glances between the cousins.

The silence held long enough to finish eating, although somewhere in there she lost her taste for the food. She sipped the controversial tea. At least it was hot, and free of drugs.

Nate finished about the same time as she, Bannion soon thereafter. Shoving his plate aside, he fixed a steely look on her and made a steeple of his fingers. "Enough of this fiddle-farting around. My patience is about worn out. You know what I want. Start talking."

His attitude grated, especially considering he sounded like a hard-assed cop and she a suspect. Suspected of what crime, she had yet to decipher. Absently, she picked at the new scar on her arm and forced her mind away from even *thinking* about how it got there.

"I told you yesterday," she said. "You all know my name is Lily Turnbow. I'm a Border Patrol agent with the Spokane sector. My base is Metaline, which is where we first heard about the drop set to take place on the lake a couple days ago. Since my supervisor and I were the ones in contact with the snitch, we were included in the task force. We, along with local enforcement, the DEA and the FBI set up along the shore Halloween night. After the float-plane landed and our suspects met on the dock, we went in to arrest them. The suspects started shooting, and all hell erupted. I saw another suspect up in the old graveyard, gave chase, made contact—" She picked at the scar again. "—and then . . . then . . ."

She stopped, sweat breaking out on her forehead. Tremors quivered through her hands again. "Something happened. Like being struck by lightning, a sonic boom exploding inside my head, and taking a knock-out punch all at the same time. Then multiplied by a hundred thousand."

Bannion slammed the flat of his hand on the table, making Neila jump nearly as high as Lily. "Mag shit!"

"What?"

"You heard me. A load of crap if I ever heard one. What do you take us for, Lily Turnbow? We may not be Techs or Traders or Cross-up people, but we're not stupid."

"I don't know what you mean. I've answered exactly what you asked." Lily enumerated, touching the tips of her fingers. "Name, where I'm from, who I work for, what I'm doing here. I believe that covers it. I'm sure you've seen my ID," she added.

"Oh, my Lord. Bannion?" Neila's dark skin paled as she whispered her cousin's name.

"You're hiding something. What is it?" Bannion demanded, his gaze not straying from Lily.

"I'm not hiding anything," she said. "I'm just trying to make sense of you folks. No offense, but you're coming across as very, very strange."

"We are?"

"You are. All this talk of techs and traders and cross-ups and whatever. This whole place. Then the Mags. For God's sake, the Mags." Lily's voice rose. She stood, swaying a little, and grabbed onto the table.

"Bannion, " Neila said again.

"What?" He sounded angry, impatient even with the healer.

She bent over and whispered in his ear.

Lily heard, trying to keep any reaction from showing on her face.

"I know who she is," Neila said. "Impossible, but true. It just hit me. We need to talk."

"You know her?"

She shook her head, quieting him in mid-sentence, but she spoke to Lily. "Excuse us a moment, Ms. Turnbow. Have another cup of tea. Come with me, Bannion, Nate. Outside. It's important."

Reluctantly, Bannion got to his feet, allowing himself to be ushered from the house. Nate went more willingly, with a slight nod at Lily. A blast of cold air came through the open door as Neila paused to snatch a jacket from a hook. It seemed winter had arrived in the day or so Lily had been in the O'Quinn infirmary.

But more than a change in the weather struck her. She got a clear view of the inner compound, too, before the door slammed shut between them. The glimpse showed the front of an old log barn and a rickety lean-to shed attached to its side.

Lily's legs, in the few frozen seconds in which her vision had time to focus, then fade, turned to jelly before collapsing beneath her. She fell to the floor on her knees, her hands clasped under her chin as if praying.

"No," she breathed. "Can't be. "

But it was.

Chapter 12

Bannion turned his back to a wind that whistled around the corner of the infirmary. Felt like the time had come to shake out his winter coat and hope it had been properly stored. He didn't want mice taking up residence in the lining.

"It's cold, Neila. What's so all-fired important we had to come outside?" He turned to face Neila. Placing his body between his cousin and the wind, he glared at her, not troubling to hide his annoyance. "Don't you know better than to interrupt an interrogation? All you're doing is giving her an opportunity to think up more lies." That reminded him of the Mag on hold in the cell under the old barn. Leave'im alone much longer and he'd chew his own arm off. Wouldn't be the first time.

A shake of Neila's head signified impatience with his concerns. "Listen to me, Bannion. There's something funny going on."

"No lie."

"I mean really funny, as in strange…weird," she insisted. "I told you. All this time I thought her name sounded familiar, then it struck me and I remembered."

"You remembered what? C'mon, Cuz. Hurry it up."

Instead of answering out loud, Neila pointed so insistently Bannion stared off in the direction her rigid forefinger indicated.

After a moment, realization hit him. The muscles in his face gave an involuntary twitch. He was so accustomed to the damned old thing being there he didn't even see it anymore. Probably no one did except Neila—and Nate. Nate, who leaned against the house wall and turned up his coat collar, a half-smile on his face.

"A trick," Bannion said. "She's pulling an elaborate trick, that's all. She must've seen it earlier and thought to take advantage."

"I don't think so." Neila ticked points off on her fingers. "Remember the labels in her clothes? They aren't something she just sewed in yesterday. Believe me, they've been there through several washings. There's what she keeps calling her ID. And then there's that picture, the photograph in the archives." She stumbled over the unfamiliar word before continuing with more confidence. "The photograph of Heathen. Do you see what I mean?"

Nate crossed his arms.

Bannion saw. "Shit." Oh, he got what his cousin meant, all right. But Neila must be wrong, because there wasn't any way she could be right. Somebody needed to dig the picture out of wherever it'd been buried so they could refresh their memories. He'd be glad to prove himself, and her, too, fallible, just this once.

"I think she's real, Bannion. Somehow, after all these years, she's real. This changes things, doesn't it?"

Yeah, and he didn't like it any better than she did. He kept his expression bland. "Maybe. Maybe not."

The lines around Neila's mouth deepened and she whispered, "What is she, cousin?"

"Cross-up," Nate said so softly he was easy to ignore. "Newly hatched."

"We don't know that," Bannion insisted. "It's what I intend to find out."

"But will you?" The worry lines in Neila's forehead deepened. "Or can she put a hoodoo on you? Is that what she's here for, do you suppose?" She turned to Nate. "A Cross-up, yeah. That's what you called her. What Jacob called her. Even what Harrison called her. But is she immortal along with everything else?"

Bannion stared down at her. "Immortal? Are you crazy?"

She smiled without humor. "I sincerely hope so. But remember, the other Cross-ups came out in our grandparents' time. And they weren't anyone any of us knew."

"We don't know her," Nate said, staring off into space. "But, this *is* a hell of a coincidence."

"Yes."

They took a second look, silent and rapt, at the object that had caught Neila's attention.

"Anyway, most of them died right after they showed up," Bannion said finally. "That's probably why she's been so sick."

Neila nodded. "And I helped her survive."

"It's what you do." Nate consoled her.

"Take hope. I think maybe she'll die anyway," Bannion said.

Across the compound, Selkirk, taking his time, ambled toward them. He waved as he saw them looking.

"My brother isn't going to like this," Neila said quietly.

No, Bannion thought. The head of their clan, an appealing and dependable leader in working with their own people, was not so good when it came to dealing with surprises and strangers.

"Can't say as I like it much, myself," he said. "If what you're thinking the same as I'm thinking is true."

"Can you come up with any other explanation? I'd love to hear one."

"Sure, I can. Lot's of them." Ignoring Nate's shrug, he returned Selkirk's wave, motioning him to put on a little speed. Oh, yeah. Give him a minute and ideas would sprout like a farmer's wheat in the spring. For now, though, he had none that fit the situation any better than Neila's wild conjecture. And there was no way in hell she could be right. No way. Was there?

"Turned cold overnight. What are you three doing standing out here in the wind?" Selkirk asked, coming to a stop beside his sister and putting his arm around her. "Bannion, you talk to that woman yet? How is she, Neila?"

"She's all right. Maybe a bit confused." Neila shot Bannion a meaningful glance and shook her head.

He figured she meant for him to keep quiet about her suspicions until they had a little more to go on. She might be convinced she had the right of things, but there was no use in spreading unsubstantiated tales through the whole clan. To some extent, he agreed.

"We're hatching a plan of action," he told Selkirk, "and making a list of questions. The woman is a little stubborn about talking plain; keeps saying her name and giving a cockamamie story about Border Patrols and BDI and the local sheriff."

"You?" Selkirk asked in surprise.

"Don't think she knows I'm clan sheriff."

Selkirk's brows pulled together over his strong, handsome nose. "Everybody for a hundred miles—two hundred miles and maybe more—knows you're the sheriff. That's when you aren't being war leader. Or sometimes both at the same time. Where's she been?"

"That," Bannion said grimly, "is what I'm still trying to find out. You going to sit in on the questioning?"

The clan leader grimaced. "Do you want me to?"

While Neila laughed out loud and Nate snickered, Bannion fisted his cousin on a heavy shoulder. "I ain't planning on beating her up. Not in the first session, at least. Stay if you want."

"Thanks anyway." Selkirk didn't sound in the least sorry to turn down Bannion's offer. "I've got a squabble to settle between the House family and the Garcias. The Garcias are miffed because they've got two kids, but the House's cabin is bigger. Ms. Garcia says seniority shouldn't matter in this instance, and I'm not too sure but what she's right."

Bannion shuddered. "Better you than me. I'll take a good skirmish over a war of words any day."

"And that, cousin, is why you do what you do, and why I do what I like." With a mock salute, Selkirk continued on his way, sauntering past the infirmary, heading toward a cluster of cabins surrounding what had once been a root cellar, now enlarged into a low fort and courthouse.

Smirking, Neila watched him go. "Smart. Got out of one, didn't you? You know my brother so well. Which means avoiding any situation where he's out of his depth."

"And yet, except for Nate, there's no man I'd rather have at my back in a fight." Bannion drew a deep breath. "Do this for me, will you, Neila? Fetch that photo. We'll face her with it. See what she has to say."

"Good idea. I know just where it is."

"Yes." Bannion's voice hardened. "Last page in the book. The final day."

"Final day." Face sober, Neila went off with a purposeful stride toward the small outbuilding they used to store artifacts from the earlier age, before the Event.

Bannion breathed deeply of the cold air. Above him, a single snowflake floated out of the darkening sky, melting as it touched his forehead.

"Weather's changing," he noted with a questioning look at Nate.

"Yep. Gonna be a hard winter. I can smell it coming. A week or ten days from now there'll be a big storm blow in."

Bannion breathed out a sigh that steamed in the air. "In

more ways than one."

"Afraid so."

While Bannion may have given Selkirk the impression he looked forward to questioning the woman, Neila's discovery had shocked away some of his confidence.

Of course Lily Turnbow was a Cross-up woman; no doubt about that. He saw her throwing fireballs himself. He'd also seen a traveling showman do a similar trick once, but that had been accomplished by deftness of hand. An illusion capable of fooling most of the watchers, but not him. What this woman created out of nothing had been real fire, and worse, she seemed as bewildered by the trick as anyone. The thing is, if she could conjure fire by the simple expedient of thinking it, what the hell else could she do? *What did she want to do? What were her intentions?*

Before entering the house again, he took another look at the derelict object Neila had pointed out. The paint on it had faded to practically nothing. Twenty-five years ago, when learning to read, the words on the metal cart had been clearer. *Horse trailer,* he corrected himself, not metal cart. He remembered what those words were. "Heathen," the first line read. And then, below it, in heavy black script, "L. Turnbow."

A story went with the object, of course, handed down these many years. Guess it was time he found out if the woman knew the tale. Sighing, Bannion reached for the doorknob and motioned Nate to precede him inside.

*****

Lily felt as though turned into ice, kneeling there on the floor with the wind blowing through a crack under the door. Cold. So cold. Yet she couldn't find the strength to rise. Not just yet. It felt as though her very blood had frozen, hardened in her veins, arteries, capillaries, stopping her heart.

Impossible thoughts raced around her head like a chipmunk in a cage. Was she alive? Should she be? If so, she wished for the memories to stay buried instead of ballooning up out of a dead world.

She'd been their friend, the people who owned this ranch. When dispatch radioed her about the multi taskforce action set up for Halloween night, she had Heathen with her, taking the mare home after a three day stint traipsing through the rough country between the U.S. and Canada. She and her partner Jason had been searching for an Asian family reported to have jumped the border. Found them, too, and sent them back to Canada.

Unwilling to leave Heathen cooped up in the trailer while she attended to this new assignment, she stopped off at Kettle Creek Ranch, fortuitously located only a few miles from her destination. Imposing on the Poundstone's friendship, she left the horse there. She'd boarded Heathen at the ranch a couple times before. They treated the mare well and as a courtesy, they offered a space where she could leave her horse trailer.

Lily swayed, her head buried in her hands, watching the scene through her mind's eye. To her, this had happened only a few days ago, but was also lost in the distance. What, for God's sake, was true?

This much, for certain.

The horse trailer was only a year old, its tires new. Painted a pearly white, the writing along the sides stood out in metallic charcoal contrast. L. Turnbow. Heathen. She recalled parking it and leaving Heathen with a pat, time for only a quick word with the Poundstone's before hurrying to get in position down at the lake before dark.

She remembered the ranch set-up well. Brian Poundstone owned the place. It had been in his family for a hundred years, a matter of great pride to him. He and his wife had a thirteen-year-old daughter, and more than once Brian had bemoaned the fact he had no sons to carry on.

"What about Ginger?" Lily had asked once. Thirteen going on twenty-one, Ginger worked alongside her parents pitching horse manure and dragging hay bales—when she wasn't taking prizes all over the Northwest in barrel racing. She seemed to love the place every bit as much as her dad did.

"Name'll change when Ginger marries," Brian had said. "Damn depressing if you ask me."

Lily had flinched at his remark. She was the last of her bloodline, too, her grandparents' north Idaho farm her heritage. This same cussed lament had swirled around her all her life, as if a woman had no existence apart from a man. Didn't Brian realize a woman didn't *have* to take her husband's name? She'd never been able to convince her granddad it was legal.

The similarities between her own and Ginger's situation had struck home. Both descended from old-time homestead-ers, although farmers built with brick and lumber, north country ranchers with logs. Barns, as usual in an earlier era, were always bigger than the living quarters. Just like her grandfather's place, Brian kept Kettle Creek Ranch in tip top shape. As were all their possessions—or possessions left in their care. Like Heathen and her trailer.

And yet—

Moving as if she were eighty years old, Lily rose to her feet, bracing herself with a hand on a chair. Of course she felt a sense of *déjà vu.* Why not? She was in the old Pound-stone ranch house right now, the one they'd turned over to their hired man—a young guy named Nate—when they built the new one. Nate Bell, for God's sake.

The "bells" inside her head were deafening.

The house was smaller than she remembered. And the barn across the way? Was it the same barn into which she'd led Heathen the night . . . that night . . .

Her mind stuttered. *When?*

Take the shed directly opposite this door. The same shed beside which her trailer sat. The exact same now dented, rusted out hulk sitting on cement blocks under a sagging roof someone had built over it.

If she squinted and used her imagination, she could still see the identifying words. L. Turnbow. Heathen.

If only she were dreaming.

But there it was. Old. Beat-up. *Dead.* Like she was supposed to be.

*****

If Bannion thought the woman pale when he left the infirmary, it was nothing compared to how she looked when he strode back in. As though drained almost of life, her hazel eyes were huge in a haunted face.

Despite his intentions, she gave him pause. Especially when she shifted her attention to him, to Nate, then back to him with an obvious effort and said, "Who are you people? Where is Brian Poundstone? Or Linda? Or Ginger?"

He came close to swallowing his own tongue. "How do you know those names?"

"They're friends of mine. Where are they? What are all you goons doing here, letting everything go to hell?"

"Friends of yours, you say? That's about the stupidest thing anybody ever said to me. As far as—"

The door slammed open and Neila burst through, Nate and Harmon on her heels. Bannion forgot what he's started to say, because Neila was waving a book over her head, an aged book, falling apart at the spine.

"I found it, Bannion," she said. "Before you say another word, you've got to see this."

The woman, Lily, stared out at the hulk across the way until Harm shut off the view. Then she swallowed, coughed, and sank slowly into the chair nearest her. It was where Bannion had been sitting earlier, but she drank from his half-full cup of tea as if grasping at a lifeline.

A picture, no, Bannion corrected himself, *a photograph,* floated out of the book from between pages, settling on the floor equidistant from each of them. It was quite a large photograph and, considering the relic's age, the image clear. Distinct enough, in fact, to recognize the setting, and even the people, if one were to see them in real life.

Harm, being young and quick, darted in and picked up the photo. "Here, Mom." He gave it a fleeting look. "What's so great about this old thing? Flett can draw better pictures."

Harm's confidence in Flett's abilities, Bannion thought, though commendable, was a little misplaced. His under-standing was that photographs captured the image in an instant. This old picture contained details it would take Flett a week or more to replicate.

Neila handed Bannion the photo. "What do you make of this?"

He studied it a moment before squatting beside the wom-an in the chair and, holding it by his finger pads, tipping the artifact for her to see. She flicked it a glance then, jumping to her feet, snatched the photograph out of his hands.

"Where did you get this? Nate—" Her forehead puckered as she gave *their* Nate a hard stare—which Bannion noticed he returned blandly—and she continued more slowly. "Nate *Bell* took this with the new digital camera Ginger got for her thirteenth birthday and immediately printed it out. Look. There was still a glimmer of sunshine before the storm came in. Makes Heathen's hindquarters shine as though coated with wax." She met Bannion's eyes. "Where are these peo-ple now, Mr. O'Quinn? What have you done with them? And where is my horse?" Her fingernail clicked against the photograph. "This horse."

"What do you mean, that horse?" Harmon glared at the Turnbow woman. "Mom, is she crazy?"

Neila's eyes flashed. Amusement? Bannion wondered. Or wonder touched with fear? Most probably, some of each.

"Impolite," Nate admonished.

"But, Uncle, Mom just got that picture out of the—"

"Harmon, quiet. You haven't earned a place in this discussion. Speak only to answer questions." Nate's quiet reprimand stopped the boy.

"Aw," the boy muttered. Fortunately, the habit of obeying his elders was strong enough to mute him.

"See now," Bannion said to Lily, "this is the kind of thing that gives me fits."

"You should let the boy talk. Maybe we'll get somewhere with him running the show." She nodded to the boy. "What makes you think I'm crazy, kid?"

Harmon, respect for Nate's reproof sinking in at just the wrong time, answered before Bannion or Neila could stop him. "Because these people have been dead since the Event."

Lily shook her head.

"Big Bang," Harmony clarified. "Most of them have, anyway. Except Ginger and Nate. 'Course they are now. Dead, I mean." His chin lifted proudly. "They're my great-grandparents."

Neila inhaled deeply. "Great, great," she corrected him.

"Yeah. Great-great grandparents." He didn't seem to see Lily turning dead white, or notice the way she quit breathing.

"And that horse, Heathen," Harmon continued. "She's part of the found—uh—foundation line of the Bell/O'Quinn stud. Years and years and *years* ago."

"Are you done bragging?" Nate asked, tousling the boy's hair.

Harmon batted at his uncle's hand.

Bannion barely noticed the interplay between his male relatives, because of his own grim realization being reflected in Neila's face. The photograph was indisputably of the same Lily Turnbow standing right there with them now. She even wore the same clothes as in the picture, her brown hair in the same thick braid.

But no. He was mistaken in one thing. She was no longer standing, because her eyes had rolled back in her head and before anyone could catch her, she thumped onto the floor at their feet.

"Well," Neila said in obvious surprise. "Well."

Chapter 13

Lily's head pounded like the big bass drum in a marching band when she came around a few moments later. Nate Quick, to her surprise, had her in his arms carrying her down the hall like a baby. The floating sensation added to her stomach's distress.

"Which room?" Nate asked Neila who followed them, and at the jerk of her thumb, headed toward the little room Lily'd escaped from only an hour ago.

Nate's golden eyes met hers. "Okay?" he asked, so softly she wasn't sure but that he only mouthed the words.

At first she couldn't answer. *Okay?* Hell, no. Shocked, embarrassed, afraid. Sick! Not okay.The whole of her predicament flooded in. What a revolting development. At this rate they were apt to lock her up for the rest of her life as a dangerous lunatic, though a physically weak one.

"Hold on," she said, surprised when her voice came out scratchy and faint as an old 33 1/3 record, ancient history even to her. The irony of the simile didn't escape her. According to these people, Nate Bell and Ginger Poundstone, teenagers less than a week ago, had somehow become the grandparents, a few times removed, of the boy traipsing along behind them, his eyes big with wonder at this intriguing morsel of information.

Which meant that she—

The concept was too much for her pea-brain to cope with, let alone a boy's. Yeah. The kid had figured out the impossibility of it all just as well as the rest of them. Didn't quite mean as much to him as it did to her, of course. The thought of being something like a hundred and thirty years old set one back a step, for sure. Because, of course, such a scenario could not be a viable possibility. *Could it?*

"Put me down." Her demand came out louder this time. Nate didn't stop though. "Hey, guy," she said. "Wait a minute. I'm all right now." They were already at the door to the room.

"It won't hurt you to lie down a few minutes," Neila said, coming forward and working the door. "I'll bring more tea with honey in it, and a cold compress for the back of your head. You hit pretty hard when you fell."

Yeah. As if she didn't know.

The rest of the gang trooped in behind them. Already tiny, the room became seriously overcrowded with the addition of three men, the healer, and the boy.

Nate put her on the cot and stepped back. Despite her best intentions, Lily liked the soft pillow beneath her aching head, and even the sagging mattress poufing around her body. She wanted to sink into what comfort the rather Spartan quarters afforded and forget the conclusions scampering around in her brain like a bunch of crazy rats.

Not a good idea to let herself relax, she knew. Not for a moment. Wincing with pain, she sat up.

"You want to tell me how you got hold of that picture?" she asked Neila.

"You want to tell me how you seem to be part of it?" Neila countered.

Bannion's head jerked agreement, as the boy, Harmon, looked bewildered. Nate, once again, had stepped back and taken a position leaning against the wall. The boy, dark-eyed and sharp-faced like his mother, stood behind his big relatives, watching and listening. Banded together, the four of them filled the room to overflowing and surrounded her in a ring of suspicion.

"I don't know," she said, her voice flat. "But I think you people have a good idea. It might be helpful if you let me in on the secret."

Neila's mouth tightened. After a full minute of silence, the healer grimaced and motioned for Bannion to accompany her out of the room, leaving Nate and Harmon to baby sit.

Making sure she didn't escape, Lily thought. Unnecessary. The door seemed well-guarded and the single window only big enough for a skinny cat. Looked as if it was painted shut, anyway. Through the window she saw Bannion and Neila pacing up and down the patch of dry grass between the infirmary and a gravel road leading to one of the barns. She saw their mouths moving, their expressions intense as they seemed to be arguing about something, but even with her superlative hearing their words were beyond her.

"Why is Mom mad at Bannion?" Harmon asked, looking to his older cousin or uncle or whatever relationship lay between them.

Nate shook his head. "She's not mad at him," he said with a lift of one shoulder. "She's just upset. Worried. Freaked out by this whole business. The usual."

"Yeah, the usual." The boy scowled.

There, Lily thought, was another of those anomalies. Sometimes these people used the idiom as if born to it; other times their speech took an unfamiliar turn. Such as when Nate smiled at her and said, "Looks like you've been walking the void a long time, Lily Turnbow." And, as if that wasn't an obscure enough statement, he added, "Have you always been her—Lily—I wonder, or is this a new incarnation?"

She stared at him, her brows drawing together. "What?"

"I'm told Cross-up people used to just pop up out of nowhere, like you'd been hiding under a rock. Other times, the elders say you'd take some poor sucker over and try to do the rest of us in. Which category do you fall into, Lily Turnbow?"

He didn't sound so genial now, and the personable smile was missing.

"I have no idea what you're talking about," she said. "But it doesn't sound promising."

"That's because it ain't," Harmon said. "My cousin Bannion don't like Cross-up people. And neither does Uncle Selkirk, or Ma. Me neither. None of the O'Quinns or the Bells do."

Because Nate's strange eyes kept drawing her attention to him, Lily noticed the way his mouth pursed, then relaxed.

He ruffled the boy's hair. Lily judged it a sign of appreciation for his loyalty, kind of like a man patting his dog in "atta boy" approval. Saved him the bother of having to explain.

"But I'm not a . . . whatever you call them," she began, then stopped. Maybe she was one of those Cross-up people they kept yammering about. Because what other explanation was there? *"Pop up out of nowhere, like you've been hiding under a rock. Didn't I, literally, push out from under a rock?"* And those damned fireballs, tossing them around like they were nothing, right where everyone could see her. When she thought about it, Cross-up fit her situation to a tee. Only she had a hunch the description should be *crossed-up* person.

She pressed her head back against the pillow, almost wishing for the darkness to reclaim her. How was this predicament even possible? Like Rip Van Winkle—or maybe Sleeping Beauty; she was female, after all—she'd gone to sleep, or, technically, been knocked out by a cataclysmic event in one time, and awakened in an entirely different era.

That noise. The flash. The unbearable pain. A sensation of being scattered into pieces. Maybe she had, and now, somehow, been put back together.

Not Sleeping Beauty, then. Humpty Dumpty.

When a little later Bannion and Neila entered the room Lily referred to in her mind as "her cell," she kept her eyes closed and her back turned. She pretended to be asleep, even as her mind raced. *Why the hell had she ever awakened?* That was the question she kept asking herself.

"Wake up, Lily Turnbow." Bannion coughed loud enough to wake the comatose and when she couldn't stop her eyelids from flickering a response, started in on her again. "Tell us about the horse, Heathen."

A trick, Lily thought. Why should they want her to speak of the mustang? What difference did it make now? She kept her breathing deep and regular. Had she heard him? Sorry, no.

"Oh, let her sleep," Neila said impatiently. "I've got things to do and she isn't going anywhere. Have someone keep an eye on her. Harmon can sit outside and take first watch."

Not that she needed it, but here was proof of incarceration. Lily almost took comfort from the affirmation. At least she knew where she stood with the O'Quinn clan.

As the door closed behind the healer and the two warriors, she determined to let sleep become the reality. What else was there to do? Besides, her mind was so very tired.

*****

Before long, as was Lily's intention, the boy Harmon grew bored with his assigned task. At first he'd sneaked into her room when no one was looking and tried to talk to her. She had no doubt she could've gotten a great deal of information from him, but it just didn't seem worth the effort. When she remained silent, he went to drink tea and eat cookies in the kitchen. Not much excitement in watching a woman sleep, she smirked to herself.

Thereafter, she slept through the day watch. Someone brought food and left it on the bedside table. She ate. At night, her guard dozed. That's when Lily, silent as a shadow, took the opportunity to slip from her room and look around. Although a padlock, in theory, kept her corralled, she found it surprisingly easy to jiggle free.

Moving on light cat's feet, she found Bren, the night nurse, stretched out on a sagging couch. The woman never heard her creeping about. Lily questioned the woman's effectiveness as a caretaker. Once she blundered into a table holding jars and bottles filled with medicinal preparations. The glassware clinked and rattled, but Bren snoozed on.

Snickering to herself, Lily peered through a window at the starlit compound. Bright stars, shining in a way she'd never seen before.

Overcome with the desire to breathe fresh air, she unlocked the outside door as easily as she had her room. She jiggled, the lock released. But before she could open the door, she heard footsteps approaching and drew back. As she held to the doorknob beneath her hand, it jerked, stopped, was still. She fancied she heard breathing before the footsteps retreated.

Oh, yes. A prisoner indeed.

What's the use? she asked herself. The O'Quinn leaders appeared determined to keep her apart from the rest of the clan, their distrust of her plain. The feeling was mutual, the only question she had concerned what they intended to do with her—and what she intended to do about them.

Two nights later, she had an unexpected visitor.

*****

Bright moonlight streamed across the quilt on Lily's bed as she awoke and tossed back the covers. New energy flowed through her, urging her body into motion. Same as the past couple nights, she jumped from the cot and began exercising her cramped and underused muscles. Arms reaching high overhead, twisting sideways, hamstrings stretching until she groaned. The floor, as usual, was cold beneath her bare feet and she shivered, fumbling to pull the bedside rug into a more accommodating position.

A soft catch, then exhalation of breath was the first clue she wasn't alone.

Whirling toward the sound, Lily gasped. "Who is that?" Then, "What are you doing here?"

Nate Quick arose from where he'd been seated in the room's darkest corner and mimicked her arm reaches. "Right now? Admiring the scenery."

"What?" She eyed him warily.

His hand lifted. "Make that waiting for you to wake up. I want to talk to you, Lily Turnbow. I hoped we could have a civilized exchange of information."

"Really. A civilized exchange? I hadn't noticed much in the way of civilization going around."

"We live a hard life," he said, an agreement of sorts. "Most every day is a challenge just to stay alive. Remain alert and watch each other's back. That's how we do it. We suspect everyone we meet is an enemy until he, or she, proves different. Hard for you to understand, I guess."

"Might not be quite so hard if someone would just explain things to me."

He came forward, into the same moonlight that bathed her. Snagging the quilt from the bed, he wrapped it around her, his hands gentle. "That occurred to me," he said. "It's why I'm here. Ask away. I'll try to answer."

"Now that you're covered up."

Lily felt heat climbing her cheeks. Even though he hadn't said that last sentence out loud, it had certainly been broadcast from his mind. But no, she added a second later. If that were the case it would mean she was a mind-reader as well as a whatever else she was.

Horrified, it occurred to her that what she wasn't was any kind of modest, having gone to bed wearing only her light t-shirt. And that barely covered her butt even when she wasn't stretching for the ceiling. She hugged the quilt more tightly.

Mr. Nate Quick hadn't seemed offended by her attire, or lack thereof. He seemed more . . . distracted.

And she, Lily thought, was just the girl to take advantage of it.

She plopped down onto the cot and patted the space beside her. Smiling with a wry twist of his mouth, he sat, perching on the very edge and crossing one leg over the other.

"Your relatives—brothers, cousins, whatever they are— keep calling me a Cross-up. I want to know why. I want to know what that is. I want to know what happened. Not," she added, shaking a forefinger under his nose, "that I'm agreeing with any of the labels you people are putting on me."

"Cousins," he said. "We're cousins. I'm not sure you know this, but Selkirk is clan leader. He runs the outfit, day-to-day. Neila is his sister. She's the clan healer and all around wise woman."

"Wise woman. Jacob called her that and was offended when I asked if that meant herbal healer or witch woman."

"Better not mention anything about a witch woman. I think you might call her an advisor."

"Hmm. But hardly a diplomat. What about Bannion?"

Nate cocked an eyebrow. "Bannion keeps everyone else in order. He and his patrollers fight our battles. He's the sheriff and warleader."

Her fingers plucked at a thread on the quilt. "And you, Mr. Quick? What do you do?"

"Me?" He shrugged. "This and that. I'm a go-to kind of guy. I do stuff nobody else wants to do."

"Such as?"

"Such as scout a little, fight a little, help out where I'm needed."

Lily decided this meant Nate was either a small cog in the O'Quinn wheel, or an outrageously important one. And it didn't look like he meant to tell her. Her next question struck closer to home.

"What are Cross-ups, exactly?" She met his eyes, dark and fathomless in the moonlit room. "It sounds like an accusation, an abomination, when you people call me that."

He sighed. "Because Cross-ups, taken as a whole, aren't the goodwill type. Maybe, somewhere, there are good people among them. Around these parts...well, we haven't seen any." He blinked. "You might even put them in the same stew as witch woman."

Lily's breath caught. "But what are they? *Why* are they? And why do your people think I'm one?"

"How many people did you know...before...who could throw around missiles made of fire?"

She couldn't speak, couldn't tell him the truth. *None, of course. None.*

But he knew. "That's what I thought," he said. "As to what they are? People who came back, later, with the ability to do," he hesitated, "to do things no human being should be able to do. Just like you."

Sick, Lily couldn't meet his eyes. Yes, like her. Even to jiggling a lock open. "How many of us are there?" she asked at last, voice shaking.

He rose, leaving her feeling even more chilled as he walked around the tiny room. He seemed restless. Caged.

"Around here? There've been four or five. Only two now. Well, three, with you. You're the first I've heard of for at least a generation." He smiled briefly. "Cross-ups have a habit of killing each other off, you see. Or die because something about the process doesn't click."

"I see."

"No, I don't think you do. Not yet. As for the other part of your question, *why* Cross-ups came into to being, as far as I've ever heard, nobody knows. The Event stopped the clock, Lily. Some things quit, other things started. That's the only answer I have."

"Not very helpful."

"No, I suppose not."

Standing to make herself appear taller, stronger, she felt her lips tremble and fiercely clamped her back teeth together. "I may be what you say, Nate. A Cross-up. But I'm not a bad person. I believe in law and order and justice and in taking care of people. It's my job."

"Yeah? Maybe. Today, anyhow." His jaw clenched. "In a year or two, when you've got a feel for your power, who's to say?"

In the room beyond them, they both heard the night nurse, Bren, stir, rise from her kitchen cot, and walk into the bathroom. Nate, without speaking further, slipped from the room noiseless as a cat. Even Lily couldn't make out his footsteps down the hall, although she was aware when the outer down latched behind him.

She sank down on her bed gripping the quilt around her for warmth, more disheartened than ever. Even so, Nate's visit had been an unexpected act of kindness. Unless, of course, it had been a simple scouting expedition. Did she fall under the *this and that* designation?

Lily rather thought so.

Chapter 14

Standing at the head of a welcoming committee, Neila watched the line of heavy wagons and strings of pack animals wend their way across the meadow to the compound. A guard seemed to be pointing out the irregular burn spots in the grass where a little more than a week ago there'd been a battle.

In only a few days, word had gotten around the countryside that the clan was in winter residence. A code of drumbeats here, a flash of heliograph there, a system of messengers both on foot and riding horseback spread the news.

The decisive victory that had cleaned out such a huge and dangerous nest of Mags was, naturally, the most welcome news. It made the area safer, if not risk free, and as expected, traders were already taking advantage of the situation. The trader caravan approaching the compound now was the first company of the season, arriving at the west end of Frying Pan Lake.

They were, Neila saw, shading her eyes against an errant sunbeam, escorted by a squad of mercenary guards riding alongside merchandise-laden wagons. Early in braving the risks of the trail, they'd received a boisterous greeting and a prompt invitation from the outer circle watchers to approach headquarters. More than one of the trader's guards came from the Bell/O'Quinn clan, so for some it was like a family reunion.

Neila's own anticipation grew as a few of the people became identifiable.

Of course, after the long summer in the mountains, everyone needed to shop. Clothing had worn thin, pretties gone out of style, imported foodstuffs grown scarce. Neila had a list as long as Sliver's tail of supplies necessary to see their people safely through the winter.

"Hey, sis! Neila. Hello!" An ebullient cry drew Neila's attention to the slim woman heading up a string of dozen horses, each laden with covered packs swaying three feet above their withers. A small child sat in front of the woman, and Neila's heart caught with joy. She hadn't seen her sister Pauline since last year this time, when the child had barely gained his feet.

"Pauline! I'm so glad to see you. Are you well?"

A nudge from Dark Bill Shandy, Kira's father, reminded her of her duty, and she called to the leaders, "Dismount, all of you. Selkirk O'Qinn, leader of the clan bids you welcome to Kettle Creek Ranch. We've cleared the dance floor in the big barn for a display area. Tables have been set up, curtains hung for dressing rooms." Spotting the education representative she smiled warmly. "You've brought my order of reading materials, haven't you? School is about to start."

His thumbs up relieved her of one concern.

A big man, his arms and shoulders heavily muscled and shown to advantage on this occasion by his coatless state, gave her a salute and a wink as he rode by. Even as he directed the wagons toward the barn, his eyes never left her.

Pike. Neila's breath caught and she shivered with anticipation at what she saw in his face. He'd proved a thoughtful lover last year and his heated gaze indicated he hadn't forgotten her.

She pulled her attention back to her sister. "I hope you've brought the medical books and supplies I ordered. We're running short on antibiotics."

"Got'em." Pauline dismounted and ground-hitched her nag. "But I warn you, they're more expensive than ever."

"Stuff goes up every year," Dark Bill muttered under his breath. "Damn traders want everything we've got." Strutting with importance, he stalked off to assign traders a display space in the barn.

Amid the cacophony of excited animals, yammering people, and the clatter of packs dropping to the ground, Neila embraced her sister, baby Alonzo and all. He was Pauline's third living child, lucky, lucky woman.

"Are the girls with you?" she asked. "Can you stay and visit a while this year?" Tenderly, she patted Alonzo's pink cheeks. "How you've grown, little man."

Oh, how she wished Pike would plant a cousin for Alonzo, a brother for Harmon, in *her* womb this year. If she had her way, it wouldn't be for wont of trying.

Pauline laughed, thrusting the child toward her. "I wish. Regretfully, we'll have to move on with the caravan. I hope you can corral this one while we're here, Sis. He's off and running the second his feet touch the ground. And yes, the girls are here somewhere. With Jinx, I think." Jinx was Pauline's husband, of the Trader Nordman clan. "Or they may be with Pike's family," she added, looking around.

Neila froze. "Pike's family?" She choked on the words, though her sister appeared not to notice.

"Yeah. His mother, his son, and a younger brother are with him. I thought you two got together last year, Neila. Didn't he tell you about his family then?" Pauline grinned knowingly. "I guess you were too busy doing other things to spend time talking."

A son. Neila barely heard the rest of Pauline's teasing;

the part about how Pike had been the first to sign on to the caravan when he heard it was headed this way.

Stiff with the resentment surging through her, Neila caught sight of Lily Turnbow, *the Cross-up,* standing near the artifact shed by herself, her face quite expressionless as she watched the trader's arrival. What with anger warring with the cutting disappointment of Pauline's revelation that Pike was married, Neila's voice was sharp as she called to Lily over Alonzo's head, breath stirring his mop of black O'Quinn hair.

"You. What are you doing out here? Get inside and stay there." She headed purposefully toward Lily, Alonzo still in her arms.

The Turnbow woman had been sick—or so she claimed—ever since she realized she lived by some freakish accident of time, or space, or something. Nobody really knew the why of her presence. While she wasn't the only Cross-up person the clan knew about, she was the most recent one by far, and the only one ever to appear in O'Quinn territory. Cross-ups had always been more likely to emerge where there'd once been big cities, in zones that had escaped the fires, if not the quakes of the Event. And then the over-whelming variety of diseases, the resultant mass die-off, and the following mutations.

Nate, and to a lesser degree Selkirk, had had a hard time convincing Lily this was all real. Stupid woman. She didn't want to believe the evidence of her own being.

Conveniently for everyone, since Bannion had finally turned her loose, she spent a lot of time in the artifacts shed, looking through the few remaining diaries and journals chronicling the years after the Event. Neila never had made it through all of them. Too depressing by far, and she much too busy trying to save the lives of her people in the here and now.

Lily had told her yesterday she should've studied them, adding, "Maybe then you wouldn't always be trying to reinvent old technology. After all, it wouldn't have failed if it'd been practical in this time."

Neila had come close to slapping the sour bitch.

But now, to all appearances caught up in the excitement of the trader's arrival, Lily stood her ground as Neila stomped toward her. The rest of the clan gave her wide berth, swirling around the Cross-up woman as if she wasn't there. They were foolish, too, Neila admitted, as well as frightened by the thought of irking the woman and causing her to produce a fireball aimed at one of them. They'd been warned not to tell the traders about her, but to leave making her introduction to Selkirk and Bannion when the time was right. If ever.

She snorted. Fat chance of that. Neila was willing to wager the news had already spread. This kind of news was damn hard to contain. And now, with a strange woman standing in plain sight, questions would soon surface.

Neila took Lily's arm in a firm grip, turning her. "We decided you'd stay out of sight. If there's anything we don't need it's a dozen strangers knocking on our gates wanting a look at you. Then the Techs will show up, and the Cits and the Cross-ups beholden to them. Your presence alone is enough to start a war."

Neila's low-voiced, though heated rebuke didn't visibly affect Lily. She shook her arm loose as if twitching off flies. "You and your brothers or cousins or whatever they are decided. Nobody discussed it with me. I do agree not to give any details, but I need to meet these people, see where they stand in this whacked out world for myself."

"You *need* to do as you're told."

Lily lifted a single eyebrow. "Really? Are you going to force me into a show of strength? Well," there was another of those seemingly careless shrugs, "there's a nice audience, which I'd say is to my advantage." She flicked her fingers suggestively.

Alonzo stared in bewilderment at his aunt before his face puckered and he began crying.

"You're pinching the kid," Lily said, and to Neila's intense mortification, she was right. The baby whimpered, saying, "Owie."

Neila hadn't known he could talk. She was surprised when the Cross-up woman turned a crooked grin on the baby and said, "Hey, squirt, you're a pretty cute kid, aren't you?"

Tears immediately stopping, the baby grinned back and held out his arms, wanting Lily to take him.

Automatically, Lily reached for him. "I'm Lily. Who are you?"

"Lonz," the baby said.

"No." A twinge of fear struck Neila and she twirled Alonzo away, but he squirmed and squirmed until she was forced to set him down. Once again he made a dive for Lily, grabbing her around a leg. Shocking Neila completely, the magician bent and hugged him back before letting him go.

Neila knew her mouth was gaping open like a pop-eyed fish out of water, but she couldn't help herself. Was that all for show, or was the Cross-up woman a half-way decent human after all? And then Pauline was there beside her and Alonzo transferred his affection to his mother.

Pauline stared at Lily in open curiosity. "Looks like Alonzo has taken a liking to you," she said. "Who are you? Have you married into the clan?"

It was an explanation for Lily's presence no one had thought of giving, not that it would've served, because Lily, back to her unsmiling self, nodded to Pauline and said, "I'm Lily Turnbow. They—" an encompassing gesture took in headquarters and the people, "say I'm a Cross-up woman, whatever the hell that is, and no, I'm not married."

Pauline gasped.

Neila, if a crossbow had been ready to hand, would cheerfully have sent a bolt right through Lily about then, because Pike, his ears tuned, was leading his first wagon into the barn at that moment. He'd have had to be deaf not to overhear.

Sure enough, he stopped in mid-stride, staring at the Turnbow woman before turning his gaze on her. "Neila?" he said.

"Damn you," she told Lily. "Ignorant troublemaking interloper. You're going to get us all killed."

She didn't appreciate her sister pointing out her face was flaming red with fury and that she didn't need to worry about somebody else killing her because she was about to give herself a heart attack.

*****

Whoever had set up the archives, Lily discovered, had been systematic enough to file notebooks according to date. Or did in the early years, anyway. Along about 2030 the order had gone to pot and it took another twenty–five years for anyone to make a new attempt. Or so she surmised from the misfilings and omissions during those years. Documents filed in the last ten were most precise. Trouble is, the quantity and quality of the documents had fallen off rather drastically. As a matter of fact, all the volumes, regular school issue notebooks, were on the slim side.

Sitting in a dangerously rickety chair, over the past couple days Lily had spent hours pouring over the notebooks. One by one, she laid them out on the small desk. She found the photo someone, Neila, probably, had haphazardly replaced in the first notebook. The quality of the photo was rapidly deteriorating, she noticed. Soon there'd be nothing left to tie her to these people.

Except for the two notebooks on a separate shelf, found yesterday. They made her smile. Someone, Ginger probably, had kept excellent records of the Kettle Creek Ranch stud. It started off with fewer animals than Lily remembered around the barns and corrals. Two stallions, one she remembered as on ornery S.O.B., the other a tough, though smallish quarter horse. Only seven mares had survived the Event. One of them was Heathen, and it was her foals that eventually became the basis of the ranch's continued existence.

When Ginger turned sixteen, as the only remaining Poundstone, she hooked up with young Nate Bell, who'd also lived through the cataclysm. Certain paragraphs in the record led Lily to believe Nate had fought tooth and toenail—literally—to keep the girl alive in those post-apocalyptic days. Eventually, Seamus O'Quinn and his wife had wandered in from the north and the two couple's linked together for protection. Gradually, Lily read, a few other survivors joined them. Armand Quick Water, for one. Lily supposed he must have been one of Nate Quick's ancestors. In the fourth book she found her guess was correct.

Anyway, the union grew over the years. The blended families fought off everyone who wanted what they had. The stud grew. The Mags, mutants of undetermined origin, flourished even as the regular population struggled with a low birth rate.

Technology died without the means in people, material, or common knowledge to retain it. People reverted to a 19th Century type society, or at least the lucky ones succeeded in doing so. Only in the last twenty years or so had any sort of widespread commerce, like the traveling Trader clan in the compound now, begun.

Lily finished the final volume, sat back and rubbed her burning eyes. The little artifact shed was dark with only the weak flickering of an oil lamp. Absently, a flip of her fingers sent a small light hovering above the desk.

The door swung open, allowing her a glimpse of the frenetically busy yard where traders and clansfolk talked and bartered. Nate strode in. When he saw her, he halted and let the saddlebag he carried over his shoulder clump to the floor.

"I wondered if you'd find your way here," he said after a moment.

"Mr. Bell let me have a key." If a defensive note crept into her voice, Lily couldn't help it. In plain fact she was still smarting from Neila's earlier animosity and had come in here to hide. Not that her own deliberate provocation toward the healer had her chest swelling with pride. What had gotten into her? As much as she hated to admit it, she needed these people on her side. And Nate, it occurred to her, had saved her life. At the least, she owed him civility.

"Didn't figure you broke in," Nate was saying. "Learning anything?"

She nodded. "This and that, all of it sad."

"I guess, to you. To us, it's just life. We don't think about the old days much. Except me. Kind of turns my crank."

The expression made Lily smile.

Nate picked up his saddlebag, putting it on the desktop as Lily got up to shove the current notebook back on the proper shelf. He cast a glance at the fireball spinning overhead. "Handy," he said.

"At times."

"You're apt to be interested in what I've got here." Nate patted the saddlebag.

She leaned closer to the desk. "What is it?"

With a flourish, he reached into the bag and pulled out not one, but three books, hardcovers, all in fairly decent condition except for what seemed to be a blood splatter on one. The blood, while dry, looked quite fresh.

"Books are a great prize," Nate said. He paused to read the back cover blurb of one. "This sounds good. It's about a racehorse."

Lily, gazing at the cover, smiled. "It *is* good. They made

a movie of it." The book was *Seabiscuit*, by Laura Hillen-
brand. The second book was by her, as well. And the third
was a how-to book on primitive pumps, which probably
made the slim volume the most valuable find of them all.

"A movie?" Nate was still reading the back cover. "Soon
to be a major motion picture, it says. That's the same thing,
right?" He looked up at her. "I've read about movies, but
haven't figured how the hell they put pictures into motion."

Although tempted to tell him, "by magic," she refrained.
She thought a moment. "Simplest way to explain it, I guess,
is for you to imagine thousands and thousands of single
photographs all lined up and put on a reel. The reel spins,
advancing very fast and projecting the pictures onto a flat
surface. The photographs look as if they're moving." Visions
of pre-1900 film clips ran through her memory. Crikey!
Hard to believe this society was even more primitive.

"How many people will read these books?" she asked,
picking up the one titled *Unbroken.*

He shrugged. "Me. Harrison. A few others, during the
winter. Many more over the years."

"But not Neila." It wasn't a question.

"No. Probably not." He gave her a questioning stare.
"She giving you a hard time?"

"Nothing I can't handle." Lily thought it prudent to
change the subject. "Where did you get these?"

"Found somebody's hidey hole. Happens every now
and then even after a hundred years." He reached into his
saddlebag, withdrawing two spiral bound school notebooks.
"Paper is scarce these days, too. This is a real prize. And
so is this." This time he brought out a ten-pound spool of
copper tubing. "It'll make the hooch from Black Jack's still
a whole lot safer."

Lily snorted. "Hooch. I might have known." She sobered.
"This is what you do, isn't it? Make discoveries, preserve

history where you can."

To her surprise, he turned pink beneath the warm olive of his skin. "Among other things," he replied tersely, striking her as being on the defensive. Why?

But he didn't tell her what those other things were. She didn't think he would've even if Selkirk hadn't hailed him just then from outside the artifact shed. Stretching her neck, Lily saw Nate's roan hitched to the rail with a most peculiarly shaped load tied on behind the saddle. The clan leader was looking at the load, too.

"Nate," Selkirk called. "What have you got here?"

Nate, his pink color fading, motioned for her to precede him outside. "Maybe you can tell me exactly what this thing is," he said to her.

Her curiosity aroused, Lily stepped into the sunlight, shading her eyes and trying her best to ignore Selkirk's hard stare. He, no doubt, disapproved of finding her together with his cousin.

Nate apparently took no notice of the stare, nor cared what Selkirk might think. "See," he said, busy with the pack. "Metal. A bonanza. Enough to keep our arrowhead makers busy for a while."

Nimble fingers yanking open knots, he flung back the deer hide cover. Revealed was a length of silvery metal, bright, uncorroded, beautiful.

Lily reached out and touched it, hefting the loose end in her hand and finding it surprisingly light for its size. "Titanium," she breathed in delight. "Part, I think…" she surveyed the piece, estimating the point at which the metal had snapped,"…I think it may be part of a helicopter rotor," she finished. She smiled at Nate's hidden excitement. "Metal that'll make great arrowheads if you can rework it. Is this the only piece you found?"

"There's more," he said. "I saw this glinting and dug

it out of the ground. I'll go back later with a pack horse."

Even Selkirk was pleased. "Well done, cousin. Is there enough to trade?"

"Trade?" Nate frowned. "Seems to me we should keep this for us."

Selkirk's gaze drifted over Lily. "Bring in the rest and we'll see. You'll have to go tonight. Traders won't be staying long."

That isn't what Lily had heard. Studying Selkirk, it didn't take long to figure him out. He just wanted to get Nate away from her, that's all. What an asswipe! As if she could ever be attracted to—

A little part of her stuttered to a halt and she took a second sneak peak at Nate as he leaned against his horse.

On the other hand, maybe she could, given a certain set of conditions. A startling idea.

Chapter 15

Lily, in her room brushing her long brown hair into a soft cloud, figured she was the only one in the whole compound not actually invited to the party being held that night in the big barn. Not that she planned on letting the lack of a formal invitation stop her from showing up. No indeed. She planned on attending just to spite the clan. Her only regret was the dearth of party gear. A brush of her pants and a swift polish of her boots would have to do.

The party was in honor of the Traders, the second celebration in the seven or eight days the clan had been home.

And yet, as she approached the barn, a part of her wished to retreat to that dour little room in the medical building. In fact, she turned around once, but getting hold of her nerves, forced herself across the compound to where music soared from an open doorway.

Slipping around an oblivious group of young men at the barn entrance, she saw where the trade good displays had been pushed to the side, freeing the thick plank floor for dancing. Even with the doors open the cavernous space was warm. Guys wore shirts unbuttoned to show brawny, or otherwise, chests, their sleeves rolled above the elbow; girls stripped down to short skirts and tank tops that struck Lily as absurd paired with their moccasins. The old building quaked under thirty pairs of feet pounding in a kind of dance she could never have imagined. It was a mixture of hoedown, American Indian powwow dancing, and hip-hop. Dust motes left from when the barn had been filled with hay floated in the lantern light. Watching, she had to laugh.

She gathered parties were an important part of the culture. These people lived on the edge, aware that at any time an enemy might try to wipe them out, so she supposed they welcomed any excuse to drink, dance, and sing. When they weren't fighting, anyway. Apparently, they enjoyed that, too, along with some free and easy bed-hopping. Their visitors, the traders and the mercenaries who guarded them, made no bones about liking the last part very much indeed. As far as she could tell hardly anyone slept alone. Even Bannion, according to overheard gossip. But not Selkirk or the mysterious Nate.

And now her.

She'd also heard enough talk to know the outwardly promiscuous behavior was because most of the younger women, along with a few older ones, were constant in their endeavor to bear children. The clan needed population, and these outsiders helped widen the gene pool. She learned that when she listened in on Neila. Neila the bad-tempered, the hard-assed, the dedicated hater of anything outside her personal realm, who had been whining to her sister about miscarrying another child last year after Pike's visit.

"I took every care I know of, Pauline, and still I lost it. You're so lucky with three healthy children. I don't know what's wrong with me. I'm strong. I'm healthy."

"You want it too much, Sis." Pauline had hugged her sister. "You're so tense your innards just bind up in a knot."

Lily thought Pauline might be on the right track. Though the subject had never been of primary importance to her, she had read a few articles along those lines. She ought to start a general information magazine for these people. Open up a new occupation for herself. *Living Beyond the Grave* sounded like a good title. Give them some insight by one who'd lived in the information age into what had gone wrong with them.

Her mouth twisted into a wry smile. Hell, judging by Nate's glee over finding two old notebooks, there wasn't paper in quantity enough for a magazine, which might open her up to yet another necessary profession if she could only remember what all went into making cheap paper.

"Do we strike you as funny?" a deep voice asked from beside her. "Or contemptible?"

Lily started and shrank farther against wall nearest the door. She hadn't been aware of Selkirk's approach, odd, since he was such a large man. Light on his feet, though.

She took a breath and faced him. "Funny, yes, at times. Contemptible? Never. I don't hold anyone in contempt who has the ability and the desire to kill me."

"And you think we do?"

"It's not much of a secret, Mr. O'Quinn. There's a certain faction in this compound that's all for it. So far, none of them want to get their hands dirty."

"Aside from the fact they're afraid of you."

"Which I suppose is why they want to kill me. Round and round it goes. It isn't like I've done anything to harm anyone here. Quite the opposite if memory serves me correctly.

His eyes, which she noticed were every bit as hard as his cousin Bannion's, glinted down at her. Usually he hid himself behind a wall of natural bonhomie. Right now he was letting his true self show through. Or maybe he wasn't consciously letting it. After the encounter yesterday afternoon, she thought she saw him in a way other people didn't.

"But you're not afraid of me," she added.

"Should I be?"

The question warranted thought. "Depends," she finally answered. "If attacked, I'll fight back with every weapon at my disposal."

"I know you will. I've been warned."

"By whom?"

He shrugged. "Maybe I saw it in a dream," he said, watching the dancers twirl past, his toe tapping the rhythm.

But Lily wasn't inclined to let the matter drop. "All I want is for the people here to respect me and allow me my space. Help me and I'll help you. It's as simple as that."

"Ah, but wait until word gets out about you."

For a moment she couldn't think what he meant. Then she did. "Oh," she said, her tone flat. "Because of that."

"Because of that, yes." His expression lost any vestige of softness. "Come the time one of my people gets killed fighting over you, or for you, then we'll see if you're so positive regarding your space and your respect."

"Why should anyone be killed?"

"Foolish question from one such as you." Selkirk folded his arms over his massive chest. "But here's the answer. Everyone will want a piece of you. Have you thought about that?"

Lily recalled the trader's wide-eyed interest yesterday, and the surreptitious visit by the wagon master and then the leader of the mercenary guards. Oh, yes. And Neila's reaction when she heard about the contact.

Avoiding Selkirk's eyes, she said, "I don't know what you mean. Why should they? I refuse to hide myself away. To tell the truth, a change of address sounds pretty good right now. No one here speaks to me. I'm treated as if I have some communicable disease. Why?"

Selkirk's shoulders hunched. "Come now, Lily Turnbow.

You can guess. You're far from dumb."

"And you're avoiding the issue. Why not be straight-forward and tell me what's going on? I'm sure your cousin would, if he'd hold still long enough to hold a decent conversation. With him, everything is a confrontation."

"Who, Bannion? Then you should try harder." It sounded as though he had no great fear of that happening.

Impatient with the way he avoided a direct answer, she snagged a lock of hair behind her right ear, not caring if it gave her a lopsided look. "The traders want me to go with them when they head out," she said. "I guess I will. There's nothing for me here except distrust and animosity. If I leave, you won't have to be afraid me or worry about what I might do."

"You think not? You're not being very realistic. I expect your leaving would only make matters worse." With this, which left Lily frustrated beyond belief, Selkirk slipped away, cryptic as ever. At the beginning of the next song, she saw him dancing, squiring a young woman nearly as tall as he around the dance floor, and acting as though he hadn't a care in the world.

Music pulsed over Lily, fortunately not at the ear-splitting volume she was used to. Or had been, in the real world. Her world. There were no amplifiers in this age, just the sound natural to the instruments, fiddle, guitar, pipes, hand drums. Clan Bell/O'Quinn unplugged.

Although angry with Selkirk, her body longed to join the dancers. She wanted to fling herself into motion and lose herself in joyful abandon. Standing alone on the dance floor's edge, she was conscious of many eyes on her. Watching, someone always watching her. That's why the light, almost tentative touch on her arm made her jump like she'd been poked with a pin. Spinning, she found Jacob Felix grinning at her, his teeth flashing in his dark-skinned face.

"Did I scare you?" His eyes twinkled.

"You guys are entirely too good at sneaking up on people," she grumped, glad in spite of herself to see a half-way friendly face. "Got a real talent for it."

"Thanks. Who else snuck up on you?"

"Selkirk." She bit out the name.

"Him? Hell, he's like an old woman. Wait till the boss gets after you. Or Nate. He's the best."

"The boss?"

"Nate. But Bannion is only a hair behind."

Oh. Sure." She should've known.

Jacob, taller than she by a few inches, was rigged out like the other men in open shirt and denims. He had his dancing shoes on, fancy moccasins beaded with an intricate geometric pattern in green, blue and red. For a moment she wondered where these people got their beads, but the thought was lost when he held his hand out to her.

"Come on and dance, Lily Turnbow. I seen you bouncing up and down. You're feeling the beat, ain't you?"

Lily hadn't known she was so easily read. Embarrassing. "No, thanks," she said, denying the music's siren song. "I don't know the steps."

"It's easy. I'll show you."

"I'd as soon not make an ass out of myself, if you don't mind. And I don't think your people would appreciate me barging in on their fun. I should go." In full retreat, she turned to leave.

"You scared of us?" he asked. "Got reason, I guess. Me and Harrison, we've told the folks you're okay, but they need to get used to you. If you can dance, they'll warm up sooner." He held out his hand. "C'mon. It's a good way to get acquainted."

So what if he was a kid making trouble for himself in associating with her? Or so Lily excused herself. Young or not, he had a streak of practicality to him. Blunt, too. And not a bit shy. His advice, when she pondered it, made sense. More than the clan leader's, she suspected, coming as it did, in a manner of speaking, from grassroots level. Besides, Lily wasn't much on foregoing a challenge when she heard one. Narrowing her eyes at him, she took Jacob's outstretched hand. It was warm, but not sweaty like most boys his age. Of her acquaintance, anyway. This kid had no nervous qualms. Made sense for a warrior like him. *He* wasn't afraid of her.

"Okay, pal," she said, feeling better at the thought. "You asked for it."

She had no trouble with the steps, just the patterns, and after a few minutes she got onto that, too. Soon she was able to relax and lose herself in the rhythms, and rise and fall of the fiddler's tune. She loved dancing. Loved music. After executing a particularly tricky step she picked up watching Jacob earlier, she grinned at him.

"Good one. Told you," he said, just before the answering grin faded from his face as he glanced over her shoulder. "Uh oh."

"What now?" His alarm barely registered with her before Bannion O'Quinn twirled his partner to a stop beside them. The girl was the same one who'd earned his praise at the battle's aftermath a few days ago. Kira Shandy. The one Neila thought Bannion should...er...court.

Still in unison, Lily and Jacob's dance came to a halt.

"What the hell do you think you're doing, Felix?" Bannion growled, his voice low. "Parading this woman around is asking for trouble. You should know better." He shifted his glare to Lily. "And you. I'd think you have sense enough to stay out of sight. Are you deliberately trying to stir folks up?"

Her temper flared. "I'm not trying to do anything but dance." She didn't trouble to hide her anger. "I figured it was time to get acquainted with the people here. Nothing wrong with that, is there?"

"What's your motive?"

"I don't know what you mean. The only motive I've got is getting out and meeting the people in this new world. It's as simple as that."

Jacob exchanged a puzzled look with Kira. "We're just dancing, boss. That's all."

"I'll want to talk to you tomorrow, Felix. Drop by the house in the morning."

Lily surmised Jacob was due for a butt-chewing. He knew it, too, because his shoulders jerked straight and a set look came over his face. "Whatever you say."

"Don't blame Jacob for my transgressions," Lily said. "I was intrigued by your unique dances and wanted to try them for myself. That's all. I picked Jacob to be my partner, and he was gentleman enough to indulge me."

"The hell," Jacob said. "I talked you into it, Lily. You don't gotta fib for me. Anyway, boss, she ain't in jail, is she?" His eyes flickered, then settled on Bannion. "Is she?"

Bannion's answer was slow in coming. "Been keeping her close for her own protection, Jacob. I thought you knew."

Lily made a sound somewhere between laughter and disgust. "He means he's been trying to keep my presence here a secret, Jacob, though I don't quite understand how he ever thought he'd succeed. Anyway, it hasn't worked. A dozen or more people saw what happened in that meadow. Were they all sworn to silence? Did you trust each one to keep such news totally quiet?" She spoke to Jacob, but her words were meant for Bannion. "I don't think so. These traders showed up a little too promptly, wouldn't you agree? Anyway, what difference does it make?"

She turned thoughtful. "Although from what I understand, people nowadays don't interact much, what with the lack of communication." She faltered, adding wistfully, "Very different from the world I knew, with our Internet service and cell phones everywhere."

Bannion waved that away. "A hundred years gone. What happened then doesn't mean anything to us now."

"Yes, except from what I can tell, everyone left is still fighting one another." Lily swept on, "Which goes to show nobody learned *anything* from whatever disaster struck." After days of denying the premise, saying it aloud didn't make the facts any more believable. Not even reading Ginger's journal, taken from the Bell family archives, helped make her situation real.

"Doesn't change the fact every clan in the country is going to be fighting over you, Lily Turnbow. They'll all want you throwing fireballs at their enemies."

"I have no intention of throwing fireballs at anyone," Lily said.

Bannion snorted. "No intention, huh? Until somebody, Mag or human, comes at you wanting your blood. Because that's the other thing. If you're not with them, they'll want you dead."

That hadn't escaped her. "Including Clan O'Quinn."

He gave a tiny, almost involuntary inclination of his head.

Damn him. She knew that if the situation demanded it, she'd fight to live. She'd pretty well proved that already. And he knew it, too.

"Well, shoot, boss," Jacob said. "That don't seem right."

The girl, Kira, didn't seem too broken up, but she touched Jacob's arm.

Around them, the background of music and stamping feet ceased. People shifted, clothing rustled, voices whispered. One voice came clear. Pike, speaking to Neila. "Aw, c'mon, honey. What's it going to hurt? Boss Trader Frin already asked her to come with us. Look at him. He's spreading the news to his people quick as his tongue can wag."

Not such good news, considering her present company. Lily hadn't answered the trader one way or another.

Still, Lily wasn't surprised when, over Neila's protest, the clanswoman and Pike joined them. The trader's caravan guard, big, blond, and battle-scarred, though still a good-looking man, gave her a thorough once-over. His regard was more invasive than Bannion's had been, and she hadn't thought that possible.

"Miss Lily," Pike said, spreading his smile over the entire group and acting as if he couldn't sense the tension between them. "Frin thinks he has a little problem with what ya'll were talking about. Wonder if you can fix it for him."

In fact, Frin had such an acute stutter, Lily wasn't sure she understood him when he cornered her this afternoon and spoken his piece. And in view of Bannion's—should she call it a threat?—she wished Pike had kept his mouth shut.

Over by the stage, a woman was soloing on a hand drum. After a few beats, voices joined in practiced harmony. Beside her, Lily sensed Jacob's discomfort. Poor kid. He'd taken pity on one he thought a fellow warrior, and been drawn into a situation beyond his expectations. Beyond hers, too, if only he knew.

Lily took a breath. "I doubt it," she told Pike curtly, then smiled at the kid. "Lets get closer to the music, Jake. That style is something new to me. Sounds like a cross between a powwow dance song and a Celtic round."

"A what?" Jacob asked, moving at her direction across the puncheon floor, their backs turned to the others. Bannion, having said his piece, and Pike, because he didn't quite dare annoy the area sheriff, let them go without further comment.

But if Lily had planned on that as a nifty exit strategy, her acting was spoiled when one of Bannion's younger posse members, or patrollers or whatever they called themselves, popped up in the open doorway yelling his head off for the boss.

"Nate says to tell you there's a whole bunch of strangers coming, Mr. O'Quinn." He sounded more excited than scared. "He says they're Techs. And they have that Cross-up guy from Spokane Sector with them."

Jacob stopped. "Hooey! You stay here, Lily," he said. "I gotta go get my bow."

"Your bow? Why? What's going on?"

"Gonna be trouble, I betcha."

Apparently he was right. Within a couple minutes, Bannion had assigned more scouts to work with Nate and gathered a squad of almost silent warriors around him. They left the barn, their speed just short of a trot. The music had come to a standstill at first warning. Folks stood silent, their faces stiff with tension. Lily felt herself withdrawing, alone, though surrounded by those left behind as they began talking to each other, ignoring her. More, they avoided even looking at her, almost as if she were invisible or didn't exist.

After a few moments, she walked over to the coat rack and found a jacket, putting it on before slipping out through the big barn door where people gathered in knots. Drifting past them, the flame in the lantern one carried flickered. No one paid attention.

This was the most freedom of movement she'd had since her arrival here. Reveling in her liberty, she glided toward the stable where the fighters were saddling their horses. Grim, they worked in silence.

Bannion was there, talking with his cousin Nate. With them standing together, the similarity between them became more obvious. Although, she decided thoughtfully, the resemblance may have stemmed more from the strong, tough aura surrounding both men than their physical looks. Nate, with his amber eyes and brown hair; Bannion with black hair and dark eyes.

The big lineback dun Bannion had been riding the day of the firefight was tacked up and ready to go. The horse tossed his head as she came close and laid a hand on his neck.

"Easy, Nog," Bannion said, as off-handed as though she weren't standing there for him to notice. He waved as his cousin rode off ahead of the patrol. "Mount up," he directed his posse.

Jacob, looking eager for the fight ahead, checked his bow and supply of arrows before springing to the back of a nondescript bay. He must've been too nervous to pay her any attention, for his fierce smile went over her head.

Within moments, the patrol was ready to go. She could only conclude by the speed of their preparations that they'd lots of practice. Shaking his fist in a follow-me gesture, Bannion rode out of the yard. Soon, men and horses had been swallowed up by the night. One by one, lanterns within the barn were doused, the helpers scattering to their homes.

No one spoke to her. No one harried her. No one saw her.

When she looked down, she couldn't see herself, either. Not her feet. Not her arms and hands, although she felt her hands clench. And though she cried out in appalled fear, the sound was only in her mind.

Chapter 16

"What d'ya got for me, Dak?" Bannion steered the sweating scout into the center of the group of patrollers gathered around him. He wanted everyone, Rongo, Kira, House, and several of his older warriors to hear what Dak had to say. "Where are the Techs now? What's their status?"

Dak wore a self-satisfied grin. In running flat out the four miles from old Highway 20 located south of the compound, he hardly needed to catch his breath, conditioning Bannion freely acknowledged was due to Rondo's training. One of the slight, fair-haired O'Quinns, Dak could easily outrun a horse through the woods and no spindle-shanked Mag—his very words—stood a chance against him in a foot race.

"I found 'em about five miles out," he said, "taking their time like this is a Sunday stroll. There's a white flag waving at the head of the troop and their weapons are stowed, so it doesn't appear they're looking for a fight. Not right off, anyhow. Got a Cross-up man with 'em, just like our outpost reported last night. It's that dwarf guy, the one who calls himself 'Phil Barnes, the Screenmaster.' He's riding along in one of those rubber-tired sheepherder wagons. Even got a staircase up to the driver's seat." His lip curled over strong teeth. "Got four blooded nags hitched to it that look like they're about to keel over."

Bannion grunted. "Nate, what do you know about The Screenmaster?"

Nate, having met with Dak on his way in, had returned home only minutes ago after spending most of the day scrounging the titanium metal per Selkirk's orders. Nate was designated, among his other duties and avocations, clan intelligence officer. He kept up with the news via a string of friendly contacts, and a few flyers that came into his hands. "Know your enemy," was a favored mantra, a piece of the old-fashioned jargon he often used. If anyone knew about the Cross-up wheeling along with the Techs, it would be him.

"Those horses white?" Nate asked Dak.

"Would be if they weren't hog dirty from the road."

The patrollers grunted their humor. Dust or mud or sweat, primitive roads and white horses didn't mix well if one was trying to make an impression.

Nate, mounted on the strong-looking red roan he called Pigeon, grinned. "Sounds like Barnes, all right. As I remember, he's the one came out from around some little farm town in Oregon fifty or sixty years ago. A vicious little bastard. Been selling his talents to whoever pays the most in tithe. Tell the boss which Tech unit he's with, Dak."

"Those crazy coots that put wind sails on their saicles."

"Them," Bannion said on a note of disgust.

"No wonder those horses are done in," House said, showing just a touch of admiration. "Pretty hard to keep up with saicles."

"Maybe on the flat," Rongo said, "or downhill, but they ain't worth a shit going up a mountains."

"Neither are four horses on a heavy rig like Screenmaster's," Dak said. "Uphill, downhill, or anywhere in-between."

Bannion held up his hand before differing opinions escalated into a discussion they had no time for. "Could be worse. The saiclers'll try to talk you to death before they shank you in the back, but they don't generally carry a lot of armament."

"Eh, boss," Nate said, "Dak says they're pretty well loaded down this time. They've got five four-wheel carts they're hauling along, and they're stacked high."

"With what?"

Dak answered for himself. "Don't know for sure. They got tarps over them."

Scanning his patrollers, Bannion issued a call for volunteers. "Who wants to find out what they're carrying?"

"I'll go," House said.

"As will I." Kira waved her hand, earning Bannion's wink of approval.

"Both of you," he decided. "Watch each other's back. Don't take any chances. What's this Screenmaster guy's specialty, Nate? Do you know?"

"He sets a shield of some kind our metal points can't penetrate." Nate shook his head. "Intel is that he's a cocky SOB, but fat as an old boar and slower than molasses in January."

Kira stared at him. "Slower than what?"

Nate shrugged. "Molasses. Read it somewhere. Don't know what molasses is for sure, but I get what it means." The roan he rode stirred restively.

"You're the only one," House muttered.

"Means he's *real* slow," Nate explained. "If it comes to a fight, we want to get our licks in before he has a chance to set his shields."

"Good to know." Bannion nodded at House and Kira. "Patrollers, get moving. Stay out of the saicler's and that Screenmaster's sight. Report in two hours. If you're not back by then, we'll be coming after you."

"Gotcha, boss." House spun his horse, gigging it into a trot. Kira trailed him as they set out through the woods along the same shortcut Dak had used on foot.

Bannion watched a moment before pointing at Dak. "I'm borrowing you from Nate. Get yourself a horse and follow them. I want you on hand at the Tech caravan in case anything goes wrong with House and Shandy. Keep 'em out of trouble if you can."

Dak nodded and jogged off to find a mount.

"Now what?" Fingers on the hilt of his sword, Rongo showed yellowed teeth in a grin. "You plannin' on taking these saiclers on, boss?"

"Up to them. We'll try talking to them first. Pick a crew, Rongo. I want the road blocked at Wolf Point. And use all due haste. They may have scouts ahead of the main body and I don't want them getting there before we do."

"You got it." Rongo called out a dozen names and thirty seconds later his party galloped off at a tangent from the direction House and Kira had taken.

This left Bannion, Nate, and a couple of the youngsters from the meadow fight to bring up the rear. More warriors had been assigned duty at the compound, in case these Techs and their Cross-up proved more hostile and harder to fight than anyone expected. Others were watching the old road north and some of the bigger easterly trails for anyone trying to slip in through an unexpected direction.

Bannion swung Nog around. "Nate, come with me."

Riding abreast, the pair loped toward the clan compound. Bannion's mind raced. Grateful for Nate's customary silence, this brief interval gave him time to plan his strategy and stir his enthusiasm for leading his people into battle. Again. They'd barely settled into winter quarters and here they were, preparing for yet another scuffle. All within the first ten-day home. All that damn Cross-up woman's fault.

His mood was grim as, back at the compound, they pulled up in front of Selkirk's house, seat of authority in clan Bell-O'Quinn. Trouble of some kind had been bound to come, given the rebirth of Lily Turnbow. The bigger, more sophisticated clans, whether Techs, Cits or Stayers, each wanted a piece of any newly resurrected Cross-up. But he'd hoped it wouldn't happen so soon. These Cross-up people often didn't make it through the first month. If no one helped them, they most likely died within that time. Or somebody aced them. Those few that survived were fighters. And angry. Coupled with their unexpected and un-natural powers, that made them doubly dangerous.

Selkirk opened the door, waving Nate and him into the house almost before they could hitch their horses to the porch rail.

"Who and how many?" he asked. "Do I need to draw the folks in from the outlying areas?"

Bannion shrugged, leaving it to Nate to answer. "Wouldn't hurt if they were to pack their stuff and be ready,"

"Dammit." Selkirk scowled. "They've hardly had a chance to unpack. Are you looking for a siege?"

"Not if I can help it." Bannion hesitated. "I'm taking the Cross-up woman to Wolf Point with Nate and me. See how she reacts when she meets another of her kind."

Nate leveled a questioning stare on him, but didn't protest.

Selkirk was not so reticent. "That could be a little chancy, couldn't it? What if Screenmaster recruits her somehow? They get together, they can do a lot of damage."

"Better out there in the open than in the compound," Bannion said. "And I only know one way to learn what she'll do. She makes one wrong move and I'll take her out. Or Nate will." He didn't ask, didn't discuss. It was an offhand order from the war leader, one to be taken seriously.

"What do you consider a wrong move, boss?"

The formality of Nate's address brought Bannion's stare around to fix on him. "You don't agree?"

"Didn't say that. But now that you mention it, I don't believe she means us any harm. Not without provocation, anyway."

"How the hell do you know?"

"I've talked to her, a little. She's all right."

A sharp chopping motion of Bannion's hand stopped Nate. "We're not going to argue, cousin. Get a mount saddled and fetch her. We haven't got all day."

Nate saluted as he left, the gesture almost mocking.

"Don't ride him too hard," Selkirk warned as their cousin quietly closed the door behind him. "Or he's apt to disappear on one of his winter jaunts just when we need him most."

"He won't leave. Not with this going on." Bannion sat down on one of Selkirk's cushioned chairs and closed his eyes for a moment. No sleep and likely a battle to come. A man rested whatever minutes he found. "Nate knows we need him. He can sense if anything starts to go wrong and he'll grab her. Give us the time we need. Even if he doesn't like the idea."

"You know him best." Selkirk's brow rose questioningly. "Think she can ride?"

"She can if she's who she says she is." Truth be told, he was used to the idea, deny it how he may. The old photograph had passed from hand-to-hand amongst the clan for everyone to see. The evidence was clear. The name of Heathen had already been familiar to every child born into the clan. Those newly accepted for citizenship were learning. It only remained to see if Lily Turnbow retained any ties to the O'Quinn people. If not, he'd take her out, plain and simple. He or Nate. And though Nate might protest, he'd do whatever he had to. Nate was family.

Chapter 17

Lily huddled beneath the blankets sheathing her narrow bed, shivering with cold. She knew it was very early, daylight just a thought in the morning sky. Wide awake, after startling awake by crying out in her sleep, a heavy, strange feeling had settled over her. It felt a lot like impending doom.

Last night. What had that been? How had she managed to make herself invisible?

"Uh!" Forcing that thought away, she stuck both arms out from the beneath the covers and ran a hand over the disfiguring scar the terrorist's thrust had left on the left one. Drawing her fingernails over the ragged keloid, the ridge rose in a raw strip of nerves. Last night, when she got back . . .home, for lack of a better word, she hadn't been sure she was real. She couldn't get that strange sense of disconnect out of her mind.

Tucking her arms under the blankets again, she savored the warmth. Her room in the infirmary had Spartan comforts at best; the sheets rough, the blankets coarse and thin. The only reason the towels in the bathroom were soft is because they'd been washed a thousand times. She smiled ruefully. Damn, but her moods had changed since this damn apocalypse, or whatever it was, had happened. Fairly sunny of disposition before, she found herself grouchy these days, as full of complaint as a princess who'd lost her tiara. For shame. This wasn't her first time facing rough circumstances, distrust, and dislike. That was part of her profession. She ought to be used to it. What had happened to her toughness?

Stirred by a feeling she couldn't name, Lily sat up and stretched, thrusting her feet over the side of the cot, touching the floor. Immediately, goose bumps popped up on her exposed skin. Odd how she felt the cold so much more than she ever had before.

Before doomsday hit.

Any chance of sleep fled, and when she heard someone knock on the kitchen door, be greeted and invited in, she hurriedly drew on her trusty cargo pants. The visitor had come to the back, which meant this wasn't a medical emergency. But the fact he didn't just barge in also indicated this wasn't his normal hangout.

Lily tensed as a pair of voices came to her. Part of what they said was lost, but not all. Thrusting her arms into the heavyweight flannel shirt someone had donated to the infirmary, she reached for her boots, fingers flying to untangle laces knotted when she kicked the boots off last night.

"She's not up yet. I haven't heard a peep out of her, so I'm counting my blessings. She scares me." Bren, the night nurse-guard-caretaker-whatever you want to call her, was saying in an unnaturally breathy voice.

Must be Bannion with her after all, Lily thought, smirking a little as she decided the shoe strings could wait and she buttoned the shirt as fast as she could. She had no doubt of the identity of the "she/her" the woman referred to. The new arrival, whoever he might be, had come for her.

"Get her up, dressed, and ready to ride, Bren, please."

Lily paused in the buttoning. To her surprise, the man

wasn't Bannion. Way too soft-spoken to be the forceful sheriff. She knew the voice, though. Nate Quick. A little shiver—anticipation?—ran through her.

"Has the fighting started?" The woman sounded fearful, with reason considering the to-do last night.

"Not yet. Bannion's asking the lady to ride with us, is all. He wants her to take a look at this Cross-up fellow traveling with the Techs."

"Now?" asked Bren.

"Yep. Right now."

"All right. I'll fetch her. You should wait in the kitchen, Nate," Bren said. "There's fresh tea in the pot. Help yourself. I doubt you've even taken time for breakfast."

The man murmured again and Bren said wryly, "Sure you got time. This gal doesn't move very fast without she has her tea first. Pour her a cup to cool while you're at it."

Lily's lips twitched again. Damn right, she didn't move fast. No point in letting the O'Quinn tribe know she could move quickly enough if she had to, or wanted to. Harrison and Jacob knew, but no one else. Go ahead and build a reputation that said otherwise. These people were not her friends.

She had no friends. That much was clear. A frisson of unease traversed her spine. But everyone wanted something from her, just the same. The memory of the Trader captain and his offer came to her, and she added it to what she'd heard about the Techs.

Bren pushed the door open without warning, and strode in as if thinking to take Lily by surprise. The lamp she carried turned back the gloom, showing the mussed bed, but no occupant. She sucked in a breath and called, "Nate!" on a panicky note as if ready to announce her prisoner had escaped.

Or that's what it seemed like to Lily.

"Are you looking for me?" she asked from behind the woman. As if she didn't know. "If you are, it would be polite to knock."

Bren almost dropped the lamp as she spun around. Lily caught it with reflexes faster than she thought possible. These old wooden buildings, though. It wouldn't take much to burn the place to the ground. Best not let a fire get started.

"What are you doing up?" Bren asked, taking back the lamp and inadvertently touching the clear chimney. She winced from the heat, glaring as though the pain were Lily's fault. "How'd you know Bannion wants you?"

An imp of mischief, or maybe the fact she was fed up with the whole weird O'Quinn clan and their constant drama, made Lily smile smugly. "Guess the sheriff will have to get in line. I've got a hot date with Nate that takes priority." She batted her eyes for emphasis.

Date with Nate. A cutesy catchy rhyme.

Grabbing her coat from a hook beside the door, she slipped past Bren and went to meet the man. Better to go for a ride than to hide away in this room.

A thinner, slighter representative of the clan, Nate radiated whipcord strength doing nothing more than standing at the stove. He wore heavy brown jeans, a jacket that looked too light for the weather, and a floppy-brimmed hat jammed over his longish brown hair. His hands must've been asbestos-lined, for he held the tea kettle with bare fingers as he faced her. Dark circles cast shadows under his amber eyes. She didn't think he slept much the night before, either.

"Bren says you need tea to crank your engine in the morning," he said, filling a mug and holding it out to her.

Surprised, Lily took the cup. Sipped. Swallowed. Oh, for a simple cup of coffee instead of these bland herbal concoctions. She needed caffeine.

"You used that phrase once before. What do you know about engines?" she asked. "A little before your time, weren't they? Unless you're a whole lot older than you look."

Nate shook his head. "Nope. Not me. Born in 2088 right

here in this building. I talked to someone who'd seen one and been told about them first hand, though. And I read the old books, when I can get hold of one. I wish there were more. A lot of them have been burned over the years."

Lily shook her head. "What were people thinking? Books are the repository of all knowledge. Didn't people need them to get civilization going after the Event?"

"People were too busy trying to stay alive to think about books at first." Nate smiled as he used another of his *oldisms,* as Lily soon learned he called them. "But now you're preachin' to the choir. I take it on myself to scout for old texts."

Left out of the conversation, Bren's face turned sullen. "Preach to the choir? What are you talking about, Nate? You're not making any sense."

"I know it, Bren. Sorry. I'm here for a purpose. Guess I'd better mind my manners."

Lily slurped from her cup, relishing the bite of the herbal tea. His cool humor reassured her, though she couldn't think why. "So, where are we going, Nate?"

"Boss thinks you can help us with a little problem." Showing no reaction to Lily's use of his first name, he set his empty cup on the drain board of the sink and buttoned his jacket. "We're going to take a little ride out to where the Techs and the Cross-up are. See what you think of him. Cold out, though. You got a hat? Gloves?"

Excitement quickened Lily's pulse even as she shook her head. "I'll be fine. My coat has a hood. I'll pull it up." Ride out of the compound to meet the Techs and the Cross-up man? Why? Much as she longed for the learning experience, she wondered just what Bannion O'Quinn and the clan wanted from her. One way to find out, she supposed, wordlessly zipping her jacket.

"Let's go, then," Nate said. "Bren, thanks for the tea."

"Come back anytime, Nate." Bren's voice purred, heavy

with a more meaningful invitation.

The big red roan gelding hitched to a post was the one Nate had been riding the last time she saw him. Pigeon. She remembered its name. Next to it was another animal that looked like his horse's little sister. Evidently, Nate had provided her with a mount from his own stock. She stepped forward, longing suddenly to be in the saddle, journeying into the frosty dawn.

"They say you can ride." Nate handed her the reins to the smaller mount.

"Huh. Last time I checked." And when Lily put her foot in the stirrup and swung into the saddle, she knew nothing had changed. She felt comfortable, as if this was where she belonged. Only then did she discover the saddle was her own, the leather worn, but soft with soaping and oiling.

Although she wanted to thank Nate for this unexpected kindness, the words froze in her mouth and they'd traversed the short distance across the compound before she had a chance.

Bannion was waiting outside the headquarters main house where Selkirk lived, scowling as she and Nate rode over. "Took you long enough," he grumped, stepping up onto Nog. "Let's go."

Wearing a worried expression, Selkirk waved them off, his eyes fixed on Lily.

More distrust, as if afraid she could, or would, do something to harm them. But why would she? What were they so afraid of?

The horses moved quietly over the soft earth, leaving Traders and clan members still asleep after last night's excitement to rest undisturbed, provided they could sleep at all. But once the three of them were on the trail, an old and overgrown secondary road, Bannion urged Nog into a trot. Lily gigged her horse into a matching gait. Nate rode a stride behind.

"She gonna fall off that nag?" Bannion called past her to Nate, like he didn't care if her feeling were hurt at the insult.

Nate grinned when she scowled back at him. "Don't look like it. Let's step on it, boss. Sun'll be up before we make Wolf Point."

Their speed kicked up to a lope, Lily ignored the hunger gnawing in a stomach she just couldn't seem to fill lately. She breathed in air moist and fresh from the lake below the winding trail. Their route took them through forested rolling foothills. Except for the pounding of the horses' feet, the woods were quiet, if not silent. Once they startled a deer from the under-brush, a nice five-pointer. Other than that, Lily noticed birds, lots of them, maintaining a constant twitter as they swirled like blowing leaves in the sky above the rider's heads.

"What's the matter with those starlings?" she asked Nate, pointing at the small black birds. They'd reached a place she could slow and let him pull in at her side. She'd noticed right off that while Bannion took the lead, Nate formed a rearguard, keeping her sandwiched between them. Somehow, she doubted it was for her safety.

"The birds?" He nodded to Bannion. "Ask him."

She didn't think she would. The sheriff's expression was too grim for her to break his concentration. No one spoke for the next hour, not until they broke over the ridge into the open.

"Wolf Point," Bannion said. The main highway still ran here, the asphalt long since eroded and broken into a choppy one-lane trail. "We beat them."

Nate squinted against the sun, glaring in orange and blue glory through darkly billowing scattered clouds. "Break out the checkered flag. It was a close race. See their sails?"

Sails? Lily peered into the distance, where activity stirred beneath a cloud of dust. What was he talking about?

Wolf Point was an intersection notorious, she recalled upon recognizing the place, for a horrific number of high speed collisions and resultant fatalities. There'd been a convenience store and gas station here last time she passed by. All that remained was a tumbled pile of broken concrete and cinder blocks, mostly obscured by encroaching box elder and scrawny Jack pine trees.

Hearing voices before she saw anyone, she discovered Bannion's patrollers hidden with artful concealment in the ruins. However, although the patrollers were well camouflaged and spoke no more than necessary, she imagined any halfway competent leader would expect ambush at this site.

"How many fighters do you have?" she asked, eyeing the dust cloud in the distance.

Nate answered in a vague sort of way. "No fret, Lily. The boss figures we have plenty of warriors on hand to take care of these Techs. If it becomes necessary."

Cagey, she thought. "They're not as bad as Mags, are they?" Bad? Scary? Fearsome? Please, no more mutants with filed teeth and three eyes.

"Mags?" he asked, as if surprised. "You think they're bad?"

"Don't you?"

"There's worse."

Lily could only stare at him in astonishment. "Worse than Mags?" She didn't miss the glance Bannion shot Nate. A warning?

"Get her under cover, Nate," Bannion said abruptly. "Keep her quiet and don't let Screenmaster see her. You can hand your horses over to Carina. She and Jacob have the rest of them corralled down in the draw."

Lily held back "Wait a minute. What do you mean, get me under cover? What kind of trouble are you expecting? And what do you want me to do about it?"

Bannion's cool gaze scraped against her, raising the hair at the back of her neck. "Depends," he said.

"On what?"

"Screenmaster. This bunch of saiclers. You." Turning his

horse, he rode off to where a second squad of his patrollers were busy erecting a road block out of downed logs and some large pieces of broken concrete. They greeted him with cheers.

Nate reached across and took control of Lily's reins. "Come on. Might as well do as he says. You'll find my cousin is an immovable force when he's got his mind made up about things."

"Me being one of those things." Lily made no attempt to keep the bitterness out of her voice. "Regardless of my actions."

"Afraid so. Unless you can prove he doesn't need to worry."

"I thought I did that the other day," she said, to which Nate didn't reply.

A few minutes later, Lily found herself squatting in a cramped space between a couple of rusted off gas pumps, watching the aforementioned saiclers approach. For the first time since awakening from her long sleep, Lily laughed aloud.

Saiclers, she discovered, followed precedents set by the creation of words like smog and blog, taking their name from a combination of cyclists and sailors. Their method of locomotion looked especially funny as they approached the crest of the barren hill, with the riders standing on their pegs and pumping hard. A light tail wind pushed against a small square sail rigged from a mast attached to the rear fender. They looked absurd.

"What so funny?" Nate asked, and one of the nearby warriors peeked around a fallen wall and stared at her.

Lily's laughter ceased. "What in the world are those ridiculous little sails flapping in the breeze? Do those things actually work to push them along?

"Yep," Nate said. "Sure do. Sometimes, anyway. Saiclers can move pretty fast when conditions are right. Faster than horses over a long run."

Lily spared a thought for the Tour de France. Those guys hadn't needed floppy canvas sails. "Do you take them seriously?"

"Don't pay to discount anybody, Lily, when they got a

sword at your throat."

"Cripes, all they need are tight little Speedos," she muttered. "What a picture."

However, as the bike riders came closer, she saw short spears, and bows and quivers of arrows bristling from carriers fixed to the saicyle's, if that's what the vehicles were called, fenders. In a bin in front of the handlebars, chains with spiked balls on the ends were coiled like rattlesnakes. The riders wore helmets, fashioned in a medieval manner, leathers, and what looked like chain mail vests. A half dozen massive dogs ran alongside the leaders. Pitbulls, she thought. Supersized ones. Sliver would have a hard time with one of those. Her fit of humor subsided.

Some distance from the O'Quinn's roadblock, the cyclists formed up in ranks four abreast and drew to a halt. There were a lot of them, she decided, making a try at an accurate count. They were waiting for a rig that looked like a camp trailer with an outside driving seat. It was pulled by four white horses straining to catch up. On the seat, reins in hand, was a little person, a rotund little man person, garbed in clothing like a roman centurion plus baggy pants. Except, Lily thought, her eyes going wide, this person was not so benign.

"You're not laughing now," Nate whispered out the side of his mouth.

"No." Shock effectively dried Lily's ability to speak beyond the monosyllabic croak. She'd seen this little man before, and the context did not thrill her. Chill her, yes. If she wasn't mistaken, in the weeks before the . . . the so-called Event, his trial and sentencing had made big headlines in newspapers across the country. CNN, CNBC, FOX, all the television channels and the internet news had carried lurid stories about him. That he had survived the catastrophic event had to be some kind of cruel cosmic joke.

Except, as Nate said, she wasn't laughing.

Chapter 18

"Fifteen, eighteen, twenty-one." Counting by threes, Nate enumerated the saiclers aloud. He was counting the forces lining up against the O'Quinn clansmen when Lily's breath hissing in and out in a disturbed fashion claimed his attention. His hand went to his knife as he spun around, only to find her hunkered against the rusty debris surrounding them as if wishing to disappear. Her face had drained of color.

"What's the matter?" he asked, loosing count. No big deal. The saicler group was almost past anyway. They numbered somewhere around forty.

Her breath released. "You're right. There are worse things than Mags. They, at least, have the excuse of genetic mutation screwing with them. Your Cross-up has always been a mutant. A man without conscience."

"Screenmaster? The Cross-up?" His narrow-eyed gaze followed the dwarf riding high on his wagon. "You mean you know that runt?"

Peering around the edge of the concrete shelter, she squinted for a better look at the little man in question. "Not personally, thank God. But if that's who I think it is, everybody knows his story. His picture has been shown non-stop over every media outlet known to man for the last six months." She swallowed. "Was shown, I mean."

"Eh, Lily, remind me. What's media?" Hating to stop her flow of information, Nate nevertheless asked the question.

She made a little throwaway motion. "Television, newspapers, the Internet, phone services."

He nodded in semi-understanding. He'd read the terms, and even seen some of the equipment, but the concept still boggled his mind. His attention snapped back as she said, her expression sad, "Technically, I guess that was a hundred years ago."

"Not many people remember back that far." Even he knew the quip was weak, and that the humor failed to move her.

"This Screenmaster, do you know his given name?" She asked as though she hoped for a different answer than the one she had percolating in her mind.

They spoke together, one voice overrunning the other. "Phil Barnes."

"That's who he says he is, all right. So what did he do? Back then, I mean. Rob a bank?" He spared a thought for banks, one of those old time institutions almost forgotten in time. His people had no need for such. Hell, they had no money, though Pike said gold and silver coins had begun circulating in the city and larger towns and a Cit had brought up the concept of monetary loans.

Lily hooked a stray lock of brown hair behind her ear. "I never heard him called Screenmaster in those days. I guess it might figure, though. He's got a revolting past. When details of his crimes came out, he became known as the Blue Prairie Pig Farmer."

"Pig farmer?" He started to laugh, then stopped at the look on her face. "How so?" he urged when she fell silent.

Lily's hazel eyes met his. Her upper lip curled in disgust. "He killed women. Lots of women. Little girls, young mothers, a seventy-year-old grandma. Didn't matter to him as long as they were female. He met most of them online, enticed them into meeting him, and if they passed his criteria, he had sex before he murdered them." She paused. "And after he murdered them, too. He tortured them first, and when he was done with their bodies, fed the good parts to his hogs. Which he then sold to the local butcher shop. He spread what was left on his pasture for fertilizer."

Nate's gaze darted to where the little man was now standing on the driving seat, pumping his fist in the air and shouting what sounded like exhortations to the Techs. He couldn't hear what Screenmaster was saying, but judging by Lily's expression, she had a good idea.

"What's he yammering about?"

"Blood." Her head cocked to the side. "O'Quinn blood. He says kill the men, keep the women for later. And—"

"And?"

He waited.

Finally she muttered, "He says save the Cross-up woman for him."

"I think we'd better tell Bannion this story." He got ready to move. "Might make some difference in how he negotiates with these people." As an afterthought he added, "And in how we fight."

"I remember hearing he, Barnes, was very strong," Lily said. "Don't let his size and shape fool you."

"Yeah." Nate shoved a rolling bit of rubble aside with his foot. "I've heard something about that. He's a regular little Superman. Wait here, Lily." Flat on his belly, he crawled from the rubble and wormed a way beyond the concealed entrance. "Keep your head down," a whisper wafted back.

With a little slick maneuvering, Nate remained out of sight from anyone watching the road, and ghosted over to where Bannion, Rongo, and a few others were working with all due speed.

"We need a little palaver," he said.

"Kind of busy here, Nate." Bannion laid hold of a log, helping a couple boys heave it into place. "Doubt if that little bastard is going to wait for us to get all snugged in tight and cozy. I hear he isn't too patient."

Nate ignored this as drivel. "This can't wait, Sheriff." Deliberately, he used Bannion's most formal title. It earned him a sharp glance and drew his cousin over to meet him out of the patroller's hearing.

"What's up, Nate? More bad news? Did something happen to Dak and the scouts?" Worry etched new lines in Bannion's face. He glanced over his shoulder as if hoping to see his scouts. "They should've been here."

"Far as I know they're okay, but you're right. I expected them to check in before now. Their absence isn't our only worry." Talking fast, but keeping his voice low, he outlined what Lily had told him about the man they knew as Screenmaster.

Bannion listened in silence, the muscles in his jaw working, his eyes snapping fire.

Nate finished talking and watched his cousin.

"She sure about this?" Bannion asked a few heartbeats later.

"Seemed so. Looks like this character scares her pretty bad. She tried to hide it, but I could tell seeing him shook her up."

"Ain't this just ducky," Bannion said. A second later he called over to Rongo, telling him to get that last log in place and have the fighters hunker down behind it. "I'd as soon have something stout between us and him. I don't know how much actual power he has, but I don't want him practicing on us. And if what Lily says is true, he has to be kept from the women at all costs."

"You ain't just awhistlin' Dixie," Nate agreed soberly, drawing a hard stare from the sheriff. "This is apt to be worse than just scaring off a few Techs."

"Get back in position." Bannion's jaw tightened. "Hold your archers until we can get the enemy between us. Take out the dwarf if you can. Tell your fighters he's first meat."

Nate nodded.

"It's the best we can do." Bannion strode off, summoning Sergeant Rongo Zelnor to him with a gesture.

"I'm thinking the boss might've bit off more than he can chew with this outfit," Nate said when he slipped in beside Lily again, so quiet he made her jump at the sound of his voice. "We could use more fighters. I'll be glad when our scouts get back. Be good to know if the Techs have a company waiting on the sidelines." He didn't let on he was wondering now if Dak, and House and the girl were even alive.

"Might they?" she asked. She studied the terrain, a curious, if convoluted mix of newer trees interspersed with burnt stumps. "Yes. A flanking movement," she decided, and pointed. "From over there," her thin finger moved, "and there."

"They've been known to use that tactic." Nate rested his elbows on a flat piece of concrete and held a small pair of antique binoculars to his eyes.

Lily raised her brows, which made him grin despite his worry. "Jacob brought them up to me," he said. "He thought they might come in handy. That boy's got good warrior instincts."

"Hmm," Lily agreed. "It's nice to know something from the old time still works."

Nate, although he heard her, didn't answer. Taking the binoculars from his eyes, he cocked his head. "Well, you had'em pegged. The Tech's have got a few men working up from the main body on either side. Not many, and they're on foot. Guess I'll wander over and see if I can shut some of those boys down. Stay here. Don't come out unless Bannion or Rongo calls for you." He frowned. "You got that?"

Her mouth pursed. "I hear you."

It wasn't exact agreement, a point he didn't miss. Lifting his hat from his head, he handed it to Lily. "Keep this for me until I get back. Make sure you don't lose it."

Automatically, she grabbed the hat's floppy brim and set it on her own head where it sank around her ears. "Sure." Her lips twitched. "I don't suppose you'd like to explain?"

"Hard to sneak through the underbrush wearin' a hat, especially when the wind comes up."

"The wind isn't blowing."

"It will be. And snow soon after."

*****

Everything but the job he assigned himself dropped from Nate's consciousness as he drifted into the woods. There wasn't time to fill Bannion in on his plan. Using his normal caution, he'd have the Tech scouts nullified before the skirmish began, preventing them from flanking the O'Quinns. If he didn't succeed with that, he could still raise some kind of commotion. Give the clan folk warning, so they wouldn't be taken by surprise. Anyway, Bannion would be watching the birds. He always did, and they seldom failed to alert him to any strangeness in their domain.

A rabbit raced hell-bent in front of him, almost under his feet. Nate froze. Whatever had startled the animal, its fear of Nate was less than for what it fled. Nate heard something, too. A nearby bush rattled, a downed log thumped hollowly, a branch cracked as it broke. He glanced upward. Yes. Birds were avoiding this region of the sky.

Nate drew his long fighting knife, holding it unsheathed in one hand. Dropping to his knees, he parted the branches of a low bush in front of him with one cautious finger and peered through the opening.

A sudden breeze stirred the pine needles above his head,

and whispered in the dry leaves clinging to the snowberry bushes. Cold air blew under his coat collar, down his neck, and through his uncovered hair.

He sniffed the air. An odor foreign to the forest mixed with the natural earthiness. The fetid stench of man. Or more specifically, the smell of a man—or men—who'd been sweating heavily, dried, then sweat and dried in a cycle several times over. Saiclers or saiclists or whatever the hell they called themselves, worked hard, pumping their wheels up the hills, even though they coasted on the way down. His nostrils flared, taking in the scent. This particular man had been eating onions.

The odor led Nate straight to the nearest Tech scout, a term that almost caused Nate to snort out loud. A rail thin man, dark rings showing under the arms of a close-fitting shirt, was blundering through the underbrush, walking bent over like he thought it made him invisible. Twenty yards beyond him was another man, and then, at a further twenty yards, another.

Nate smiled in satisfaction. City boys, all of them, a long way from being woodsmen. If they only knew, they'd have been better off staying together. As it was, he could take them out one at a time, all without the others knowing until it became their turn. They wallowed through the woods oblivious to their surroundings. In a way, he felt almost sorry for them. But not quite.

For Nate, it was a simple matter of dropping to his belly and wriggling forward beneath the lowest branches of bushes and trees. The soft rustle of his clothing dragging against the dirt was hidden by the breeze through the pine tree's branches. He came up behind the first man who died unsuspecting, as though the hold that snapped his neck came out of the blue. Nate shuddered in sympathy.

The second man died harder. At the last moment, he

sensed Nate behind him and turned around, his mouth open to shout a warning. It was the breath he took first that spelled failure. Nate's sharply honed knife dug into his throat and ripped to the side before any sound escaped, the resultant spurt of blood drenching them both.

It was all so easy Nate got careless in the last encounter. It might've been the crackle of a leaves under his moccasins, or even the smell of blood clinging to him, but the man—a kid, really—spotted him before he was set. Fortunately for Nate, the kid, instead of immediately sounding the alarm, sprang at him, the hum of his whirling spiked ball and chain loud as it passed over Nate's head a fraction of a second after he ducked.

But he had gone against these weapons before. Ugly damn things that did a lot of messy damage if they connected. They were designed to keep an opponent at a distance, a strategy he had no patience with. Instead of ducking a second time, he dove beneath the chain at the kid's legs, bringing the youth down and knocking the wind out of him. After that it was simple, if it's ever a simple thing to watch the light fade from a man's eyes.

In the end, he wasn't even breathing hard.

After that, he made haste to cross the road at the bend just beyond the hill's crest. The first two flankers on this side had even less chance against him than the others, him with the blood lust boiling in his veins already. But then he discovered the last of them was a woman, which made Nate almost hesitate an instant too long.

She came at him teeth bared, her eyes ferocious, as wild as any animal in the woods. A big woman and tall, she outweighed him by a good twenty pounds. She had him down and was within an inch of breaking his neck when he, flailing his legs with all he had in him, got his foot hooked under one of her knees and pulled her loose enough to stick his knife blade into a kidney.

"Dammit," he whispered when she finally stopped moving and he got his breath back. Rolling her flaccid bulk to one side, he rose to his knees, placing his forefinger on the carotid under her ear. Nothing. Her blood soaked his britches, sticky and bright. Not a good color for camouflage.

He hated killing females, even, although the failing was something he never admitted to his cousin Bannion, a Mag female. Women, and their ability to bear children, carried responsibility for the species. Someday, he felt certain, all people would be joined under a banner of humanity, as they had been in the olden days. *More or less.* But that was a hope for another day, not this one.

After this maudlin thought, what his eyes had focused on struck home. The woman's clothing was as bloodstained as his own, although her shirt had dried enough to stiffen. And that meant the blood didn't belong to her—or to him, for that matter. So whose blood was it?

Nate's head jerked up, a sudden frisson sending a warning through him. How had these flankers, clumsy town dwellers at that, managed to get this close to the O'Quinn's without being stopped? How had they gotten past Dak and Bannion's other two patrollers, each fairly experienced in scout work? *Where the hell were those scouts now?*

From the direction of the Wolf Point Crossing roadblock, he heard voices calling back and forth. Bannion, for one, he thought, and at least two others. Techs, or the Screenmaster. Both, maybe. That was good. Keep'em jabbering. No need to rush this thing. He needed time to catch his breath and think what his next move should be.

Anxiety over Lily Turnbow churned in his gut. He shouldn't have left her alone this long. Bannion would have his head if she pulled any kind of unpredictable stunt. And although he was intrigued by her wicked sense of humor and felt an unaccustomed pull of attraction, he didn't trust her. Couldn't trust her.

Whose side would she come down on? This coming battle depended on that. Now more than ever. If she—

The spreading puddle of the Tech woman's blood at his feet decided him. Nate wiped his knife, jamming it into the sheath on his belt. Studying the ground as he moved, he took off at a trot, following the signs the Techs had left as they threshed a trail through the woods wide enough for a two-year-old to follow. He found where one had taken a leak, where another had loosed an arrow and brought down a squirrel, then left it to rot.

It didn't take long for him to pass beyond the last saicler straggler. The woods quiet around him, he broke into a run, his moccasins silent on the forest floor. At the foot of the long hill leading to the crossroad, he started hearing a sound that raised the hair on the back of his neck. An up and down wail he wasn't certain was human. Then he found a small mess where someone had vomited, and thirty yards away, another.

The keening grew in his ears until it about broke his skull. And his heart.

He found House first, the young patroller's flesh slashed to ribbons with enough blood drenching the soil a man would think a horse had died there. The wounds in his hands and across his face told he'd put up a terrific fight. They'd cut out his eyes. And cut off his testicles.

Nate swallowed on his own bile, anger burning through him hot enough to start a fire. Sonsabitchin' savages! As bad as the Mags even if they weren't technically cannibals. What need of this?

A repeat of the agonized wail that had drawn him here carried over the wind and through the trees, closer now. Soft-footed, Nate followed the sound. It led him to a clearing where a big old cottonwood tree stood in what had once been a stump rancher's dooryard.

Kira Shandy hung suspended from one of the branches. Her body spun in slow circles as the rope looped beneath her arms and around her chest twisted with the convulsions racking her.

"Christ!" Hyper-alert senses assured Nate no one had been left to watch the girl die. Knife out, he approached the tree and the girl's broken body. "Kira. Kira Shandy. Can you hear me?"

Another unintelligible cry. Her lips were mashed and swollen, bitten through by broken teeth. Her eyes were open, aware and watching him. Blood had flowed copiously from a ragged cut in her scalp, flooding her face and down her shoulders. Bone showed through a gap where her hair had been torn from the roots. Her hands, below the tightly bound ropes, were purple, swollen blobs. Both legs, he noted, had been beaten and broken in numerous places, as though they'd strung her into the tree, then used her as a living piñata.

"Christ," he said again. "Hold on, Kira. I'll cut you down."

"D...d...d..." she breathed, the rope spinning with another spasm.

Nate took a few deep breaths, forcing his racing heart to slow while he figured out how to lower her without doing more harm. His only choice seemed to be to climb the tree, which he did. The limb, when he crawled out on it to cut the rope, creaked dangerously under his and Kira's combined weight. He dropped the girl as gently as possible to the ground, the slack in the rope sliding through his hands, raising blisters.

Her wail became a scream, then shut off.

Nate jumped down beside her. Her eyes had closed now, and he could hear the labored sound of her breathing, fighting the rope's constriction of her lungs. Within moments, he sliced through the hemp, freeing her.

"D...Dak?" she whispered.

She didn't ask about House. Knew what had befallen him, probably. Couldn't help it, if her eyes were open. Nate had seen the boy's body from the branch where she hung, the details all too clear.

"Haven't seen Dak," Nate told her. For one of the few times in his life he felt helpless. They needed a whole healer team for Kira, right now, and there was none to be had. Hell, he didn't even have any water with him to ease her throat.

"Dak." Kira forced words past her broken teeth. "Rocks."

Nate glanced around. The rocks she must be referring to were stones gathered onsite and used, way back when, to make the foundation of a barn. Long since destroyed by weather or fire, the mortar holding them together had moldered. Fallen rocks now formed a two-foot tall mound.

"I'll look," he told Kira, wondering how she remained conscious, and wishing, for her sake, she's wouldn't.

A body lay a couple dozen yards beyond the rock. It wasn't Dak. Rolling the man over, Nate saw another saicler, this one with his guts spilling onto the dirt beneath him. Studying the splatter of blood, disturbed soil, broken sticks and whatnot, he narrowed his eyes and followed the pointers until thick underbrush stopped him. Shrugging, he returned to the rocks and stared down at them. "Dak," he said. "You here?"

Silence. Cold wind blew down his neck, making Nate shiver, then a pile of dry, fallen leaves rustled and a hand poked through.

Chapter 19

Every minute Nate remained away from his assigned post seemed to last forever. Or so Lily thought as she forced herself to sit without fidgeting. His absence grew to a half-hour, then forty-five minutes. More than enough time for him to have completed a scout. The sheriff and the leader of the saiclers were bound to cease their dickering—or bickering—soon and get down to the business of war. Judging by the increasing noise of the saiclers, they were all rested up and ready to fight. And when that happened, Bannion was going to want his cousin on the firing line.

Nate better not have gotten himself killed. Lily couldn't help the pang the thought gave her. Not that she actually *cared,* but he had been friendlier to her than anyone, excepting only Jacob and Harrison. And technically, she supposed, going off on his own without telling the boss was wrong. Bannion's orders were probably comparable to any commander's, even though the clan seemed to cooperate with less stricture and a great deal more independence than say, the United States Army or the Border Patrol. And yet from what she could tell, duties of both those outfits appeared in his job description.

Meanwhile, the argument between the saiclers and the O'Quinns escalated to the level that most parts were audible, the negotiators no longer attempting to mute themselves.

"Give 'blank blank' up," the tough appearing saicler leader said, and Lily wasn't sure if he was talking about clan territory or her. Bannion's reply lent no more clarity. "Gather up these go-boys of yours and get back to your city," he said. "There's nothing for you here but cold death."

"We take what we want." The saicler's gesture, even at a distance, showed disdain for the clan's defiance.

"We'll chase you back to Spokane like the whipped apes you are," Bannion shot back, "and those we don't kill we'll leave to the Mags."

The saicler laughed. "Ha, you cow breeding, in-bred bumpkin. Loose all the arrows you like, they can't hurt us. You have no weapon like ours." There was a growl of sound from his forces, and a chant began. "Screenmaster, Screenmaster," repeated over and over like speech generated by robots.

What kind of world had this become? One in which neither side had appeasement in mind, that much was sure. Violence and death apparently were every day facts of no great importance. Strange and sad, Lily thought, that with a such diminished population, these people were so eager to kill each other off.

The so-called Cross-up man, Barnes, kept his mouth shut, something of a surprise. She remembered his trial being quite the show, with him pleading his own case after firing one attorney after another. This silence struck her as suspicious and worrisome. What was the old murderer plotting? Or had he brainwashed these saiclers into mindless obedience, ready to do whatever he said?

Yes. Probably so. Or, more likely, frightened them into doing so.

In plain fact, her nerves were about to fail her when Nate finally appeared, slipping between piles of rubble to reach her side. The rising wind had muted sounds of his approach, but she heard him coming, anyway. The only thing that really surprised her was his ragged appearance.

"What happened?" Taking in his bloody clothes and weary expression at a glance, she bit her lip. "Are you hurt?"

"I'm fine. Had a little trouble, is all." He found his hat and clamped it on his head. "Bannion says to tell you he appreciates you staying put like I asked. Surprised him."

Lily scowled. So he stopped by his cousin's position first, huh? "Really. And why is that?"

"He hasn't had much call to trust anyone but family. And sometimes you can't trust them. Bannion knows it."

"Oh. You mean this world isn't all Utopian? Imagine that. And is family the reason you look so . . . so devastated?" Something in the way he held himself, the tension in his face, the glitter in his smoldering eyes showed his foray into the woods had had repercussions beyond his expectations. Whatever he'd encountered out there had not been pleasant. She almost regretted her sarcasm, but not enough to call it back.

If Nate meant to give a rebuttal he didn't get the chance, because a sudden, swelling roar claimed their attention. The noise set the butterflies in Lily's stomach fluttering.

"Sounds like talking time is over." Nate took out his whetstone and slid his knife blade over it, front and back, front and back. "Bannion kept it going longer than I expected. Guess my report put an end to his patience."

"What—" she began, even as he interrupted.

"Our scouts. One dead, butchered, The other two cut up real bad. There'll be no quarter given today, from them or from us. Soon as the fighting starts, get yourself out of the way. I won't be able to look after you. " He pointed with his blade toward the coulee where they'd left their horses in a side gully with Jacob. "Go keep the Felix kid company.

He'll be champing at the bit to get in on the fight, but unless they get past our lines, his job is fixed. You'll probably need to remind him every now and then."

Lily shrugged. "Whatever you say. Not that I need anybody to look out for me. But Bannion seemed pretty hot on bringing me along on this party. What made him change his mind?"

Nate tested the edge with his thumb, then slipped his freshly sharpened knife in the sheath and took up his other weapons. "I don't think he was expecting quite this level of intent."

"No time to put me to the test, in other words."

"That's about it." He took her arm and turned her away from the sight of saicler archers nocking arrows. He gestured. "Over there. Go now." Without waiting, he slithered through the narrow opening in the rubble, silent as a ghost.

"Stay safe," Lily whispered after him.

The night her world ended replayed itself in Lily's memory. Even without the dark and the rain this situation felt similar, helped by steadily increasing clouds and blustery wind. Add in the waiting and tension and it missed only the exhilaration she felt the first time around. The Mags had chased that feeling out of her. Now she got to meet yet another group of bloodthirsty freaks. This must be her lucky day.

Backing out of the sheltering rubble, Lily glided soundlessly in the direction Nate had indicated, gathering shadows around her like a blanket as, yielding to the war chief's wishes, she made her way along the gully to where Jacob had the warriors' horses in care.

From somewhere within the saicler ranks, a drum, its tone deep and gut-wrenching, began a rhythmic pounding. The noise was damn scary, like the war drums depicted in that gladiator movie a bunch of years back, done up in Dolby sound. Before a curve in the gully cut out her line of sight, she turned for one last look.

Saiclers had formed a line of men five across and four deep in the road in front of the Screenmaster's wagon. He stood on the seat, his arms raised to the heavens and speaking gibberish in some kind of showy incantation. She didn't believe it. Abracadabra bullpuckie, that's all it was.

The whole scene became even more unreal as the baying of dogs rang out in conjunction with the drums.

"Take no prisoners," Screenmaster yowled from his perch, dropping the gobbledygook, but with his voice strangely amplified. "Use their women. Kill. Kill. Saiclers, you are invincible. I am with you."

Lily's stomach churned and she fled.

A couple hundred yards down the gully, where the curve muted the human sounds to near silence, she found Jacob sitting disconsolately on a downed log, his unstrung bow propped beside him. He was singing a tuneless little song in an attempt to soothe the picket line of horses in his charge. Perhaps thirty feet beyond Jacob, she saw an even younger warrior with another picket line, perhaps two dozen animals in all, which tallied with her estimate of clan warriors. A girl was helping him. All the horses but Nate's two roans, and that included Bannion's big war horse, Nog, skittered every time the drums made an extra thump. Lily sympathized. The sound hurt her ears too.

"Hi, Jake," she said, stepping over the log to join him. "I've come to keep you company."

Jacob jumped to his feet. "What the hell! Lily! Where'd you come from? You about scared the holy living crap out of me."

"Sorry." She checked her arm. Yeah. Living color. Good thing she dropped the now you see me now you don't thing before showing up. "I should've yelled, let you know I was coming."

"But I was—" He shook his head. "Some fighter I am. Can't see what's right in front of me."

Poor Jacob. And yet, she didn't think she'd say any-thing to disavow his words. Bad enough coping with the O'Quinn's distrust because of what they already knew, or thought they knew, about her.

"You're distracted," she excused him. "Those pounding drums. They make a pretty good scare tactic. Sure have the horses freaked out."

"Are we going to fight?" he asked, stroking a horse that showed signs of bolting, and blowing in its nostrils. He answered his own question. "Sure we are. O'Quinns don't back down from anybody, even somebody with a Cross-up like Screenmaster." He brightened. "But we've got you. Shouldn't you be up with the patrollers, ready to go toe-to-toe with this guy?"

She smiled. "Bannion doesn't trust me, I'm afraid. He sent me back here to keep me out of mischief."

Jacob gaped at her. "You're kidding, right?"

"Nope."

Lily cocked her head, listening as the regular thudding of the drums picked up a cadence implying urgency. They seemed louder, stronger, now, pounding like an out of whack heartbeat. Her ears hurt, but the pain multiplied at the first agonized scream. She jerked, drawing Jacob's attention away from the horse.

"What's the matter, Lily? You just turned dead white."

"Can't you hear it? The fighting has begun." Her last words were loud in the comparative silence as the drums reached a crescendo then quit. Screams and fierce yelling picked up, carried toward them on the gusting wind. Dogs barked, and over them Lily fancied she heard Bannion's strong voice, muted by distance, shouting orders. She knew Screenmaster, Phil Barnes, remained unharmed, although surely he was the O'Quinns prime target. His exhortation to "Kill, kill," came loud and clear.

Jacob heard them now. He stared toward the sounds of battle, his expression fierce. The other boy, although farther away, turned toward them, watching Jacob's reaction with alarm. The girl had grabbed onto his arm.

A kind of guilt sneaked into Lily's mind. She should be up there with the fighters, doing what she could to kill that murderous dwarf since she stood a better chance than any of them. It would come that. She knew it like she knew her own name. The much respected Bannion O'Quinn wasn't using his resources efficiently, she thought snidely. Besides, ridding the world of Phil Barnes was a job held over from her time. Her job. She hated waiting.

And she had to pee.

With the cessation of the drums, the horses quieted, standing with ears pricked toward the fighting. Jacob climbed onto the log, as if the couple of added feet of height would give him a clearer picture of events.

"Rory, Fanta." Clearly excited, he yelled and waved his arms, drawing his fellow horseholder's attention. "The fighting has started."

Rory disengaged Fanta's hand and waved acknowledgment.

"Shouldn't you keep your voice down?" Lily snagged him by the pant leg as he started to slide from the log. "If the saiclers have scouts out, they'll try to come through us to get behind the clan. You don't want to draw their attention."

Struck by their isolation, she felt an itch along her spine. A kind of dread of things to come, as if she were psychic and could see into the future. The hair on her arms rose in dread.

Jacob stirred. "I ain't scared of them."

For a moment Lily debated telling him how Nate had found their own scouts tortured and butchered in the woods, then decided bad news came better from one of his own. "I am. And you ought to be," she said. "If they're any kind of fighters at all, they've got people out here looking for the right opening."

Fanta, a girl whose Indian heritage showed in her skin and eyes and straight black hair, ran over to join them in time to catch Lily's words. "How do you know?"

"That's what I'd do. Wouldn't you?"

Jake thought about it. "Yes."

"Yes," Fanta echoed.

"Look at the sky," Lily said, another idea occurring to her.

Fanta's head raised and she scanned the patch of blue overhead. "What am I looking for?"

"Birds." Lily heard Jacob suck in a breath.

"There aren't any," the girl said.

Jacob slipped his bow from his shoulder and strung it. "That's the point, Fanta. You haven't finished training yet, but you'll find one of the boss's first lessons is to watch the birds. They always tell him if the woods are safe."

"Or not," Lily added. She might not care for Bannion, but she couldn't fault his powers of observation.

"Yeah. Or not, and these woods are too quiet." He went through a ritual of checking his quiver full of arrows, loosening the knife at his hip, and touching the one in his boot. "I'm gonna go talk to Rory. Maybe I'll look around in the woods a little. You here to watch our backs, Lily?"

Their situation might be dire, but amusement bubbled in her. "That wasn't my mission, Jake, but now I'm here, I might as well." There being no place safer, what difference did it make? What other choice had she?

Lily had thought Jacob would convince Rory to go into the woods with him, but after a short discussion he scaled the side of the gully by himself, leaving the other boy to take charge of the horses. Jake was good, Lily noted. One moment he was there, outlined against the horizon. The next he was gone. He faded into the background nearly as well as she with her cloaking abilities.

Inappropriate laughter bubbled up again, leaving her wondering if she was a little touched in the head. Except...

cloaking abilities reminded her all too strongly of Klingons or Romulons or some such out of the Star Trek movies. She doubted these people would get the joke. Maybe Nate. Nah, she told herself. Not even him.

"Ms. Turnbow?" Fanta, who had taken over Jacob's horse-holding duties, had followed Jacob's lead and strung her bow, too, leaving it propped against the log. "What should we do if the saiclers try to get the horses."

"Stop them," Lily said, thinking, why ask me? The girl's hands were already shaking and her smooth young face pinched. No need to add to her distress.

"What if we're outnumbered?" Fanta persisted.

"We'll still try to stop them. You don't want to run away, do you?"

Fanta pulled at her upper lip. "No."

Lily tuned the girl out, listening with all her might to the clash of battle. That night at the lake, the fight had been noisy, gunshots, men shouting, the boat and airplane engines roaring across the water. This was different; quieter, but just as deadly. The *whing* of steel swords, screams of agony, dogs howling. A weird music, like glass singing, came to her.

"Do you hear that?" the girl asked.

"I hear it."

"What is it?"

"I don't know."

Fanta's hand crept into hers, tightening as for a brief moment all noise ceased. Then a huge bestial roar seemed to shake the trees.

"Uh-oh." Lily didn't need to see what was happening to know. The O'Quinns had been overrun. There was no other explanation.

Down at the far end of the gully, with his back to them, Rory nocked an arrow, took aim, released. The arrow's flight took it into the brush nearest the off horse. A dog's yipe answered and one of the saicler's big pit bulls staggered into the open before collapsing. Smelling blood and worried by the dog, the horses started snorting, crowhopping, and fighting their ties.

From within the far woods, a quick yodel rang out.

"That's Jacob," Fanta gasped, numbing Lily's hand with the strength of her squeeze. "His family does that. Did that to identify themselves. It means—"

Lily swallowed. *Did?* "What does it mean?"

"He's killed an enemy."

There was fierce pride in Fanta's voice, a pride Lily could echo. "Go, Jake," she said. But the three of them had more to do than let Jacob protect them. Or stand and wait for the saicler war party to search them out. Do that and the O'Quinns might be left with no resources. And Jacob had left her in charge, hadn't he?

He had.

"Untie these horses, Fanta," she said, pulling away from the girl's clinging hand. "And mount up."

"The boss said to stay here and keep them safe," the girl said, but Lily cut her off.

"The boss isn't here. I am and I'm giving the orders. Mount up." Her head turned toward the crossroad, listening. "Hurry. I can hear them, coming this way. We have help them."

The girl gaped, then, as the portent of Lily's words hit, did as she was told, choosing the roan mare for her mount. Lily didn't care. She groped for the stirrup on the nearest saddled horse and swung her leg over, only then discovering it was Nog flouncing under her unaccustomed weight.

"Settle down," she told the animal, reining it in. "Fanta, take the horses and join Rory. It's more open at that end. We have more room to maneuver there." Nog shook his head as she gathered the reins. He sensed her tension, maybe smelled blood. The horse reared as one of the O'Quinn's, or maybe the Bell's, Karelian Bear dogs shot into the clearing, running so fast his white belly skimmed the ground. Lily barely kept her seat.

Finding the horses, the black-and-white dog darted in between them, yipping as though giving orders. Since the effect on the horses was calming, Lily thought maybe he had.

The girl wasn't moving fast enough. "Hustle!" Lily snapped, pulling a long mullein stalk from the ground as she rode past it and slashing out at the horses with the dry, flowered end. Startled, they broke into a lope, the dog running behind. Birds swooped and called, risen from their perches in the woods beyond the horses where they'd hidden. Jacob, she felt sure, was not the cause of their alarm.

Eyes swiveling side to side, trying to see everything at once, she was aware when, from her right, a swarm of birds fluttered into the sky and shot off to the north.

"Hell," she breathed. They'd been flanked. And Jacob, in taking the fight to the saiclers, very likely was cut off from the three of them.

She joined the two kids holding the strings of excited horses barely in check. Hoping her façade appeared calm, she grinned at Rory. "You were hoping for a little action, weren't you?"

"Action, hell! The folks. They've been overrun." Anguish marked his pale face. The kid was one of the light-skinned side of the clan, like Nate.

In trying to soothe the dancing Nog, Lily's spirits soared when she discovered Bannion had left a spare sword hanging from a saddle sheath. She jerked it from the scabbard, hearing the metal sing as it slid from the leather. It was, she thought, modeled after an old cavalry saber. So how did one use a saber? Chop and hew, or poke and jab? Only one cutting edge, she saw. Which probably meant chop and hew. If only the cursed thing weren't so heavy.

"Miz!" Fanta shrieked. "Look." She pointed into the woods surrounding them where a couple of skinny guys wearing saicler type duds darted from tree to tree.

Fanta's bow hung slackly from her arm.

"Shoot'em," Lily ordered crisply.

"Ma'am," Rory said, his voice cracking. "Ahead of us. Here they come."

The saiclers were on foot, as Lily had imagined they would be, the coulee's floor an unsuitable surface for bicycles. She saw four, then a couple more stand between them and the rest of the clan. At least one saicler was wounded and dripping blood from a gash in his arm. At the edge of the little meadow they paused, another three joining them. Sloppy. Evidently without an officer to direct them, they slowly formed into an advancing line. Some laughed, making lewd suggestions when they saw Lily and Fanta.

"Get ready to turn the horses loose," Lily said.

Rory stared at her. "What? Ma'am, we can't do that."

"Sure we can. We are three, they've got three times that many that we can see. But if you add in twenty-four horses, and a dog, we've got them nicely outnumbered. We'll use the horses to break through and join the O'Quinn warriors. They'll be wanting their horses." *If any were still alive to want anything except a decent burial. Nate. Jacob.* No. She wouldn't think of them.

Light dawned in Rory's eyes. "Whoee, ma'am. That's smart."

She hoped so. She'd copped the idea from one of her grandpa's old western novels. "When I say go, turn the horses loose and run'em over the top of those bastards. If they're like most city guys they'll be petrified by a half ton of horseflesh running toward them. Keep the horses moving. They must not stop. Don't let anyone stop *you*. Rory, keep an eye on Fanta. We don't want her to fall into their hands."

"No, ma'am," Rory said emphatically.

No more time for talk. The saiclers were reaching into their quivers for arrows.

"Let'em go!" she cried, and the kids dropped the leads, allowing the rope holding the horses together to slide through rings under their chin straps. Before they could break apart, Lily gouged Nog hard with her heels, using him to prod the horses into motion. "Go," she screamed. "Go, go, go."

Rory yelling, Fanta with her high-pitched shriek, and the black-and-white dog barking at their heels, the horse stampeded.

Chapter 20

"Loudmouthed little bastard, isn't he? You know what they say?" Bannion injected a trace of amusement into his voice and pitched it so the nearest patrollers to hear.

Nate raised his eyebrows.

"Man who talks loudest has . . ." the rest of it faded away.

A small, though nervous, chuckle rewarded the boss' efforts.

"Guess we'll see," Nate muttered.

"Yes, we will, cousin." Bannion turned, checking the placement of the patrollers for the fourth time in a single minute before gesturing one boy and one girl drawn too far apart to close up ranks. Too scattered and they could get cut off. Too crowded and they'd get in each other's way. "Wish I didn't believe Lily Turnbow has him pegged, but I imagine she does."

"Yep," Nate said. "He scares her plenty bad. You can put your money on it, boss. She won't be joining up with the saiclers. Not by choice."

Bannion snorted. "Money? What do you think I am, one of these newborn city boys?"

"Bet your favorite horse on it, then."

"You better be right." Bannion checked his bow string and loosened the sword in his hip scabbard. He whistled, a piercing four note sequence that meant "get ready to attack."

He hadn't expected a Tech force of the numbers gathered against his people. They'd started out with twenty-four of the clan, to face more than forty of the Techs—plus Screenmaster. *And one of us dead already and two more cut almost to pieces.* Made him madder than hell and hurt his heart at the same time. Beautiful Kira, her smooth skin cut to ribbons, her straight white teeth...Godbedamned Cross-ups, anyhow. Made a man wonder what he and his people had done to deserve this.

The Tech's big drum, its thud amplified and reverberating in his chest, ended on a roll like thunder. In the sudden silence, the Screenmaster's bellow carried all too well in a orgy of blood lust. "Kill, kill," he screeched. "I want the woman. Give me the woman. Kill them all, but bring me the woman."

It seemed certain he meant Lily Turnbow. No wonder Nate said she was afraid of him.

Bannion heard that peculiar singing sound again, and Screenmaster's diatribe became muffled. Aha, he thought. That's what that sound is. He's put up his famous screen. Which means this fight is about to begin.

"Arrows ready," he roared in a voice cultivated to carry over a battleground and the screams of the dying. He stood up, his bow already drawn. "Fire. Fire. Fire." He loosed the first arrow, ignoring what he knew would be the futility of aiming for Screenmaster, and going for the saicler's leader.

His flatbow, crafted last winter of seasoned hickory with reinforced tips and sporting an elk horn hand hold, drew at one hundred and twenty pounds. Supposing good razored-steel tips, he could drive an arrow clean through an elk or penetrate plate armor. Which was a good thing, because now he knew what was in those heavy carts the saiclers had been guarding so carefully. Chain mail torso covers and iron helmets.

The head saicler dropped, dead before he hit the ground, Bannion's arrow buried all the way to its red and white fletching in his heart. Had he mentioned razor-sharp tips?

"Better get their *money* back if they paid much for those vests," he muttered to Nate.

Nate took on the man to the leader's left. That one screamed, dropped his bow, and clutched the arrow protruding from his gut, a few inches below his short mail cuirass.

"I'd say so," he agreed.

Behind them, a saicler crawled away with one of Sergeant Zelnor's yellow painted arrows stuck through his jaw.

One of the clan girls, drawing a bow of no more than seventy-five pounds, had her arrow turn as it hit the metalwork under her target's shirt and skitter down his arm, slicing through tendons and arteries. Assuredly dead in the near future, Bannion thought, but not just yet, and if a man wasn't dead, he was dangerous.

"Put him away," he ordered.

She obeyed.

The saicler casualties helped, but it wasn't enough. More crowded to the fore as those few dropped.

"Aim low, below their breastplates," he called between shots. Ripped guts wouldn't be pretty, but they did tend to stop a man.

Beside him, Nate drew and released, drew and released, his face calm, his aim steady. There were plenty of targets, but the O'Quinns weren't going to have time to take full advantage.

Secure behind his transparent singing screen, Screenmaster's face was fiendish as he bounced on his wagon seat. Then he did something with his hands and the screen expanded, ballooning into a barrier between the saiclers and the O'Quinn arrows.

Some of the patrollers shot in futile anger, the arrows recoiling uselessly off what looked like a thickening of the air.

Bannion had expected no less. "Hold fire. Shields up," he bellowed. "Watch their arrows."

The words barely left his mouth before a hail of missiles dropped out of the sky, proving the screen worked only one way. The enemy could shoot through it while blocking the O'Quinns. Saicler arrows thudded into the clan's heavy bullhide shields held like umbrellas over their heads. Some points penetrated and, though none went all the way through, some slipped between the shield edges. Several of his fighters went down, one dead instantly when chance sent a ricocheted arrow into his jugular. Two others were seriously hurt, one sobbing in agony with an arrow through his thigh. Another, a girl with her hand nearly severed at the wrist, stared at the open bone in silent shock. Three or four fighters had minor wounds. Bannion himself was unscathed. Nate bled a little from a notch cut between his neck and his shoulder.

Over the clank and roar of battle, he heard Screenmaster laughing, urging the saiclers to advance. "More blood, I want more blood," the dwarf shouted.

"More blood, eh?" Bannion whispered to himself. This was a fight his patrollers had no chance of winning. "Nate, Josh, Black Pete," he called. "Flank those suckers. You gotta buy us some time."

Nate, he could see, realized the futility of staying here and dying. His cousin's face was grim as the three whose names he called dove into cover along the road, Nate on one side, Black Pete and Josh taking the other.

When he saw them safely away, Bannion motioned to his sergeant. "Get ready to pull back, Rondo." He took a breath. "Leave the two seriously wounded." It was a wrench, contrary to both his personal and clan code. *We'll be back for them.* He made the promise to himself, the question being if they'd still be alive.

Grimly, Rondo nodded, yelping as another flight of arrows descended, one cutting a furrow across his forearm when his shield canted to the side. Another man, a Bell, went down. When the wave eased to a trickle, he ran along the scattered line of patrollers hunkered in the road block's inadequate shelter. Nods, along with some protests, acknowledged the order.

Another kid, one of the Shandys, died in the next hail of arrows. Screenmaster's voice never quit, the "kill, blood, kill," of his exhortation becoming monotonous, meaningless. When the last arrow either hit the ground or thudded into the raised shields, Bannion gestured the clan's walking wounded to retreat and make their way up the coulee toward the horses. Knowing their efforts were ineffectual, the remaining patrollers set up a covering fire, arrows bouncing off the screen. He tried the saicler's trick, shooting high for the arrow to drop, but Screenmaster had prepared for that.

Made them duck, anyway, Bannion thought with grim humor. Then finally, Screenmaster dropped the overextended, wavering shield behind the fleeing patrollers, and loosed the war dogs in pursuit. Saicler fighters swarmed forward, shouting hoarsely, swords swinging, pikes thrusting.

Bannion and Rondo stayed where they were. Calling four men to him, Bannion set them as rear guard. His people were horsemen, a little lost without their mounts. Lacking the strength of their trained war horses, this might not be a battle they could win.

Meeting the saicler front, Bannion wielded his sword in great swooping cuts. Horse or no horse, he could take a few of the enemy with him into the land of the dead, by God. His bloody sword cut the legs out from under a thin saicler whose attention was on one of the O'Quinn girls, and finished him off with a blow to head. Sweat ran into his eyes, his hand became slick with the enemy's blood. The muscles in his arms and shoulders strained.

*****

Nate forced his mind to blank out the action spreading around Wolf Point crossing. His heart beat fast, and although the clouds had blown in and it was spitting snow, the cold never touched him.

It wasn't difficult getting around the saiclers. O'Quinns on the run kept them fully occupied. Barking dogs, battle cries, and the clink of sword blade against sword blade covered any slight noise he made working his way into the woods at the rear.

He came to one of the mounds that dotted the roadside and climbed to the top, its five-foot elevation giving him a clear line of sight. Taking a handful of arrows from his quiver, he stabbed them into the ground in front of him, close at hand. A mild ping told him the tip had touched the metal roof of an abandoned vehicle, grown over the last century to become more a thing of the earth than a man-made object.

Forcing all thought from his mind, he picked his first target as the saiclers surged down the road. A big, muscular man bent over the O'Quinn girl with the severed hand. Nate's bowstring twanged, sending an arrow into the man's back. Another thudded into him before he could fall, and across the way, Nate caught sight of Black Pete, already nocking another arrow. Pete nodded.

With their leader dead, the bewildered saicler fighters scattered, seeming unaware of the danger at their rear. But they ran forward when Screenmaster ordered them on. He, surrounded by his conjured shield, remained impervious to danger atop his wagon as he lumbered past. The dwarf, as far as Nate could tell, had no weapon except his magic. And that, gods rot it, was enough to protect him.

Nate couldn't figure the Cross-up. The little creep must be aware of his own men dying in the crossfire, but he just laughed and urged them on, ignoring him and Black Pete as if they weren't even there. If they couldn't hurt him, and they couldn't, they didn't matter.

Able to draw, aim, and release a shaft every three seconds, between him and Black Pete, the pair of them managed a lot of damage—until their arrows ran out. Nate jumped from his mound down to the road, drew his sword and prepared to follow the running fight. Just then a bushy-tailed squirrel ran from somewhere inside the mound and darted away. Dodging the horses' hooves and the big wooden wheels, it passed safely to the opposite verge where it sat chattering at him.

It took a moment for what that vision meant to sink into Nate's brain.

"Pete," he yelled, careless of who might hear, but the saiclers were too intent on their prey to pay attention, and Screenmaster didn't care. Well, he'd see if he could change that attitude. "Pete."

Black Pete ran across the road behind Screenmaster's wagon. Together, they stood in the open as though out for a Sunday stroll.

"You got any arrows left?" Nate asked.

"Not a one. Why?"

Nate told him.

"No lie? Underneath? Well, hell. Where's Josh? I ain't seen him in a while. Maybe he's got arrows."

But Josh was not to be found. Either he'd been killed, or he was on the saicler's right, following the crowd and trying to get in a few more licks. Either way, Nate's frustration boiled. He needed a weapon. The right kind of weapon, he amended, if only he knew just what that would be. Which is when the sound of twenty-four horses' pounding hooves running flat out reached his ears.

*****

"Hi, hi," Fanta screamed, her high-pitched voice carrying over the noise of horse's hooves thudding and clicking on rocks. The herd grunted with effort, a few neighed. Rory bellowed, deeper, calmer. Lily just slapped at the nearest beast, the loose stirrups of the saddle on its back flapping wildly. Scared it into running, all right, the chore being to keep it pointed in the right direction.

Going at a flat-out run, they swept from the gully's mouth into the wider part of the coulee. Just at the turning, Lily saw people on foot, limping toward them. More specifically, she saw bloodied patrollers helping each other along as they retreated. And not an orderly retreat, either, but a full rout.

"Get out of the way," she yelled, and when Fanta would've slowed the horses to help her kin, Lily hollered "hi, hiya," and whipped her now battered mullein stalk all the harder. They couldn't stop until they reached the front for those still able to ride and mount a cavalry charge. If there were any.

A hundred yards farther on she found the remaining O'Quinns fighting a rearguard action in which they were sorely outnumbered. They were pretty good, she admitted, even though the swords in their hands horrified her. There was just something about a blade. The gaping wound of sliced open flesh. Guns, now. Guns were pretty clean compared to the slash and stab of edged weapons.

But it was time, and she took Bannion's sword from the scabbard, its weight dragging at her arm. She set herself to stabbing and slashing, knowing herself awkward and as much a danger to friend as to foe.

Meanwhile, the horses, no longer being chased, slowed and milled, allowing O'Quinns to find a mount and spring into the saddle. Saiclers, unaccustomed to the snorting beasts, were trampled underfoot.

Lily, whacking about wildly with the heavy blade, searched the area, trying to see everything at once. No Bannion. No Nate. No Rondo, no Jake.

No Nate. Cold settled around her heart.

She jabbed at a saicler trying to grab her leg and poked him in the cheek with the sword point. A cut opened up like a tear in a pair of pants. Merciful heavens! Bannion's sword was sharp as a surgeon's scalpel. Permanently discouraged the leg grabber, for sure, as he dropped his weapon and ran away, screaming and holding his bloody face.

But there were so many of them, stinking and sweating, cursing and bleeding. The horses gave the O'Quinns an incalculable advantage. Enough to allow her a second's breathing room, in which she became aware of arrows and swordsmen dispensing cold death from behind the saiclers as the invaders were caught in a crossfire. She lifted her voice, yelling encouragement to the O'Quinns.

From the superior vantage being on horseback gave her, Lily saw that one of the archers was Bannion. His face set in cold fury, he drew his bow and shot arrows like an automaton, quick, quick, quick. A man fell for every arrow. She counted four in the space of seconds as she rode Nog toward him. The other man, the sergeant called Rondo, bled from several wounds, but he held the ground around Bannion so the sheriff had room to shoot.

Her admiration for the O'Quinns shot up.

Knowing their war leader survived, full of fight and no give to him, provided the clan with new life. Enough they fought with renewed vigor.

Lily saw Fanta unhorsed, but as she headed toward the girl, one of the older warriors reached down and swooped the girl up where they stood back-to-back, slashing out with sword and long knife against three young saiclers. In a blink, two of the three faltered beneath clan blades and the last one ran.

And then Lily reached Bannion and hauled on the reins.

Nog slid on his haunches, stopping beside the war leader. Unceremoniously, Bannion yanked Lily from the saddle and threw himself into it in her place.

"Take her, sergeant. Find Nate," he ordered, and jerked a thumb. "He's back there, trying to stop the Cross-up. Go help him."

Lily, sprawled catawampus across the dead and very bloody body of a female saicler, barely avoided being skewered by the sword in her own hand. Pushing away from the corpse she nodded, deciding right off to find a hole and crawl in first chance she got. To hell with this. It wasn't her fight, and she'd done all she had any intention of doing, help or hinder.

Sergeant Zelnor may have seen this resolve in her face, for he pulled her to her feet and said, "You heard the boss. Come on."

Lily shook off his hand. "What if Nate is dead?" *Please not.*

"He ain't dead."

"And you know that how?" She drew back.

Zelnor pointed. "Look there. See those skinny little shits with arrows in their backsides? Those running away? That's Nate's work. Nate and Black Pete."

That there were more of Nate's arrows than Pete's gave Lily an odd sense of satisfaction. He could be funny and gentle, but it seemed he could also be ruthless when the lives of his family and his home were at stake.

A kind of empty feeling crashed through her, then, leaving her weak and disoriented. She had no one to care for her in this world. Knew none of these strangely altered humans or their living condition. She had no family and no home. Her life didn't make any sense.

How could anyone sleep for a hundred years? Sleep and then awaken in a strange hereafter? It was impossible, that's what. She felt herself drowning in the sudden bewilderment and disconnection.

"Wake up, woman."

A rough push in the middle of her back brought Lily's wandering mind back to the present.

"C'mon," Rondo Zelnor said. "What the hell're you doing? Can't blank out on us now."

"Want to bet?" Still, something clicked in and, sword dragging at her side, she staggered in the direction Rondo pushed her. Battle cries and the clang of blade against blade faded a bit as they emerged onto what had once been the main highway. Unfortunately, that meant almost bumping noses with the white horses hitched to Screenmaster's wagon as they plodded down the middle of the road.

No thanks to Rondo, she stepped aside in time to avoid being trampled. The whole set up, horses, wagon wheels, harness, were encased in a peculiar silence. What the bubble didn't muffle was Screenmaster's voice.

"You're her," he hollered down to her from his high perch as though delighted. He ignored Rondo as if the sergeant were invisible. "I know you're her. You've got the look. Our look. Come here to me, sweetheart. I want you."

Lily didn't dignify his demand with an answer. She was too taken with seeing through the transparent screen, Nate and another man trailing Screenmaster's outfit. Each wore an identical look of frustration, until a slight smile flicked across Nate's face when he saw her. Barnes himself seemed unaware of the men. Or perhaps, knowing he was secure behind his shield, he just didn't care.

Barnes stopped his team beside her. An odor emanating from the screen warned Lily that she was closer to it than she liked, but curious, she put out a finger and touched it. Cold, sticky and, what was that smell? It stank of something awful, like old death.

Her nose wrinkled in reaction and she stepped back, but it was already too late.

The bubble expanded to trap her inside.

Chapter 21

"Well," Philip Barnes, Screenmaster, said, staring down at her from the high wagon seat, "that was easy. You walked into my sphere like a trusting little mouse. I expected more from one of the 'Fighting O'Quinns.' I hope you'll be a little more active when I, no, make that when *we* start to play."

Lily opened her mouth to tell him she wasn't an O'Quinn, then closed it again. Not smart. No point in giving him any information.

He watched her, grinning with a show of bad teeth. It was an attribute unchanged in the last one hundred years. She remembered his lack of dental care from seeing him on TV.

"What's the matter, woman? Cat got your tongue?" He giggled at his private joke. "Yum. Tongue." His own darted out to lick his thick lips.

She swallowed. One of the notable things, repeated endlessly on the news, about his last killing spree was that he severed his victim's tongue and ate it raw as the woman watched. Sick bastard.

"Do you know who I am?" he demanded.

Finding her voice, she answered more boldly than she

felt. "Of course. I could hardly avoid it, seeing you've been making announcements every couple of minutes."

"Then you know I'm running this show. You know I'm the king of the Cross-ups. The most powerful Cross-up to come down the pike, to be exact. All others are subject to my whims. When I give an order, people obey. You got that?"

"More fool them." Eyes narrowed, she watched for any effect her words might have. It was said he got off on listening to his female victims scream, possible without a tongue even if speech was not.

Her lack of reaction evidently displeased him, though he must have seen something of what she was thinking in her face. His voice raised an octave and grew several decibels louder. "When I speak, woman, *you* obey. I am the power here. *Capisce*?"

Against her will, Lily sensed a kind of inner pull, a force the nasty little man managed to exert. Even she, warned and aware of what he was, had to fight against it. Screenmaster's bubble seemed to take her breath away, her lungs laboring to use the air trapped within, stale and seething with evil. Beyond him, Rondo had joined Nate and another man. They were conferring in whispers, Nate gesturing, the one she didn't know nodding, and Rondo turning to stare at Screenmaster's gear. None of the three appeared quite as dismayed at her captivity as she felt warranted.

"Well?" Philip Barnes, murderer and magician, reclaimed her full attention. "Answer me."

"I'm sorry. Did you ask a question? I guess my attention wandered."

"Ho." Barnes laughed down at her from his high perch. "Do I sense a little attitude in you? I hope so. You might test my mettle after all. Excellent."

"You think so? You're an arrogant little—" Lily searched for the proper word, "—outlaw, aren't you?"

"You have heard of me, haven't you? Well, of course you have. Everyone has heard of Screenmaster." He preened, smoothing his rough hair like a parakeet nibbles its feathers.

Lily shrugged. "Oh, that. Not so much. I was thinking of your past as a condemned criminal. How, I wonder, did such an unmitigated horror as yourself manage to survive the catastrophe that caused us?" Anger suddenly flashed through her. "No. That's not right. What I really wonder is *why* did you survive? It just doesn't seem right. You were within a couple days of execution, if memory serves me. It's too bad the state of Washington didn't move a little faster."

All traces of Barnes' grotesque smile faded from his face. "You have a sharp tongue, bitch. I'll have to curb that. Permanently. You know what I'm saying?"

"I'm not some old lady or drunken bar bunny," Lily said. "Maybe not such easy prey. Think about it, dwarf." She used the word as an insult, remembering how furious he became at his trial when one of the witnesses called him that. It had induced in him a childlike tantrum. The less clearly he was thinking, the better she could fight him. Or so she told herself.

But he must have learned a thing or two in the last hundred years, and although his face reddened, he held on to his temper. "You have some lessons to learn, I see. But for your information, woman, no. I have other plans for you. That other thing?" He fluttered his pudgy fingers in the air. "There are plenty of that simple kind around to satisfy my, um, call them urges. I told you. I expect more out of you. Now," he patted the seat beside him in invitation, "come up here. Let's get better acquainted."

She didn't move. "No, thanks."

His voice, deep for such a small man, hardened. "I insist."

"A gentleman would come down." What advantage that would give her was questionable, but her argument felt right.

He appeared to consider. "Okay. I will. This once. See how agreeable I am?" Wrapping the reins around the brake lever, he began the climb from the tall seat, the bizarre robe he wore hindering movement. Made of heavy velvet, stars sprinkled the background, shining with some kind of glitter. Lily thought it looked like a Merlin the magician Halloween costume. Theatrical maybe, but silly, too.

The horses stamped and blew, tails frisking at a few late flies trapped in the bubble with them.

Lily's heart beat faster as Philip Barnes jumped from the last step of a stair specially built to accommodate his short legs. Nothing he wore could cover a certain stiffness in the way he carried himself. A row of throwing knives peeked above the collar of his robe like a short picket fence. Under the swirl of fabric, she saw the gleam of metal armor.

Knives, she remembered, were his thing. Not so silly.

He circled her, eyeing her like a prospective buyer judges a mare for his breeding stable. He paid special attention to her backside, and when he was finished, he posed in front of her, one hand on his hip, the other tucked across his body Napoleonic style. "You're a fine looking woman, you know that? Got good teeth, too. I admire that in a woman." He nodded grandly and said, "We shall be partners and rule the world. You'll like that, won't you? Of course, I'll be the senior partner, but you can sit at my left hand. I throw with my right."

Lily knew he lied. The slant of the sheathed knives told her as much.

Outside the bubble, and off to the side, Nate had borrowed one of Rondo's arrows. It was nocked in his bow, but strangely, the bow pointed at the ground in a oblique position. He was making faces and gestures, none of which made sense.

Or did they? An idea glimmered.

Her attention shifted back to Barnes. What had he been saying? "You want to make me your consort?" She laughed, surprised when it sounded almost natural. "And what, little man, makes you think your powers are stronger than mine?" She walked around him as he had done to her, finally placing herself between him and the massive wagon so that his back was to the O'Quinn contingent. "Perhaps we could turn the idea around and I'll have you at *my* left."

He roared with laughter, showing a disturbingly unpretty snaggle of teeth. "No one is stronger than me, dear. And you're not a rogue. Not yet. But you haven't tried to stop this fight, either. I'd know if you had. I can smell the use of power."

Yuck. Lily hated thinking they could relate on that score. She wanted *nothing* in common with this little toad. "Did you ever consider that our magical powers should be used to benefit people, not to harm them?" she asked.

Barnes swung the arm previously tucked in his robe in a grand manner. "Oh, please. The power benefits me. If you've got it, flaunt it. That's what I always say. And you will too, when you get over this American Way, apple pie, and mother shit that's been ground into your head. I'll teach you."

"I knew you'd say that, but Mr. Barnes, there is nothing I want to learn from you." Watching him carefully, she unzipped her jacket, displaying the badge clipped to her belt. "Sir, you are under arrest."

He stared up at her, his pale eyes bugging. "What?"

She stepped to the right. "Place your hands on the side of the wagon where I can see them." His face puckered until she though he was going to cry, but what came out of his mouth was laughter. Great bellows that left him gasping, his froggy face red.

Voice level, she said, "Hands against the wagon, Mr. Barnes. Do not make me tell you again."

The laughter shut off like the turning of a faucet. "You're pretty funny, you know? Got a real sense of humor, which I warn you, could get old fast. Just out of curiosity, on whose authority are you making this claim? You're behind times, woman. There is no law in this world. Not as you think of it. Here whoever is strongest makes the law." He paused. "And that is yours truly. Your little stand means nothing. To me or to anyone. Not even the O'Quinns, I wager."

He was telling the truth, both about his strength and about the O'Quinns. Not that it mattered to Lily. Not when it came to Philip Barnes.

She shrugged. "I guess I'm still stuck in the 2020s."

Lily watched his hands. The paper had reported he was deceptively fast, that he almost killed an officer once with a thrown knife before they could taser him and bring him down. She had to be ready.

"Last I heard, I hadn't been fired and I'm not on vacation or sick leave," she continued. "As far as I'm concerned, I'm still a Border Patrol officer, bound to uphold the law. So, hands against the wagon, Mr. Barnes. And I'd suggest you drop this shield bologna. I'm not impressed." Okay, that all sounded silly even to herself. So what? It was just talk. *Watch for any sudden move. Be ready.*

Of course he refused either to spread himself against the wagon or to drop the shield. She expected nothing else.

"So this is the way it has to be." He grinned. "Just as well. I've never found another Cross-up I could trust. You have no idea what I've been through. There were one or two over the years that even made me lose an hour's sleep. It'll be fun, killing you right in front of them," he nodded toward the clansmen, "and nothing they can do about it except watch. Do you think they'll weep over you? Hmm. They're O'Quinns. Knowing their reputation, probably not."

After that, Barnes—she refused to name him Screenmaster even in her own mind—ignored the three O'Quinns outside his bubble as though they were invisible. She, on the other hand, kept them in sight, although it didn't seem wise to let them distract her as the little man began a slow circling movement around her. In truth, she couldn't imagine why Rondo kept making gestures indicating she move away from Barnes, while the man she didn't know pointed at her feet, and Nate—Nate just looked worried.

He wasn't the only one. Lily was worried too. What would it take for Barnes to drop his shield? Since she couldn't seem to rile him into it, only one other likely reason came to her, which meant one way or another, she was on the spot for his capitulation. A smile tugged at her lips, probably looking like a frightened grimace to anyone watching. But really, it was funny. Here stood Lily Turnbow with, among other things, a newly discovered talent of disappearing from plain sight. The knack was in opposition to Phillip Barnes who, keeping himself in the limelight, could build a shield around himself preventing anyone's approach. Polar opposites.

Stranger yet, Barnes threw knives, while she threw fire-balls. It would come down to a duel. She felt that truth in her bones. So she might as well begin now, before the afternoon waned and dark descended upon them. She needed the day-light in order to watch Barnes' hands.

Outside the conjured screen, snow began falling. Great flakes that floated gently on a slight breeze. They settled on the dead, turning red as they melted in the fresh blood. Lily flinched from the sight as Barnes took another step to his left. Steel sang an eerie song as she lifted Bannion's saddle sword in her left hand. The action appeared awkward, she knew, but not as awkward as it felt. Didn't matter, anyway. This was not her weapon.

"Put down that sword," Barnes said, confirming her guess. "It looks silly. What does a hundred-year-old Border Patrol agent know of sword fighting, for Gawd's sake. There's nobody can beat my knives. Nobody."

"Scared, are you?" Lily asked softly.

"Of you? Don't be ridiculous."

But he watched the sword and her with narrowed eyes. Amusing, really. Hadn't anyone told him about her little talent? Was he confident enough of his own powers that he didn't care?

She followed his circling dance step for step until one of his horses whuffed the back of her neck. She doubted Barnes would deliberately stab one of them, but it was possible that in his egotism failure in his aim wouldn't occur to him. She tensed, her heart beating faster. Anger roiled, a heat in her blood.

Nate knelt outside the bubble's edge. The shield's circumference, she noted with some surprise, had shrunken. Nate had some wild creature in his hands, a bird, fluttering in terror. Suddenly, with a flapping of wings, it slipped beneath Barnes' screen, ran a couple of yards, then turned and scooted right back out between Nate's feet.

Ah. Now she knew what he was trying to tell her. Without looking directly at him, she dipped her head once.

The first knife came at her so fast she barely had time to shift the inch required to avoid it. The horse standing behind her squealed, threshing wildly in the harness, the knife protruding from its shoulder muscle.

So. Barnes was willing to sacrifice the horses, after all. She wasn't.

"Not nice," she said, thrusting with the sword so that by some quirk of luck his next knife clanged off the blade and clattered to the ground. She couldn't count on that happening more than once. The sword wavered, impossibly heavy and dragging at her arms.

Hand blurring, he reached again behind his neck. His teeth bared and he snarled like a wild animal as the next blade came free. Mad, feral eyes glowed with excitement.

Lily dropped the sword. No more fooling around. Time for a show of her own. Her fingers flicked. A mote of fire

zipped off the ends and struck Barnes in the chest, burning
a hole in the snazzy purple fabric. With an angry howl, his
next knife came free. At the same time, his screen shrank,
leaving her outside and free of its poisonous air, while it
built and thickened around him. His velvet robe smoked.
He was panting.

"My robe," he said, brushing at the charred area. "My
beautiful robe. You bitch. Think you're clever don't you?"

She should've been watching more closely, but the fact
is she was a little unsettled by his crazy eyes. And so she
missed seeing the knife in time to entirely avoid it.

Barnes' bad karma was being a dwarf. An angry, excited
little person in this case, and instead of throwing, he hacked
out like a wild man. He missed her gut by a hand's width,
slicing instead across the top of her thigh. The pain brought
Lily down in a heap, and immediately Barnes stalked toward
her, the blade gleaming through the falling snow.

Without pausing to think, she rolled beneath the nearest
horse's belly, dodging its kick by an inch. Maybe not the
best choice of shelter seeing it was the horse that'd been
stabbed. It danced around her, squealing with pain and fear.

"Hah!" Barnes roared. "Got you. Come out." Slashing
at her with his palm knife, only the short length of his arms
saved her. Disgusted, he threw the blade down and snatched
up the sword she'd let fall. His thick lips curled in a smug
smile, certain there was nothing she could do to harm him.
His magical screen wrapped him in security from head to foot.

The horse jigged from side-to-side, restrained only by
the harness. One oversized hoof knocked against the side
of her head, making her vision blur as Barnes jabbed with
the sword between its feet. Damn. Damn! Impossible to stay
clear long enough to fight him.

Timing the horse's movement, she scooted backward
until she reached the open space between the lead pair. Re-

gaining her feet brought fresh blood pouring down her leg, which trembled beneath her. Safely beyond Barnes' reach for the moment, her position served to madden him further. His thick lips drew back over clenched yellow teeth as he drew the sword back and took a hack at the horse.

A chunk of flesh torn from its side, the agonized beast screamed and lunged forward, drawing the rest of the team with him. Lily hobbled between the lead pair, a hand on each bridle helping keep a precarious balance. At any instant she could be jerked off her feet and trampled. A precarious state of affairs to be sure. She had to stop Barnes. Now!

The dwarf stabbed at her again. Frightened by the blade flashing in front of their eyes, the horses reared, lifting her into the air before dropping her down again. She hit the ground with a gasp of agony, her wounded leg faltering beneath her. Then Nate was there, filling her vision as he grabbed the horses, stilling them with what she thought was shear will power.

"Hurry," he said. "Get clear."

Rondo's arrows bounced off Barnes' magical armor as the dwarf bounded toward Nate, his stubby legs deceptively fast. He flung the sword at Nate, who dodged easily, but he was already reaching for a throwing knife.

Lily crawled. No time. No time.

Barnes' hand came out from behind his ear holding a short knife by the blade. His piggy eyes narrowed on Nate.

"No!" Careless of the rearing horses, she flung out her hands. Fire shaped into molten zigzags of lightning shot from her fingertips. One hit Barnes in his shielded face, rolled slowly downward, the fire dying and leaving Screenmaster unscathed. But it caused him to blink, which skewed his aim just enough for the knife to miss Nate and skitter harmlessly into the brush a few yards distant.

How many more of those damn blades did he have? It

seemed an unending supply, because he was grabbing for yet another. Her choices had run out and so had his. Gathering herself, she stepped forward and pointed downward. Fire rained from her fingertips.

Screenmaster lost his smile as the bottom of his loose britches exploded. Orange and blue flames leapt up his stumpy legs. His eyes bugged, reflecting shock.

She cast more of the tiny spheres. Ricochets bounced from the old paved road, flying beneath his shield and into his clothing. The balls glowed fiercely before flames burst into being. Wherever they touched, they blossomed.

The edges of Screenmaster's wizard's robe smoked, then burned hotly as though fed by a propellant. Caught within his screen, sparkling embers flew around his head. His hair erupted into a fiery halo. The screen dropped. Clamping both hands to his head, he tried to run.

And then it was just Philip Barnes, no longer Screenmaster, but only a man on fire, caught in real human panic. A man with no third chance at life.

After a time Lily thought would never end, he toppled onto the wet road, his body jerking and smoking within his armor. His charred flesh, she noted somewhere at the back of her mind, stunk of fire and brimstone. Fitting for one of his kind.

She gave a great shuddering breath and fell to her knees, closing her eyes against the sight. As though from far away she heard Rondo shout, "Clear the way. Those sonsabitches are running for home. We beat them."

"Into the wagon," Nate said. "Pete, get that door open. Hurry."

Someone, she knew it was Nate, lifted her in his arms. In a hurried, leg-jolting dash, he carried her into a dark place and laid her on a cot inches too short even for her small frame. She smelled the bodies crowded in with her. Sweat, blood, maleness—and Barnes.

She muttered a protest when what she wanted to do is scream her pain.

"Be still," Nate said. So she was silent, listening as the few remaining saiclers, thoroughly defeated, fled back toward their parked bicycles and pushed off the way they'd come. So far as she could tell, not one stopped to mourn their Screenmaster.

Chapter 22

Bannion seized Screenmaster's wagon, drafting it into ambulance service for the trek back to O'Quinn headquarters. Too many of the clan were incapable of either riding or walking.

"Damned lucky to have it, too," he told Nate, helping cut the wounded horse out of harness.

Lily, sitting on the low step leading to the wagon's driving seat, looked on.

"Don't know how else we'd get the injured home," Bannion continued. "There's not enough of us to lug stretchers." A worried glance spelled out his particular concern. Kira Shandy, moaning softly even though unconscious was in a condition sure to twist anyone's heart.

Lily knew clan members selected for medic duty had done their best. In her opinion, that wasn't saying much. Someone handed her a sterile pad with instructions to exert pressure on the deep cut on her own leg. Not much, she told herself, compared to poor Kira Shandy. What a horrible, sad case *she* was in.

Drawn by the remaining three big white horses, the wagon was soon overloaded even though several of the injured fighters rode horseback when they should've been carried. Six bodies bound face down over their saddles followed the sad cavalcade. It was an appalling number of casualties for such a small force.

After that first fainting spell, Lily counted herself among the lucky ones able to ride. Nevertheless, she had only vague impressions of the damaged horse being led away. Nate had done that. She'd heard him talking to the horse, soothing, apologizing as he tied it to the wagon's tailgate. Bannion had wanted to put the big animal down; Nate insisted it would be good as new, given a few days rest and care.

She was glad when Nate won the argument. Glad, too, when he took on the chore of seeing she didn't fall off the roan horse once she was helped up. Then came the eternity of wending their way along the old rutted road. She wasn't the only one unable to hold back a groan when her mount stumbled, as it did every now and then.

Eventually, all the wounded ended up outside the little hospital. Neila and her medical staff began triage, and the mourning of the dead began. Sobbing filled the expansive compound; grief drew the falling darkness around the bereaved. And that, Lily thought sadly, meant nearly every one, this being an extended family. Only the traders drew back. And Lily.

Lips tight, faces drawn, Neila and Bren went about the business of selecting Kira Shandy, grotesque in her injuries as their first patient. The second was the girl with a severed hand. The scout Dak, third. Others followed.

Lily came in dead last. No more than she'd expected.

She sat on the lobby floor with her head leaned against the wall and her eyes closed, waiting, only half aware of the sometimes frantic activity around her. Even a semi-conscious state couldn't keep what she'd seen and done this day from playing in her mind's eye like a particularly vivid horror movie.

She'd torched a man. Not a good man, but a man none-theless. Made of flesh and blood. Watched him burn. Heard his screams. Felt no real remorse. And that was only one of a series of new experiences. Nothing in her career had prepared her for this. In her previous life she'd seen a couple gunshot wounds, been on the scene of traffic accidents, walked into one or two nasty domestic violence situations, both arguments over drug running. But today had been war of a truly primitive, bestial kind.

Take the young guy—House, she remembered his name after a minute—whom the saiclers had caught scouting along with Kira and Dak. Lord, his injuries looked like wolves had been at him, his body drained of blood, his toothless mouth agape in a rictus of agony.

And now the aftermath. The crying, the sorrow, the rage. And the pointy finger of blame. Oh, she heard mutters, all right, about how it was her fault. By her resurrection, she'd drawn the enemy down on the hapless O'Quinns. But most of all, she was a Cross-up and O'Quinns hated Cross-ups. Even one who'd fought on their side.

Damn all ungrateful fools, she thought resentfully, rolling her head from side-to-side as a fresh wave of pain flooded through her. It was like blaming the rain for muddying your road. Her awakening wasn't anything she'd planned, for God's sake. They must know that, consciously or unconsciously.

Or not. The O'Quinns made their own rules, saw only what they chose to see. Either way, she remained quiet, making herself small in the corner. Sometimes she wrapped an illusion of invisibility around herself and to all purposes, disappeared from the minds of those nearby.

But at last she was the only patient waiting. Bren called her name and, hoisting herself up by grabbing onto a chair, she limped into Neila's operating theater under her own power.

"So," Neila said, stretching her back, her haggard face

cold and unwelcoming. "You again. At least you managed to kill that other one, or so I hear."

Lily knew "that other one" meant Screenmaster. "Yes."

"I'm surprised you didn't join with him instead." Neila snapped on a fresh pair of thin gloves without meeting Lily's eyes.

"Are you?" She sucked in air through her nose and damped down her frustration. "What you must think of me! Why? Your family and I were always good friends, before the Event."

Bren looked up from opening a new package of auto-claved sterile needles, thread, and bandages. "Has no one told her?" she asked Neila with a puzzled frown.

Neila shook her head sharply.

"Told me what?"

"Cross-ups." Neila injected a wealth of scorn into the word, never mind that it rang a little false. "The clan has met up with two, no, four now, counting Screenmaster and you, and the first three were pure evil. As for you?" Her shrug conveyed reservations. "When in doubt, err on the side of caution. That's what I always say."

Bren bobbed her head in vigorous agreement.

Pain of a different sort shot through Lily, leaving her wondering where her professionalism had gone. What Neila thought, or what the entire clan thought of her shouldn't matter, but apparently it did. "You don't know me at all, do you? Or even care to think I might be someone who only wants to help."

"So you say now. In five years, ten years, you're apt to be singing a different tune." Neila jerked her thumb. "Get those britches off and climb onto the table. I'm tired and want to finish up here. I've family to check on."

As much as she wished to walk out the door, Lily knew she didn't dare. Couldn't, most probably. In fact, she had to accept Bren's help with her pants and shirt before climbing onto the table. Almost before she'd settled, Neila stuck a canister with an open top under her nose. "Here, take a whiff of this. It'll help a little. We're out of ether. The worst casualties have used up most of the supplies we just got from the traders." She nodded to Bren. "Make a note. Don't let the medical wagon leave. I'll beg Frin for more medical supplies even if it means I have to owe him."

"It'll be costly," Bren warned.

"I know. Maybe Pike will speak for us."

Lily pushed the canister away. "What is this?" She couldn't help the distrust that crept into the question.

"Aroma therapy," Bren said. "Lavender, in this case ."

Marginally reassured, Lily sniffed the sweet-smelling vapors, only to find it did nothing to ease the pain when Neila swabbed, then pinched the edges of Lily's wound closed and inserted a neat row of stitches.

Lily, drawing air through her nose in short bursts, refrained from either screaming or passing out. A matter of pride. Apparently, since she felt every stab of the needle, and every tug of the thread through her flesh, a real, working topical pain reliever didn't exist. None they were telling her about, anyway. She wouldn't put it past Neila to save the good stuff purely for the clan's use.

Ignoring her gasp of pain, the healer jabbed home an antibiotic injection. One technology they'd retained from the old days, perhaps handed on by Linda Poundstone who'd been a nurse practitioner. She wondered if Neila even knew that, about her long gone relative.

"You'll do," Bren said brusquely, helping her sit up as Neila turned away, tossed her gloves in a receptacle to be laundered, sterilized and then used again. No more disposable latex, Lily noted. Another item lost in time. But at least they hadn't neglected basic sanitation procedures.

Neila gathered more gloves, bandages and spare needles for her set of glass syringes and prepared to make rounds. She barely glanced at Lily, who stood clad only in her underwear with her head buzzing and legs shaking.

"Is there a robe?" Lily asked. "I'll go to my room and stay out of your way."

"That room is full." Neila shed her bloody lab coat and found another, pristine white.

"Then where shall I go?"

"Every available bed is full with our own people. So are all the spare cots. I don't care where you go, Ms. Turnbow. I've done the necessary. Maybe there's room in the barn." She walked out, shoulders stiff with weariness.

A slight smile tugged at Bren's thin lips. "I guess your outing with Nate didn't turn out so well."

Lily found her shirt piled on top her ruined cargo pants, both dropped carelessly on the floor. Her movements jerky, she pulled it on and fastened buttons higgledy-piggledy, intent only on covering herself. Bloody and torn britches followed, and her coat. Only when she was fully dressed and her boots tied did she turn to the other woman who stood back and watched.

"Oh, I don't know." She made her voice as sweet and smooth as honey. "Nate defended me with all his might, then picked me up and carried me to safety. Not so bad for a first date."

Her perfect squelch might have been more effective if she hadn't had to cling to the wall as she staggered out of the hospital into the night.

Where do I go from here? She breathed deeply, trying to clear the dizzying effects of blood loss and pain. The frosty air felt sharp in her lungs, but it was clean. Blessedly clean. Snow blanketed the ground away from paths which, due to increased foot traffic in this emergency, had been trampled to mud. Lights showed in the barn where last night—could it possibly only be last night?—laughter and dancing had warmed the night.

Lily peered across the yard. The trestle tables piled high with trade good yesterday, now bore a different burden. Seven bodies lay side-by-side, wrapped in stained sheets. From deeper in the barn she heard the scrape of saws and a pounding of hammers. Building coffins, she expected. The O'Quinns would take care of their own. The enemy must still lie on the battlefield where wild beasts would scour their bones.

Cold, crackling like ice shards in water, ran through her in waves. What the hell was she supposed to do now? She wanted to leave this place. She wanted her old life and a civilized world.

A man's figure materialized wraith-like out of the night and headed toward her. Who now? Someone else coming to lay these deaths on her?

"Come with me, Lily," he said. "I've been sent to fetch you."

Nate? For a moment her heart leapt, but then she recognized Jacob Felix. So he'd survived his scout into the woods behind the horse herd. Praise be.

She gave a shuddering sigh. "Better not be seen with me, Jake. I told you that last night and it's even more true after today. I'm *persona non grata* around here."

His feet shifted, uncomfortable at the pathos in her voice. His glance toward the infirmary was troubled. "Don't believe I know what that is, person not grot, but I can take a guess. Not everybody thinks like Neila, and not everybody blames you for what happened today. Most folks know you were fighting for us."

Had she been fighting for the O'Quinns? Or only trying to save herself and rid the world of the abomination of Philip Barnes? Part of both, maybe.

"Fanta, for one," Jacob continued over the buzzing in her ears. He sounded far away. "And Rory, some of the others whose butt you saved when you used the horses against the Techs. Lucky they don't know shit about animals. And killing Screenmaster, well hell, that makes you a hero to the rest of us, the fighters out there today."

Lily swayed, putting out her hand to hold herself steady, surprised by how cold the porch rail felt against her fingers. "I didn't kill the dwarf for the clan, Jake. I want you to know that. I killed him because I was scared and because he needed to be destroyed. Call me the executioner who finally carried out Philip Barnes's sentence, but don't call me a hero."

"Well, sure you were scared. Who wouldn't be?" Apparently Jake forgave her this minor transgression. He reached for her arm, holding her upright. "Come with me, Lily. It ain't far."

Her voice rang in her ears like a faraway gong. "Where are we going?" A kind of agreement, she supposed.

He must've thought so, because he tugged, got her moving, one foot in front of the other. "Where nobody will give you a bad time. You'll see."

A blur of motion joined them; Sliver, his black-and-white coat echoing the colors of the ground beneath her feet. The dog stuck his wet nose into the hand not clinging to Jake's strong arm, as if he, too, would help her along. "Hey, dog," she whispered.

They went in the opposite direction of the barn, out where the only light was that reflected from the snow and where a few small houses crouched like toadstools beneath the trees.

"Don't think I'm going to make it," she said after a while. Black dots danced in front of her eyes. Her heart felt like a rundown clock, going slower and slower.

"You'll be all right." Jake bent to Sliver, gave him some instruction, whereupon the dog raced away. "Hang on now," he told Lily, and she did for as long as she could, wobbling and panting and about half bawling. Until finally she was plucked off her feet and carried swiftly toward the farthest house.

Wow. She hadn't been giving Jake enough credit, she thought muzzily, only to find the face staring down at her as they pushed through the swirling snow belonged to Nate, his expression even grimmer than when he'd helped her into the infirmary.

"Anybody see you?" he asked Jacob.

"Don't think so. Everybody is either busy or staying close to home. Women are fixing food for the wake. Tomorrow's gonna be bad." The boy strode along beside his longer-legged relative.

"You got that right." Nate's breath poofed out in a steamy cloud. "Best if she just disappears for a day or two."

"Yeah."

They went past two houses, finally reaching the last one. More of a cabin than a house, it had walls of peeled cedar logs, a roof of split shakes. Lily smelled wood smoke coming from the chimney, and now they were closer, she saw pinpoints of light blinking beyond heavily shuttered windows. Jacob darted ahead, knocked, and opened the door for Nate and her. Sliver slipped between Nate's legs, beating them inside.

A blast of welcoming warmth hit Lily in the face. The source, a fire crackling in a cast iron stove that sported a glass door, had a cooking pot spewing steam and a delectable aroma into the room. A single lamp showed Harrison Bell sitting in a big leather chair, a book in his lap. He creaked to his feet as they entered.

"Welcome to my home, Lily Turnbow," he said.

Sliver ran over and smiled up at his master who said, "Good dog," and then to Nate, "Lily is not as ambulatory as I was told."

Nate shifted his burden. "She's been running on pure grit, I think. Or maybe pride."

Harrison nodded. "Have much trouble persuading Neila to cut her loose, Jacob?"

"Hell, no." Something like disgust showed in Jake's dark eyes. "Neila kicked her out. I found her on the porch about ready to take a header into the snow."

Bell's face twisted. "Poor Neila. She's a changed woman since my son died. It's like her heart has been shrunken and dried into a knot."

"Grinch," Lily muttered, a reference none of the men understood.

"Where do you want me to put her?" Nate asked after a brief wait for her to explain, which she didn't. Too many unnecessary words; too much trouble to speak.

Bell pointed. "There's a bed in the loft. It's warm up there, and if I have visitors her presence will be less abrasive."

"Out of sight, out of mind." Nate used another of his oldisms, one that had been a favorite of Lily's grandma.

"Exactly." Harrison lit another, smaller lamp with a punk fired by the larger one, and handed it to Jake. "Show them way, Jacob. I'll dish up the stew. Have any of you eaten today?"

"Not me." Nate laughed. "Never gave it a thought."

"I don't remember," Jake said, yanking on the rope lowering the pull-down staircase to the loft. "But I'm hungry enough to eat magpie stew."

"We haven't come down to that yet," Bell answered, moving toward a wall cupboard. "I believe this is beef and vegetables. Your aunt Doris made it."

"It'll be good then."

"Always is."

Stew sounded good to Lily, too. She hoped Harrison included her in the invitation.

Bell's idea of a bed varied a bit from Lily's conception. This was a pallet made up of a sheep wool affair that looked like an extra long dog bed, with a couple hand-woven blankets tossed on top and a thick puffy pillow. Adding to the dog bed resemblance, it was laid out on the smooth plank floor.

Nate's knees creaked as he set her on the pallet, then rose and stood looking down at her. "I hope you heal fast, Lily."

She heard a kind of portent in his tone, more meaningful than his words. Was he hinting of another round of trouble coming her way? So who cared? For now she only wanted to sleep, or even to lapse into unconsciousness deep enough to hide the pain and fear nagging at her.

Without speaking, she settled on the pallet, finding it less uncomfortable than she'd expected. Warmth rose from the room below. Presently she heard the clink of forks on plates as the men dipped into Doris' stew pot and sleepily, allowing her eyes to drift closed. Maybe they'd save her some for later.

Sometime later, she jerked awake at a preemptory rapping on Harrison Bell's door.

Chapter 23

With Lily settled, curled on the pallet like a tired puppy, Nate cat-footed his way down the staircase to where Harrison had pulled another chair up to the table. Dipping slabs of sourdough bread into the thick stew, the three concentrated on eating. Harrison ate with an old man's curbed appetite, Jacob as if he were on the verge of starvation, and Nate somewhere in between. The three ate silently, withholding conversation until Harrison, replete, pushed back his chair and sipped at his steaming tea.

"All right, nephew," he said to Nate, "tell me. What am I to do with her?"

Nate had been wondering this himself. "Keeping her out of Neila's sight will do for a start. After that? Who knows?"

"What if they decide to kill her?" Jake asked, and when the older men stared at him, he said defensively, "It ain't my idea. I overheard Bannion say something about a death sentence—not mentioning any names—when he told Peter Shandy to come to meeting tomorrow night. First order of business is for the council to figure out what went wrong with the fight."

Nate snorted and drew on one of his 'oldisms.' "It isn't rocket science, for God's sake. Outnumbered and too lax in our security. Simple."

"Rocket science?" Jake said wonderingly. "What is that?" He stopped as Harrison shook his head. "They'll finger Lily for everything," he went on. "That's my guess." He scowled. "What's rocket science, Nate?"

"Hell, I don't know. Not for sure." Impatiently, Nate waved him aside. "You been called to council, Harrison?"

"No."

"Me either. You sure about the when and where, Jake?"

"Yep. Headquarters. Bannion told me to have Selkirk set up chairs for a dozen."

"Closed meeting," Harrison said, frowning. "And they're leaving us out, Nate."

Nate's glance went toward the loft where Lily slept. "Trying to. They're gonna pull a shitty on her and don't want any argument."

"Neila's doing, I'm afraid. I don't know why that woman has grown so bitter. Or why she's taken against Lily Turn-bow the way she has." Harrison shook his head.

A rapping on the door, the thuds hard and angry like the beating of closed fists, brought Nate to his feet. He reached for his knife before remembering where he was and halting the motion. "You expecting anybody, Harrison?"

The old man's face set in stern lines. "No."

The thuds came again, louder.

"Your visitor is a impatient," Nate observed.

Harrison's lips clamped. "Get it for me, please, Jacob, before our guest is awakened. Be polite. We don't know who it is."

"Sure we do," Nate said, as though he were certain. "Bannion."

True to Nate's prediction, when Jake opened the door, Bannion stood on the porch. his fist raised for another hammer blow.

Also, as Nate had forecast earlier, they saw the snow was falling harder now, dropping out of the sky at a rate that soon would cover the dead at Wolf Point Crossing. The twin lines of Nate and Jacob's footprints had already almost disappeared.

Bannion pushed past Jake, snow scattering from his shoulders and the brim of his hat. He gave Jacob a hard stare. "What are you doing here, Felix? Shouldn't you be on guard duty?"

Harrison clicked his tongue, remonstrating without words. "You know the boy stays here a good part of the time, Bannion. Cut him some slack."

"And I ain't on duty, boss," Jake said. "I did my share at the fight. You ordered the junior patrollers to stand guard."

"Argh." Bannion ignored the excuse and stood, surveying the room. Nate barely wiped the smile from his face before his cousin started in on him. "What about you? You stay here a good part of the time too, Cuz?"

"Just visiting and staying warm. Kept me from cooking my own supper."

"Sit down and eat," Harrison invited in a cool voice. "Aunt Doris fixed our supper and she made enough for a haying crew."

For a moment Bannion looked as if he'd take the older man up on it, but then he brushed the invitation aside. "I'm looking for Lily Turnbow. Bren said the woman left the infirmary under her own power, but now nobody knows where she is."

A quick shake of Nate's head stilled Jake's intake of breath.

"She left, huh?" he said. "I wonder how that came about? Hope somebody friendly took her in. I think she's had a somewhat trying day."

Bannion gave him a hard look. "I don't want her running loose in the compound. Hard tellin' what'll happen if she thinks somebody is insulting her."

"Is *somebody* planning on doing that?" Nate asked, innocence personified.

Harrison's gaze sharpened, while Jacob's dark eyes blazed with understanding.

"Mind if I look through your house, Harrison?" Bannion had already taken a step onto the stairway to the loft.

"As a matter of fact, I do." Harrison rose to his feet. "I'd consider it an abuse of my hospitality."

Bannion stopped with his foot on the lowest rung. "I know you think you owe this woman something, Uncle—" He used the reference of respect. "—but I'd say the debt has been repaid."

"Would you?" Harrison smiled. "Perhaps I hold my life in greater esteem than you do, nephew."

Bannion had the grace to flush. "That isn't what I meant. We've taken her in, given her medical care, food, a place to stay. That cancels out your debt."

"Don't presume to cancel my debts, Bannion. I make those decisions."

"What about her killing Screenmaster and saving all our asses today?" Jacob cut in, low, beneath his breath and barely audible. He'd come back to the table and slouched in his chair where Nate hoped he'd stay.

"That's what we want to talk with her about," Bannion said.

"*We*, cousin? You and who else?" A trace of anger crept into Nate's voice.

"Don't try me, Nate," Bannion said. "This hasn't been my best day, either. And let me remind you *I'm* the sheriff. Our people rely on me to keep them safe. I know Lily Turn-bow has helped Harrison and the clan. If I thought she meant us harm she'd be dead by now with no chance of coming back. But she's not one of us. I'll thank you all to remember that. She's not like us." Ignoring Harrison's irate motion, he continued up the stairs, his tread heavy.

Nate waited for the outburst sure to follow, but other than the shuffling of Bannion's footsteps overhead, there was silence. He looked at Harrison, whose face wrinkled in puzzlement.

"What the heck?" Jake began with a puzzled look, but Nate shushed him as a few moments later Bannion clomped back down the stairs.

"My apologies, Harrison, cousins," Bannion said. "I guessed wrong, thinking you'd taken her in." He turned even grimmer. "So where the hell can she be? Gonna be trouble if she isn't there."

Nate kept himself from leaping to his feet only by strenuous effort. He hoped his expression wasn't quite as dumbfounded as Harrison's or Jake's. How could Bannion not have seen Lily? "Trouble if she isn't where?" he asked.

"At the meeting tomorrow. At Selkirk's house. You'd better be there, too." He glanced at Harrison. "Both of you."

Shifting attention to Jake, the sheriff's dark eyes looked like they were trying to bore a hole through the kid, probably the weakest link if only because he hadn't yet learned the art of deception—or of controlling his expression. "You know where she is, don't you, Felix?"

Jake's feet did an almost imperceptible dance. "Me? No. Hell no!" He may have sounded a little too emphatic.

"Yeah, well, if any of you happen to see her, tell her some of us want to talk to her about what happened today."

"Could be Lily's not up to a long conversation," Nate reminded him. "She's hurt worse than you or Neila seem to think she is. I expect she's gone to ground somewhere to lick her wounds."

Bannion hmphed. "Makes her sound like a dog. Neila said her wound wasn't much."

"Neila has her own axe to grind, Bannion. You've seen how she is, mean as a maverick cow. And Neila wasn't around during the fight. Lily lost a lot of blood."

The sheriff's hard stare encompassed them all before he went to the door and opened it—none too soon in Nate's opinion. He seemed oblivious to the blast of cold wind he let in. The lamp flames flickered behind their globes. "She's got until tomorrow noon, then she needs to show up at head-quarters," he warned them. "Maybe you'd better see to it, Nate, since you've become her champion."

"Who, me? I'm nobody's champion. But I figure fair's fair." He rose to his feet and sniffed the freshening wind. "There's a big storm coming." He tasted the truth of it on his tongue. "You got that right," Bannion said as he left, banging the door behind him in a minor fit of temper.

Nate didn't know if he meant the weather outside, or the difference of opinion regarding matters certain to shake clan O'Quinn, but right now it didn't matter. He turned to Harrison and Jake, his face full of bewilderment. "Well, now. This is a strange kettle of fish. Do you suppose Bannion is losing his eyesight?"

But Jake was already talking over the top of Harrison. "Why didn't he see her?" he said, drowning Harrison's softer, "Where can she be? There's no place to hide up there."

Moving together, the three pushed forward, mounting the stair two at a time to the silent loft.

*****

Lily, drifting in and out of semi-consciousness thanks to recurring twinges every time she moved her leg, became fully alert in time to hear Bannion giving his speech about the responsibility he bore his people. Pontificating, she thought wryly, like every other political being she'd ever heard. A smile hovered. *Wonder what he'd think if someone pointed that out to him.* Except his emphatic declaration of her outsider status wasn't quite so amusing.

It was a tossup with one side of her brain thinking sarcastically about how devoted that made him, not that he knew any other way when it came to his people. Meanwhile, the other side was thinking, no, wishing, she could be part of this clan and come under his protection. What he'd said about a meeting though. She neither liked the sound of that, nor wanted any part of it.

So, hearing his approach, she stifled a groan and rolled off the pallet, straightening the covers with a sweep of her hand. Crawling into a niche formed in the space between the outside wall and the stone chimney, she crunched into a ball. At least it was warm there, in the shadows. Not entirely hidden, in the normal course of things, but nothing much was normal anymore. Silently, she drew the cloaking illusion she'd started calling her "you can't see me" trick around herself. The core of her presence faded to vapor. Bannion didn't see a thing, although he stared hard a couple times into the narrow space where she sat. If he'd poked into the seeming void with a finger, she would've cried out, the illusion lost

But he didn't. No birds here to speak to him, she thought with a touch of humor. Then, even after he'd gone she sat still, waiting for Nate, Harrison, and Jake. A grin quirked. Another surprise to spring on them. Should she—or should she not?

They climbed through the floor opening and stared around, gaping like backcountry bumpkins at a circus. Great. And she was the main act. She gave them plenty of time before a small huff of breath escaped. Nate's head jerked around from where he'd been looking out the small window, locked from the inside.

What had he been thinking, that she'd jumped from the second story window?

"Lily?" Jake whispered.

She sighed and dropped the illusion. "Here."

Nate was looking right at her when she became visible, and she could tell he wasn't particularly pleased with her little trick. Jake, naturally, admired the ability.

"I don't suppose you could teach me how to do that?" he said wistfully.

"Doubtful, Jake, since I don't know how it works myself. Sorry. It just happens." She stretched her hand out to him. "Help me up, please."

But it was Nate who reached her first, drawing her to her feet and steadying her shaky stance. "You thinking of becoming the next Screenmaster?" he asked and, sensing his disapproval, she kept quiet.

"I suppose you heard what Bannion had to say," Harrison said. He seemed less taken aback by her ability than the other two, but perhaps he hadn't quite caught the full effect.

Lily smiled a little. "Yep. Couldn't help it. What do they want with me, Mr. Bell? Should I be concerned?" She noticed Jake's fidget. "Or scared?" She made her way back to the pallet and, stifling a groan, eased onto it.

"If you listened to Bannion, then you know the same as we do. But I'd advise resting while you have the chance." Harrison flipped the blanket over her. A heavy woolen thing with two red stripes, it effectively warded off the cold.

Which she needed since his words were not exactly re-assuring. And she was too tired to think about Bannion and his prejudices anymore.

"Old army trick for warriors. Eat and sleep when you can," Nate said, earning himself a puzzled look from Jake. "Read it somewhere."

Lily's eyelids fluttered shut, wishing she could blot out this whole damn world with the dark. How could it even be real? What other trials were forming for her to bear? Her grandma always quoted a grand bit of philosophy saying, "what didn't kill you made you stronger." Grandpa insisted the quote came from some song lyrics and Mom, who'd still been with them then, said it was a cliché.

Grandma's theory sounded a like so much hooey to Lily, set forth by someone who had no concept of this altered world, complete with mutants and war. Gran frequently came up with stuff like that. She would've gotten on well with Nate, the two of them spouting clichés and weird quotes. Lily could hear her now, her face lit with fun and her gravelly voice countering Mom's complaint by saying clichés came into general usage because they were true. Lily hoped Gran was right this time, but judging from the tension in this room right now, she wouldn't bank on it.

Harrison had been watching her. "Lily's exhausted, " he said. "We'll let her get some sleep. You boys come back in the morning and we'll go to Bannion's meeting together."

But solitude and rest, she discovered, wasn't actually what he had in mind. Nuh, uh. Five minutes later, having shooed Nate and Jacob from the house, he returned, bearing two cups of strong tea, a bowl of the stew, and a determined expression. In a way, she didn't mind. Not in view of Bannion's news…demands…warning…whatever.

"This secrecy," he said, settling himself on a wooden kitchen chair that had lost its back, and handing her the dish, "has gone on long enough. Both sides, you and us. I don't know what Bannion's thinking about, keeping you in the dark. My opinion, Lily, you deserve answers."

At last— this was for real.

"Two days ago I would've settled for just knowing the history of the last hundred years," she said. "I wanted a grasp of what my options were for the future."

"And now?"

"Now I doubt that I have any future. I think they want to kill me." There. She'd set it out baldly, let him know she was aware of which way the rope twisted. She lifted the spoon to her mouth.

"I'm afraid you may be right about some of our people. Let

me see if I can explain where Selkirk and Bannion are coming from." He fell silent, staring down at the gnarled hands resting on his knees as she chewed. "The clan's experience in dealing with strangers isn't good, Lily. In the early years, or so we're told, we tried to help all comers. They had a nasty habit of being untrustworthy. A newly fledged Cross-up, for one, who almost destroyed us. He came to the compound—the Quicks, O'Quinns, and Bells had already joined forces by then—and we took him in. So happens he had an army of Cits waiting to attack when he'd spied out our defenses. Except for the first Nate and his dad, the Quick family was wiped out. Of course, so was the Cross-up. And the Cits, to the last man."

Lily drew in a shaky breath. "I see. Makes the way the clan views me sound almost reasonable."

"I'm glad you understand."

"It doesn't make me any happier about the situation."

"No. I expect not."

"What can I do, Mr. Bell?" Food forgotten for the moment, she sat straighter in her nest of blankets. "I've fought on the clan's side. I've been wounded in their service. I've even killed a dreaded Cross-up. Is there anything that will win hearts and change minds? All this distrust seems a self-perpetuating state of affairs. Coming and going, fighting and killing. Somebody needs to take a step forward and try to make peace.

"Not everyone is as suspicious of you as Selkirk and Bannion."

"And Neila," she interrupted.

Harrison nodded gravely. "And Neila. But keep in mind Selkirk and Bannion have the task of keeping the clan safe. If they falter, the clan suffers, maybe even dies."

"So I'm to be a sacrifice, willing or not. A continuance of your isolation." She pounded the floor with her fist. Down below, the dog barked in alarm.

"Easy, Sliver," Harrison called to him, hushing the animal. "And we do take in strangers upon occasion. Jacob's people most recently. The House group, twenty-five years ago. The Shandys about the same. We have strictly avoided becoming in-bred. And Nate makes friends when he goes trekking. Sometimes he brings people in. Sometimes one of us goes out."

"But I'm not welcome." Lily couldn't help the bitter tinge in her voice.

"No Cross-ups."

Time to change the subject, she thought, unable bear this one any longer. "About the Mags . . ." Just thinking about them made her ill. "They are—or were—human, weren't they? Does anyone know what caused some people to turn into whatever they are now?"

"The Mag mutation was just getting into full swing when I was born. Scientists, if we still had any, could probably tell you. For us it's just guesswork, but we've heard various reasons. A worldwide release of chemicals; some kind of plague; cannibalism, among others." He ticked these items off on his fingers. "None of us know exactly why some people mutated and some passed on the best traits they had. We've been too busy trying to stay alive to find out."

"What has happened to the rest of the world, Mr. Bell?" This question had been burning Lily and no one she'd asked knew the answer. Bren, the medical aid merely scowled at her and shrugged; Jacob said he didn't know; Pike, the trader, remarked that in the last ten years a few goods had started arriving from across the big ocean. From a far-off island nation came stuff like a big fruit with a spiny top, which Lily deduced was a pineapple, and real coffee the dark-skinned trader called Kona. And from "Yrp" came bolts of cloth and medicines and metal goods.

"We don't know about the wide world. The story passed down from generation to generation is that most of the earth burned. The huge cities, which fared the worst; many of the forests; the grasslands. Burned, then froze. For ten years it was cold and dark and dry. Only small folds of land survived." He waved his hand in a circling gesture. "Such as this one. Like I told you, local families gathered together here, fighting off bandits who tried to take it from us. We bred within these families and we stayed clean and protected our resources. To this day, as you can see. On the outside, disease took many who survived the big bang and first fires, then the cold and the famine took more. Soon there was nothing for them to eat, except each other. But not us." Well-earned pride shone out of his dark eyes. "Then it got better, the sun came out. Rain and snow watered the land, grass grew again, and trees and food crops. And we became as you see us now."

Lily shuddered. Three hundred forty million people in the United States alone. How many had died? *No.* How many had lived? That was the question. Her grandparents. What about them? She couldn't absorb the story all at once. She'd known—and yet she hadn't. With Harrison's telling, the event became all too real. She closed her eyes.

"I don't think I want to hear anymore," she said. She'd meant to ask about Cross-ups; now she didn't care.

Harrison rose to his feet. "No, I don't suppose you do. But I thought you needed to know what's out there, beyond our boundaries. In case—"

She looked up. "In case I get lucky and Bannion and Selkirk decide to banish me instead of killing me?"

He pursed his lips. "We'll try not to let that happen. Nate and I."

"Try?"

"Nate won't let them kill you, and I, though old and not so important to the clan anymore will back him up." Shrugging, he edged toward the stair. "Finish your stew, then get some sleep, Lily. Regain your strength. I think you're going to need it."

Sleep? After what he'd told her? Never happen, she thought, but when she'd polished off the stew, quite suddenly, strength sapped by her wound, against all odds, she drifted off.

*****

In the way people have of sleeping through fire truck sirens and train whistles, then awaken at the slightest footfall, Lily's eyes snapped open at the click of the outside door latch. The room below was silent except for a slight noise she finally recognized as the dog lapping water.

She lay still, feeling the empty house around her. Harrison had gone out and she believed she knew where. She had no idea how many hours she'd been asleep. It felt like a long time. In fact, daylight shone through the small attic window, so it must be the next day.

Which meant Bannion's time limit may have already come and gone. The meeting. That's where the guys would be. Where she should be.

Feeling better, stronger, for last evening's food and the rest, she yawned, stretching her arms overhead before tossing the blanket aside. Her head was clear as she sat up and pulled on her packer boots, deliberately ignoring the recurring ache in her leg. Neila's stitches were holding.

Traversing the steep staircase proved a bit of a problem, but she made it without falling, wondering how Nate had ever gotten her up in the first place. The dog waited for her at the bottom step.

"Hey, Sliver. Hey, boy." She caressed his perked ears and gave him a friendly pat. Nose twitching at her scent, his tail wagged a single time.

Conscious of Bannion's meeting already underway, she took a moment to investigate Harrison's home, Sliver padding behind her. There were only two doors off the main room. One led to a small bedroom, kept spic and span with a well-made bedstead and a beautifully crafted chest of drawers. The other to a bathroom of the approximate size found in most camp trailers. She used the facilities, washing her face and combing tangles from her hair before clubbing it back in a neat ponytail. A glance in Harrison's shaving mirror showed her face drawn and washed out, looking several years older than the twenty-seven years she claimed. *One hundred and twenty-seven years.*

And then, although she'd been running on instinct, she poured herself a cup of tepid tea from the kettle keeping warm at the back of the stove, and sat at the table with the dog at her feet.

So, they, meaning Nate, Harrison, and probably Jake, young as he was, had gone over to the meeting. *Meeting!* She scoffed at the bland word. Were she to show up, it'd be more like a trial, with her the defendant. Who would be the judge, she wondered. Bannion? Or big, cold-eyed Selkirk, the clan's headman?

An inner voice urged procrastination. Let Nate handle his cousins, if he could. Let Harrison, as elder statesman of the clan, speak to his people on her behalf. Lily cast a longing look toward the loft where the pallet, warm from the heat risen from the stove, beckoned. And then, sighing, she set her cup aside, the pottery clicking against the hard wood table, and stood.

Whatever the meeting—trial—brought, she'd take the verdict first hand. No secondhand news. Better to meet trouble head-on than let it sneak up on you from behind. That's the kind of woman her grandparents had raised. That's the kind of woman the Border Patrol had trained her to be.

Chapter 24

The dog slipped outside in front of her when Lily opened the door. Met with thumb-size snowflakes flying in her face in dizzying spirals, she stood a moment, acclimating to the cold and wind and utter darkness. A couple hundred yards to the south a single yellow light winked, shining intermittently through the storm.

"What about it, Sliver? Is that where I'm supposed to go?"

Snuffling his nose through the loose snow, Sliver grinned up at her and shook flakes from his fur. Lily took it to mean yes.

"Lead the way," she told him and, as if only waiting for this release, the dog bounded off. Lily followed as quickly as her leg allowed, struggling to keep to the trail he broke.

Nate had wanted to spare her this meeting, she knew. Likewise Harrison and Jake. For some reason she had gained these three as allies, and the last thing she wanted was for them to be ostracized by their own people. Inadequate reward for their partisanship. If Bannion and Selkirk, with Neila's agreement, would give her time to heal, she'd leave here willingly. Or, and here honesty got the better of her, maybe not so willingly. This was a dangerous world now for a newby alone, let alone a Cross-up woman. But she'd come to the conclusion this was the only correct solution. The O'Quinns didn't want a Cross-up in their midst? Fair enough. She had no desire to stay where she wasn't wanted. And it wasn't as if she didn't have a destination calling to her. She did. The need to see her grandparent's old home—her old home—drew her in like a fish on a line.

A blast of wind drove snow against her face as she pushed through a drift, a shiver pulsing in her aching leg. If the O'Quinns banished her right now, how would she survive? She had no resources.

Alone and surrounded by Mags. A scene right out of one of grandpa's western novels. But were the shrieking savages the Mags? Or were they the O'Quinn clan? She suspected she'd find out soon enough.

Sliver led her straight to headquarters where Nate and she had met Bannion yesterday morning. Even through the heavy door she could hear voices raised in dissension. Brushing a film of snow off a side window, she peeped into an ordinary dining room. As many as a dozen men and women were standing or sitting around a large dining room table. Highlighted by oil lamps hanging from the ceiling, their shadows bounced on the snow-covered porch as periodically one paced across the room. One man waved his arms, looking like a boxer sparring with an invisible opponent.

She heard Jake's voice, and although even she couldn't make out what he said, he was loud enough Sliver growled in distress. It seemed her cue to fling open the door and step inside on a blast of cold and snow.

The immediate effect was that everyone quit talking. Lily had time to see the appalled look on Jake's face, and the resigned look on Nate's. Harrison, if she wasn't mistaken, actually had a little twinkle in his eye, and it was he who spoke first.

"You have a sense of the dramatic, Ms. Turnbow. Nicely done. We were just discussing you."

Unsure whether to claim this as a compliment or not, Lily nodded. "I believe I'm the guest of honor at this party. The least I could do is show up."

"Very clever," Selkirk said. He sat at the head of the table, a cup of tea and a half-eaten piece of pie in front of him. "What Nate calls a play on words, if I'm not mistaken."

Nate, leaning on the back of the wooden kitchen chair in which Jake sat, shrugged. He didn't appear all that playful to Lily.

"More a use of irony," she said, "not that it matters."

Bannion glowered from where he stood propped against an elaborate oak mantelpiece. Lily remembered it from the Poundstone's last remodeling of the house, old even then. With a sense of shock, she realized the place must be almost two hundred years old by now. Ancient in Northwestern terms. The O'Quinns and Bells had taken good care of things, one item in their favor.

Occupied in memories, she missed Bannion's sharp question. "I beg your pardon?" she said. "My mind was wandering, thinking of how this place has stayed the same all these years. The last time I was here…"

A slash of his hand cut her off. "Do you think this is a game, Ms. Turnbow? It's no game to any of us. I asked where you went after you left the infirmary? I spent an hour looking for you."

"Out of concern for me, sheriff?" she asked softly. "How nice. Or did you have a different reason?"

He never batted an eye. "Both."

Hmm. What to say? She wasn't about to admit to hiding out in Harrison's house. A thought occurred. "I took Neila's advice. She mentioned a barn as the proper place for me, so I found a spare stall."

"Which barn?" Bannion's voice was hard. "I searched them all."

"Really?" she said coolly. "I guess you weren't as thorough as you thought. Although, after a day like the one yesterday, you have plenty of excuse. What difference does it make? I'm here now."

Despite her careless fib, he cast a suspicious eye on Harrison who never so much as blinked. She thought she was the only one who noticed Jake's tiny twitch.

"So what is it you want of me, sheriff?" she asked, reclaiming his attention.

He exchanged a look with his cousin Selkirk, the clan leader. Whispers among the others hinted at disagreement in the ranks of decision makers. She recognized a few, namely Bannion's own Sergeant Zelnor, and another whom she had supplied with a horse during the great stampede. Neila, thank goodness, had skipped the meeting although, Lily suspected, only because the wounded claimed all her attention. She may have cast a vote in absentia.

But Lily was tired of pussyfooting around. Almost too weak to stand, she'd brought the question into the open, although her heart sank at the stony stares the others fixed on her.

She managed a short laugh. "Not to pin a medal on my chest, I see. Not even a 'well done, Lily. Thanks for helping out.'"

"Screenmaster and his saiclers wouldn't have showed up if it weren't for you," an older man said. His arm was severed just below the elbow, an old wound, the sleeve neatly pinned back.

"Maybe, maybe not, Garrett." Nate spoke out of turn. "Rondo's prisoner indicated they'd planned to come in the spring anyway. Said he wished they'd waited."

"O'Quinn territory has grown big enough everyone wants a piece of us," the horseman put in, an ambiguous statement that might have meant anything.

"Or will try to test our mettle," Selkirk agreed unexpectedly. "If Ms.Turnbow was to remain here, we'd have'em coming at us every time we turned around, their forces ever larger." He pushed his cup away, sloshing liquid over the side. "They're gonna want her powers to use for themselves. I don't see any way around it." His jaw set. "And I won't stand for it."

Lily's knees shook and she locked them, hoping no one had seen. Like a kitten cornered by coyotes, she dare not show weakness. "That sounds remarkably like a threat, Mr. O'Quinn. You have two choices that I can see."

"Do I?" he said, almost whispering. "And what would those *two* choices be?"

Lily's voice dropped to match. "You can either take me into the clan, or—" For a moment, she couldn't bring herself to say the other.

"Or?"

In a corner of her mind she was aware of Jacob saying to Nate, "What does she mean, Nate?" and Nate saying, "Hush," on a ragged note.

"Or you can kill me here and now. Or try," she finished. A collective indrawn breath kept everyone silent, except Jacob, who said, "What?" After a few heartbeats, she went on, "Not that I will take that lying down, mind you. I hope you won't forget I have a few weapons at my disposal." There. She'd made herself clear.

"Yes," Bannion said. "We're aware of that. But understand this, Lily Turnbow. We're only one family. If you stay, a bigger family, or a warrior cult or another group like the saiclers is going to want your powers. They're going to come after us and, I fear, eventually, win."

A man at the far end of the room scooted his chair away from the table with a heavy scraping of legs, then reversed that action. Someone said, "Sweet Jesus," on a prayerful note, and the rest fidgeted and coughed and made restless movements with their hands. Only Lily and Bannion were immobile, their eyes locked.

Nate, his voice laconic, broke the silence after a minute. "A Mexican standoff," he said.

Bannion moved impatiently. "Make sense."

"He means we're at a stalemate." Lily smiled. "And he's right." A movement of her pinky finger sent a fireball the size of a pinhead to the old oak floor at Bannion's feet where it charred a disproportionately large hole. He ground the burn with his boot sole before a blaze could start and glared at Nate as if the situation were his fault.

"Here," Selkirk said. "Don't you be tearing up my house."

Lily ignored him and sucked in a deep breath. "Of course, you could try making some of these factions into allies. Join together, fight together for the common good."

"We'll not be taken over by anyone," Selkirk said unequivocally.

"Hence the meaning of *ally*," Lily said, "and I speak of negotiating from a position of strength, either real strength or assumed."

"You don't know what you're talking about," Bannion said.

Seemingly careless, she shrugged. "Well, then, there is a third option I can suggest."

She'd thought this offer over carefully on the way to the meeting. Even now a hollow feeling in her gut warned of the loneliness, the danger, the isolation that was in her future. That's if she had any future at all.

The council members stirred, but said nothing, leaving the question to the sheriff. He obliged. "What option?"

"Give me a horse, some supplies. I'll leave the ranch." Her head lifted. "I want to check out my grandparents' place. See if anything is still there. If there are bones, I'll bury them. Maybe my cousins lived. Maybe—"

"You'll carry a grudge." Bannion dropped his casual stance by the fireplace. "The clan can't sleep as soundly at night with you out there. They'd always be wondering when you'd take a notion to drop a fireball on'em."

"Take a notion?" Lily's eyes blazed, sudden wrath showing no matter that she tried to veil the signs. Some of them might be afraid of her anger. "I'm a Border Patrol agent. I joined the force to serve and protect my country and its people. I took an oath that means the world to me! Why should this purpose change? From what I've seen, this country, no, this world, needs more people with genuine altruistic objectives."

Someone whispered, "Altruistic?"

"Humane," Lily snapped. "Selfless. Forgiving. Giving!"

Selkirk stood up, started to speak.

She flashed a hand at him, making him dodge as though expecting another fireball, and she shook her head pityingly. "Look at you, on tenterhooks looking for an attack in your own home.

"Liberty and justice for all. We used to say that. Has anybody here even heard of the Pledge of Allegiance? Those words were part of it."

A few of the O'Quinns looked to Nate, who jerked his chin. "I read it in a book. Sorry to say the words might be fine, but they don't mean much, Lily. Not now."

Stretching her leg, she tried to ease the ache. "They do to me, Nate. They mean I won't drop a fireball on anybody who isn't attacking me." Staring hard at Bannion, she added, "They mean I won't bomb Spokane just because a few saiclers from there followed a madman here. They mean I won't slaughter Mags for the pure hell of it. If I find they need hunted, I'll hunt them, but I require proof. Liberty and justice for all."

Selkirk snorted. "Ain't that fine, though. Sounds about

what a Cross-up would say just before lambasting you with something nasty."

"Then perhaps," Lily said, her voice pitched low and warm and sweet, "Bannion can ask his birds to watch his back, or Nate can call down a protective storm, or Neila can shut off a blood supply as an act of mercy or should a patient prove inconvenient. Perhaps Harrison can watch the horizon with his eyes closed and you, Selkirk, can practice plausible deniability to cover them all. Folks will believe you. They always have. You have the knack." Her gaze swept the room. "You all have the *knack*."

She didn't need her extra sharp hearing to make her aware of butts shifting uncomfortably in chairs. For a moment she would've recalled her words—until Nate chuckled.

"You aren't supposed to have twigged to that, Lily," he said.

Selkirk stuck a fork in his leftover pie like he wished it was a saber slicing through Lily's gut. "Nothing to twig to, Nate, and you know it. We're not mages." He glared around the table. "We're not. We've learned to read signs. To pay attention to what's going on around us. That's all."

Lily recalled Bren's panic and the look of concentration on Neila's face when the girl with the severed hand had begun spurting blood again. Then the abrupt, seemingly miraculous easing of the situation. Nope. She wasn't mistaken. Neila had used power. Lily had felt it, even tasted it in the air. And Neila had known what she was doing, nothing accidental.

"Oh, please," she scoffed, low in her throat. "Do not try that on me."

Bannion refused to meet her level gaze.

Suddenly, her leg buckled under her. Lily grabbed the back of the nearest chair, whose present occupant leapt to his feet like he'd been singed by fire. Damn the O'Quinns, she thought muzzily, groping her way around and collapsing onto the seat. Making everyone afraid of her, as if the method she'd used to defeat Philip Barnes hadn't drawn enough unwelcome attention.

As though the man's relinquishment of his chair was due to good manners rather than the flash of fear she saw cross his face, Lily murmured, "Thank you."

Ignoring what sounded like a whole hive of bees droning in her head, she glanced around the room. Several of the council members refused to meet her eyes, choosing to fiddle with tea cups or cough or whisper to whomever sat beside them. She'd known herself to be the subject under discussion when she walked in, but the way they avoided looking at her increased her tension. At some time or another over the past several days, she had exchanged greetings with most of them. A few words, pleasantries.

Anger flashed like bright lightning behind her eyes. The clan didn't act terribly appreciative of her efforts on their behalf. Nor even sympathetic of her wound. Or if they were, they hid their support well.

"So," she said, controlling her voice with an effort. "I'll require a horse and a few days supplies. I've earned the supplies in return for my services. And, according to your own records, the success of your horse herd over the years can be attributed in large part to the strength of my mare Heathen's mustang blood. I believe you owe me a replacement."

"Hold on," Selkirk said, but Harrison quieted him with a shake of his head.

"I, personally, owe you more than that, Lily," he said. "I owe you my life. It'll be done. Your pick of a horse out of my portion. A mare?"

"By preference. Thank you."

"You're taking a lot on yourself, Harrison." Selkirk rested his fingertips on the table and stared down at each of the committee members in turn. "We should put this to a vote."

"I vote we keep Lily with us." Jacob, his young face paler than it had been during the midst of the fighting, spoke up.

"You don't have a vote," Selkirk said. "In fact, I don't know what you're doing here."

Jake glared at the clan leader. "I'm the last of my family, Selkirk. I inherit their vote."

"You're sixteen, Jacob. Talk to me in two years."

Harrison heaved his thin body off the straight-backed kitchen chair, rubbing his chest where his wound must've been bothering him. "I'd vote for you to stay as well, Lily, but I sense you wouldn't be comfortable among us. Not that I blame you."

"Think they used to have something they called an attitude adjustment," Nate said. "We need to learn the technique. I vote she stays."

He was funny without meaning to be, Lily thought, smiling crookedly at him, but as she studied the grim faces around her, she knew how the vote, now it had been called, would go. Nor was she wrong, not completely. More of the voters, who'd also been fighters today, turned a little more compassionate than she anticipated.

But there was Selkirk, who hammered his hand on the table and said strongly, "We should kill her."

And Nate, who said just as strongly, "Who you got picked to do the executing, cousin? Yourself? Because I won't do it."

Bannion muttered, "Damn it, don't look at me," which caused a twitch of Selkirk's brows and took Lily by surprise.

The clan's verdict came as a surprise when counting the influence Selkirk and Bannion held over the rest. Banishment, they said, conceding her right to a horse and supplies. The time frame was not as lenient.

"We ought to make you leave tonight." Bannion looked tired as he said this, and just a little stricken, as if he realized the injustice of their decision but was impelled by his duty as sheriff to enforce Selkirk's and the family's edict. "But tomorrow will do. Go back to whatever hidey-hole you found, Lily Turnbow. I don't want to know where it is. Meet me at the horse barn in the morning." He looked up. "This meeting is adjourned."

Almost as one, the committee members rose stiffly from their seats and began stuffing arms into coats sleeves and jamming hats on heads. They were a silent group. Only Nate remained still, and after a period of consideration where he tapped his teeth and stared at her, finally spoke.

"Hold it," he said. Everyone jerked around to look at him. Dropping what Lily knew was a casual pretense, he took his place beside his cousin at the fireplace, his shoulders set in an aggressive posture. "Seems to me somebody needs to do a little of this negotiating Lily mentioned."

Selkirk and Bannion wore matching scowls. "Negotiate what?" Selkirk demanded.

"Lily killed Screenmaster. In my opinion, the spoils of war belong to her."

"Spoils of war?" Selkirk demanded. In the background, the others whispered.

"Screenmaster's wagon, his horses, his supplies." Nate winked at Lily. "He had a regular little rolling home. It's every bit as good as Neila's camper."

"Excellent idea," Harrison said approvingly, while Jacob, a knit hat crumpled in his hand, nodded and grinned. Most of the others shrugged.

"Wait a minute," Selkirk's scowl grew more fearsome. "How do you figure she's entitled. She gets a horse and enough supplies for a week. That's enough."

Nate shook his head. "She's earned much more than that, Selkirk, and you know it."

Lily's heart felt squeezed as gladness poured through

her. Not friendless. Not completely alone, after all. The connection between Nate and her meant something. She knew it now.

Selkirk protested again, before Bannion said loudly, "Call a vote."

"What?" Selkirk's question was a protest.

"Call a vote," Bannion repeated, making Nate smile. "She rode Nog, you know. Nobody rides Nog but me. He won't let'em. If she can, she ain't all bad." His dark eye caught at the others. "What do you say? Rondo? Let her have the 'spoils of war?'"

Sergeant Zelnor was already at least halfway in Lily's camp. "All right with me," he said. "Can't imagine anybody here'd want anything that belonged to the dwarf anyhow."

"You know where I stand," Harrison said. "Aye."

"Aye," voted the head of the family whose daughter had lost a hand.

"Aye," said the Shandy patriarch, evidently remembering Lily had given up a bed for their daughter.

"No," said a woman who stared with longing eyes at Selkirk.

"Aye," Jacob called loudly, making his opinion known whether it counted as a vote or not.

Lily was shaking by the time it was all over.

Banishment, but not destitution. It could've been worse. It wasn't a death sentence. Not yet.

She'd never been more frightened in her life.

Chapter 25

Daylight brought a drop in temperature and a surcease of the snow. Nate, wet to his knees from wading through drifts blown up against the barn door, was slathering a purple potion on the horse Screenmaster had stabbed. It flinched, hide rippling at his gentlest touch.

"Whoa, boy. Easy now." He murmured soft nothings until it relaxed and went back to mouthing the handful of oats scattered in the manger.

Body heat from the animals lucky enough to be under shelter helped warm the barn, keeping Nate's bare hand from freezing as he ministered to the horse. A draft of cold, along with a brief display of sunshine, announced he had a visitor. Boots stomped away snow before approaching the stall where he worked. The boots, and the man wearing them, stopped behind him.

"Checking up on me, Cuz?" he asked without looking up from his chore.

"How's the horse?" Bannion, voice loud in the cavernous building, gave Nate's question short shrift.

Straightening, Nate patted the creature's rump before turning to face his cousin. "Better than I expected. Glad

I didn't put him down. He isn't up to hauling that heavy wagon yet, but he will be in a few days."

"She goes today. We decided. She agreed."

Nate snorted. "Hell, yes, she agreed. The woman isn't crazy, in case you haven't noticed. Lily knows she has no choice. Given this particular set of circumstances, if you'd been warned you'd be killed otherwise, wouldn't you? No matter what the cost?"

"She agreed," Bannion insisted, stubborn and unthinking as an ox. Or so Nate considered. Also just like him to have left the door unlatched, for it flapped open again briefly in an errant gust of wind.

"It isn't right, sheriff." Nate used the title deliberately "Turning her out in this weather, under these conditions. She's wounded, beat down, and running a fever. Also smart enough not to stay here any longer than it takes to recover her strength."

Bannion sighed and stuffed his mittened hands in his coat pockets. "I know it, cuz. I do. But Selkirk is letting Neila call the shots on this one. Guess he's hoping it'll help drain the venom out of her. He figures it's all caused by this baby thing she's obsessed with all the sudden. You know she's always blamed the old ones for what happened to her, and any way you look at it, Lily Turnbow is an old one. And female to boot." His voice hardened, "I agree it's best she goes. She's made just enough friends in the clan to split us right down the middle. You don't want this to spiral down to a family squabble and endless infighting, do you?"

Damn it, Nate thought. As much as he hated to agree, Bannion was right. There wasn't a thing either of them could do about—or for—Neila, and Selkirk had given up trying. Bannion felt the clan's pulse all too accurately. The family had only been at headquarters two weeks and here they were, bickering back and forth like it was already spring.

He corked the pot holding the horse's medicine, wiped his hands on the rag he'd brought along for the purpose, and made one more try. "The folks just need the chance to get used to her. That's all. Given inspiration by their leaders, I doubt it'd take too long."

"I don't want any family division, and Selkirk won't stand for it. Final word, Nate. Get those other three horses hitched to the wagon. Awkward, I know, but it'll have to do."

"We don't even know if she can handle a team. Let her have a day or two to learn. I'll keep her away from the folks. Talk to Selkirk. Persuade him."

Bannion hesitated before shaking his head, and Nate was pretty sure he detected a tad of regret at the decision.

"Noon," the sheriff said. "That's the best I can do." He turned and strode away, kicking at a pile of loose hay outside a mare's stall. This time the door latched behind him.

The barn was quiet when he'd gone, except for a horse chewing and slobbering, and Nate's own breathing. "I suppose you heard all that," he said into empty space. He scowled toward the shadows at the rear of the barn.

"Yes." Lily dropped her "you can't see me" cloak and limped forward from where she'd been silently communing with a barn cat. She came to stand beside him, resting her arms on the stall gate, inside which the white horse, eased by Nate's doctoring, now drowsed. "I don't understand why Neila blames me for her problems. She has one son, so obviously she's fertile. Seems to me her barrenness now could be a matter of inverse consequence."

"What's that" Nate tried the phrase on his tongue.

"In this case, bad luck. Or fate." She studied him. "Being in the right place at the wrong time. Women, in case you didn't know, are only fertile at certain times of the month. The sex act has to take place at that time. Or, could be her age is against her."

Nate had known that, in an off-hand way. Being a single man, it hadn't particularly concerned him until now. He was jolted by a sharp urge in his loins. Damn. Lily was standing close enough he caught her clean scent.

"While it's logical for Bannion and her brother to support her against me," she said, thankfully oblivious to his sudden discomfort, "the logic doesn't make me feel any better."

"I don't suppose it does." Deliberately, he turned away, wrapped the pot of medicine in an old sack and put it on an upended wooden box where it wouldn't freeze.

"I'm having trouble getting my head around what I've become, myself," she admitted.

She didn't look happy, for true. The corners of her mouth drooped like a child about to cry. Nate hoped she wouldn't. Crying women made him nervous.

"In all fairness," she added, "if, back in my time, I'd met someone who could toss fireballs or disappear at will, I'd be leery, too. But I will not become the goat for whatever caused the meltdown all those years ago, or assume the responsibility behind humanity's mutations. From what anyone seems to know, it may even have been something out of nature. An errant asteroid knocked the planet askew on its axis or something."

But he could tell she didn't think so.

She fell silent, staring at, or through, the horse as if it weren't even there. Finally, her forehead drew together as if she were in pain. "And I certainly didn't ask for…for resurrection." Her mouth clamped shut and he saw her throat working.

"The majority of Cross-ups embrace their talent, you know," he said, guessing at her pain. They stood side-by-side, tension between them like useless static electricity. "After a while, most of them decide they want more from the plain people around them. Demand extra this and extra that. And get it."

"Yeah. So I've been told. Repeatedly." She reached out and touched the horse's rump, her hand looking very small against the massive animal. "This Sleeping Beauty thing—An Old fairytale," she added, at his puzzled look. "Gal slept for a hundred years and awakened at her lover's kiss." She shrugged. "No kiss for me, so I have no idea what woke me up. No idea what has resurrected even my flesh even to previous scars. It's something that shouldn't be possible. You'll never know how much I wish it hadn't happened. My world is gone and I'm not ready for this one. Not strong, not tough, not hard enough. What's more, I don't want to be."

He forced himself to grin at her as if he thought she was being melodramatic. "I think you're a whole lot tougher than you know, Lily. You'll learn fast." Truth to tell, he wondered about that. She seemed shrunken to him this morning, her hazel eyes dark and shadowed, cheeks hollow, skin pale, listless and without energy. Almost as bad as right after they found her and she'd been so ill with the resurrection sickness.

"Well," she said, turning brisk and throwing back her shoulders. "I've come to tell you I've never driven a team of horses in my life. Worse, I've never harnessed a team. Perhaps I should do as Selkirk wanted and leave Screenmaster's wagon here. I can use the horses as pack animals." She laughed suddenly, the sound high and mirthless. "One thing in my favor. Since I have no possessions but the clothes I stand up in, it won't take me long to pack."

This earned her a glare. "Don't you think for one minute Harrison or Jake or I will send you off destitute. We won't."

A faint smile touched her mouth, finally turning the corners up. "Thank you. I haven't said so, Nate, but I appreciate you standing up for me last night and negotiating on my behalf." Her voice grew softer. "And for taking me at face value."

Abruptly, as though the action was beyond his control, Nate wrapped his arms around her and drew her close, cheek to cheek. She roused a wanting in him, a need he'd never felt for any other woman. She resisted for a moment, and he sensed a fear about her, as though she didn't quite trust him. He tilted her head back with a finger under her chin until she met his eyes.

"Don't be afraid of me, Lily," he said. "I promise I won't double cross you."

"I'm not afraid of you. I believe you'll *try* to be straight with me." Her lips twisted. "You carry a lot of baggage around with you, though. I—" She stopped as a line creased his forehead. "I mean you've got a big family to answer to, like it or not. I never had much in the way of close family. After my mom died, just my grandparents and a couple of cousins. But I listened to friends who did. They all say . . . or they said . . . their families are difficult to deal with at times. Families don't necessarily do what you want. Every person has about six different ideas on any given subject. And they all want you to come down on their side. Sound familiar?"

His shoulders hunched. Yeah. It did.

She relaxed and leaned against him. Nate wondered if she liked the way he felt. He enjoyed her body touching his, the way she just seemed to fit. "You should marry me," he said out of the blue. "Then my people would have to accept you."

The vein in her throat visibly jumped and started pulsing faster.

Oh, Lord! What had he said?

After a pause that lasted a little longer than it should've, Lily forced out a laugh. "Love me, love my dog?"

He recognized the old quote, but before he could say so, she shook her head. "What if they disowned you, threw you out? Sorry payment for all you've done for me. And they'd hate me twice as much, especially Bren, for taking you away from the family. Pretty soon you'd hate me, too."

She shivered and her arms went around his waist. "But I thank you for the offer."

Reaching up, she gave him a little peck on the lips, at least that's how it started out. But when she would've drawn away, he caught her with one hand behind her head, holding her steady while he took his time, savoring the touch of her soft lips. Pretty soon he discovered she was pressing closer, her mouth open under his.

Then, as if she had a sixth sense, Lily jerked away as the barn door opened again. "Hey," Jacob's voice floated over to them, "anybody here?"

Nate drew in a deep, shuddering breath—let it go. Lily, her eyes dark as they searched his face, stepped apart.

"Here," he called to Jake. "Did you bring the stuff I asked for?"

*****

The butterflies in Lily's stomach soared into flight as she climbed the steps to the seat of Screenmaster's wagon. The backs of the three big horses hitched to the camper looked enormous from this perch. What on earth let her ever think she could drive a setup like this?

But Selkirk O'Quinn was standing at one side of the wide barn doors, with Bannion on the other, both in identical poses of stiffly folded arms and sour expressions, so she knew there'd be no reprieve. Her allotted time was up, and this a "do or die' situation. Only Nate had an encouraging smile for her. She quivered, thinking of the kiss they'd shared. Already she felt his loss.

"You'll be all right," he said now. "Just take it easy and remember what I taught you."

She cleared her throat. "I will. Thanks." She loosed the reins from where they were wound around the brake lever and threaded them through her fingers per his instructions.

Time to go.

"Hyah, giddy-up," she said, voice barely rising above a whisper. Even so, the horses understood the message of reins flapping against their backs. They leaned into their collars and started off together at a slow plod. *Single tree, double tree, collars, hames.* The meaning of the terms, though known to her previously, now seemed a blank inside her head.

Jake ran beside the wagon. "Don't forget, Lily," he called up to her, "you gotta hobble the horses tonight when you stop. And put that string of bells up around your camp. Most of the Mags are afraid of bells, so you'll have time to wake up if you have to fight them."

She flicked him a glance, opened her mouth to ask why Mags were afraid of bells, then decided it didn't matter. "I won't forget," she assured him. "Thanks for everything, Jake."

"Anyway, if you don't smell them from a mile away, the pup will."

This remark almost forced her to stop. "Pup?"

His grin was as wide as a friendly jack-o'-lantern's. "You'll see."

As her outfit cleared the barn, she saw Fanta waving shyly at her from between the infirmary and another building. As it turned out, Fanta and the girl with the severed hand were sisters, and the family was grateful to Lily for saving the girl's life. They'd contributed a newish shirt and spare pair of pants, gifts of tangible gratitude, to Lily's outfit.

Lily nodded and forced a smile as Rory came to stand by Fanta. He'd lugged in a fifty pound bag of oats for the horses; another family had filled the bin at the end of the wagon with good grass hay.

Neila, her face set, watched Lily's passage from the infirmary window, Bren hovering at the healer's shoulder. No love lost there.

She was relieved when headquarters finally disappeared behind the crest of the hill overlooking the lake. After an hour, as she came up on what looked to be a well-used turn off, Lily took her first deep breath since starting out and tugged the horses to a halt. Nate had drawn her a map, showing a route passable for the wagon. It wasn't the same as in the old days, he said. By the time the great die-off ended and population stabilized, the old roads had become impassable for the most part; overgrown in spots due to lack of use; burned away by fire in others. Only after trade had started up were some cleared and used again, but those were not necessarily the ones she needed now.

Nate's forefinger had traced a course for her, zigzagging across country and avoiding the worst of the areas still black and dead, killed by what could not, she realized, have been regular cleansing fire. She stopped at what she believed was the first zig. The new trail had deep ruts, headed southeast and downhill, and carved through a stand of scrub timber whose branches drooped with heavy wet snow, melting now. Dismal, facing the ordeal on her own. Her innards did an earthquake dance.

"It's about a hundred miles to your grandfolks's place," Nate said, confirming her own guess. "Probably take you ten days or so to get there. That's if the weather holds." He looked out at the sky and sniffed the wind. "But it won't. This storm isn't finished with us. Look for a foot of snow along about the day after tomorrow. There'll be plenty of wind. Hole up here." His forefinger had touched a mark on the map. "You'll find a sheltered spot. Stay until the storm passes. Give it a couple days, then you should have fine weather. But be on the watch. That's when the Mags'll be out."

The funny part is, when he said that about the weather, she believed him. That old O'Quinn family mojo everyone denied having at work. All he did was look at the sky and quaff the air, but Nate knew.

"Phooey on all O'Quinns, Quicks, and Bells," she muttered to herself now. "Bitch about me being a mage when they've got the same damn disease. Bunch of frigging hypocrites."

Grousing made her feel a little better as she went over the route again, then, certain this was where she should make her first turn, lifted the reins. A stirring in the wagon behind her halted the motion.

"What in the world? Who's there?" The noise had been faint. Most people would never have heard it, but she picked up on a curious little whine. After a brief silence, she heard it again, along with a quick, repetitive thumping sound.

"Whoa," she told the horses, wrapping the reins around the brake for a second time. Nate had told her to make the action a habit and she was trying. Crouching, she opened the cubby door behind the seat, which led into the body of the wagon.

The dark interior made it hard to see. No matter. She smiled. No one here to be offended by the use of one of her tricks. A flick of her fingers provided light until she could touch the wick of a lantern. Once the flame came up, she looked around for the source of the sound. At first she saw nothing to account for it, then, in a space under the cot, she spied movement and the gleam of a bright eye. More telling, a puddle of yellowish liquid spread across the floor.

"*Pup*," Jake had said.

"Looks like somebody has had an oopsie," she said conversationally. Entering the camper, she lifted the edge of a ratty quilt and peeked under the cot. "Would that be you?"

The black-and-white puppy—a miniature Sliver—advanced an inch or two and licked her face.

"Oh, ho. An apology?" she asked, and in answer, the pup emerged from his hideout, sat and scratched energetically at an ear with a hind foot. Lily recognized the sound from before. "I hope to God you don't have fleas. If you do, I'll probably have to burn the bed."

The puppy barked, a baby bark, and instantly, Lily's heart melted. "That darn Jake. What does he think I'm supposed to do with you? How am I to feed you?"

Wishing for a big roll of paper towels, she looked around for a rag to clean up the puddle. Upon locating a dirty towel, leftover from Phillip Barnes' ablutions she supposed, since it was hanging from a rack beside the bowl obviously used as a sink, she mopped the puddle. Stirred by this activity to attack her hand with sharp little teeth, the pup bounced around in the floor's open space. A collar was buckled around his neck, evidently what he'd been scratching at. She spotted a bit of precious paper stuck beneath it. Pulling the wrinkled document out, Lily unfolded it.

Lily, the note said. *Hope yu like the dog. He's Sliver's full bruther, only a few years yunger. Like I told yu, he'll warn about Mags. Harrison put some of the trale rashuns he makes for Sliver in a powch, but the pup'll soon learn to hunt his own food. Nate said I should tell yu that becuz back in the old days, dogs ate some kind of stuff peeple bought in a store for them. He lernd that frum a book he fownd in a ruind howse. The powch is in the cupboard by the door.*

The note made her smile, and lament the fact that Jacob Felix's spelling left something to be desired.

Paper. She underlined an item on her mental list. *Schools and teachers, emphasis on spelling.*

But there was no time to play with the pup. Finding a length of rope in one of the drawers in the commode, she tied it to the pup's collar.

"Your first lesson, puppy, is staying on the wagon seat without strangling yourself." Lifting the little duffer, more solid than she first thought, she took him out, placed him beside her, and admonished him to stay. Then, picking up the reins again, she hollered to the horses and they started their slow, steady pace.

Dark had gathered under the trees when at last she reached the area Nate had marked on the map for her first camp. Climbing stiffly from the wagon seat while carrying a pup who wiggled to be free, and contending with a leg screaming with pain, she paid Barnes gratitude for his stair to the ground.

With the pup gamboling around her heels, she unhitched the horses, brushed dirt from their white coats while they lipped up a measure of grain. She affixed the animal's hobbles, then spent half an hour arranging the lengths of bells. The puppy loved that, barking and growling as she dragged the strings of bells around the wagon, attaching them to hooks Nate and Jacob had screwed into the wood.

"Always take care of your stock first," Nate had said, "no matter how tired you are. Then set the bells. Your life may depend on it."

By the time she finished, she could barely walk, her leg throbbing as she gathered an armload of firewood. No big deal for that. Fallen limbs littered the ground under the tall fir trees. Nate's map showed an overhang where, preferring the outdoors for her meal than the dark and stuffy camper interior still smelling of Philip Barnes, she built a fire and warmed stew left from Harrison's meal last night. The pup dined with her, his belly round and replete, and later, in the wagon, he curled against her in a cocoon of blankets.

She didn't sleep that night—no surprise—but lay and listened for the bells, which never rang, while staring into the darkness filling the camper.

Before dawn, a meager breakfast eaten, with some trial and error, Lily hitched the horses and started off along Nate's planned route. Miles traveled rolled out behind the wagon wheels, the terrain dropped lower, into foothills sketchily covered with sere vegetation. She saw plenty of wild game: flocks of geese squawking as a huge V formation flew overhead; a moose, standing with its head submerged in the shallows of a small lake; chillingly, what appeared to her shocked senses to be an African lion. It paid her or the puppy, who stood with his hackles raised barking a challenge, no mind, its attention on the moose. Frightened, she urged the horses into a jog and drove past the campsite Nate had marked on the map, traveling on until she found a place more open, where the horses had better graze close to the wagon.

She hobbled the team, set the bells, and turned in. By morning, the storm Nate had predicted arrived.

Chapter 26

Philip Barnes' camper, built on springs lifted from some well-preserved antique car, rocked in the blustery wind. The motion set the bells chiming. Lily started awake at the first sound, heart thudding, her mouth open in a silent scream as she sat up. The pup, curled against her with the tip of his tail covering his nose, opened one eye. He appeared unalarmed.

The wind. Only the wind. No mutants hammering to get at her. Lily swallowed. The motion was making her a little seasick.

"Looks like Nate had the weather pegged," she informed her companion as the camper shook again. Outside, the bells pealed. A scatter of fine snow blew under the door at the next gust. The temperature had dropped considerably in the last few hours. Shivering, even though wearing her pants and a shirt, she drew a pair of wool socks over bare feet. The fire in the small stove had gone out, the camper's interior turned glacial.

She had no idea of the time. Exhausted from a full day of driving the cumbersome vehicle over the almost obscured remnants of ancient roads, she'd been sleeping hard. Was it the middle of the night now, or morning? Night, she decided. The atmosphere had that feel.

Scratching a deep layer of frost from a corner of the tiny window above the bed, she peered through the hole. Ambient light reflected off the snow. Everything beyond the horses, which were hobbled only a few feet away, was indistinct, lost in a fog of swirling white. Poor creatures, they stood with hindquarters turned to the wind,. There was nothing she could do for them, at least until daylight.

Meanwhile, her concern over a possible Mag attack faded. Harrison had told her the mutants stayed inside in weather like this. They wore only bare essentials when it came to clothing—having apparently degenerated until they were more animal than human—and were without the sense to stay warm. The O'Quinns said they found a few thawing corpses every spring, dead of exposure to the elements.

Lily lay back down with the blankets pulled around her ears as the camper grew more chill. The walls were but thin protection against falling temperatures and the blizzard outside. Afraid to either fall asleep or to start the fire in case the chimney vent plugged and carbon monoxide fumes poisoned her, she shivered through long, lonely hours, listening to the bells. At that, she only knew it was morning because the pup stirred and demanded to go out.

"Are you kidding?" she asked. "You'll get lost in this snow."

The whine grew more determined.

"All right, all right, contain yourself a minute, you hear me? I don't want any more puddles on the floor."

Holding the top quilt around her, Lily found a clean pair of the dwarf's socks, pulling them on over her own in a double layer before thrusting her feet into packer boots. A second shirt went over the one she'd slept in, her coat over all, zipper pulled all the way up. Hat, gloves, something around her neck. Lastly, she found a fifty-foot length of rope.

"You're going to be sorry about this," she warned the pup. Hauling the door open against the iced sill used all her strength. A gust of frigid air took her breath away. Turning her back to the wind, she tied one end of the rope to the door handle, and held the rest of the coil in her hand. Not that she planned on getting lost only steps away from the camper, but with visibility almost non-existent, she was darned if she'd let herself lose her only shelter.

Shaking the idea away, she stepped off the back of the wagon, promptly sinking to her waist in a drift. Stomping snow, she broke trail for the dog. An eerie feeling, as though she heard her grandfather speaking, reminded her that she depended on the animals and they would need water. Impossible. She hadn't the heat source to melt any. The supply of wood stored under the wagon bed had dwindled to practically nothing already.

The pup plunged along beside her, burying himself at first in the powdery snow, then leaping upward onto bare ground where the wind had cleared a short stretch. He barked, black eyes shining with delight, and squatted.

"Silly baby," Lily muttered, her words puffing into the frigid air.

A chiming of the bells attached to the horses' halters with the idea they'd guard against Mags, led her to where the horses had taken refuge from the wind behind the camper. They stood, ghostly shapes with snow frosting their backs, icicles hanging from their lips and nostrils. The biggest gelding stamped and whickered miserably at her approach.

The only shelter for her stock was the wagon, and it wasn't helping much. Snow blew in around the wheels caking the animals' legs before sweeping over the rounded camper top in a tornado-like whirl. Last night, she'd seen a thick band of trees a long arrow-shot to the south, and deliberately stopped short, thinking it better to face either Mags or African lions in the open where she could see them. A mistake, she realized now. There would be a creek over there, and a windbreak. Nate had seen to it her route followed water.

But though she squinted through narrowed eyes against the icy prickle of blowing snow, the trees were indiscernible. Visibility stopped just beyond the camper.

Lily brushed a blanket of snow from the first horse's back. Try as she might, she felt no warmth coming through his skin, but only a few rippling tremors. The others were in like condition. They'd soon die at this rate, and then where would she be? Stuck in the middle of a howling wilderness, that's where. Providing *she* made it through the storm.

"This isn't going to work, is it?" she crooned to the wretched beast. "I've got to get you fellows out of the wind and find water." Dark eyes dull, the leader blinked through a crust of ice.

Slowly, wincing from the need, Lily removed the glove from her left hand. The flick of her fingers was slowed by cold, but enough to bring up a flare of witch light. Her arm extended, she peered into the fog beyond the glow. Was that dark blur the trees, or only a figment of her imagination?

The little dog gamboled between her feet, apparently impervious to the weather, but entranced by the light. The blanketing snow muffled his sharp yap.

Behind her, one of the horses stumbled against the other. Both grunted. Long hours in the cold had drained their strength. She needed to get them to safety—and make it quick.

Letting the light die, Lily bent and fumbled the hobbles loose. Only then did she slide her almost frozen hand back in the glove. *Good Lord, she could barely feel her fingers!*

Using the rope looped around her wrist, the wind pushing at her, she pulled herself back to the camper door. The puppy scooting ahead, she scrambled inside where she put down his food and water, preparing to leave him behind. The horses were enough to contend with. She didn't need another animal depending on her.

Although the interior of the camper had seemed freezing earlier, now it felt warm. From here, even the bells sounded less intrusive, more comforting. She had an almost over-whelming desire to curl up on the cot and cover her head.

*****

At one point Lily imagined she was carrying the horses on her back, they were that heavy. Alternately yanking the lead ropes, then vocally urging them on, her voice grew raspy in the cold. The animals' steps were plodding, barely lifting from the ground, getting stuck in even small drifts, forcing her to break trail.

Wind-blown snow muffled ordinary sounds. The small troop had gone, at Lily's best estimate, no more than a hundred yards before she lost the sound of bells chiming at the wagon. The pup, locked in the camper by himself, howled piteously at first, a noise that lasted another dozen or so strides and then faded.

Lily blundered on, praying she was still headed in the right direction. Praying she could find her way back to the camper. Periodically she removed her glove and made witch light, casting the glow ahead. Each time, the cold drew warmth from her fingers, until they became like nubs of blue ice.

Plunging through tall drifts used every bit of breath she had, until her lungs, seared by frigid air, felt like bloodied rags in her chest. The wound in her leg pulsed in pain, until at last she couldn't feel it as a separate entity anymore. Just a burning, but one of severe cold rather than fire.

Three times she fell, pulled herself up by the lead ropes under the miserable horses' noses, and forced them all to go on. As her energy waned, each instance became more difficult. The next time, she believed, might well be her last.

And yet, when she slipped and tumbled again, some indomitable strength made her lift her head and summon light one more time. There! She nearly sobbed in relief. There was something ahead. A dark blur. Lily rubbed her eyes on her coat sleeve.

Yes. It was still there, and as though the wind paused for just a second in encouragement, she glimpsed the ragged edges and pointed tops of trees nearby.

"Hallelujah!" Pushing to her feet, Lily yelled at the gelding, startling him into shaking his massive head. "C'mon, horse. We're getting there. Don't you poop out on me now. Hihihi. C'mon."

Obedient to her chivying, the animals hopped toward the blur, dragging her along. They reached the trees less than a minute later. Abruptly, the wind cut off, allowing the gurgle of a nearby creek to reach their ears. At least Lily heard the rush of water, the horses may have smelled it. Lunging forward, their hooves pushed through a ragged rim of ice at the water's edge. Like greedy children, they stuffed noses into the icy torrent, snuffling with pleasure.

Lily, licking her own cold and dry lips, didn't blame them a bit. Blundering over to a snow-topped stump, she brushed it bare and sat. Legs as flaccid as cooked noodles could no longer bear weight. Breath burning, her heart pounded.

Though it seemed serene here, out of the wind's full force, she knew the apparent safety could be deceptive. Good enough for horses, as she saw one go from slurping water to pawing through the snow. With a snort, he reached the dry grass underneath the crust and began grazing, already more content.

One mission accomplished.

Troubling her own peace of mind, Lily recalled Nate's map with the hive of Mags hidden in this area clearly marked. Stick of graphite in hand, he'd drawn a heavy circle around the place, warning her to stay well away.

"Hurry through this part early in the morning." Mags didn't stir much then, he told her, recommending she camp north of here. Good advice, if only a lion hadn't already occupied the site.

And now? God knows where the Mags were. God knows where she was, when you came right down to it, or when she'd be able to move on. But putting all other consider-ations aside, she thought, lifting her weary head and peering out at the blank wall of falling snow beyond the trees, she had to find the camper again.

Slowly, fatigue dragging at her heels like concrete overshoes, she stood up. If she didn't start now, that might never happen.

To Lily's relief, backtracking herself proved a snap—at first. Between the three horses and herself they'd cut a fair-ly wide swath on the way over, so she made fast progress returning along the beaten trail, even trotting a little to help keep warm. But then she reached a place where her tracks were already partially filled, and within moments the last of them disappeared. Carrying on, she went another ten strides, then ten more. Now her feet dragged.

Floundering, she stopped. Wind buffeted her. Frozen shards of snow struck like BBs at her face where it was exposed, pinging against the skin with tiny buzzes of sound. The towel wrapped around her neck only partially covered her chin and cheeks.

Frostbite. She couldn't feel her nose. Couldn't feel her lips, either, not even when she bit down on her lower one.

Her heartbeat quickened. People died in blizzards. They always had. *Will I be next?* No. She damn well would not. Not as long as the camper turned up soon.

Think, Lily.

Scared, she jeered at herself, trying to remain calm and ignore the way her heart clattered in her breast. *Tough old Border Patrol agent like you, and you're scared?*

Damn straight, she was.

Think.

When she came to the place where the hoof marks had begun filling in, she was fine, her feet pointed in the right direction. She stayed on track then, that much was fact. And even as the trail petered out, she kept going the same way. What made her think so? Because the wind had been blowing into her left eye when she started out. Since then, she'd been holding it almost closed—a form of protection. And still was.

So keep going. It was all she knew to do.

The way grew harder. Lily bent into the wind until at times she was nearly swimming over the tallest of the drifts.

Lord, she was cold. So cold. Mindless, unthinking now, she fought on.

And then she slipped and fell, outstretched hands too numb to catch herself. Air whooshed out of her lungs as she belly-flopped onto the frozen earth. Head jolting, she was barely aware of colliding with a snow-covered stone. Vision blurred, she lay stunned.

After a while, it occurred to her how good it felt to just lie there relaxed, resting her tired bones. If only the little voice yammering in the back of her mind about how she had to get up and go on would shut up. What was the big deal, anyway?

The wind passed above her prone body, no longer buffeting her back and forth like a straw dummy. Those heavy gusts must've been the reason she felt so cold earlier, but now she was warming up nicely. Too nicely, in fact.

She loosened the muffler around her throat. Keep this up and she'd need to take off her jacket.

No. Must not do that. Someone had said— She couldn't remember what, or even who "he" was. They'd been discussing storms, she knew that. More precisely, blizzards.

And dying. Most of the time she thought the man's voice belonged to her grandpa, other times, to Nate.

Nate was smart about weather. A regular weather wizard. A small chuckle gurgled in the back of her throat. *Weather wizard, get it?* One of the ilk the O'Quinn professed to hate so much, even though half of them were well on their way to becoming the very thing they detested so much. Bunch of damn hypocrites!

This time Lily snorted, which, along with the sudden flare of ire, roused her into rolling over.

What had she been thinking? Oh, yes. Hot.

Or . . . no, she wasn't. Not hot at all. Some part of her recognized the sensation as an illusion along the same lines as cloaking herself in invisibility. Only in this case, unlike the cloaking, the illusion could be lethal.

"As the victim nears the end," that *someone* had said, "the body shuts down. Goes numb. He gets sleepy. Imagines things." He'd laughed. "Get like that you'd better start ringing your own wake-up bell, 'cause if you give in to it, that's all she wrote."

Who *had* said that? Didn't seem like Grandpa, after all, and not Nate, either. They hadn't had time together for conversation to flow so widely between them. Good grief! Had it been that slimy buzzard Lopez, her Border Patrol boss? Not that it mattered. She yawned, but with her mouth clamped shut, it wasn't very satisfactory.

Bells ringing.

The sound of the telephone wrenched Lily a little way back to consciousness, maybe because the musical, though somewhat tinny notes were so welcome. Wahoo, she thought as she drifted on a sea of imagination. She was back in civilization where she belonged and where cell phones worked properly.

Not really aware, her hand groped toward the pocket of her coat. *Wake up, Lily. Wake up. This is an important call.*

The bell chimed again, louder this time.

Hello, she heard herself saying. *Hello.* And then that inner voice came again, *Wake up, Lily!*

Gotta do it, she thought. Gotta do it. Something is wrong.

She stirred, rolled up onto hands and knees and rocked forward. *Not hot. Cold. So awfully cold.*

But from out of the gusting winds she heard bells again. Not the telephone, she realized suddenly, but Nate's anti-Mag device around the camper.

What had she been thinking?

She turned her face into the driving snow once more. Safety lay only a short distance farther along. All she had to do was follow the sound, if only her sluggish body would respond. Slowly, stiffly, forcing numb feet and muscles to work, like a Phoenix born of ashes, she staggered upright.

The wind gusted once, twice more, before abruptly dying. The bells went silent.

It was almost as if the world had ended yet again, though without the pain or crash of thunder of the last time. Or so the thought flashed through Lily's mind. The meaning of the sudden silence seemed clear. The owner of this universe was trying to tell her to let the cold win this battle. Death should be easy and final. No more resurrections into a dreary, distant world where everything she thought she knew turned out skewed. Humanity. Time. Magic. Even love. No man had ever gotten close to her heart like Nate had in these last few days.

A shock went through her. They hadn't even slept together. Their only kiss had been interrupted. How could she trust the warmth that infused her at the mere recalling of his touch?

Warmth. Nate. *Nate.*

The last thing he said to her after Jacob walked in on them was that he'd meet her at her grandparents' old place. "Wait for me there," he said. "I'll catch up with you before winter sets in."

She believed him, trusted him. Hard telling why since it could've been just a line to get her out of his hair. But somehow—

Lily surfaced to discover herself plunging through a drift, headed in a straight line toward the camper whose rounded top she was finally able to pick out of the fog of snow. The realization of what instinct and superlative hearing had been telling her for the last few minutes while she dreamed of Nate struck. No bells, although they'd gotten her a certain distance, but now she unconsciously picked up on something else.

The little Karelian Bear dog shut up in the camper was having a fit, and with his steady, high-pitched puppyish yipping was complaining to the world. To her.

Gasping, crying, Lily made it to the camper and, hands too numb to actually feel the latch, blindly fumbled open the door. No longer able to stand, she sprawled inside, nudged the door shut with a ten-ton foot, and let the welcoming dog kisses lick some warmth back into her frozen face.

*****

Two days later, the horror of Wednesday's sharp brush with death still playing havoc with her body, Lily finally forced herself to crawl from the cot. Joints aching, a glance in the mirror suspended from a nail over the wash basin showed just how close she'd come to dying in the whiteout.

Her nose was only now regaining normal skin color, thanks, no doubt, to the slight protection the cloth wrapped around her neck and face had yielded. Aside from a certain amount of pain, the biggest damage seemed to be over her cheekbones where a scattering of blisters had sprouted. Most were clear, but two small ones were filled with dark fluid. Not a good sign, if she recalled her first aid courses correctly. Dry skin sloughed like dandruff. In addition, the fingers on her right hand, from which she'd pulled the glove a few times while making witch light, were swollen and stiff.

"Great," she sighed, eyeing the damage and carefully wrapping a clean cloth over the worst spots. God knows she didn't need an infection. "Just ducky."

Sunshine glared out of a vibrant blue sky when she and the pup ventured from the camper at his demand. The temperature had climbed to what she figured was a balmy fifty degrees, almost summer after what had gone before. The air had never smelled so clean and pure. From the trees a quarter mile away where the horses were stashed, the creek gurgled with the rush of melting snow water. Between, a couple of what had been the tallest drifts sat in a muddy loblolly.

A Chinook had come in not long after she fell, strength at an end, into the camper. Now, soggy bare spots showed like mange on a dog. But not a dog like Blizzard, that being the name she'd hung on the pup. What could be more appropriate?

Blizzard tended to the demands of his training by running a perimeter check around the camper before answering his personal needs. Judging by his reaction, all was well, so Lily stepped to the ground from the camper steps.

Glory, she moved like she was a full hundred twenty-seven. Haha. Joke. How did one count the years before resurrection?

Squinting, she made out the shapes of the horses over in the band of trees, where they were still content to graze the dry grass alongside the stream. Today she had to walk over there, make sure all was well, probably put the hobbles and protective bells back on. Right now, the prospect called for more energy than she had.

"Hey, Blizzard, go check the horses," she told the pup, a smile in her voice. *As if.*

Consequently, when he raced off in the direction she indicated as though he understood, she about fell over.

A real clown, he made her laugh as he leapt rapidly melting drifts like he wanted to fly. But then, at the mid-way point, he stopped dead. Nose pointing into the breeze, ears pricked forward, he froze. The hair on his back rose like quills on a hedgehog.

Enemy! Lily scanned the woods with as much tension as the dog. Who? Where? She didn't see anything. Didn't hear anything, either, which didn't mean much considering the dog's sensitive nose was a more reliable early warning system. So what bothered him? Lion? Or Mags?

In either case, at all costs she had to protect the horses. If they were lost, she was well and truly stuck.

How close was the danger? Blizzard continued to test the wind currents, but didn't signal further alarm. Still, the hair on his back didn't flatten either. Urgency crowded her. She had to get the horses hitched and make tracks out of here—now—and trust the ground was firm enough the heavy wagon didn't sink to the axles.

Reaching into the camper, Lily grabbed the crossbow and quiver of arrows from a peg by the door. Feeling as if a target were nailed to her jacket, she forced unwilling legs into a trot, Blizzard bouncing alongside her.

Chapter 27

Expecting an ambush either by hoards of screaming mutants or a pride of hungry lions, Lily sped toward the band of trees, a quarrel nocked in the crossbow's groove. Her abrupt appearance set the startled horses to shying as she and the pup interrupted their placid grazing. There was no sign of danger. Not yet. Releasing pent-up breath, Lily released the bow, slung it over her shoulder and went about collecting the team.

"Whoa." She used a no-nonsense tone when one shook his massive head and attempted to sidestep her. Blizzard stood guard as she linked a lead rope through the horses's halters, found a downed log from which to mount the smallest, and tugged the others along behind as they lumbered toward the camper. The pup followed, turning often to stare off toward the west, testing the air with his nose. His ears twitched; once he whined.

Lily jerked the lead rope, nearly going over backwards as a horse pulled the other way. "Hustle it up, you slugs."

Blizzard ran beside the little cavalcade, his growl a low, constant rumble.

"Good boy, Blizzard. I hear them now." She did, too, a

strange, blood chilling ululation. Her heels thudded against the horse's sides, urging more speed.

Mags, then. Not lions. The high-pitched cries remained faint, but edged closer. Probably didn't matter much if you got right down to it, one being as wild and dangerous as the other. If her luck was in, maybe they were far enough away she still had a chance of eluding them.

Lily was gasping, the pain coursing through her already abused body taking a toll. They drew up beside the wagon, chunks of mud flying from the horses' hooves. Dismounting and landing heavily on her healing leg, without pausing, Lily flung open the harness storage bin and hauled out gear. No time to lay the parts out. She had to get it right the first time. *Collar, hame, trace, crupper.*

The horses would not be hurried, but at last, sweating, shaking, Lily got them hitched to the wagon. She climbed the steps to the seat. Granted, she could've driven from inside, but she had not the option of enclosing the rig, complete with horses, in a security bubble like Barnes had done. She had to prevent the Mags from attacking the team, and leave herself room to fight.

'Hiyah," she called softly. "Get-up."

The yodeling Mags were closer now. Individual shrieks and screams became clear. "Kill. Blood. Man."

Dreadful creatures. How did they manage to work together long enough to kill anybody but each other?

"Hiyah." Pulling the whip from the holder by the seat, Lily lashed out at the single lead horse. Surprised by the sting, he pulled hard against the sucking mud. Blizzard, who'd evaded her when she tried to put him in the camper, chased alongside the team leader nipping at its heels, harrying them all into a shambling trot.

But even the dog's best efforts couldn't force the heavy equipage over the ground fast enough to crest the hill before the first of the Mags broke into the meadow where the camper had sat for the last three days.

Lily, looking over her shoulder at the sound of more blood-curdling ki-yiing, saw a tall, nearly naked beanstalk of a mutant gesturing several of his brethren on. "Kill," he shouted. Then, "Woman. Blood."

Woman? How had he known? And were those the only words they knew? Best not stick around and find out.

As she watched, he beat a fist against his chest. The mutant gave chase, long, praying mantis-like legs covering ground as though he ran on a groomed lane instead of a muddy track. Outdistancing his companions, every stride brought him nearer.

Heart going like a trip-hammer, Lily whipped the horses again. *Dammit. Dammit!* Half-frozen ground sucked at the horse's hooves, clutching at them like quicksand.

Silence made no difference now. Finding her voice, Lily yelled encouragement to the team. Even so, as they started down the other side of the hill, she turned and saw the Mag gaining on her. He'd soon catch up.

"Pointy-toothed bastards." Gritting her own teeth, Lily gave the lines some slack and wound them around pegs at the front of the foot box. Wear showed where Barnes had done the same when without need for guidance. She didn't know about the guidance thing, but definitely needed the use of both her hands.

Dropping her gloves onto the seat, she loosened the big survival knife worn as a matter of course on her belt, and picked up the crossbow. Enough bolts? Every one had to find its mark.

Glancing back, she saw the creature already only a dozen yards behind, his long legs pumping like steel pistons.

Lily's team, though steady goers, had no great turn of speed. Flicking the whip again, she shouted to them, cocked the bow and set a bolt. The wagon swayed, skewing and slipping, as it rolled over a melting drift.

Seconds later the brown-skinned mutant caught up with the wagon. Staring up at her and grinning, he grabbed the hand rail and easily swung himself onto the suddenly not-so-convenient stair.

Lily loosed the arrow nearly point blank, just as the Mag slipped on the unaccustomed step and fell to one knee. The bolt flew over his head. She reached for another, never completing the motion. The creature's stench made her gag as, recovering his balance, he lunged at her, a wickedly sharpened axe with a short handle raised to whack her head.

Without conscious thought, fire zinged from her bare fingers. The Mag screeched and clawed frantically at the fiery pellets blinding him. Lily kicked out at him with her good leg, her foot sinking ankle deep into his belly and booting him from the wagon. The heavy vehicle bumped over his writhing body. His cries stopped.

They sped on, if you could call the horse's even trot speeding. To Lily, it felt more like wading through chest deep water. She readied the crossbow again, setting another quarrel and sliding across the rig's seat at the next jolt. And even as she fixed her eyes on the next grade, willing the horses on, a Mag wearing moccasins, short pants, and a fur shawl type thing over its shoulders, dashed into the trail ahead of them, brandishing a straight, four-foot spear sharpened to a pencil point. The creature, female, judging by its piercing cries and semi-exposed breasts, drew back her throwing arm, prepared to drive the spear through the lead horse's chest. The animal tossed his head, eyes rolling white, and tried to turn.

"Hiyah," Lily yelled. Fire would probably scare the horse as badly as the Mag. Instead, she grabbed the crossbow, took aim, released. No miss this time.

The Mag had no chance of evasion, almost seeming unaware of the danger until the arrow stabbed through her middle. Then the creature plucked at the shaft, drawing it out with a cry, her guts spilling around thin fingers before she staggered out of the horse's path and fell to the ground.

The female was only the first. More of the hive swarmed the wagon, thumping the heavy wooden sides with clubs and spears, a couple even chopping at the wheels with their war axes. A cacophony of screaming, blurred words, and the whirl of weapons accompanied them.

Lily screamed along with them, until her throat became sore and hoarse. She hollered at the horses, at the dog, at the clustering Mags. Caught a spear in a net of fire no more than six feet from her chest. Knocked a knife-wielding male sliding over the camper's top to the ground with a well-timed blow with her own, larger blade. Time after time, she drew fire to her fingertips, flinging it down onto the Mags in a blistering hail.

The horses took a few glancing wounds, until their white hides were zebra striped with blood. Blizzard ran using only three legs, taking cover now beneath the wagon where his sharp teeth snapped at any Mag who too closely approached the stair.

A blaze, ignited by a stray flicker of witch light, tore through a few straggling pines at Lily's right, the conflagration chasing two Mags from cover into her rain of fire.

And then, quite suddenly, there were no more cries, no more spears or knives or savage teeth to dodge. No more reeking Mags to kill. Only a litter of dead sprawled along the back trail, abandoned by the wounded who crawled away.

After one look, she drove on without stopping.

*****

Come noon, Nate Quick dismounted in the lea of a gigantic basalt boulder, the hallmark of this traditional camping area. The spot had, he knew, been used in the same way even in the old time, a resting place for travelers. This is where he had expected to catch up with Lily, he and Jake having made better time than the big camper wagon could manage. The storm had delayed them some, but not as long as it would've her.

"So where is she?" Jake asked, looking around and hunching his shoulders as a dollop of melting snow fell on him from a tree branch.

Nate was asking himself that same question. "Don't know." He poked at an oddly shaped pile of stones, the base of which was held together by mortar. He believed it had once given a name to this place. "Get down. Let's see if we can pick up her trail. That camper is heavy enough to leave traces even on frozen ground."

Swinging off his horse, Jake scanned the area. "There's wood over by the fire-pit. Think we can make tea? I could stand something warm in my gizzard."

Scouting the five-acre patch would take a little time. Long enough to make the fire worthwhile. "Good idea," Nate said, leading his horse over to a second, smaller ring of stones. The Screenmaster's recovering draft horse, carrying a pack designed to avoid the wound in his side, followed his roan.

He and Jake set about knocking snow off wood and digging into the pile to find dry stuff. Shouldn't have been anything left to burn, he reflected uneasily, if Lily had made it this far. They knew she'd been only a few miles away and on the proper course, but then the storm had come in and wiped out any sign of her passage.

The kid hunkered beside him while he searched for a match. "Too bad Lily ain't here. She'd have this fire roaring in a flash."

Nate forced a grin. "I hope she'd be more cautious than to do that. There's a Mag hive somewhere close around here. Smoke is apt to draw them like flies on fresh kill." Which was why he was building his small fire under a tree where the smoke would be lost among the branches. Nothing he could do about the scent.

While they waited for snow water to boil, Nate took one side of the rest area and Jacob the other, pacing out a grid searching for traces of her. To Nate's chagrin, he found nothing.

"Think she beat the storm out of here?" Jake had returned to the fire and was peeking into their small pot to see if the tea was hot. Finding it was, he poured them each a tin cup full, the fragrant steam rising in the cold air.

A chill was settling in Nate's innards that had nothing to do with the weather. "I told her to wait here until it was past, but I can't see where she even made it this far."

"She can't have got lost, can she? Not if she kept to the map you drew her."

Nate didn't want to talk about the alternatives. Too restless to sit like a fireplace granny and drink tea strong with rose hips, he gulped down the steaming liquid even as Jacob warmed his hands around his own mug.

"I'll water the horses," Nate said abruptly, setting his cup aside for Jake to pack in his saddlebags.

The stream was where he discovered a possible reason for Lily's absence.

"Jake," he yelled, "get your ass over here."

Dropping his cup, Jake got. "What'd you find, Nate?"

Nate, hunkering beside his discovery, pointed. Tracks been made when the soil was thawed and damp, then frozen firm, and now, with the return of warmer temperatures, showed as indentations filled with water. The sign was clear enough to read, however.

"Oh crap," Jake said. "Lion. An old male and a couple

females." He pointed his nose and sniffed. "Not here now. Can't smell'em."

Standing, Nate stared off toward the southeast, wishing for a glimpse of the round-topped camper. "She saw them and went on without stopping. They didn't run wild before the Event, you know."

"So I've heard. Those big cats must've scared her plenty."

"Hell, yes. They scare me." Nate fingered the sword hilt poking over his shoulder, the handiest, most comfortable way to carry it when riding. "Mount up." he said.

Towards evening they found where Lily had spent the storm. Discovered the chewed down grass by the creek where her horses had grazed, and wondered that the wagon tracks stopped in the clearing.

"Squatted out here in the middle making sure Mags or those lions didn't sneak up on her," Nate said.

"Smart." Admiration showed in Jake's nod. "You'd think she was one of us instead of a Cross-up. Most of those folks don't know hardly anything practical."

"She was friends with our people," Nate reminded the kid, "back in the old times."

"I forget she's old, except for when Neila and Selkirk hound her about it."

Lily had obviously survived the storm just fine, Nate figured, packing up and heading out when the weather cleared.

They camped by the creek that night, sure they'd come up with her the next day, but feeling no particular pressure to hurry. That came the next morning when, having crested the hill beyond the meadow, Jake noticed a strange thing.

He'd been eyeing the evidence of Lily's passage with a furrowed brow, and finally broke his silence. "Does it look to you like these horses are being pushed?"

Nate's gaze sharpened. "Pushed?"

"Yeah. See where the horses' stride changed? Looks like

she was trying to make 'em run. Why would she do that?"

"Guess we'll find out. Keep your eyes peeled." A sour spot was forming in Nate's belly. Lily was hardly an expert teamster. She wouldn't be asking those big horses to do any more than walk steadily if she had her druthers.

In the end, it was his sharp eyes that first caught a glimmer of the trouble that'd hit Lily. A glove, one of the few items brought through in her resurrection and precious to her for that reason. It lay a few feet beyond the track left by the wagon. She would've come back for it if it'd gone missing by accident.

But the glove in itself wasn't the only thing that gave him the collywobbles. That took the narrow, elongated print of a man's foot on top, grinding it into the mud.

"Mags." Jake's voice was hushed.

Nate swung down from Pigeon and retrieved the glove, shaking the blue leather and Gore-Tex free of dirt before tucking it into his belt. His face grim, he remounted without saying a word, heeling his horse into a trot. They rode on.

"Birds on the wing," Jake said soberly, pointing ahead. "Circling and diving. Something dead." An apt student of Bannion's lessons, he noticed things like that.

Nate grunted, having seen them as well.

They went down the other side of the hill and back up another. From there they could see the trail ahead. There was no trace of the camper, but there were some Mag-sized lumps in the trail.

"Dead Mags," Jake announced on a note of pride as they stopped to examine the first, a scarred mutant cut nearly in half by the camper's steel-bound wheels.

They found more, three, four, seven, on the road as it unwound in front of them. Jake pumped his fist as though responsible for each one, but Nate felt none of his young friend's ebullience. He wouldn't be satisfied until they caught up with the big camper wagon and he saw Lily alive and well for himself.

Gonna kiss her again. As many times as she'll let me. A promise he made himself. *And then, by God, I'm gonna try to get laid. She's gonna be my woman.*

"You plan on standing here all day?" he growled to Jake. "No more talk. Move it."

Chapter 28

Lily guided the three-horse team along what once had been Highway 95, reins slack, letting the animals set their own pace. From time to time she called encouragement to them, mostly just to hear the sound of her own voice. She thought it comforted the horses, too, in some way. The animals had been severely tried during her running fight with the Mags a few days ago. Superficial—thankfully *only* superficial—cuts were healing on their hides.

The sun beat down on her bare head. Hard to think a week ago a blizzard had piled snow high. Now, only small heaps remained on the north side of the rolling hills. Blizzard the pup, his left hind foot almost healed from the injury the day of the Mags attack, sat beside her on the bench seat. Every now and then, he barked at low flying birds.

Bless Jake for giving her the dog, she thought, for about the thousandth time. Aside from having saved her life with his warning of the Mag attack, the little Karelian Bear dog gave her someone to talk to.

These last few days of the trip had been peaceful, almost boring, considering what had gone on before. Except that she was having a hard time reconciling herself to the emptiness of a landscape once taken up with towns, homes, farms, highways filled with people. Here and there she passed through areas still bleak and blackened from that hideous night her world ended. Even so there were signs of the land recovering. Give it another hundred years. Maybe even only fifty.

Would she still be here to see it? The question worried her. Were Cross-ups immortal, unless deliberately killed, like Philip Barnes?

The one caravan she met eyed her with suspicion only slightly mollified by her lone status. Their group, consisting of two camper wagons much like the one taken from Screenmaster, only smaller, and six outriders harrying a small herd of cattle, had no doubt feared a trap.

No surprise. She viewed them in exactly the same way, and felt only relief when they disappeared in the distance. She slept very little that night. Bogeymen appeared whenever she shut her eyes, not all of them with the brown mottled skin and sharpened teeth of Mags.

Her sense of aloneness kept her staring into the dark corners of the camper, around which she never failed to set the bells. Who was there in this world to care for her? Easy answer. One smallish dog—and maybe the three horses who whickered and nuzzled her when she gave each a handful of oats.

She rose that morning thankful to open the door and let a fresh breeze blow through the wagon while the dog barked at the horses.

Occasionally she spied columns of smoke rising into a clear blue sky marking the fair weather Nate had promised. Up until now she avoided any meeting with whoever lit those fires, but then at last, and pretty much according to the schedule he'd worked out, she came down out of the hills into what had once been the rolling farmland of the Coeur d'Alene country. Almost home.

Excitement built inside her as she rounded the last bend leading into the little town she'd grown up in. She'd gone to grade school here, in a burg already shrunken to barely more than a tribal smoke shop, a post office, a restaurant just skimping by, and a grain elevator.

An involuntary moan escaped her lips as she reached the outskirts of town, sadness welling up to clog her chest.

"Damn," she breathed. "Damn."

Blizzard climbed onto her lap and licked her chin.

The town was gone, except for a few dangerous mantraps the gaping old basements had become. They were scattered amongst an emerging hardwood forest of maple and oak, no doubt grown up from seed scattered by shade trees from the past. Like so much else in this long changed world, it appeared fire had once destroyed everything that would burn.

Of course, basements didn't burn, or not the concrete or rock walls anyway, although most had filled with debris over the years. A closer look showed a few were occupied. So, the old village wasn't quite a ghost town. She didn't know whether to be glad or sorry. Glad, because not everyone was dead. Sorry, because as she saw furtive movement between the scattered ruins, she trusted no one. Who knows what these people had become? Not Mags, at least, because she saw where roofs had been thrown over the basement walls, with chimneys rising above them. A reinforced door appeared likely to keep strangers, like her, at bay. A few had log palisades thrown up around them. Patches of land dotted with standing corn stalks and wheat stubble showed where the occupants had grown crops over the summer.

Definitely not a Mag hive, then, she noted with relief, although without damping down her watchfulness. Nate had told her about those, that they were no better than a bear's winter lair, and smelled even worse.

Blizzard, limping only slightly, ranged over to investigate the new odors, until she called him back. Even then no one came to meet, or even question her, though she was aware of eyes tracking every move. Once the hair on the back of her neck rose, and she was certain she came close to death in that moment. Only at the last second did something change the hidden watcher's mind. Maybe the fact that she turned the horses and the camper wagon onto what memory told her had been the road to her grandparent's farm.

This area had been part of the Coeur d'Alene Indian Reservation. In 1909 homesteads had been apportioned out via a government lottery, the land, mostly timber, cleared. Lily's grandfather's family had been one of the original homesteaders, a point of great pride. There'd been Turnbow's here for over a century—or could she make a claim for two?

Anyway, in the years since the Event, the timber had started to come back, forcing Lily to steer the wagon on a zigzag path, finding her way. The road, never great to begin with, had disappeared in time. But she knew the number of hills to the home place. The first long rise to where Mitchell's place once stood, then Drummond's, also gone without a remaining trace. Restor's, a vestige of the house still, then Schulman's, burned to the ground, their big barn a mossy heap of rubble. Then, and at last, she made her final stop.

There'd been a fire here, too, she saw at once. The ranch house had been brick, already sixty years old in her day, though built to last forever. It hadn't, but the remains still littered the ground like the blackened bones of an old corpse.

She'd guessed as much, hadn't she? This was not so isolated a country as the Poundstone's, now O'Quinn's, Kettle Creek Ranch had been, and had suffered accordingly. There'd been no one left to preserve or rebuild here. Lily swallowed, and swallowed again, trying not to let weak tears blind her.

"Whoa," she called softly to the horses, tugging them to a stop where an asphalt driveway had once circled the big front yard. Blizzard, running beside the wagon, sat and looked up at her when they stopped, his head cocked questioningly.

"This is it," she told him. "End of the line. No more traveling, baby dog. Time to rest your weary feet."

There'd always been tall pines in the yard, scattering a hailstorm of pine cones every time the wind blew. Kept Grandma busy, picking the cockeyed things up and her cussing like a trooper the whole time. It was almost as though Lily could hear her voice in the susurrant whispering of the re-emerging trees.

"Gran, Grandpa, I'm home," she called.

She sat there for a moment, listening, but then the sound faded and she took a deep breath. The voice wasn't real. The wheel of time had turned and only ghosts remained. She counted herself one of them.

A hollowness invading her core, she set the brake on the wagon and climbed down from the high seat. A rotting snowdrift left from the big storm barred the way to where the back door to the house had been, just as drifts always had. Heart heavy, she waded through it and stood looking.

Nothing to see really. It'd been too long. *She* had taken too long to get home. Reaching down, she picked up one of the bricks, hardened nearly to glass by the destroying fire, and threw it hard into the middle of the house. Some small, living things scrambled away.

Blizzard, instead of chasing them, leaned against her.

"It's pretty damn sad, isn't it?" Her voice was thick, as though her throat would swell shut. "I don't even know if they got buried. If they were in the house when it burned. Or if the crazy ones got them. Sweet Jesus!" The exclamation came out a croak. Maybe it was a prayer "What if *they* turned into crazy ones? Into what became Mags." But she didn't believe it. Couldn't.

The dog sat on his haunches and pawed at her knee.

"It's all ours now, Blizzard. Yours and mine." The small pines, in their whispering, mocked her and she looked up and stared at the sky. "Who else's?" she asked with a bitter little smile. But there was no answer to that.

The short afternoon was already waning when Lily set about unhitching the horses and giving them each a good drink from the water barrel on the wagon. Their muzzles dripping, she led them over to a sugar maple grove sprouted up where the corral had been and hobbled them, patting each on the rump. There'd been no trees before, except a lone English walnut tree at the corner of the barn.

A vision flashed in her mind's eye, of Heathen lounging hipshot, drowsy-eyed in the sunshine, right about *there* where grass stood tall among the trees, and her heart ached.

She thrust the hurt aside. But at least there'd be no worry about feeding these animals for the next few days. After that?

The thought served as a reminder. "C'mon," she called to Blizzard. "Let's find us something to eat. Tomorrow we start cleaning up around here. Grandma and Grandpa would be ashamed."

*****

Dark came early in November, a constant even in this changed world. Lily had gone to bed soon after a meager supper and fallen into exhausted slumber. Hours—minutes—the timing escaped her, Blizzard startled her awake with a *sub voce* growl. The dog jumped from the cot where he'd been warming her feet, and padded to the door, sniffing at the fine crack.

"Hush, boy. What is it, Mags?" Tossing the blankets

aside, she reached for the crossbow, better for close up work than the regular bow, cocked it and inserted a bolt.

Although the mutants leapt first into her head, further thought indicated the dog wasn't making enough stink for him to have scented Mags. Nor lions. She listened with all attention, head cocked identically to Blizzard's. Nothing pointed to the horses having been disturbed.

"It's those people from town, isn't it? Has to be."

Well, and who could blame them for checking her out? Hadn't they as much cause to distrust her as vice versa? At the same time, give them an inch and who knows what else they'd try to take. Life, apparently, didn't have much of a price tag anymore. And, by golly, the hours of darkness were *not* a good time for friendly visiting. Not in this age. Not in any age.

What to do?

Time for a little hoodoo, she suspected, if not for all out war. Kill one and she would probably have to kill them all. Damn. She didn't want to do that. For better or worse, they were her neighbors and true human beings.

Slipping into her coat and boots—she always slept in her clothes nowadays, wrinkles be damned—Lily admonished Blizzard to guard the camper. Then, pulling her handy little illusion of "you can't see me" about her, opened the door and stepped to the ground outside.

The silence was almost heavy enough to feel. Breathing softly, just at the top of her lungs, Lily listened, her superlative hearing soon picking up traces of alien presence.

A nervous intake of breath revealed someone over by the horses, a muffled cough at the corner of the old house another. Beyond them, a pair of people hiding behind trees spoke in low tones. And then there was the brush of feet on the ground headed her way.

She stood still, a smile touching her lips. They'd seen the

door open, then close, but they hadn't seen her. Nor would they. Not quite yet. Let the anomaly work on their nerves while she gained the high ground. Soft-footed and keeping close to the dark side of the camper, she moved around to where a skinny man, shivering a little in a thin coat, stared nervously around, his eyes blind to her.

Slow and easy, that's the way. I'm two feet away from this guy and he can't see me.

Knife in hand, the guy flailed out once as though sensing her, but she slipped past him and mounted the stair to the wagon seat.

"See anything?" the man by the horses whispered to the person closest to him.

"Nothing," the woman at the house replied. "Just . . ." But her voice trailed away.

Showtime.

Standing on the bench, Lily flicked her fingers at the sky, quick, quick, quick.

Glowing balls of witch light shot up, blazing in the dark sky like the Fourth of July.

Gasps, a couple cries, an arrow loosed by an archer shaken at the spectacle, gave her an adequate response.

While they were all looking upward, Lily spoke, her voice carrying and deliberately unearthly in the still night. "Who are you?"

Dead silence. The witch light died.

"What do you want?" she called.

The two in the trees, women, she saw as they moved, cried out. "Cross-up!" one said. "Run!" yelled the other.

A finger motion sent another display of fireworks into the sky, breaking above their heads in a shower of sparks, freezing them in mid-motion.

"Answer me," she shouted at her loudest volume, which, she noted with satisfaction, sounded very loud indeed given the cold and darkness. Although the visitors seemed mesmerized by the show, she prepared to duck in case they loosed their arrows in her direction.

But they didn't. After a while, the man below her cleared his throat and said, his voice quaking. "We're from town. Had to see where you was headed. Had to see who you are."

No need to lead them astray. "I am Lily Turnbow," she said. "This is my grandfather's farm."

"Fah," said one of the women. "Ain't nobody lived here *ever.*"

"Oh, I assure you they did," Lily said.

"Ever for a long, long time." The man below her was looking up, finding her location by voice, but she kept the illusion of invisibility in place.

She forced a chuckle. "You seem to be right about that. But I claim this land as mine. My inheritance. Does anyone have a quarrel with that?"

"You gonna magic us? Take our steads?"

"I only want what's mine. You keep what is yours. Simple. Honest." *Honest.* Would they even recognize the concept?

A pause showed they were wondering if they could accept her word—or what to do about it if they could not. Finally, the man nearest to her, apparently their spokesman, lowered his knife. "No weapons," he instructed his people, and to her relief, arrows were reclaimed, bows reslung at their backs.

"Where you hiding," he asked then. "Come out. We ain't gonna shoot you."

So she came out, enjoying their awe when she materialized in front of them and they realized another of her powers. Another burst of light reinforced their opinion as open-mouthed, they stared up at her standing tall on the wagon seat.

"Go home," she said. "Come back in daylight if you want to visit. You'll be welcome then."

So they did. And no one was more amazed than she.

*****

In the midnight hours, ghosts came to haunt her sleep and preached to her about the practicalities of the situation. She couldn't stay here, surrounded by these desolate ruins. Grandpa's voice got into her head and told her so.

"No water here, kiddo. Always did have to pump it uphill from the well. And without electricity or a generator? Guess you know that ain't gonna fly."

Yes. She remembered the inconvenience even short power outages caused. But she also recalled how the draw where the well stood in its rock pump house was always sub-irrigated, and that they got two, sometimes, three cuttings of hay from there during the summer. Putting up the crop for winter feed was always darned hard work. Many a time she'd drawn the job of stacking bales in the big barn loft. Yeah. The same barn that now was only a bump of debris out by a non-existent corral.

"Oh, that well." Grandma joined the ghostly conversation. "Did we tell you that an entrepreneur from Seattle wanted to buy us out and set up a bottled water facility? Said it was the best water in the west." She laughed merrily at the idea.

The west-side entrepreneur had been right. Lily could almost taste the water, icy cold to cut the dust when they were hauling hay.

The well, the well. Words that echoed throughout her restless sleep remained in her mind in the morning. They meant something more, she thought, something that lay beneath the surface. And so, after a quick breakfast of oatmeal sweetened with honey, she tied Blizzard to one of the camper's wheels with a length of rope long enough to allow him shelter under the wagon. She set a pan of water within his reach and optimistically instructed him to watch the horses and gear. Arming herself with bow and arrows, she set out to check over the next hill.

In the years before rural electrification, Grandpa had told her, there'd been a windmill there with a mechanical pump. Surely something as simple as that could be resurrected, parts found or manufactured.

Grandpa had laughed, calling the pump house his fortress. Said he built it to last three hundred years. He even constructed a small room at the front, a handy place to rest during harvest or haying when the work got a little too much for him. He wasn't—hadn't been—getting any younger, after all. But even as he joked, he made certain to keep the little building in good repair. The farm's only source of water, they would've been in a pickle if the system failed.

Speaking of pumps, the one in Lily's chest beat faster as she topped the hill. A breeze blew through her hair; sunlight once again warmed her shoulders, the familiar hills rolled off into the distance.

A pleasant day. If she closed off her mind, she could almost imagine a world untouched.

At first she thought her short hike would turn out to be mere exercise for her nearly healed leg because at first glance the wide draw was empty of everything except a bunch of young cottonwoods flourishing between rotted stumps of older trees. The cottonwoods hadn't been there in her day, but the tree was notorious for its weed-like qualities, taking root wherever enough moisture allowed, apparently seeding itself by magic.

Squinting, she saw a small mountain of rocks grubbed out of the fields over the years punctuated the whole. She had contributed to the pile herself, helping her grandfather clear the land each spring. Freeze and thaw cycles always threw a new crop of rocks up during the winter. God knows where they came from, sprouting from the dirt like weeds.

But then she took a closer look. That mound of rocks. The placement didn't look right. Hadn't it been closer to the fence row to the south? And what was that poking out from the middle of the heap? It looked like a vent.

Joy broke over her like a starburst. Of course. The pump house had been hidden in plain sight, covered by an artistic arrangement of rock mortared over the original building. Grandpa would've done that, when the world failed. Her grandparents' last resort.

She heard his chuckle as she hastened down the hill, anxious now to find out if anything had survived the century as she…slept.

Caution borne of recent experience slowed her steps as she neared the disguised pump house. Snow still blocked the door on the north side. Grandma had always complained about a north side opening, making Grandpa grin. "Now, Helen," he'd say, "what difference does it make to you? You haven't been down here in fifteen years."

Lily smiled. Lack of information had never kept Gran from having an opinion.

No tracks showed in the snow in front of the building, nor, she found as she scouted an ever widening circle around it, had anyone been there since the snow began. Or only a couple deer who evidently called the draw home.

"Enough," she whispered to herself, retracing her steps to the pump house. Time to see what was there, if only her heart would quit pounding in her ears.

"We'll keep the key here," Grandpa had said one day as they walked down from the combine working the slope above the draw. *"You and me are the only ones know where it is, kiddo. Let's keep it that way."*

Of course she agreed. One of their many pacts.

It took Lily a few moments to discern the key's hiding place. A tremor in her hands made forcing the key into the old steel lock difficult. But when she gave a twist and felt the tumblers releasing after all these years, a strange reluctance prevented her from completing the action and pressing the hidden latch. What awaited behind that door?

Whatever did, any immediacy was long past.

With a strangely angry gesture, she thrust against the unyielding barrier, harder and harder until the rusty hinges broke free with a loud protest.

Squealing, the door opened.

Chapter 29

Stale air escaped from the long closed, tomb-like room, forcing Lily outside until it cleared. Peering in, the insides remained a mystery. The fortress was dark, without windows or other means of light. With her talents, nothing she need worry about.

Another cautionary look around outside assured her that she was alone, except for the

two deer feeding at the other end of the draw. The insistent honking of a V of geese drew her gaze upward, reminding her of days when jet contrails laced across the clear blue sky.

Lily realized she was procrastinating, but she couldn't help herself. What would she find here? Answers to a few of her questions, or only more pain?

Nerves tense, she created witch light and ducked through the doorway. In the first shattered moment, the light died.

No, she told herself, blinking. She must be stronger than this. Summoning the light again, she thrust her arm high, illuminating the room in every detail.

A mummy sat propped between the arms of a wooden desk chair facing the rough table. *Grandpa.* She closed her eyes, willing the sight away, opening them again almost immediately, hoping for a mistake.

No mistake.

She recognized his clothes, the red suspenders he always wore, the western snap button shirt, its colors still discernible. Thin white hair crowned his head, sprouted along his jaw. He'd gone unshaven for many days before he died. She recognized the once thick, work-worn fingers arthritis had left twisted, desiccated into thin bony digits. Lily took a shaky breath, the light she held high wavering.

"Hi, Grandpa," she whispered.

He looked just like that dried cadaver who'd been on display in a Seattle gift shop for fifty years or more. Her grandfather's state of preservation proved the old man had been a master builder, even to making the place air and water tight. He must, she believed, have planned the time of his death.

As she looked around, she saw evidence of his last weeks of life. A cot. A water jug. Storage bins for food stacked one on another, a few of Grandma's home-canned items remaining. A rack with his favorite books, some being those old westerns she remembered. Self-help books were well represented. *How to Survive the Apocalypse.* Ironic.

Her jaw clamped. Hadn't worked. No one could write a book with answers to that. Some lived while most did not, and at least one slept for a hundred years.

Walking forward disturbed the light coating of dust furring the concrete floor. Motes glinted in the witch light as she touched her grandfather's shoulder, hard and dry and feeling like papier-mâché beneath her hand. A yellow legal tablet lay face up on the slab table, his elbow resting across a corner of it. The top sheet was covered with dark writing, and even at a distance, she caught sight of her name. *Lily girl.*

Breath coming shallowly, she pulled the tablet from

under his arm and blew away the dust blurring the surface. Her mouth trembled as she took the tablet and went to stand where sunlight slanted over her shoulder onto the paper, sharpening the writing.

Her grandfather had begun the letter with a strong hand.

March, 2021

Lily girl, it said. Are you ever coming home, kiddo? I've been waiting for you, but it doesn't look like that's ever going to happen. Don't guess I'll make it much longer either. It's been five months since the flash. At first a little news got around, and the last I heard they figured that particle collider thing in France blew up. Recreated the Big Bang, only sort of in reverse. Don't know if it's true or not. Hasn't been official word of anything since the fires and the plague began. Guess there aren't too many of us left to wonder.

Whatever happened, life as we know it has come to a stop. Damned inconvenient, I can tell you, trying to carry on with no electricity, no working engines, no gas. Nothing works anymore but stuff that my granddad might've used. I ran out of ammo for my guns. Guess this tells you I've had to use it more than I ever wanted to. Got no protection now unless I'm close enough to use my old 12-gauge as a club. Been better off if I'd taken up archery or that kung fu stuff.

Word is millions died in the first wave after the flash. Whole cities, New York, L.A., London, Paris. All burned to the ground, and now the sickness is taking most everyone else. I been hoping you're holed up someplace far away from this. The people left around here are acting real strange, like they've been turned inside out. Not quite human, a lot of them, maybe because they've been eating each other. The Reston's, they've gone that way. Think they finished off Schultz and his last son, Johnny. I know they turned on your grandma and me.

I gotta tell you, Lily, that on our last trip to town, Helen insisted we stop and try to help the Reston young ones, their folks having died in the flash. They attacked us. We escaped, then, but not before they cut Helen up pretty bad. She caught something after the youngest girl bit her, and died the next day. I think maybe she willed herself dead so's she wouldn't pass whatever it was on to me. I buried her up on the knoll, where the wind blows free.

April, 2021

Another month gone. Reston boys came around last night again. They don't hardly look human anymore. Hard to describe the change. Don't think I want to try. I'm next on their list, I suppose, but they gotta catch me first. I intend to see they don't. What a world we've come to, kiddo. What a world.

What had been a firm hand, suddenly squiggled into loops.

May

If you ever read this, the letter continued, the writing fainter now as though without pressure, know your grandma and I are proud of you as we can be. Always have been. Take care of yourself, Lily. You're our last hope for the great hereafter, and your grandpa loves…."

The last words straggled off the page. The pen used to write his message of love was in her grandfather's hand, frozen in time.

Lily willed herself to stillness. The tragedy was old. No need to cry now. No need to cry.

A dog barked, sharp and high, and she jumped. Blizzard! He dashed into the room, trailing frayed rope behind him.

"How'd you get loose?"

Her question went unanswered.

The sound of soft footsteps stirring the grass and stones outside the pump house spurred her to action. She dropped the letter on the table and strung her bow. A fight would feel good, she thought. A way to vent some of the pain raging through her.

Turning, she faced the doorway, but before she could nock an arrow, a figure filled the opening. Even through the shadows she knew his form.

"Nate! What are you doing here? How'd you find me?"

"We've been looking for you, Lily," he said simply. "We found your camper and just followed the dog when he chewed through the rope. He nosed out your trail. Are you all right?" He peered beyond her at her grandfather's body.

"Am I all right?" She didn't mean her laugh to sound bitter, although it did. "Relatively speaking, I suppose."

"You sure? We saw people in the town, and stranger's tracks around the camper. We found an arrow on the ground not of O'Quinn making."

"The tracks—I had visitors last night. People from town checking me out." She bit her lip. Her heart beat fast. "I didn't expect to see you." *Ever again* remained unspoken between them.

"Didn't you? But here I am. I said I'd find you."

"Me, too." Jacob Felix grinned at her over Nate's shoulder. "Aren't you glad to see us?"

At last, something she didn't have to ponder. "I am glad, Jake. More than I can say."

She sucked in a breath. "My grandfather was here, waiting for me." Tears, unwanted, unforeseen, flooded down her cheeks. "All these years."

Nate shook his head at Jake's questioning look, stepped forward and drew her, bow and all, outside into the light and the circle of his arms.

*****

"I'm surprised the family let you go," Lily said to Nate later, when they'd returned to the camper. The fourth of Screenmaster's white dray horses was hobbled beside her team of three. Blizzard pranced importantly back and forth between Jake and her.

"I spend every winter searching the ruins for artifacts," Nate reminded her as he lifted his roan's hooves checking for stones before tightening the cinch. "We need all the books I can dig up, for our teachers. Sometimes I find good reworkable metal like the helicopter rotor you identified, or implements suitable to supply the traders. For instance, there's good profit in nails. I talked Selkirk and Neila into letting Jake come with me this season. He's got a big mouth. I was afraid he'd make trouble for himself if he stayed at the compound."

Jake looked over at him and blew a raspberry.

Lily frowned. "Because of me?"

"Partly."

Another sin to lay at her door.

Jake busied himself hitching the horses, a complete team with the now healed fourth animal back in harness. They were preparing to move the wagon over the hill, away from the ruined building to the only remaining one on the Turnbow property. They had a burial to see to.

Sighing, Lily closed up the camper and climbed to the driver's seat as Jake handed the lines up to her. "There used to be a couple of machine sheds across the road," she said, pointing. "Maybe you'll find metal there. Better yet, maybe you can find a working plow the horses can pull. There used to be one. In the spring, I'll need to put in a crop—if I can find seed. Maybe my new neighbors have some they'd be willing to sell to me."

Nate gathered his reins, his back to her. "You plan on staying here?"

Lily thought she heard disappointment in his muffled voice. "I have no where else to go, Nate. Besides, I owe my grandfather. You read the letter."

He hesitated, mounting his horse before he said, "He put no bonds on you, except for the hope you'd know what happened. A strong man, your grandfather. Looks like you take after him. Family trait, maybe."

His words brought a measure of comfort and she smiled. "That's nice. I always wanted to be like him."

Picking up the whip, she gave it a pop above the horses' broad backs. "Hiyah," she called, and with Blizzard bounding alongside the wagon, the team leaned into their collars, heading over the hill, the two men as outriders.

Nate had meant to say something else to her. She saw the look he exchanged with Jake, as though they shared a secret. What could it be? Hope jumped up waving a flag. Had Selkirk removed the banishment edict per chance? Or had, Nate and Jake and Harrison between them, convinced the head man to accept her after all? Be honest, why did she care so much?

Easy answer. How was she to live, surrounded by distrust and always, always, looking out for people who wanted to kill her? To most, Cross-ups were fair game. She needed someone who'd watch her back, someone she could trust. She needed Nate and, she admitted to herself, wanted him in every way a woman wants a man.

*****

They carried the fragile remains of her grandfather to the knoll above the pump house where the ground was soft and buried him there, facing the morning sun. None of the three spoke words over him. Lily couldn't and Nate and Jacob hadn't known him. Lily said a final, silent goodbye and motioned for the men to fill in the grave, the crumbling clods of rich soil filling the hole around the old man's shrouded body.

They spent the rest of the day in the fortress-like room, cleaning and airing until the smell of old death was blown away on a brisk breeze. Lily noticed there seemed an element of promise in Nate's work as he opened vents, fashioned new hinges for the door, and studied the old mechanical pump stored on a shelf in the inner room with admiring eyes.

"Can you fix it?" she asked.

He rubbed his beardless chin with strong brown fingers. "Maybe, if I can find the tools."

"There's a set of tools in the camper. Apparently, Philip Barnes went well prepared." She swallowed, asking, although she wished she didn't sound so eager, "Will you winter here with me? You and Jake?"

He paused in the act of tying wet rawhide around the joints of the cot legs where, as he explained, it would dry and perform reinforcement. He studied her intently before going back to his task. "I don't know. Think I can find anything to make it worth my while, Lily?"

Her throat went dry as bright neurons seemed to fire inside her veins. Something about the way he said that seemed promising. "Worth your while?"

"Uh hmm." He didn't look up.

"That might depend on what you're looking for," she said.

"You know what I'm looking for."

"Yes. I remember." She felt as though she were frozen in stasis, waiting for plainer words. Glory, she wasn't any good at this kind of thing. "Books," she croaked at last. "Metal, trade goods. I might be able to show you places that have been left untouched. If you want to stick around, that is. You and Jake."

"Do *you* want us?" He smiled crookedly, his amber gaze holding hers. "Do you want *me*?"

Her breath caught in her throat. It didn't take words, after all, but only a certain look to make his meaning clear.

Have him stay with her? Make love at night? Make life during the day? Beyond words, she nodded, feeling what had felt like a steel cage collapse from around her heart.

His smile grew. "Silly woman. Why else do you think I followed you as soon as Bannion turned me loose? Why else would I draw a map for you to follow?"

"Almost follow. Too bad you didn't warn me about lions."

He shrugged. "Say it out loud," he demanded.

"Say what?"

"That you want me to stay."

Behind him, Lily saw a shadow cast ahead by the sun stop, freeze, then retreat. Jacob Felix, wise beyond his years, hearing their voices and knowing this part wasn't meant for him.

"Please, stay with me." *What if he was teasing? What if he said no?*

But he didn't.

There is, she thought in a daze of delight as he folded her against him and pressed his lips to hers, only one real way to awaken a sleeping beauty.

A Look At:
The Woman Who Built A Bridge

Spur Award Winner for Western Romance.

Shay Billings is pleasantly surprised at discovering a new bridge over the river, as it cuts several miles from his trip into town. Ambushed and left for dead, he has even more cause to be grateful when the bridge-builder saves his life. Shay's savior turns out to be a mysterious young woman with extraordinary skills. More importantly, she's a strong ally when he and a few other men are forced to defend themselves and their ranches against a power hungry rich man. Marvin Hammel seems determined to own everything in their small valley, his intention to gobble up not only their homes and their livelihoods, but the water that flows through the land.

January Schutt just wants to be left alone to hide her scars. She's rebuilt the bridge that crosses the river onto her property, and lives like a hermit in a rundown old barn. All that changes when she takes in a wounded Shay Billings. Now she's placed in the middle of a war over water rights. But has she picked the winning side?

AVAILABLE ON AMAZON

About the Author

C.K. Crigger was born and raised in North Idaho on the Coeur d'Alene Indian Reservation, and currently lives with her husband, three feisty little dogs and an uppity Persian cat in Spokane Valley, Washington.

Imbued with an abiding love of western traditions and wide-open spaces, Crigger writes of free-spirited people who break from their standard roles.

Her short story, Aldy Neal's Ghost, was a 2007 Spur finalist. Black Crossing, won the 2008 EPIC Award in the historical/western category. Letter of the Law was a 2009 Spur finalist in the audio category. The Woman Who Built a Bridge was the 2019 Spur Award winner for best western romance.